WOULD-BE WITCH

SLIGHTLY SPELLBOUND

KIMBERLY FROST

BERKLEY SENSATION, NEW YORK

THE BERKLEY PUBLISHING GROUP
Published by the Penguin Group
Penguin Group (USA) LLC
375 Hudson Street, New York, New York 10014

USA • Canada • UK • Ireland • Australia • New Zealand • India • South Africa • China

penguin.com

A Penguin Random House Company

SLIGHTLY SPELLBOUND

A Berkley Sensation Book / published by arrangement with the author

For information, address: The Berkley Publishing Group,
a division of Penguin Group (USA) LLC,
375 Hudson Street, New York, New York 10014.

ISBN: 978-0-425-26754-7

PUBLISHING HISTORY
Berkley Sensation mass-market edition / May 2014

PRINTED IN THE UNITED STATES OF AMERICA

10 9 8 7 6 5 4 3 2 1

Cover art by Tony Mauro.
Cover design by Rita Frangie.
Interior text design by Kelly Lipovich.

For my dad, Chris

ACKNOWLEDGMENTS

Many thanks to David Mohan, my friend and critique partner, for reading this book and giving me feedback. Also to my editor, Leis, whose insights were incredibly valuable. Thanks to the entire team at Berkley, especially the copy editor and art department whose wonderful work I've seen firsthand. I owe a debt of gratitude to my terrific agent Liz and the team at McIntosh and Otis for all the things they do on behalf of the books and my career. And finally, always, thank you to the readers of this series. Your emails, reviews, and support mean the world to me.

1

NO MATTER HOW many times people try to kill me, I never seem to get used to it. That goes for spying, too. I'm always startled to find a Peeping Tom . . . or Craig . . . or fire warlock creeping around. The thing is they'd better not let me catch them at it. I'm a redhead. I'm armed. And I don't take kindly to interruptions when I'm trying out a new cake recipe.

I didn't always have a hair-trigger temper, or a hair-trigger weapon tucked in the top kitchen drawer behind the salad tongs, but a couple of months ago, my life changed.

My name is Tamara Josephine Trask, Tammy Jo to most of my friends. I'm twenty-three years old, and I'm a witch. Or I should say I come from a long line of witches. Until recently, I thought the family magic skipped over me. It turns out that I actually got a double helping of magic and that my two types of magic, like the creatures they come from—witch and faery—don't get along. It might have stayed that way, with the two magicks canceling each other out, if I hadn't had a close encounter with a wizard named Bryn whose own magical heritage is also mixed. From the moment my magic met his, it was trouble for us and anyone within a twenty-mile radius.

Now it was late December, and the supernatural drama had died down. Country music Christmas carols played on the radio, and in my kitchen I was minding my own business as I sometimes do. I wore a white T-shirt, boot-cut Levi's, and a black apron with a Julia Child quote in white letters that said, *If you're afraid of butter, just use cream.*

I was in the middle of stirring cake batter that had both butter and cream in it when the trees started kicking up a fuss. I don't speak tree, but after an unfortunate incident involving pixie dust, I'm usually able to get the gist of what they're trying to tell me.

Woody limbs scratched the roof and scraped against the kitchen window, making me look up from the bowl. I slid open the window and said through the screen, "I'm not coming out to visit right now. I'm busy being a regular person."

The leaves crackled, and I rolled my eyes. A chilly breeze blew in. I shivered and closed the window. When I turned up the radio, Martina McBride drowned out the trees.

My ocelot, Mercutio, who'd just woken up, strode into the kitchen. It seemed like God couldn't make up his mind when. He painted ocelot fur. There are stripes on their faces and necks like little tigers, but spots on their bodies like leopards. One thing's certain, they're the cutest cats of all, big or small, foreign or domestic. A person might say I'm biased and that person would be right, but that doesn't mean I'm wrong about ocelots being extremely cute. Just ask the Internet to show you some pictures.

"The racket woke you up?" I asked as I dripped a couple of drops of cream on my finger and held it down to him.

He licked and swallowed. Another scrape against the roof made us look toward the yard.

"For foliage, that's pretty pushy," I said. "I'm not fixin' to go out there with bare feet. It's full-on winter and that ground's cold."

Mercutio tipped his head down, touching his nose to the top of my bare foot.

"I meant I wouldn't go *outside* barefoot. In the kitchen with the oven on is fine," I said. "In here it's seventy-five degrees. Out there, it's forty-eight, and rumor has it it's going down to thirty. By Texas standards, that's blizzard cold. Now I ask you, would anyone in her right mind go out in a blizzard without socks and boots?"

Mercutio cocked his head and opened his mouth to answer.

"I meant that to be rhetorical, Merc." I leaned over the bowl. I added finely chopped Texas pecans, a dash of chili powder, and another splash of cream to the cocoa cream cake batter. "Besides, I'm real busy." I stirred and then dipped my finger into the bowl. As soon as the batter hit my tongue, I smiled. *Now we're talking.* I added pinches of nutmeg and pepper.

Mercutio jumped onto the counter, nearly knocking the mixer off, and darted to the window that's above the sink.

"Watch your step," I said, moving the mixer to the middle of the counter.

Mercutio's low growl raised the hair on the back of my neck. When it comes to announcing trouble, Mercutio's more accurate than a police scanner. I reached into the corner and turned down the radio, then opened a bottom drawer and pulled out a flashlight. I turned it on and shined it out the window.

I jumped when I caught a glimpse of a figure in the tree. I instantly lowered the light and yanked open the top drawer. Reaching behind spatulas and tongs, I closed my fist on the handle of my gun.

I tucked it into the back of my jeans and moved away from the window. I yanked on the socks that were sitting next to my cooking clogs and slipped my feet into the shoes.

"What do you think, Merc? A neighbor boy trying to sneak a peek at me in my undies again? Or real trouble?"

Mercutio crossed the counter in two strides and pounced down to the floor. I watched him approach the back door. He kept his body low, in full-on stealth and ready-to-rumble stance.

"All right, then," I said, and reached over to turn off the kitchen light. "Someone more sinister than a teenage boy it is."

I crouched next to Merc. "Even with the lights off, he'll see the door open. So we'll have to move fast," I said, and then rolled my eyes at myself. I didn't need to tell Mercutio about speed. He could give lightning a run for its money.

I moved the flashlight into my left hand so it was ready to be flipped on and gripped the door handle with my right. I took a deep breath and opened it.

We burst into the yard. Claws out, Mercutio went up the trunk. I drew my gun with my right hand and shined the flashlight at the treetop.

One glimpse told me the figure was all wrong. For a split second, I froze, staring at the gaunt face. His skin was so thin I could see stark white bones beneath the surface as he gnashed his teeth at me. Was there even flesh on those bones? Or just a translucent phantom covering? *Is he alive or dead?* I wondered frantically.

A bright flash of light blinded me as the man—or whatever he was—jumped. I dropped to my knees and rolled for cover. He didn't land on me—or the ground, that I heard.

Tangled among the azalea bushes, I pointed the flashlight beam at the treetop. Mercutio howled a protest at the fact that the intruder had escaped before he'd gotten to him. I moved the light all around the yard, scanning every inch. I also checked the sky and the fence. No sign of the peeping skeleton.

Mercutio returned to the ground, strolled past, and padded into the house.

My heart thundered in my chest. "What the heck?" I muttered, rolling onto the patio. "We're done, Merc?" I asked, following him inside. "Just like that?"

Mercutio meowed.

Apparently so. I locked the door, set my gun down, and brushed off my clothes.

"Well, what was that? I didn't hear it hit the ground. So was it a ghost, then?" I frowned. "I haven't seen all that many ghosts, but the ones I have seen look like people. A little more transparent than a regular person sometimes, but not like a skeleton."

Merc sniffed.

"And maybe I'm old-fashioned, but I think skeletons ought to be either covered with flesh and blood or buried in a coffin waiting to turn to dust as God intended. They don't need to be creeping around in a person's backyard, annoying the trees and giving me a heart attack when I'm trying out a new cream cake recipe."

Mercutio yawned and curled up on the floor a few feet from the door.

I turned off the oven and put the batter in the fridge. "I'm going to consult some witches' books. Not that I have many here to consult. But I'm not going to Bryn's house. I've made it twelve whole days without sleeping with him, and no scary skeleton standing in a tree is going to send me to Seduction Central now that Bryn's big case is finally over."

Mercutio didn't move a whisker. When it comes to fighting for my life, Mercutio's the best friend I could have. When it comes to my messed-up love life, I'm on my own.

And actually it's okay that Mercutio's not into that kind of drama. That's what the rest of the town is for.

2

THE ONLY LIVE-ACTION skeletons I found in Aunt Mel's magical reference book were zombies. In my experience, zombies were a lot squishier than the treetop creature. Not that I had vast experience with them or anything. The only zombie I'd ever met had been the reanimated wife of our town's retired psychiatrist, and probably Mrs. Barnaby hadn't been dead long enough to be just bones.

Even so, I didn't think the skeletal creature in my tree was a zombie. If he had been, I'm sure I would've heard him hit the ground when he jumped down. Zombies weren't dainty. They also didn't climb trees or run off when you threatened them with a weapon. They tried to maul you until they succeeded or you stopped them.

The creature from the tree seemed smarter than a zombie. There was also the slight glow and transparency to it, which made me think it might be a ghost.

Frustrated that I couldn't decide what I thought it actually was, I returned to the kitchen. I'd get back to what was really important: cake. I whipped the batter and added a teaspoon of Kentucky bourbon. I was midtaste when the doorbell rang.

Mercutio lifted his head and yowled.

"I'm not expecting company. You?"

Mercutio stretched and walked to the back door.

"Okay," I said. From Merc's laid-back attitude I decided the doorbell ringer was probably a person and not one who had murder in mind.

I let Mercutio into the yard, and the person at the front door knocked. I swallowed another teaspoon of batter, then did a rapid tiptoe to the foyer to confirm Merc's instincts that I didn't need my gun. I stared through the peephole, my pulse doing a two-step at the sight of the man on the other side of the door. As usual, Merc was right. A gun wasn't the kind of protection I needed. A chastity belt might've helped, though.

Bryn Lyons is ridiculously accomplished at many things, one of them being his ability to separate me from my clothes. He's blue-eyed, black-haired, and the kind of gorgeous that the devil might use to tempt a nun to sin. Since I'm not especially nunlike, for me he's like a chocolate truffle. In large quantities, I might remember he's too rich for my blood, but intermittently he's too delicious to resist. I sighed and rested my head against the door.

My hand hovered over the knob. Why was he here? I often visited Bryn at his mansion in Shoreside Oaks, taking advantage of his giant library of magical reference books, chatting over tea and scones with his gentleman butler, and curling up with Bryn on the fancy cushioned furniture, but Bryn didn't come to my house. Because I never invited him.

I'd been raised with a family prophecy that made nine families, including Bryn's, off-limits. Bryn's savvy, though, and he might have shown up unannounced because he realized my keeping him out of the old Victorian house wasn't just about following family rules. It was also a way of keeping our relationship in a holding pattern.

I stepped back as the chemistry between us thrummed clear through the door. My fingers tap-danced on the knob as his knuckles rapped on the wood. I folded like a falling soufflé and pulled the door open.

"Hey there," I said.

"Hello," he said, all sparkling blue eyes. Magic as enticing as the smell of cookies fresh from the oven surrounded me. "Would you like to help me celebrate?" he asked, holding up a bottle of champagne.

I grinned. He'd been doing battle with one of the biggest law firms in Dallas, and as the case progressed, they kept adding lawyers to the team against him. Working until three in the morning, he'd likened it to David versus Goliath, with him holding the slingshot.

"It turned out okay?" I asked, pulling open the screen door. "When I didn't hear from you I was afraid to call, but I should've known!"

Under his dark topcoat, he wore jeans and a black V-neck sweater. He looked scrumptiously casual. High-priced suits had been his daily uniform for weeks. It was nice to see him dressed down.

"I was late returning to Duvall. The client insisted on taking me to dinner to celebrate."

"She has a crush on you," I said. "I would, too! You got rid of the cheating husband who browbeat her for fourteen years. You're a hero."

"I found a loophole in the prenuptial agreement. The judge awarded her ten million dollars."

I let out a low whistle and gave him a quick kiss. "Congratulations."

A few seconds passed, and I hadn't stepped back yet to let him inside. He gave me a considering look.

"Is this an okay time?" he asked.

"What? Oh sure, I guess," I said, finally moving aside. "I'm baking." *And seeing creepy skeleton guys*. I didn't tell Bryn that. I didn't want him to worry. I'd dragged him into more than enough magical messes. He deserved a night off.

"I have to get up early tomorrow," I said. "And you must be exhausted. We should celebrate a different night when we can do it up right."

He stepped inside and handed me the bottle. "You heard he's back in town."

"Who?" I asked, pretending I didn't know what he was talking about.

Bryn cocked an eyebrow but didn't say more on the subject of Zach Sutton, my ex-husband.

Zach and I had been childhood sweethearts who'd gotten married too young. After the marriage went bust, we should've gone our separate ways, but the breakup was kind of a bust, too. We'd had an on-again, off-again relationship for three years. Then I'd needed Bryn's help with magic and in a matter of weeks, I'd fallen in love with him, too. I can't recommend being in love with two men at the same time. Knowing I'd have to choose between them had my nerves as frayed as old wires.

Bryn pulled a piece of rolled paper secured with a gold ribbon from his back pocket. He set it on the side table in the foyer.

"What's that?" I asked.

"Something for you. For the smoked salmon at midnight on Tuesday and the coffee and spice cake at two a.m. Thursday. I appreciated it."

"I was glad to do it. You were working so hard!" I said. "You didn't have to get me a present," I added, but snatched it up and pulled the ribbon strings to unravel it.

When I unrolled the paper, my heart about stopped. Sarah Nylan's secret recipe for amaretto caramel sauce is the stuff of culinary legend. The Hill Country candy maker's sauce elevates an apple crumble to a five-star gourmet treat. I'd been dying to get my hands on her recipe forever.

"Holy moly! How did you get this? I've written Sarah Nylan twice with recipes to trade and sent her samples of my pastries. I promised never to serve the sauce without giving out her website, but she never responded. I would just order bottles from her, but she can't keep up with demand. It's a four-month wait to get one jar. What in the world did you do to get this?"

Bryn shrugged with a smile.

"You went to see her, didn't you? One visit from you and

she would've handed over her firstborn. What's a little recipe for caramel sauce?"

"If you think I coerced her, you could tear it up."

"Probably I should. As a rule you should be using your powers for bigger causes," I murmured. "But I really, really want this recipe," I said, staring at it like I'd found the Holy Grail.

"I know," he said.

I looked up when I heard the knob turn. He was leaving. A wave of guilt swamped me. He'd been working like a dog, and he'd still found time to do something really sweet for me. Of course, Zach being back in town might have been part of the reason Bryn had gone so far out of his way. Bryn could teach even Nick Saban, who won back-to-back college football championships, a thing or two about strategy.

"Hang on," I said.

"Yes?" he asked, turning back.

"Oh please," I said, rolling my eyes. "Don't look so innocent. You know I'm not going to let you leave without giving you something sweet for this."

"Something sweet," he echoed. "That sounds promising. What specifically?"

"I'm about to put a cake in the oven," I offered.

"That's a good place to start," he said, and I had no doubt where he wanted things to end. I knew I should push him back out the door, but his beautiful smile reminded me of all the reasons I'm crazy about him.

"We're not going to get carried away. If anything, you're in trouble with me."

"Am I?" he asked.

"I've warned you a bunch of times to stop doing things to make me fall more in love with you, but you just don't listen."

He smiled. "Yeah, me treating you well, it's a problem."

"It is," I said, waving a hand impatiently. "You know that I made a promise not to make a decision about my love life until . . ." I trailed off with another vague wave of my hand.

He smiled and held out his arms in an "I surrender"

gesture. "All right. Have a glass of champagne with me so I don't have to celebrate alone. Then feed me a slice of cake and send me packing."

"Really? You'll behave? You won't try to flirt your way into my bedroom?"

He shook his head. "Champagne, cake, home."

"Okay, then. See how when we negotiate, we're both happy?"

"Sure," he said with another innocent expression that I didn't trust. Bryn's a lot of things, but innocent's not one of them.

I narrowed my eyes at him. "As long as you agree that the only sugar I'll be serving up tonight is cocoa pecan cream cake, we'll get along fine."

"I'd never try to force you into anything, Tamara. You know that," he said sincerely. "Glasses?" he asked, taking the champagne bottle back from me.

The tension eased from my shoulders. I'd be good for the night at least. Then I really did have to sort things out. It wasn't fair to any of us for me to keep the relationships in limbo. But it was going to be awful to choose, like trying to decide between hot apple pie à la mode and dark chocolate decadence. Each was perfect in its own way. Too bad men weren't really desserts. Then each one could have a turn.

I thunked myself in the head. *No matter how good they taste, men aren't desserts. Get over it, Lady Godiva Chocolates, before you turn into a tart yourself.*

3

I WAS HALF asleep when a soft yowl and an odd tinkling sound outside my window woke me. I rubbed my eyes and turned my head. Bryn lay next to me in all his gorgeous perfection.

"Good grief," I muttered. One glass of champagne, one slice of cake, one funny courtroom story, and here we were. We hadn't actually made love, but we'd come pretty close.

I sighed. "You don't play fair, Lyons," I whispered. "And I don't think you ever plan to."

The second yowl made me sit up. Was Mercutio trying to get my attention? Hadn't I left the kitchen window open? Merc knew how to get in that way. I climbed from bed and opened the bedroom window.

I cocked my head at the tinkling sound. It was a little like wind chimes, but none of my neighbors had chimes that sounded quite like that. It was a little too "nails on the chalkboard" to be pleasant. Maybe that was why Merc yowled. He didn't like the noise.

Bryn murmured in his sleep but didn't really stir. I was glad. He definitely needed some rest.

"Hello, biscuit."

I jerked around to face the chair in the far corner of the room. It was inhabited by the green-eyed ghost of my great-great-grandmother's twin sister, Edie. Though I'd grown up with Edie and once upon a time we'd been really close, we weren't on bosom terms at the moment owing to the fact that she'd said some pretty harsh things to me when I got involved with Bryn. I understood her point of view. It was her sister Lenore's premonitions that prompted the creation of the list of nine forbidden families.

"Hey," I said to Edie while glancing over my shoulder to be sure that Bryn was covered. The dollhouse-print quilt my granny Justine had made for me hit him midchest. It was odd for a naked man to be sleeping under that spread. While Zach and I were married, that quilt had hung like a tapestry on the guest room wall.

The irritating tinkling started again. "What in the Sam Houston is that?" I complained.

"Melanie's bluebells. They warn a witch that fae are nearby."

I frowned. "I'm half fae. They don't make that noise around me," I said, hoping she was wrong about what the ringing meant. I'd had a battle with some really hideous Unseelie fae, and I wasn't keen to bump into any more of them on a dark night. Or a sunny day for that matter.

"You have some fae blood, but you're sixteenth-generation McKenna witch and were raised in a house of witches. The spell on the plants wouldn't raise an alarm over you."

"Aunt Mel bespelled the plants? She shouldn't have. They won't like it."

"It's an Earth witch's garden. Everything in it is under our dominion."

"Not the trees," I said. "Try to make the old ash so much as bend a branch, and you'll see how much dominion witches have over a garden."

Her beautifully sculpted brows rose. "So it's true, then. You're toying with becoming a wild one? You won't survive in the Never. You're very sweet, but you're not submissive.

You can't imagine the things they'd do to a Halfling with a rebellious streak."

I drew my brows together. "What are you talking about? I'd never go live with the faeries. So far all they've ever done is tangle my hair and stab me." I grimaced. "No thanks. I'm only saying nature's got to be respected. Those trees are hundreds of years old. A witch who hasn't even hit forty ought not to mess with them. It'd be like me telling Bryn's seventy-something-year-old butler, Mr. Jenson, to shine my shoes. I'd sooner eat the shoe polish than disrespect him."

"Is that so?" Edie asked, narrowing her almond-shaped eyes. They were heavily lined with kohl, making her look like a Park Avenue Cleopatra. "After all, Jenson does work for Lyons, who's much younger than his elderly butler. It's a fact of life that those with the power are destined to make use of it. If you're not playing lady of the manor at the candy-legger's mansion, what role are you playing? The lord of the manor's peasant-girl mistress?"

"I'm not playing anything," I snapped, but an icy breeze blew in and made my teeth chatter, which took some of the authority out of my voice.

Bryn stirred.

"Go away," I said flatly. "You shouldn't be in here. You know how he feels about ghosts." *Especially you.*

One time, Bryn had even blocked Edie from reaching me. I'd been furious when I'd found out, but Bryn had reason to distrust ghosts, and Edie actually wasn't wholly trustworthy. She'd kept so many secrets from me.

Edie sighed. "Has it really come to this? After all the times I watched over you and played with you when you were a child? You'd really ban me from your life for the likes of him?" She floated from the chair and rested on the bed next to Bryn. "I admit he's quite beautiful. But those black Irish good looks come with a black Irish heart. He can't be trusted."

"I say he can." *Most of the time.* I twisted the ring that had to stay on my finger. To save Bryn's life I'd made a special vow that tied us together. The day after, I'd woken with a ring on my right middle finger that was linked to one on his left. Removing the ring made my finger burn and ache, the pain spreading with every minute that passed. But constantly wearing it made me uneasy. Bryn claimed the oath I'd made had activated the rings and the best he could do was make them invisible to people. I worried Zach might see through the spell, the way I could when I concentrated. I wondered if Bryn was telling the truth when he said he couldn't loosen the binding spell on the rings so we could get them off without the pain.

"What do you know of Lyons's nature?" Edie demanded. "You're a prize he's trying to win. He'll suck the power from you the way wraiths suck the marrow from witches' bones. If he's charming now it's because it suits his purposes. I bet he's always *sweet*." She said it like it was a dirty word. "I'll bet he gives you lots of presents. That's how they get you. The pretty boys are the most dangerous. Take it from someone who knows."

She wasn't wrong about Bryn being able to siphon power from me, but she was wrong about him only wanting me for that. When he'd been forced to tell the truth, he'd confessed he was in love with me.

She trailed a finger over Bryn's collarbone.

He jerked his shoulder forward and back like he was trying to dislodge an insect that had landed on him.

"Don't touch him," I said.

She glanced at him and then at me. "You haven't even bothered to put on a robe. You slip toward the wild without even realizing it."

I clucked my tongue. "As if you haven't seen me like this a million times. A locked bathroom door never stopped you from floating right into the shower to tell me something. I'd have a head full of shampoo and soap in my eyes and you'd be reminding me to pick up lavender potpourri or whatever else you wanted from the store."

"And from the time you were fourteen, you always yelled at me to get out until you were dressed. But not today."

My heart pinched with fear. She was right. I'd felt myself

becoming more fae and establishing a connection to things outside myself. I longed for . . . well, I really couldn't say what I longed for. I only knew that a feeling nagged me. A sense that something was missing and I must find it. *Unsettling.*

I glanced at Bryn, biting my lip. He mistrusted faeries. I'd been full fae once under the influence of a spell, and the only thing Bryn cared about was turning me back. If I became too fae, he wouldn't love me. That thought made my heart ache, and my mind skipped through memories from the past few weeks. Baking strawberry rhubarb pies while Mr. Jenson recounted Bryn's boyhood adventures in Ireland. Trying a spell that left me covered in maple syrup. When a breeze blew papers against me that stuck, Bryn joked, "the Tammy Jo version of being tarred and feathered," which dissolved me into giggles. Most of all, I thought of lying with Bryn under the skylight in his bedroom. The *Great Gatsby* movie was coming out, and I'd said I wanted to read the book. He got it from his library and read me his favorite passage, his voice low and mesmerizing. I'd made him keep going, and we hadn't fallen asleep until halfway through. The next morning, I stayed in bed to finish it. Over dinner, we talked all about it. Daisy being fair-weathered made me mad, but Bryn defended her, and we argued about the people in the book like they were real. Finally, I got so irritated I threw a buttered roll at him. He'd shot me a look, wiping butter off his cheek, and said, "If you're going to resort to throwing biscuits, I'm going to ban food from our book clubs." I burst out laughing and he'd grinned. I never enjoyed a book that much in my life.

Standing in my room now, I stared at him. Bryn wasn't just a man. He was a whole new world.

Edie's knowing gaze followed mine, and her tone was bone dry when she spoke. "The one consolation I'd have if you became feral fae would be watching the candylegger's reaction." She smirked. "He certainly didn't think much of your personality when you were full fae."

"Well, who would have? It's kind of vague, but from what I can remember I went a little bit crazy." Normally, I smiled at Edie's use of the term *candylegger*. It was an expression from her time—the 1920s—and wasn't a compliment, but I'd always thought it was cute. Today though, I couldn't enjoy her slang. Or anything about her visit.

"The cowboy's back in town. The least you could do is go and see him."

"I've tried to talk to Zach. He's not returning my calls," I said, exasperated.

"Why would he? He heard you're living with Lyons."

"I am not living there! I stayed there a couple of weeks while this house was under repairs."

"And you don't still spend every night at his place? Cooking in his state-of-the-art kitchen? Having dinner and drinks and *sex* with him?"

"No, I don't!"

"It's like you've forgotten all about the promise you made. I guarantee Zach hasn't forgotten. And if you're not careful, you'll lose him for good."

"Likewise," I said. "And if it's anyone's fault that I'm drawn to Bryn, it's yours."

"Mine?" she spat.

"Who did I idolize as a little girl? Who had a dry sense of humor and told stories like they were movies playing on the big screen? Who had black hair and bright eyes and treated me to my best adventures? Is it really a surprise I like spending time with Bryn? He's practically a male version of you. Only sweeter."

Her phantom brows rose for a moment and then she appraised him with a calculating look. "So he's a good replacement, is he? Because I'm difficult to get along with now?"

"I'm not trying to replace you. I'm saying you should get to know him. You could be friends because you've got a lot in common."

"Trust a Lyons? Never. And so you know, the difference between your boy toy and me is that I may make a few cutting remarks, but I never set out to destroy anyone."

"Neither has he."

"Hasn't he? The town's ghosts have been wailing long

into the night. There's a spell creeping through Duvall, sucking energy from us. I'm sure the locket protects me from the worst of it, but what of the others? They lived here. They died here. This is their home. Will you let him drive them to shadow, till there's no one left?"

I shivered and cast a look at Bryn. He didn't want ghosts near us, but he'd know it wasn't right to drive people from their homes, even if they were dead. "I can't believe he had anything to do with it, but I'll talk to him. If he's cast a mean spell, I'll get him to undo it."

She bristled, throwing her arms wide. "You think you can control him?"

Her agitation made me blink. It wasn't like Edie to get riled.

"Not control him, no. But I bet I can get him to compromise."

"No, you can't. He's casting spells behind your back. Spells that are affecting even me!"

I frowned. Apparently they were affecting her. A lot.

"Okay, calm down. I'll talk to him."

Merc's latest yowl made me turn. I went to the dresser, yanked open drawers, and pulled out clothes. I stepped into a pair of purple panties and hooked the clasp of a matching bra.

"Fancy lingerie," she said. Edie was one to talk. She wore beaded dresses to breakfast.

I adjusted the sexy bra, flushing. The expensive underwear was a present from Bryn, but I sure wasn't going to admit that. I tugged my jeans on and zipped them up. I dug through the closet till I found my Texas Longhorns hoodie, which reminded me of Zach since he'd played ball there.

I knew I wasn't likely to bump into him, and it would've been more than a little tacky to seek him out after a night of celebrating with Bryn. But a part of me was sick of waiting to see Zach, and of being on pins and needles until I did.

I contemplated going to the home we used to share. *No, not tonight*, I told myself.

I pulled the orange Longhorns sweatshirt over my head

and smoothed my hair. To Edie, I said, "If you'll excuse me, I have to check on my ocelot. For all I know he's been fighting a faery out there while I've been flapping my jaws in here."

"Tell the cat I said hello. At least he's clear about which side of the Never he belongs on."

I eyed her. "Are you leaving?"

"Of course. Once you go, there will be no reason for me to stay."

"No reason other than the view," I said, glancing at Bryn.

She laughed, and it was haunting and musical.

I rolled my eyes and realized it was ridiculous for me to feel so protective of Bryn. With a few words he could probably clear Edie out of Texas let alone the house. "All right, I'm going. Don't touch my candylegger while I'm gone."

She laughed again, the sound brittle, and I caught the words she called after me as I left. "How times have changed. When you were little, you always offered to share your candy with me."

4

I PUT ON a jacket and slipped my feet into clogs before I went out.

"Merc?" I called. "Where are you?" The tinkling sound was less irritating but still rang out every few minutes. Not seeing Mercutio or hearing him nearby, I waited.

My socks seemed to tighten on my feet. I frowned, backed into the house, and closed the back door.

"There is nothing wrong with these socks," I whispered to my feet. "They fit just fine."

With the door closed, I relaxed a minute but shook my head. My feet were becoming a problem. Being from a small Southern town, I'd spent a lot of time climbing trees, hopping into swimming holes, and doing things that were best done without shoes. As I grew up I thought going barefoot was just a habit I'd gotten into. Recently though, I'd realized it was something more. Since my brush with the fae part of my nature, socks and shoes often suffocated my feet. It was hard to explain the urge that overtook me, forcing me to bare my feet and let the earth touch them, but it had been coming on more and more frequently.

The people I loved—Momma and Aunt Mel, Edie, Bryn

and Zach, even Mercutio—would think that was a disaster. So I'd kept it a secret from everyone, which was kind of lonely.

I couldn't be turning totally feral, though, I thought, chewing my lip nervously. Wild animals didn't know how to bake pies or mix cookie dough, and I was still as good a cook as ever.

I walked through the house and went out the front door. "Merc? You here?" I called. A rustle of leaves made my spine stiffen and I slowed, my knees bending deeper in case I needed to dive out of the way of an attacking faery or speeding arrow.

Mercutio is nocturnal and spends most nights hunting, but because he can also sense magic, he's helped me fight magical creatures and solve mysteries. He might be only twice the size of a regular house cat, but he's got the heart of a lion.

He yowled, and I ran toward the side of the house. A band of hobgoblins, small fae, had surrounded Mercutio, with their spears jabbing in his direction. He growled at them.

"Hey," I snapped, swooping in to grab him. I'd been poked by their small spears before and expected sharp pains in my calves, but they backed up.

Mercutio writhed in my arms, ready to fight. The hobgoblins assembled into a tight group and shook their spears triumphantly.

"You better not jeer," I warned, but they didn't listen.

A slim halo of orange morning light rose. They looked up and then turned and raced into the bushes. For a moment, I saw their small eyes glow from the darkness and then disappear.

I dropped Mercutio. He darted to the bushes, stalking in circles, searching for the tiny fae warriors.

Then he padded back to me with a complaining growl.

"I know you could've taken them, Merc, but trust me on this, those spears are sharp. They could've put your eye out."

I tucked my hands into my pockets.

"It's weird, huh? Us being able to see them now?" I asked.

Mercutio didn't disagree.

"Usually only other fae and small children can see faeries. And maybe animals—could you always see them, Merc?"

Merc eyed the hedges, but the plants had stopped ringing. The faeries seemed to be long gone.

"Well, I couldn't see them before," I murmured. "You know what else? Sometimes my skin tingles like it did when I had the faery dust on me. You think some of that's still in my system after so many weeks? Think that's why I can still spot the minor fae around town?"

Merc looked at me and cocked his head.

"I don't know either," I said, and chewed on my lip. "The only thing is . . . it seems to be happening more often. Every day this week, I've woken up with skin that—well, I think it sort of glows. Just a little." I took a deep breath. "Let's not tell anyone yet. The excess fae magic may go away."

Noticing my bedroom light flick on, I clucked my tongue. "Darn it. I think Edie woke Bryn. She is such a trouble-maker."

I hurried back to the front door and let myself inside in time to hear an upstairs door slam. Edie appeared at the top of the stairs. She flashed a smile and gave me a wild-eyed look I'd never seen before. "I never touched him," she announced. Then she faded into a pale green orb and disappeared.

"Bryn?" I called.

He arrived at the top of the stairs seconds later. He wore his jeans and pulled his sweater on as he came down. His face was a thundercloud.

"What happened?"

"I woke up in bed with a ghost instead of you, and she was whispering curses in my ear."

"But Edie can't hurt you, right? She's complained a million times that she lost all her witch magic when she died."

"She can't hurt me," Bryn said, rubbing his right ear. "It's just not the way I expected to wake up."

"Sorry," I said, touching his face. "She's still not used to you and me spending time together, and I think it rattled her to see you. This is her house, too."

"I thought Melanie had the locket that anchors the ghost to the world. If Melanie's out of town, what's Edie doing in Duvall?"

"As long as one of us wears the locket, Edie can go wherever she wants. Except for your place, since your spells block ghosts from getting in. Your spells do still do that, right?"

"Absolutely," he said, sitting down to put his shoes on.

"Would you ever consider making an exception for Edie? Assuming, of course, that I can get her to behave? You guys got off on the wrong foot, but she's—"

"No," Bryn said, standing.

"But—"

He took my face in his hands and kissed me so long and deep that I just about forgot Edie's name and my own.

"Wow," I said, licking my lips. Magic throbbed low in my belly. I shook my head to clear it.

"Come home with me," he whispered against my mouth. The pull of sex and magic was dizzying, but somewhere in the distance I heard Merc knocking over a garbage can.

"I'd like to, but Mercutio's itching for a fight. I should keep an eye on him. Before you go, though, I have to ask you something."

Bryn rubbed the back of his neck. "Yes?"

"Did you cast a spell to weaken the town ghosts?"

"No."

"Edie says you did."

"I can't think of a less reliable source. She's trying to drive a wedge between us."

"Probably, but that doesn't change the fact that she's acting a little . . . off."

"She's a ghost. Erratic behavior comes with the territory."

"No. I've known her my whole life."

"Sure, but this is the first time you've ignored her sister's prophecy. She's furious you won't obey her."

True. "You promise you're not hurting the Duvall ghosts?"

"Yes, I swear," he said, putting a hand over his heart. "Do you trust me?"

Mostly. "Yes," I said. "I'm sorry she woke you."

"It's all right. In some ways it's a good sign that I can hear her now. I assume that's because of the strengthening bond between you and me."

"I suppose," I said. My bond with Bryn didn't need strengthening. We'd gotten really close too quickly. "You're exhausted. Go on home, and I'll come by later."

"Promise?" he asked, staring into my eyes.

"Yep," I said.

He brushed his lips over mine, making them tingle. He glanced out the window. "If there's a spell affecting the ghosts in town, we'll need to investigate who cast it. I don't want to be blindsided by an interloper."

"Speaking of getting surprised by an outsider, I almost forgot to tell you about the skeleton guy from the tree."

"The what?" Bryn asked, his brows rising.

"Yeah," I said. "He was scary-looking, but he only seemed to be spying. He didn't attack us. So just medium trouble, I suppose."

The corners of Bryn's mouth crooked up momentarily at the expression *medium trouble*, but his smile was gone by the time I filled him in on my treetop visitor.

When I finished, Bryn and I went out to the yard, and he searched for traces of magic.

"There's a lot of your family's magic here. I can't find residual magic from anyone else," Bryn said.

"There's one more possibility. Maybe it wasn't a zombie or a ghost or anything that used to be human. Maybe it was Unseelie fae. They can be kind of monstrous," I said, thinking back to the horde of creatures that had tried to get into our world on Samhain. Duvall was smack-dab in the middle of Unseelie fae territory.

Bryn nodded. "Maybe. It's possible that the seal on the doors between our worlds is failing. Or perhaps a member of the Unseelie came through on Samhain and got away from the battle. He could've been hiding in the woods all this time until he was drawn to your fae magic and came to investigate."

"Well, whatever he is, I guess if he's not hurting anyone, we don't have to try to force him back to wherever he comes from."

Bryn rubbed his thumb over his lower lip. "We'll see. Magical creatures in our midst rarely turn out to be peaceable."

"I know it. But it's Christmastime; we really should all try to get along."

Bryn grinned and gave me a kiss on the forehead before he left.

A FEW MINUTES after Bryn left, I stood on the side of the house, inspecting the bushes, when a female voice said, "Hello."

I jerked around, fists raised and ready. When it comes to threats, like Mercutio, I come down on the fight side of the "fight or flight" response. But the "threat" wasn't one at all, I decided as soon as I looked at the woman who'd spoke.

She was probably a couple of inches taller than me, but it was hard to tell since her shoulders hunched forward like she wanted to curl up like a pill bug. Her dark brown hair was the color of autumn leaves and a little frizzy. She didn't seem to be wearing a dot of makeup, but her pretty brown eyes reminded me of a doe's.

"Hi," I said, offering her a smile. There was something familiar about her—her perfume, I realized. It made me feel like dancing.

"Are you Tammy Jo Trask?" she asked softly.

"Yes," I said, leaning toward her. Her shy posture and voice might have been an act; over the past few months, we'd come across plenty of fakes and phonies, most of whom had tried to kill Merc and me. But this girl I instinctively wanted to protect. The toughest part about meeting her was keeping myself from telling her to stand up straight.

"I thought it was you. I've seen your picture in *WitchWeek* and recognized your name from your time at Lampis. You did work there, didn't you?"

I blinked. "Yes, for about six months."

"There was a dessert on the menu, the Black Chambord. The one with layers of very dark chocolate cake soaked in raspberry liquor. And milk chocolate frosting dusted with ground hazelnuts. Delicious! Didn't you create it?"

I blushed, flabbergasted. "I did."

"They renamed it, you know. It's called The Tammy. No one makes it as well as you did, but it's still the most amazing dessert anyone in my family's ever had. It's the one thing my stepmother and stepbrother and I can agree on," she said, her lips curling into a small smile. She reached out like she would give my arm a squeeze, but instead pulled her hand back and clutched her hands together. "I'm really glad I've gotten to meet you. I'm Evangeline Rhodes."

A double strand of giant pearls hung around her neck, peeping out from under her silk blouse as she leaned forward. It was very elegant and didn't quite fit her shrinking-violet persona.

"Nice to meet you," I said. "What brings you to town, Miss Rhodes?"

"Oh please, would you call me Evangeline?" she asked, then added excitedly, "Or Vangie?"

"I will if you call me Tammy Jo."

She smiled, and it lit up her whole face. "I'm in town to—it's a secret. I came to see Bryn Lyons." She lowered her voice, and I had to step closer because I could barely hear her. "I can tell you that, since my being here involves you in more ways than one. You see, I always said if I got engaged, I'd try to track down the Tammy who created The Tammy, to see if you might—but maybe you'll be too busy to bake. I would pay—"

"You want me to make you one of those Black Chambord desserts? For your engagement party or something?" I asked, trying to help her get out what she wanted to say.

"I would! Yes, to celebrate. I'm getting married—shhh," she said, putting her finger to her lips. She blushed. "You know, we wondered what happened to you after you left Dallas. If I'd known that all this time I could've driven to a bakery less than two hours away and picked up specialty cakes you'd made, I would've come every week. But it's better this way. Even more special and magical that I found you right after I've gotten engaged. Do you believe in fate, Tammy Jo?"

"Sometimes." I smiled. "If I do something right, it was all my doing. If something goes wrong, that's fate's fault," I said with a wink.

She laughed, a deep throaty laugh that was completely unexpected. She covered her mouth as if embarrassed at having made noise. "You're wonderful," she said, reaching out to squeeze my arm again, and she actually did. "I knew you would be. I don't have many friends. Not close ones. Would you mind if I wanted to become your close friend?" she asked, her voice soft and earnest.

My brows shot up. I hadn't had someone ask me outright to be their friend since kindergarten. I made friends all the time but not by any kind of design or proclamation. One minute you were having a chat with someone and the next they were sitting at your kitchen table telling you about their sick dog or their nephew in the army.

Since I'd already decided I liked the whispering doe-eyed Evangeline Rhodes, I said, "Well, a person can never have enough friends."

"So true," she said. Then her fingers dipped into her leather handbag with the gold buckles and emerged with a card. Her name was printed in fancy navy blue script with her telephone number underneath. There was no mention of a job, like most people would have on a business card. I glanced at her. She looked about twenty-five. Maybe she was in school. Either taking her time at it or in something like law school, which takes longer. Only she didn't strike me as a doctor or lawyer. She was too shy and sweet for that, I thought.

"What do you do, Vangie?" I asked, trying out the nick-name.

She smiled. "I inherit things," she said, and tried to wink her left eye, but her right also closed halfway so it was a lopsided blink.

I grinned. "Now that's a job I'd like to have. What do you inherit?"

"Money," she said. "And magic. We've got that in common. I'm a witch, like you."

Not like me, I bet. A lot of my spells went crazily wrong, which wasn't typical for most witches. "Is that right? So that's what you've come to see Bryn about? Some magical goings-on that have to do with the witches' chapter in Dallas or something? You're a friend of his, too?"

"No, not really. Or at all. I've talked to him a few times. He's very . . . impressive. So much so that it makes me flustered." She shrugged. "But this time I've got an important reason to talk to him. He made a promise to protect me. I need him to honor it."

"Wait, what?" I asked. "You say he promised to protect you?"

She nodded with a smile. "I'd like you to be more than a witness at the wedding ceremony. How would you feel about being my maid of honor?"

My jaw fell open.

"You know what?" she asked, a little crease forming between her brows.

"No . . . what?" I asked, nearly struck speechless.

She fished into her designer purse again. "I didn't expect to give you this yet, but I want to. I'm not going to wait until we've known each other longer. Why should I?" she asked defiantly, and thrust a white box with an orange satin ribbon around it toward me.

"What's this?" I asked.

She looked unsure for a moment but then took a deep breath and exhaled. "Don't open it until I'm gone. It's just a little token of my friendship. I like giving people presents."

"What a coincidence. I like getting them," I murmured. "But back to what you were saying about Bryn."

"I'll let him tell you. I'm glad I came to see you first. I knew we'd be friends. A lot of people want to use me for my money. It's not the same as friendship. I've come to understand that." Her soulful eyes looked so sad. I closed my mouth on the questions that tried to spring from my tongue. "My family says it's my fault. Sometimes I try too hard and need too much. It puts people off. But I won't smother you. I promise. I won't take up much of your time. I won't be able to. I'll be newly married and that will keep me busy. Along with my magic."

"Listen, if you need protection from something, coming here and being my friend might be the last thing you should do. Lately lots of people have tried to kill me," I said.

For a moment, she looked as hard and determined as a drill sergeant. "I *will* be your friend! You're an inspiration."

"An inspiration?" I said, surprised.

"Sure! The way you stood up for yourself and your town. I've admired you ever since I read about your exploits in *WitchWeek*. I'm trying to be more confident, you see. So now when I want to try something, like driving here to meet with Bryn Lyons who's made me tongue-tied my entire adult life, I think: What would Tammy Jo do?"

Probably end up kissing him even when I wasn't supposed to, I thought. "Oh boy," I said, slapping a hand against my cheek. "I'm so flattered. I really am. But trying to think what I'd do and doing that could spell disaster. I've got good intentions and all, but I make a lot of mistakes."

"Not about the important things. I can tell," she said.

Mercutio padded to my side and looked up at her.

"Hello," she said, crouching to touch Merc's head. The fact that he let her was a really good sign. She smiled and glanced at me. "He's beautiful. Where did you find him?"

"He found me," I said. "Came down the river on a raft. Like Huck Finn."

"Marvelous." She ran her fingers through his fur. "I don't have a companion at the moment. Mine died," she said in a grief-stricken voice. "Everyone leaves me."

"Sorry," I said. Merc yowled sympathetically. "So who is it that you need protection from? It wouldn't by chance be from a skeleton guy, would it?"

She cocked her head, giving Mercutio a last pat. "Skeleton guy? No, not that I know of. My enemies are flesh and blood, and plenty of it. I need directions to Bryn Lyons's office. After I talk to him, he can fill you in since you're just his magical apprentice for now."

"I'm not his apprentice," I said. "We're magically bound together and he does have more experience, but—never mind. Bryn's not in his office this time of morning," I said, glancing at the horizon, where the sun had just shouldered its way up.

"I want to get the lay of the land. I'm staying one town over in Dyson, since there were no rooms available here."

I grimaced. WAM, the World Association of Magic, had sent its leadership to take over Duvall a few weeks earlier. Bryn and I had stopped them, but the fallout had been a flood of biblical proportions. Duvall was still recovering and rebuilding.

"It will be exciting to tour Duvall," she said. "We've heard so much about this place recently."

I gave her directions, thinking I wanted to talk to Bryn before she did.

"Thank you," she said, walking to a silver Bentley. "You have my card. Please call me anytime! And I'll see you later," she said with a hesitant smile. She opened the driver's-side door and, with a wave, disappeared inside.

"Well, there's something you don't see every day," I said. "Somebody who's nice and rich and magical and not trying to kill us. Or at least not trying to kill us yet. But she's kind of odd, huh?"

Merc meowed his agreement as her car pulled away. I slipped the ribbon off and opened the box. Inside was a rose-gold charm bracelet with a white-and-rose-gold cake charm that had tiny gems for decoration.

"Oh my gosh. Look at that," I said, lifting it up to examine it. "Isn't that the sweetest thing? You know what this means?" I asked. "I'm gonna have to drive to Dyson to get hazelnuts. Nobody in town carries them, and I need them if I'm going to make the chocolate Chambord dessert . . .

although I guess I should ask Bryn about her first, before I start making her cakes." I fastened the bracelet around my wrist, just trying it on for size. "What did you think of her?"

He gave me a satisfied purr.

"Yeah, I liked her, too, but she could turn out to be an assassin." We'd been betrayed too many times to not be suspicious of a pretty-faced spellcaster.

He yowled.

"No, I don't think so either. But here's someone who thinks I'm a brilliant pastry chef and an inspiration to other women. And she passes out gifts to people she's just met. Doesn't that seem a little far-fetched to you?" I thrust out a hand. "No, don't answer that. Let's just hear what Bryn has to say."

Merc meowed.

I walked to my car, a Ford Focus that had seen better days. After storms and floods, car chases and monster attacks, there were dents and scrapes that made it look years older than it was. I wanted to replace it but couldn't afford to. Also, I wasn't sure my hard-driving exploits were behind me. It seemed like a good idea to have a car that I didn't worry about messing up.

5

AT THE GATE to Bryn's mansion, I pushed the security console button and Steve, night security, acknowledged the ring.

"It's Mercutio and me," I said.

"Morning," Steve said.

"Did he go to sleep when he got home?" I asked as the gates slid open.

"No, he's in the pool."

I smiled. Bryn swam most mornings. I liked watching more than I should have.

I parked on the paved circular drive and let us in through the unlocked front door. Merc and I went down the hallway of fancy paintings to the door that led to the saltwater pool. The courtyard's paved with mosaic tiles and bordered by four large columns. After the state-of-the-art kitchen and the skylight in his bedroom, the pool's my favorite thing about Bryn's house.

"Hey," I said when he surfaced. His black hair gleamed in the morning light.

He emerged from the pool, gorgeous as a siren. Bryn's

so good-looking it's hard to put a finger on his best feature, but his smile's definitely high on the list. And the fact that he always smiles when he sees me makes it doubly hard to resist.

"Hello again," he said.

"Hello again yourself. What can you tell me about Evangeline Rhodes?"

"Evangeline Rhodes," he said with a slight roll of his eyes. He grabbed a towel and rubbed it over his hair. "What makes you ask about her?"

"We met. We're kind of friends."

"Since when?"

"Since about seven thirty a.m. when she said my Black Chambord dessert was the best thing she's ever tasted and that she's been on a mission to meet me ever since I left Lampis. And since she asked to be my close friend. It's hard to say no to friendship. Who am I? The Grinch?"

"You're allowed to be selective when it comes to friends. You have reason to be cautious."

"Yeah, but Vangie's not too sure of herself. I know how that feels. I was shy when I was little. And though I kick butt in the kitchen and can hold my own in a gunfight, I'm not exactly the poster girl for spell-casting competency, so I guess I think she and I have a little bit in common. Plus, she seemed so sure that I was just the kind of friend she needed. I thought she might be right."

"Tamara Josephine Trask, defender of the weak and champion of lost causes."

"Well, who am I gonna defend? The strong? They can take care of themselves, and as for lost causes, there's no such thing."

He smiled, catching a lock of my hair and rubbing it between his thumb and forefinger absently. "That attitude is what gets you into trouble." He curled the hair around his finger and tugged me forward with it. "And what makes you irresistible."

I put out a hand, my palm against his chest to prevent

myself from colliding with his body. A really good way to forget about everything was to start kissing Bryn. "So what about her?"

"She comes from a prominent and wealthy family. Her father was a wizard with a special talent for intelligence-gathering. He cast spells that allowed him to eavesdrop from great distances. WAM wanted to recruit him, but his temperament was wrong for fieldwork. He was too nervous. He restricted his data-gathering to the secrets of subjects who wouldn't kill him. Businessmen mostly. Magical insider trading made him rich.

"Vangie's mother drowned in a boating accident. Her father remarried about three years ago, and her stepmother and stepbrother moved in. The stepmother, Oatha Theroux, comes from a line of water witches. She's not particularly powerful in terms of magic, but I don't think he was interested in her for her spell-casting."

"She's pretty?"

"She's voluptuous."

"Ah."

"They were pretty passionate about each other," Bryn said, wrapping the towel around his waist.

"They were? They got divorced?"

"No, he died."

"Oh!"

"He died of a heart attack while his wife and stepson were out of town. There'd been trouble between him and Oatha the week before he died, and Evangeline claimed her father threatened to divorce Oatha. Evangeline accused the wife of killing him."

"Did someone investigate?"

"The police and coroner didn't find evidence of foul play, and Evangeline wasn't the most reliable source."

"How come?"

"She has a history of mental illness. She'd already been hospitalized twice for nervous breakdowns. Her bouts of paranoia didn't encourage authorities to take her seriously. And when she appealed to the local coven, she arrived disheveled and dressed in her great-grandmother's moth-eaten clothes. She was hysterical."

"What happened?"

"She was hospitalized again. Several of us did speak to the stepmother, though, and warned her that if anything happened to Evangeline, we would investigate with the kind of intensity that wouldn't allow anything to be overlooked. Evangeline turned eighteen in the hospital and signed herself out. A lot of people offered to house her, but she bought a condo and disappeared into herself, living like a recluse most of the time. The stepmother and stepbrother still have contact with her through the money and the magic. Evangeline uses her father's library, but Oatha won't let her remove anything from the house. And Oatha insists on seeing Vangie frequently, claiming it's for Vangie's own protection. Evangeline has a tendency to spend lavishly on friends she's just met, and several people have taken advantage of her."

I moved my charm-bracelet-clad wrist behind me.

"Evangeline also has a bad temper and questionable judgment. She once tried to mow a former friend down with her Bentley. The woman ended up with a broken pelvis. Expensive lawyers convinced the judge that Evangeline had diminished capacity, so rather than jail she spent two years in a mental institution."

"Two years," I said with a gasp.

"Still want to be her friend?"

"Hmm," I said, cocking my head. "What did the former friend do to make Vangie mow her down?"

Bryn raised his eyebrows. "Is there any argument that should be settled by hit-and-run with a Bentley?"

I pressed my lips together thoughtfully, watching steam rise from the pool. "Well . . ."

"Tamara," Bryn said, shaking his head.

"All right, so maybe she's a couple of Hershey's miniatures shy of a full bag. That doesn't mean she couldn't use a friend. And she claims she has a right to your friendship and protection."

"What?"

"She said you made a promise to protect her."

Bryn tipped his head back, staring at the sky, then looked back at me. "I promised to help her look after her assets. I've given her legal advice. And several of us vowed to help if there was cause to believe her stepmother and stepbrother were trying to hurt her. But they have control of the house and the bulk of the estate. There's no reason for them to target Evangeline. You need to understand that she has a history of paranoid delusions."

"Oh, wow. And around here, we'll never know if she's crazy or if she's right that someone's after her, since a lot of the time, magical people come to town with murder on their minds."

Bryn smiled. "You have a point."

"I tried to warn her that my life's crazy, but she wasn't having it. And when she's nervous she looks just like a baby deer. You can't expect me to shoot Bambi down. And what if she really needs help?"

"I'll look into it. But you need to remember her bouts of instability. She can be dangerous."

"How does that make her different from any witch or wizard I've ever met?" I said with a sigh.

He pulled me in for a hug and kissed the side of my head. "Just be careful."

"I'll give it a whirl."

"If I don't hear from her in the next couple of hours, I'll call her and set up a meeting."

"Sounds good. Until then, I'll be in the kitchen making everybody breakfast."

"You need sleep. The staff and I can fend for ourselves today. I sent Jenson back to bed. He's got a cold."

I waved off this plan. "Mr. Jenson needs me to make him breakfast if he's sick."

"You're not here to wait on the staff. The staff is here to take care of you and me."

"That's sure overstating things, don't you think? It's not my John Hancock on anybody's paycheck."

"Tamara," he said.

"I'm cooking the breakfast. About the only way you can stop me is if you kick me out of your house. Maybe not even then. I'd probably just ring the bell and leave a package at the gate."

Bryn smiled. "Thank you for making breakfast."

"Welcome."

6

AFTER BREAKFAST, I went home and hit the road. I delivered fresh bread, three apple pies, and two pumpkin pies to Jammers and three classic cheesecakes, one chocolate cheesecake, and two tiramisu desserts to De Marco's Italian restaurant.

With two checks for the week's catering in my pocket, I zoomed home. I'd just arrived when my phone rang and Sheriff Hobbs asked me if I had a friend named Evangeline Rhodes.

Uh-oh.

"I know Vangie," I confirmed. "Why do you ask, Sheriff?"

"Can you come on over to Delaney's?"

I raised my brows. Delaney's Furniture wasn't open at eight thirty in the morning.

"Sure thing," I said, starting my car and swinging around.

When I arrived in the parking lot, the sheriff stood next to the massive inflatable bouncy castle that was between the store and the grocery market. I hurried over.

There was a plastic sign that said the bouncy castle

opened at ten a.m. with the store. There was a theater-type rope between two posts blocking the entrance to the play area. Over the castle's doorway there was hanging fabric.

"Talk to her, Tammy Jo. See what's what."

I looked at the sheriff, who nodded at the castle.

"She's in there?" I asked, brows shooting up.

He gave a nod.

I stepped around the rope barrier, swept aside the fabric, which was a pair of silk scarves, and peered in. She was lying on her back under a blanket.

"Um, hello?"

Vangie sat bolt upright, her hair falling around her face and shoulders, and pushed up a puffy eye mask. She blinked.

"Hey," I said.

"Come in," she said.

"I think it would be better for you to come out. What the heck are you doing in there?"

"Trying to sleep, but there have been a number of interruptions."

"Vangie, that castle is for kids to play in. You can't sleep in there."

The mask slipped down so that her eyes were half-covered. She looked like a bohemian Batman.

"It doesn't open until ten a.m. The children can't use it now. And I don't want to waste time driving back to Dyson when I have arrangements to make here later."

"What arrangements? Did you talk to Bryn?"

"He doesn't believe that I'm in danger," she said with a wave of her hand. "I guess I'll have to die to be taken seriously."

I clucked my tongue. "Now that's—"

She flopped back, causing the floor to bob and for me to almost fall over since I was leaning in with my palms on it.

"Vangie, what arrangements?"

"Hair and makeup. I don't care about those things normally, but for a wedding . . . well, I guess it's such a big occasion that I should. And I've heard really good things about the hairdresser here in town. I hope I'm still alive at ten thirty. He managed to fit me in. I wouldn't like to be a no-show."

My eyebrows threatened to touch my hairline. "Vangie, tell me why you think you're in danger. Who's going to try to kill you?"

"Them, of course. Madame Lycra and her weasel of a son. I've got protection charms on my ankles and wrists," she said, her arms shooting up so I could see her bangles. "But it won't do any good. My father had a protective amulet and they managed to kill him."

"Why would they want you dead?"

"You'll have to ask them."

"Well, how do you know they want to hurt you?"

"I heard them whispering. And they've snuck into my apartment."

"How did you hear them whispering? You don't live with them."

"I have my ways."

"Did you catch them in your apartment?"

"No, I didn't need to. I know they were there."

"How?"

"My dresser. The hairbrush was moved two point five inches. And the lines in the carpet were disturbed in the living room. I had them all exactly parallel. When I came home the center lines were off."

"So you think they came in and moved your hairbrush and on their way out used your vacuum to cover their footprints in the carpet, but didn't get the lines right?"

She sat up, causing each of us to bobble.

"Precisely," she said.

I cocked my head. "I'm not too sure about that."

"Well, I am."

"Although," I said. "Hair can be used for spells."

"They won't be using mine! I don't allow any stray strands in my apartment. I burn them all so they don't fall into the wrong hands."

"Hmm—"

"Tammy Jo," Sheriff Hobbs said.

"Hang on a sec, Vangie," I said, straightening up and turning to face the sheriff.

His arms were folded across his chest.

"Get her out of there right now or I'm going to arrest her."

"All right," I said, pushing the scarves apart. "Come on out of there."

"I'm quite comfortable here. It's just for an hour."

"The sheriff will arrest you."

Vangie tilted her head. "I don't see why. I'm not hurting anything. When I'm gone, there will be no sign I was ever here. I leave things undisturbed. Unlike some steprelatives I know. Crooked carpet lines! As if I wouldn't notice."

"Oh boy," I said. I crawled in and walked to the corner to get her bag. "Hurry up now. You have to get out of here."

"I don't see why," she said, giving her covers a snap. Her sudden movement made the spot under my feet push up. I lurched forward and landed hard, making the whole floor bounce and causing Vangie to fall over.

We exchanged a look and started to laugh. "Like walking on marshmallows," I said, getting back to my knees. "Come on. I have plenty of room at my house. You can stay there until your appointment."

"Oh," she said with wide eyes. "That's very kind of you." Her shy smile widened. "All right, I accept. You're a lovely maid of honor."

"Um, well," I said. Was I actually going to stand up in this odd girl's wedding? I had a sneaking suspicion that I probably was.

Vangie collected her blanket, cell phone, and pillow and we wobbled out. She retrieved her scarves that were taped over the opening of the castle and rolled them under her arm with the pillow and blanket. Then she shuffled toward her car after murmuring, "Good day, Sheriff."

I gave the sheriff a sheepish smile and a shrug.

"You sure have strange taste in friends lately," the sheriff muttered.

"I know it," I said, because he wasn't wrong.

* * *

ONCE I GOT Vangie settled in, I began the daily baking. She came down to the kitchen after an hour and didn't seem to have combed her long hair because it was tangled and slightly fuzzy. Her clothes too were rumpled from being slept in.

"You need to borrow a hairbrush and an iron to press your clothes?"

"Nope."

"You have a hairbrush in your bag?" I asked when she picked it up.

"Nope. My brush is where it belongs, on my dresser, four point five inches from my jewelry box and at a forty-five-degree angle with respect to the edge of the dresser."

"Hmm, that sounds like a very specific place for it. But wouldn't it be better to carry it with you? So you could brush your hair whenever you needed to?"

"I shouldn't think so. Everything in its proper place."

"Sure, sure," I said, offering her a slice of warm brown bread with butter and honey. "But you're going to see Johnny Nguyen, right?"

"Exactly," she said, eating the bread. "Delicious!" She drank the glass of milk I set at the edge of the counter for her and then put her dishes in my sink. She smiled. "Thank you, maid of honor. Just out of curiosity, what kind of gemstones do you like?"

"I—you don't need to buy me anything."

She glanced around like the walls might have ears. "I was just curious," she said. "Hypothetically? Sapphires?"

"Vangie," I said, pointing to where her shirt had fallen partway off her shoulder. It was too large for her. "Do you have any clothes in your car?"

"Emeralds? Rubies? Tanzanite? You would look very good in tanzanite." She gave me a twinkle-eyed smile and strode to the front door.

"You have to comb your hair!" I called.

"Don't be silly. I'm going to see an acclaimed hairdresser. I'm sure he'll want to see my hair as it is."

"Disheveled?"

She snickered as she opened the door. "No, in its natural state."

Good lord.

SEVERAL HOURS LATER, on my way back from dropping off a mince pie in Old Town, I turned up the radio. Listening to the request hour on the new Duvall-Dyson station had become a local pastime. Who was sending out "I love you" songs? Who'd requested "I'm sorry" and "Let's not break up" or "Get out of my house" songs? We were all curious to find out. For my whole life and probably longer, gossiping's been the number one hobby in Duvall.

Red Czarsak's mellow baritone made him my favorite DJ. "And here comes some Lonestar," he said. "This one goes out to Tammy Jo. The song's called, 'Let's Be Us Again.'"

My heart missed a beat and then sped up. I pulled onto the shoulder. I licked my dry lips and listened to the words. It was about a relationship gone wrong. One that the man thought was worth saving.

While the car idled, I put my head back on the headrest and chewed my lip, anticipation thrumming through me. There was only one person who could've requested that song for me. Now what was I going to do about it? I inhaled a deep breath and blew it out.

For a few minutes after the song ended, I sat on the side of the road. I was really good at fighting with Zach and really good at making up with him. The one thing I'd never been able to do was ignore him.

I turned the car around and drove to his house. Keyed up, my heart pounded by the time I parked next to his curb. My arrival turned out to be anticlimactic since he wasn't even there. Nerves jangling, I pursed my lips. The least he could do was be home to confront me when I showed up without warning.

I probably should've left, but I have a spare key and what else is that for but to get inside a house in an emergency?

The emergency was that I couldn't take it anymore. It was okay for Zach to be mad. It was okay for him to want to see less of me while I was involved with Bryn. It was even okay if he wasn't in love with me anymore—all right, not really, at least not at first. But what was not okay, and never would be, was for him to cut me out of his life like we didn't have almost twenty years of history.

It was wrong of him to talk to me through the radio station when he wasn't talking to me in person. And I'd tell him that if he ever bothered to show up.

Because I cook when I'm nervous, or stressed, or pretty much any time I don't have anything else to do, I went straight to his fridge and started dinner. Twice I stepped back from the stove and asked myself what the heck I was doing.

I turned off the burners and glanced at my right hand. I squinted to see through the concealment spell. The gold band on my middle finger had a row of blue-violet sapphires, symbolizing Orion's Belt and Bryn's celestial magic. The white gold band Bryn wore on his left middle finger had vines, a symbol of earth magic and me. When the bands touched, our magical connection intensified, a powerful reminder of our unbreakable bond.

I shifted, leaning against the counter. Zach and I had reminders of what we meant to each other, too. A certain keepsake came to mind. No matter how angry he was, I couldn't imagine him throwing it away.

Check, I told myself. *See if it's still there. If he got rid of it, that'll say it all. You can go on home.*

I hesitated, then walked into the bedroom and dropped to my knees in front of his dresser. I opened the bottom drawer and dug under the socks. For a minute, I thought the card was gone. All the air seemed to deflate from my lungs, leaving me breathless.

When I felt the plastic Ziploc bag, my heart jumped. I fished out the bag, and there was the small card I'd given him for his fifteenth birthday. I didn't need to take it out, but my fingers worked without any specific command from my brain. Opening the card, I saw my teenage handwriting.

For your present, meet me under the bridge.

Zach's not a sentimental guy, but he'd saved that card all through the years. The bridge was where we'd had our first kiss when we were eight. And it's where we met on the night we made love for the first time. I hear that the first time's not good for a lot of people, but Zach and I had been together for years by then. We'd played around plenty, the way kids in a small town will on warm nights when school's out and there's nothing to do. By the time he turned fifteen, Zach and I had known our way around each other's bodies and when we went all the way that night, we'd both liked it.

Afterward, I'd lain next to him and said, "So you've been asking me to do that for a year. I heard TJ say it's not a big deal, and you should stick to everything else I'm willing to do for as long as you could."

"You heard that? I told him to shut his damn mouth," he said, frowning. His brother TJ had said plenty of crude stuff that night, drunk on cheap beer and revved up over a fight with the girl he'd eventually marry. "I thought you were asleep in the back of the truck. I don't want you hearing that kind of filthy talk."

I'd rolled my eyes. "He was just sore over the fight he had with that girl he's in love with."

"Who says he's in love with her?"

"Nobody has to say it. I've got eyes. Whenever she won't go out with him, he gets drunk and pretends he doesn't care about women. Whenever she will go out with him, he spends twenty minutes brushing his teeth and half an hour digging through T-shirts to find the one that best shows off his muscles."

Zach laughed. "He does do that. Asshole," he said affectionately. "So what were you going to ask me?"

"I was asking if it was worth it? That didn't have to be your birthday present. There's still time for me to buy you that leather jacket you like."

"To hell with leather jackets. This is what I want every year on my birthday." He turned his head to meet my eyes and grinned. "And all the days in between, if it were up to me."

I laughed and kissed him. "It's your birthday. Should we use the L word again?" I asked. After everyone at school had started broadcasting that they loved each other after dating for a week, Zach and I had gotten fed up and decided we'd only say it to each other on special occasions. That night, I'd whispered it to him toward the end, and he'd held me tighter.

He nodded. "Hearing you say you love me while we're together that way . . ."

"What?" I asked, leaning close to him.

He shrugged. "Anyone can give me a leather jacket. You're the only one who can give me this."

I kissed him and ran my hands over his body until we were both urgent for each other again. We'd made the most of that night and plenty of others. And over the years when we'd had terrible fights, eventually one of us would slip a note to the other saying, *When you're done being mad, send me a note to meet you under the bridge.* Even after we had a house of our own, sometimes we'd meet under the bridge to make up before we came back to it.

I put the card back and returned to the kitchen, lost in thought.

When I was with Bryn, I was happy. But Zach could make me happy, too. If he hadn't lost faith in me when he'd thought I was either making Edie up or losing my mind, our marriage might not have fallen apart. Now he knew I'd told the truth about Edie. He'd seen her. He'd accepted that magic existed and had even gone to train with people who'd tangled with the supernatural. So I wondered whether Zach and I could salvage things, if we could recapture the early days before he'd started treating me like I couldn't be trusted to run my own life. I frowned. I could never go back to him being condescending to me. But I'd missed him when he was gone, like a piece of my heart had been stolen.

I had dinner almost ready when a face popped up in the kitchen window. I dropped the skillet on the stovetop. Little splatters of butter stung my skin and I cursed.

I opened the window. "Vangie, what in the world are you doing here?"

"Providing moral support."

"Come again?" I asked.

"It's all over town that you came over here for a secret rendezvous with your ex."

"All over town," I sputtered. "Who blabbed?" I peered out the windows at the neighboring houses.

"Well, I heard it at that sports bar, Jammers. The hostess with the curly hair is a huge gossip. She stops by each table and talks for thirty minutes or more."

"Jammers is loud. There's no way you'd be able to hear half of what was said at the next table, let alone be able to follow Georgia Sue's conversations all over the restaurant."

"So you know her? Of course you do! Well, I feel like I know most of the townspeople, too, after listening to her for three hours."

"Three hours!"

"Yes, people-watching is my favorite pastime. If I could be a fly on the wall or completely invisible . . . the best thing ever. And three hours isn't that long. I had an order of hot wings, two glasses of wine that I suspect came from a box, and a slice of apple pie that you apparently made. Delicious, by the way. The way you elevate a simple fruit pie into something so heavenly—you're the Michelangelo of baked goods. Seriously, a double oven is your Sistine Chapel."

I was flabbergasted for a moment and started to gush my thanks before I remembered myself. "But I still don't understand how you heard anything with the jukebox going full blast."

"I used a spell."

I blinked. "An eavesdropping spell?" *Just like her daddy!* I thought.

She nodded. "I also hex-bombed a couple of patrons who said nasty things about you."

"People said nasty—wait, hex-bombed? You mean you put hexes on them? You can't do that, Vangie!"

She wrinkled her nose. "I can and I will if they say unkind things about my friend."

"What kind of hexes?"

"Something I picked up while eavesdropping on my step-monster, Oatha. A minor curse she was practicing. The people will just think they have the flu for a couple of days. Nothing serious."

A curse! To make someone sick!

No wonder Vangie suspected her stepmomma of killing her husband. That would make me suspicious, too. But from what I understood, killing spells were complicated and needed a lot of power. Usually only witches and wizards with a certain kind of magic—blood-and-bones magic—could perform lifesaving or life-ending spells with their normal abilities. Even if Oatha had gotten enough power to cast the spell, how would she have enough energy left to cloak the magic well enough that smart wizards like Bryn wouldn't be able to detect traces on Vangie's dad's body?

"The people will have mild fever and body aches," Vangie continued. "Although if they say any more spiteful things about you, I can't guarantee it won't become encephalitis."

"Encepha-what?"

"Brain fever."

"Brain fever!" I shouted.

"Shh!" she said, looking around. "May I remind you that you're talking to me through an open window? Your ex-husband's neighbors could overhear."

"Vangie," I said in a low voice that struggled for calm. "It was real sweet of you to look out for me and my reputation, but the thing you have to understand about Duvall is that if people weren't talking about each other it wouldn't feel like home. Also, I might deserve for people to say a few bad things about me today. After all, I cooked one man breakfast and I'm fixing dinner for another."

"So? Where's their loyalty? You saved this town from near destruction more than once. If you've decided to live your life like an episode of *Jersey Shore*, that's no one's affair but yours."

"*Jersey*—wow. When you put it like that, I really have to think about the choices I'm making. But that's not the issue now. The important thing is for you to lift those hexes this instant."

"Oh, I don't think so."

"This instant, or we can't be friends."

She rested her chin on the ledge, crestfallen.

"But we can if you just remove those curses. And I have a surprise. I made you that Chambord torte."

"Did you really?" she asked, tilting her head.

"Sure, I did. As soon as I have a visit with Zach and go on home, I'll call you and you can come over. We'll have a slice together. But first you have to undo your hexes. No spell removal, no torte. That's the deal."

"I suppose I'll have to—hey," she said, turning her head sharply.

"What?"

A bush rustled like it had been jostled by invisible cats.

"He's coming," she said, and disappeared from view.

"Who's coming? What?" I asked, standing on my tiptoes to look out the window. She was crouched under the sill scanning the quiet street. "What in the world?"

"I cast a bug spell. And by that, I don't mean insect," she added when I wrinkled my nose. "It supplies me with a supernatural bionic ear. He's listening to classic country. Hank Williams Jr. A tired choice," she said. "Don't tell him I said so!"

Vangie darted between some tall shrubs, then emerged several houses down and made her way to the street. She got into her car just as Zach's truck pulled into the driveway.

I took a couple of deep breaths to calm myself and then turned off the burners. I put pork chops, black-eyed peas, and corn bread on plates and set them on the table.

The front door opened, and I saw Zach in the doorway before he spotted me. Several things hit me all at once. First, that he was coming home from working out because his T-shirt and dark blond curls were damp with sweat. Second, he'd let his whiskers grow because he had a mustache and a bit of a beard, and third, he wasn't alone.

7

EDIE AND ZACH were talking.

Edie and Zach were talking?

As the door opened, she'd been saying something about a truck stop.

"There are worse things in the world than that bathroom," he said with a laugh. "And I'll thank my lucky stars if I never have to see 'em."

"You have company," Edie said, and they both looked at me.

Dressed in strands of enormous pearls and a feathered headband, Edie looked as glamorous and cool as ever. The spell that had rattled the ghosts didn't seem to be bothering her now.

"See you later, cowboy," Edie said to Zach. Then she blew me a kiss and disappeared.

"You're friends with Edie now?" I asked, taken aback by their cozy togetherness.

"You lost?" he asked, and shut the front door with a casualness I didn't believe. He tossed his keys on the coffee table and turned on the stereo.

"Someone played a Lonestar song for me on the Duvall-Dyson request hour."

"Wasn't me. Maybe it was the guy you're sleeping with."

"Playing 'Let's Be Us Again'?" I shook my head. "You're the only one who could play that for me," I said, setting napkins on the table.

He opened the fridge and took out a Shiner. "I haven't been listening to Lonestar lately. I've been listening to Lee Brice. A song called, 'That's When You Know It's Over.'"

"Maybe I should listen to that. Sounds like he's got the answer to the question I've been asking myself."

He leaned against the kitchen doorway, watching me. "*Are* you still asking yourself that question?"

I nodded, my stomach knotting.

He took a long swig from his beer, watching me the entire time. He lowered the bottle and tipped his head back so he looked over my head rather than in my eyes. "I heard you're living with him."

"I'm not."

"Pretty close to it, though," he said in a low voice. "What are you doing here?"

"I wanted to see you." There was a slight quaver in my voice. "I had to see you."

He nodded. "Do you remember that time Tara Moore planted one on me under the mistletoe at Jammers, and you and I had that fight in the parking lot that lasted an hour?"

"I remember. Everyone came outside to watch, like it was pregame and they were tailgating."

"You got the tire iron from the truck and busted her headlights and said next time you wouldn't stop with her car. You remember that?"

I flushed. "I have a bad temper sometimes. Red hair," I said, flicking a strand.

He walked over to me and lifted my hand. "My ring hasn't been on your finger in a long time. You're wearing someone else's ring now."

Damn it, Bryn! You swore he wouldn't be able to see it!

"It's not that kind of ring!"

"You're kissing someone else good-bye in the morning when he goes to work. Sleeping in his bed," he said, anger rolling in like the tide. "And all day long I'm this close to driving to his house with a tire iron." He breathed shallow and uneven. "I haven't carried my gun for three days because if I ran into him, I'd probably use it."

"I know it seems bad right now."

"It *seems* bad?" he said.

"Look at me," I said, grabbing his arms. "Just look at me." He did, his eyes wild with pain.

"Listen to me," I whispered. "Nothing's settled. He's in my life. I care about him. But I care about you, too. I promised I wouldn't make a decision while you were gone, and I didn't." A searing pain shot up my arms and I reeled back. Both arms felt completely numb with that "pins and needles" sensation buzzing through them like they'd fallen asleep. Zach hadn't touched my arms. I didn't understand what had happened.

"Did you try to bespell me?" Zach asked.

"Of course not," I said, shaking my arms until normal feeling returned. "I wouldn't even know how. And if I did, I wouldn't," I said, although I wasn't a hundred percent sure of myself. I didn't like seeing Zach in pain. If I had known a spell to soothe him . . .

No, I thought. Not without his permission. People needed to have a choice.

Zach pulled his T-shirt off and in the middle of his massive muscled chest hung an amulet that blazed purple and gold. Since when did he wear any jewelry besides his wedding ring?

"It's this," he said. "It protects me from magic. They gave it to me when I finished the human champion training. Like the badge I got when I became a deputy," he said.

Except a badge never almost paralyzed my arms!

He set the amulet on the coffee table with his keys. "Gone," he said. "You all right?"

"I guess so," I murmured, eyeing the amulet. As the light faded, it looked like a plain gold pendant with a purple stone.

"Now you," he said, nodding toward the ring on my finger.

"I can't take it off. There's a spell attached to it that I don't know how to undo. The ring is connected to a vow."

Zach was quiet for several excruciating moments. "You exchanged rings with him in a ceremony?"

"No, not like that. We didn't exchange rings."

"You did some ritual that involved the rings? Like a blood ritual?" he asked, unsettled.

"No, the rings came after. I just said a spell to save his life."

"When did the rings come in?"

I tilted my head. "I don't know exactly when. Sometime that night or the next day. I realized I had it on the day after I made the spell."

"Did he put it on you while you slept?"

I nodded.

"Without your knowledge or consent?" he asked in a coaxing tone of voice, like he was leading a witness into pressing charges against someone.

"I notice you took off your wedding ring," I said. "You were wearing it when you left town. You took it off when you thought I was living with him?"

He nodded.

"I stayed at his house while they were fixing Momma's."

"You could've stayed here," he pointed out. That's what he'd asked me to do when he'd left town.

"I did stay here sometimes. And I picked up the mail and watered the plants. Made sure the grass got mowed."

"Darlin', come on."

"What?"

"I've got plenty of friends and family. There's no shortage of people who'd keep the place up for me while I'm out of town."

"Including me. I'm your friend, too. Or at least I could be, if you'd let me."

He moved close. "When I was six years old, I jumped my bike from ramp to ramp to show off for you. And Mrs. Peach said, 'Like all daredevils, that boy's got more guts than sense.' And you said, 'That's why I like him.' And she said,

'One of these days he'll break his neck.' And you said, 'No, he won't. I'm keeping him.'"

Zach gripped my shoulders. "Afterward," he said, "I told GW about it and he asked if it had made me mad when you'd said that. I told him the truth. 'No,' I said. 'I liked it.' And GW said, 'Well, then I guess she is keeping you.' And I said, 'So long as I get to keep her, too.'"

Zach leaned forward till our breath mingled. He smelled musky and sexy. My belly and things lower tightened.

"We're not friends, Tammy Jo," he said in a voice infused with fierce passion. "I can get friendship from anyone. You're my girl. I'm your man. *That's* who we are." He leaned back a fraction of an inch, releasing me. "Now if you didn't come to say good-bye to me, put your arms around my neck and welcome me home with some sugar," he said, snaking an arm around my waist and pulling me against him.

It was like the million times Zach had come home from football practice in the hundred-degree heat. He'd stride in, aching and sweating, in need of a shower and food and often an ice pack for his knee. But before he saw to any of that, he'd get a kiss from me. I was that girl, the girlfriend of the football star, of the town's golden boy. I was the girl he'd lost his virginity to and the one he'd married. A thousand memories passed through my mind in an instant and my arms seemed to move of their own accord.

It felt so right to hold him. I gave him the kiss he asked for, and he gave me plenty in return.

Let's be us again. Yeah, this is us, I thought wildly as his hands slid under my butt and picked me up. With my legs wrapped around him, he pressed against me, teasing my body with his hardness that was so close to where it needed to be to do me the most good.

He walked into the bedroom and tossed me on the bed. He pulled off his shoes, tossed them aside, and joined me. The kisses were hot and wet, bruising my neck and collarbone. Feverish and frantic, we started to peel off my clothes, beginning with my sweatshirt.

He kissed me, groaning against my mouth as he moved.

"Oh, darlin'," he said. "Tell me you missed this as much as I did."

"I did."

He unbuttoned my jeans, but I grabbed his hand before he lowered the zipper. My body wanted to go farther, but I thought of Bryn and couldn't.

"I missed you, but hold on," I said, breathless and dizzy. Our hearts slammed inside our chests, almost kissing between our ribs. "I can't sleep with you until things are settled. No matter how much I want to."

"Hell." He rolled onto his back, catching his breath. "You'll be the death of me, baby girl."

"I'm sorry," I whispered.

"Me, too," he said, but there was a smile in his voice. He'd felt how much I still wanted to be with him. Apparently that counted for something.

"If it makes you feel better, I haven't been making love with him either. It doesn't seem right."

"So everybody gets to go to bed frustrated?"

"Unless you want me to sleep with you sometimes and him others."

He cast me a sidelong glance. "No, that's definitely not what I want." He turned his head and kissed me again, but he didn't try for more. "You made dinner. We best eat before it gets cold."

"Yeah," I said as he got up. Dragging a breath into my chest and letting it out as a sigh, I rose. I pulled my sweat-shirt on and followed him to the kitchen.

After a few awkward first moments, we settled in, eating and talking. It was great, but I reminded myself that Bryn talked with me, too. And in Bryn's case, I didn't just get his attention when I'd crashed a car or he'd been away for weeks. For years, Zach had taken me for granted and made it seem like the commentators on ESPN had more interesting things to say than I did. Of course, I'd been with Zach for years. How many new things were there to talk about? He hadn't cared about bakery squabbles or town gossip. I didn't much care about the New England Patriots' offense even when they played the Cowboys. There were bound to be lulls in conversations when a couple had been together since they were five years old.

Maybe after a few years, Bryn wouldn't be so interested either. The difference, though, was that Bryn was more of a talker than Zach and always would be. During Bryn's short breaks from working on the Dallas case, he'd encouraged me to tell him what was going on in Duvall. And his wise-cracks as I gossiped had left us laughing so hard I'd about come out of my shoes.

"I need a shower," Zach said, standing. With a devilish display of dimples, he added, "You could wash my back."

My body gave a little lurch of interest, but I chastised my hormones. "Not tonight, I can't. Wouldn't be right. I'll go home and—"

"Naw," he said. "Stay. He had a lot of nights with you when I was gone. We don't have to fool around, but I want more time."

That warmed my heart; he was willing to make a real effort. I nodded. "Go on, then. Wash the salt off. I'll be here."

He grinned and hauled his shirt over his head, giving me a glimpse of big rippling muscles. As he headed into the bathroom, I wondered if he'd try to seduce me into more than kissing. I shook off the thought. That was one way Zach was better than Bryn. Zach wasn't tricky. He did what he said he'd do. There were no hidden agendas.

Zach had always been the All-American Boy. Handsome, hardworking, and as loyal as the rivers run deep. I couldn't just let him go. He'd been the most important person in my life for more than a decade. Never seeing Zach would be like losing Momma or Aunt Mel or Georgia Sue. I couldn't stand it.

With a pang of guilt, I wondered, *What about Bryn? He'll deal with it.*

Bryn understood my attachment to Zach. And the vow meant Bryn and I were connected forever. Even though that complicated things, in my heart it was also a relief. Bryn might get mad about me spending time with Zach, but unlike Zach, Bryn couldn't cut me completely out of his life.

After Zach's shower, he was tired, and we ended up back in his bed. I borrowed one of his jerseys to sleep in, and we lay next to each other in the dark, talking softly, barely touching until he slipped my hand into his.

"Did you have them play the Lonestar song?" I whispered.

"You know I did," he said matter-of-factly.

"How come you didn't say so?"

"I thought you were here to settle things with me, to say good-bye so you could be with him. I didn't want to hear it. Couldn't stand to."

"Do you feel better now that you know I still love you?"

"A hell of a lot better," he said. "Instead of wanting to kill him and you and myself, now I just want to kill him."

"No one is getting killed. Everything's going to be okay now."

His low laughter was not reassuring. "There is no way everything's going to be okay. I've seen the way he looks at you. I know what he feels. If you won't choose between us, if you don't force one of us out of your life, the last man standing wins."

"No," I said as I drifted toward sleep. "It'll be all right." *I won't let either of you go. I'll keep you both in my life. One as my boyfriend. The other as a friend.*

We'll make it work.

Somehow.

8

AS I WOKE, I heard the trees whispering, "Across the sea. Ride across the sea." And I saw myself astride a galloping palomino pony. There were so many vines twisted through my hair that from a distance it looked green. Hooves beat the ground, and burning iron arrows whizzed by, cutting my thigh. I galloped faster and faster, my heart pounding. I looked over my shoulder and saw a pair of silver horsemen—the color of mercury. I sat up in bed, panting.

"What the Sam Houston?" I said, yanking the covers back to look at my burning thigh. There was a dark red mark with a few dots of blood. I looked at my hand, and there was blood under my index fingernail. I'd scratched myself in my sleep. I looked at the window, which was closed.

I didn't hear the trees say anything, I told myself as I shivered. *It was a dream. Or a vision.*

I glanced down at my skin, which had a golden glow. The color faded as I watched. Faery magic . . . again.

I climbed from the bed, wondering where Zach had gone so early in the morning. Maybe to the police station? Was he planning to come back to town for good now? To go back to work? And if he did, what would that mean for the three of us?

I winced, remembering Zach's predictions about how badly my little love triangle would turn out.

What the hell was I going to do?

Halfway to the bathroom, I heard my phone go off. By the ringtone, I knew it was a text from Bryn. I winced and shook my head. I wasn't ready to have a conversation with him yet.

After I washed my face, I went out to the kitchen. I hoped I'd find some leftover bags of semisweet chocolate chips in the pantry because if I was going to get through the day I'd need at least half a bag in my pancake batter.

"Hey, darlin'."

I jumped and spun around. Zach wore jeans and a T-shirt. Clean-shaven with damp hair, he smelled like delicious freshly washed Zach. I wanted to take a bite of him, but my conscience knew I'd better stick to pancakes.

Zach sat at the kitchen table, reading *Sports Illustrated*.

The Bryn ringtone for texts went off again.

I dug through the pantry.

"Good morning, biscuit," Edie said cheerfully from the shelf she sat on.

I lurched back from the pantry. She floated out.

"Good morning, cowboy."

"Morning, Beads. I got your magazine," he said.

I froze, watching Edie move to the chair next to Zach. A glossy magazine sat open to the table of contents. "Page ninety-four," she said. He set his magazine down and flipped hers to the page she'd asked for. My jaw dropped.

"Would you like some coffee?" Zach asked me, and got up to take out the can of Maxwell House.

I shook my head.

Zach started the coffeemaker and then returned to the table.

"Flip," Edie said, and Zach reached over and flipped the page for her before returning to his own magazine.

"What in the—? No, pancakes first. Then everything else," I whispered.

"What?" Edie asked.

I clamped my mouth shut and turned toward the shelves. "I'm sure I must have left some chocolate chips here. I really, really need some."

My phone rang, playing a Jana Kramer song I hadn't assigned to anyone. So thankfully not Bryn again. I hurried to pick it up, glad for a distraction from the surreal scene at the table and the chocolateless pantry.

"Tammy Jo?" a woman's voice asked.

"Yes."

"Oh, thank goodness. Where are you?"

"Who is this?"

"What?"

"Um—" I looked around frantically, mortified that I didn't recognize the voice of someone I was obviously supposed to know. Then it dawned on me. "Vangie?"

"Yes. Tammy Jo?"

Good grief! "I can't really talk now."

"Why? Are you driving?"

"No, but—"

"Well, you should be. Get to your car right now."

"What?" I asked. "Listen, I'm kind of busy."

"He's furious, and he's on his way over. He looked calm, but I heard the incantation . . . something about a meteor shower. All storm spells are violent and dangerous. Did you know? Get out now."

"What?" I demanded frantically.

"Bryn Lyons. I was having another meeting with him when he got your text. I really wouldn't have—but then of course, you're you, so you would."

"I would what?"

"Be brave enough to invite one of your lovers over to the other's house for breakfast."

"Oh my God," I said, spinning around to glare at Zach and Edie.

"Listen, Tammy Jo, a couple of things."

I didn't answer her because I was completely speechless.

"First, I really hope that we can get together today. I'm desperate for a slice of The Tammy torte. I dreamed about it last night. And second, I need your advice on firearms."

Oh, for the love of Hershey!

"So as soon as you finish breakfast, can you call me back? Ex-oh-ex-oh. That's hugs and kisses. I'm not sure if anyone really says that. But I used to see that on *Gossip Girl* and always liked it. All right, again, in summary, you should get in your car and drive away. But barring that, if Bryn starts calling down the heavens, take cover and use an Aetas spell for protection. Bye for now."

For a moment, I stood as still as stone, completely bewildered. I had no idea what an *Aetas* spell was or how to do one. And why was Bryn coming to Zach's?

I checked my messages. There was only one text from Bryn, and it contained two words: *All right*.

"Where are the other messages?" I demanded.

"Flip," Edie said, and Zach turned the page for her. "What messages, Tammy? What's she talking about?" Edie asked Zach.

"Lyons is on his way over," Zach said.

"Oh, he is," Edie said, sitting back in her chair with a smile. "Are you going to shoot him?"

I glared at her. She had no business egging Zach on. What the hell was wrong with her anyway?

"Nah," Zach said.

"Too bad," Edie said. "What are you going to do?"

"I'm going to let things take their natural course."

"I see," Edie said, still smiling. I wanted to throttle her.

"I don't see," I said. "What are you planning to do? To pick a fight with him?"

He didn't answer.

"Of course you are," I said, bitter as unsweetened cocoa. I really needed some chocolate to settle my nerves. I grabbed my purse and stomped through the living room and out the front door. Hopping up and down on the porch, I contemplated texting or calling Bryn and telling him not to come. But I knew he'd come anyway, and I didn't want to fight and distract him while he drove. What if he crashed?

I dug through my purse looking for anything sweet and found two miniature Mr. Goodbars. I ripped off the wrapping and consumed them in three bites.

Bryn's superfast sports car roared up to the curb, and I met him halfway down the walk.

"I didn't send you those text messages," I said.

"I figured," he said. "But it seems they were true." He looked me over, and I remembered too late that I was wearing one of Zach's football jerseys as a nightgown. Waves of Bryn's magic crashed over me, and it was hard to meet his eyes.

"Bryn, wait. It's not as bad as it looks. I didn't make love with him."

"You spent the night here. You slept in his bed," he accused.

When I didn't deny it, he walked past me.

"What will confronting Zach accomplish? He's not the problem."

"He's half the problem," Bryn said, his Irish lilt returning. It always came out when he was really mad.

He stalked into the house, and I looked around helplessly. I had to stop them. I knew men sometimes needed to let their anger out, but this was too dangerous. Zach could break a jaw with one punch. Bryn could wield magic that sliced like a knife. If they tried to kill each other, they'd succeed.

"What I really need is a tranquilizer gun." I spotted the hose. *Or that*, I thought. Crashing sounds exploded from the house as I ran to the spigot. I spun the knob and dragged the hose up the porch steps.

Halfway across the living room, I ran out of hose. I pointed the nozzle toward the kitchen and blasted the guys with it.

They jerked apart, sputtering, but Bryn muttered a spell

and Zach yanked off his shirt. I felt Bryn's spell ricochet off Zach's amulet. It slammed into Bryn, who doubled over. Pain sliced through my chest. I dropped the hose, gasping.

The amulet glowed purple and gold. I hiked to the kitchen, shielding my eyes from the bright light. Bryn rubbed his chest, eyeing the medallion. He whispered and his power reached out to the other side of the room, looking for a chink in Zach's metaphysical armor.

I squinted, my head aching like someone had tightened a vise around it. Bryn reached over and gripped my bare forearm, drawing power. I jerked back.

"No, not to use against Zach," I said, stepping out of reach.

"He's used you against me," Bryn murmured, and then he spoke in Latin and a window shattered inward. Zach spun just in time to keep a glass shard from stabbing him in the leg. It cut the skin and glanced off. Zach grabbed a piece of glass and flung it at Bryn. Bryn countered with a spell and a wave of his hand, but the amulet interfered and the glass sliced Bryn's side.

I grabbed my side. No blood coated my hand, but pain seared my flesh. I panted for breath and dropped to my knees.

"Zach, stop," Edie cried. "You're hurting Tammy Jo."

Both men swung to look at me.

"The amulet can't hurt her. She's protected from it. It's gotta be his magic in the ring that it's reacting to. Take that damn ring off," Zach said, stalking over. I shielded my face from the dreaded pendant.

"Stop. Don't come closer!" I yelled. He froze.

"Take the ring off her," Zach growled at Bryn. "You're not going to use her as a shield."

"It's not the ring," Bryn said, bending down and putting a soothing hand on my back.

I clawed the ring off my finger and cast it aside in case it was the problem. "Let me go," I said, pushing Bryn away gently. My eyes stung and my head ached. The pain in my side eased, but I thought that was more from time than the weakened effect of the amulet's power.

"Get out," Zach yelled, shoving Bryn hard toward the doorway. "Get out so I can take this thing off. It didn't hurt her like this last night. Not until you got here."

"You can't use it against me without using it against her. She and I are bound by a blood oath."

"Get the hell out of my house," Zach roared, pushing Bryn through the living room.

I closed my eyes. The two kinds of magic inside me had come uncoiled from each other. The witch magic wanted to reach out to Bryn. The fae magic wanted to stumble outside into the grass to touch the earth, to draw comfort from it, to heal. Too divided to move, I stayed where I was. My hand throbbed and burned for my missing ring.

I crawled toward where I'd thrown it. I needed to put it back on. There was too much pain coming from so many directions.

"Tamara, be still. There's glass all around you. Be careful," Bryn said.

"Out!" Zach shouted.

"Yes, go outside, Bryn. Please," I said. I wanted them apart.

I heard the front door slam and a couple of seconds later, Zach leaned over me. He picked me up and set me on the table. The headache and eye pain eased. He wasn't wearing the amulet anymore.

My hand still cramped and seared. I looked around and spotted the gold ring. I hopped off the table and stepped over glass to get to it. I slid it back on my finger and exhaled in relief. I leaned against the counter, feeling exhausted.

"I had TJ send me your hairbrush. The warlocks at the training center used the hair to code your witch magic into the amulet. They swore it wouldn't hurt or repel you. It should work on anyone supernatural except you."

"Yeah, but I'm not just a witch, Zach. I'm half witch and half fae. I think there's some iron in the amulet and when it's activated, it affects me. Also, Bryn's right. I felt every one of the wounds to him that the amulet inflicted. Our power is connected now. No one can hurt either one of us without hurting the other."

"What are you talking about?"

"I made an oath."

"What oath? You'll take it back."

"I told you that I made a vow to save his life. I did it willingly, combining my blood and his. My power and his. There's no way to undo it that I can find. I've looked it up in books and asked Aunt Mel." I shook my head. "It's for life or longer."

Zach took a step back like I'd struck him. "So you're tied to that guy? Forever? When you mentioned the vow before, you made it sound so casual. I didn't realize what it meant—"

"I don't have to sleep with him or marry him. I don't even have to see him. But if he's wounded or I am, it has consequences for both of us."

"So you have to protect each other. If someone comes to kill him, that's your fight, too."

I nodded.

"How could you do this?" he murmured. "This is worse than if you'd married him. At least then you could've divorced him. If this is something that can't be undone—" He made a strangled sound. "Then he's already won." Zach covered his mouth against an anguished groan from deep in his chest.

Tears welled in my eyes. "I'm so sorry, Zach," I whispered. "I know it's a shock, but—"

Zach shook his head, his eyes unnaturally bright. He clenched his jaw and swallowed hard. "I love you," he rasped. "I always will. But there's no way—" He shook his head again and rubbed a hand down his face, sucking in a breath. "I can't share you. One man. One woman. That's what I believe in."

"We can be friends."

"No. We can't," he said.

The weight of his words crushed me, and my knees threatened to buckle. "Okay," I croaked.

Zach grabbed my arms and pulled me to him. The hug was fierce and then we were both crying. After a few minutes, I started to have hope; he held me so tight.

Then his grip slackened, and he kissed my temple. "All right," he said in a hoarse whisper. "That's the end of it. Go on home."

He let me go and turned, fresh tears still wet on his lashes. He strode out the kitchen door without looking back. I watched him reach the fence and go over it, watched him disappear into the woods where wind rustled lonely branches.

It's not right, I thought, holding out a hand to the empty yard. *Last night . . . but now.* The thoughts were as broken as my heart.

All over? We'd never even talk? Like one of us was dead? How could I stand it?

When I came back to myself, I found that I sat in a kitchen chair, all cried out and exhausted.

I shook myself as though I could shake off the morning. I stood woodenly and walked stiffly into the bedroom. I changed into my own clothes and put Zach's jersey in the clothes hamper. I couldn't bring myself to strip the bed.

Tears blurred my eyes as I swept the glass into a pile and put it in a trash bag. I used towels to mop up the water from the floor and retrieved the hose from the living room.

I wiped the still-flowing tears from my face with my shirt as I left the house. I tossed the hose beside the house, turned off the water, and returned to the porch.

I realized that Bryn stood in the street, leaning against his car, waiting. How long had it been? He was probably upset, too, and feeling betrayed. I'd made a mess of things, but I couldn't handle a conversation about it yet. I'd just lost Zach for real and for good. I couldn't think . . . Bryn would be okay. He always was. He could handle anything.

"I can't talk," I said, my voice strangely flat. He started toward me, but I held out a hand to ward him off and shook my head.

"Later, okay? I need a little time."

He clenched his teeth but got in his car.

"I'm sorry," I whispered, but I don't think he heard me.

I turned back to the house and stared into the living room that had once been mine. Slowly, I reached in and pulled the front door closed with me on the outside.

9

FOR THE FIRST couple of hours after I got home, I was melancholy. I opened the windows, wrapped a blanket around me, and flipped through photo albums. I ignored the phone, the fridge, and the ringing bluebells.

Merc came in and lay down with me on the couch. I hugged him to me and fell asleep, which was why I woke an hour later with a mouthful of fur.

"Ugh," I said, trying to blow the hair off my tongue.

Edie sat on the coffee table, watching over me.

"Hi," I said, rubbing my face.

"Hello," she said.

"Are you all right?" I asked. "I didn't get a chance to talk to you before. Are the Duvall ghosts doing better?"

"The ones who are still around are doing fine. Did you get Lyons to lift his spell?"

"He said he didn't cast one."

"Of course he would say that. He has to keep up appearances for you, doesn't he?" she asked.

I held out a hand to ward off any more of that kind of talk. "I don't feel like arguing."

"No," she whispered, shaking her head. "I'm sorry.

You're tired and wrung out. I came to check on you, not to play the shrew. Are you all right?"

I nodded halfheartedly.

"The phone's been ringing nonstop. Feel free to ignore it, if you wish."

"Did Bryn call?"

"How would I know?"

I dug under the cushions for my phone.

Now that the initial shock and grief of losing Zach had passed, things were becoming clear. Zach didn't want me to have any connection to Bryn, but even if I'd known how Zach would react, I'd have made that oath to save Bryn's life. It was as simple as that. Also, Zach acted as though I'd betrayed him, but he'd betrayed me, too. By not believing me when I'd first told him about Edie years earlier. He'd sent me to a psychiatrist. One who'd threatened to institutionalize me someday. Zach had treated me like I was broken. Even so, when he'd realized the truth and apologized, I'd forgiven him. Why couldn't he do the same for me now? Why couldn't he see that I'd done the best I could on the night of the oath and that I hadn't hurt him intentionally?

Because jealousy isn't rational, I thought. *And it brings out the worst in people.*

That thought brought me back to Bryn, who'd been so patient and understanding for weeks. I chewed my lip. How was he now? After finally losing his cool? I tried to put myself in his shoes, seeing the person I loved coming half-dressed out of an ex's house. I winced. He was probably still mad at me, but he'd seemed calm by the time I saw him on the street.

Maybe he'd called while I'd slept.

Sixteen messages clogged my voicemail. None from Bryn. People had heard there'd been a commotion at Zach's and wanted to check on me—and to get the latest gossip. I set the phone aside.

When the doorbell rang, I found Vangie on my doorstep with a bag from DeMarco's. My stomach growled.

A loose, messy braid hung over her right shoulder with

a pen and pencil poking out from halfway down it. Between her oddly placed writing utensils and the wrinkled bohemian clothes she wore, she looked like a cross between a mad scientist and a homeless person.

"Who's this?" Edie said, floating over.

"Hi, Vangie," I said.

Vangie looked around. "I sense something. A familiar presence?"

"My double-great-aunt Edie is a ghost who lives here."

"Ah."

"She seems familiar to me, too," Edie said, scrutinizing Vangie by floating around her, as though sizing her up for a dress fitting. Edie's nose twitched. "She's too disheveled to really fit in in my time, but she has a certain vintage quality that reminds me of years past," Edie said.

Edie had been a rebellious heiress who'd been the victim of a sensational 1920s murder in New York. Edie didn't know who'd killed her, and she never talked much about her own death, or her glamorous former life in New York for that matter. Too sad, I guessed.

"Pretty Art Deco pin," Edie added.

Vangie wore a small enamel and diamond flower pin. It was a gardenia, Edie's favorite. "Gardenias are used in quite a few sex magic spells," Edie said.

My jaw dropped. She'd never told me that. Was that why Edie was partial to them? And why she'd gotten me to use frosted gardenias on so many cakes? Good grief!

Vangie looked from side to side. "Is she moving?"

"Not at the moment. She, um, likes your pin," I said, betting Vangie didn't know about any sex spells. Gardenias were such a sweet little flower. Who would ever suspect?

"A gift from my fiancé," Vangie said with a smile. "It's my favorite flower . . . for some reasons I can't talk about." Vangie blushed. For the love of Hershey, Vangie did know!

Edie rolled her eyes at Vangie's embarrassment. "The blushing schoolgirl act over a little sex magic at her age?" Edie said. "What's the world coming to? Women are liberated. You can vote and work and smoke. You can have sex for fun without consequences. If I were alive, I'd celebrate every night with an orgy, which I wouldn't regret in the morning *if* I happened to wake before noon," Edie said. "The twenty-first century is wasted on you girls." She floated toward the window.

"Where are you going? Will you drop by and check on Zach?" I asked hopefully.

Edie sighed and nodded, returning to me. She put her phantom hands on my face. "Oh, my darling," she said in the softest tone I'd heard from her in years. "He'll be all right and so will you."

I nodded, unconvinced. "I know you're disappointed about Zach and me. And about me and Bryn."

She wrinkled her nose. "I traveled with Zach as he drove to that training camp, and I stayed with him on and off in his dilapidated motel room. He was far too overbearing toward the end of your marriage, but the realizations and pain of the past few months have made their mark on him. He always had a good heart. Against all odds, he's finally got a tolerable manner to match."

Edie pursed her lips. "The calculating Bryn Lyons is another matter, but I suspect he may have bitten off more than he can chew where you're concerned. I hope so. As for me not liking him, well," she said, shrugging, "my own father was a nightmare, and I managed to live with the man for more than twenty years. I can tolerate awful men when I don't have a choice. But that spell that bans me from his house has to be lifted. Tell him to prove he loves you by getting him to remove it." She gave me a phantom kiss and disappeared.

I stared after her for a moment. Did I want to get in the middle of the power struggle between Bryn and Edie? Definitely not. But would my family ever accept him while he had a spell barring Edie from his house? No way. I sighed.

"Problem?" Vangie asked, leaning forward.

The scent of Vangie's perfume, which made me feel like dancing, hit me again, and I recognized it. It was the fragrance of some of Edie's old things. "What's that perfume you're wearing?"

"Chanel Number Five. Another gift. I like it more than I expected. Now what's the problem between Bryn Lyons and your aunt? You should tell me all about it. I've had years of therapy, so I'm practically a therapist myself."

"Oh, um, that's sweet of you. But I don't feel like talking about Edie and Bryn right now."

"They don't get along? Why not?" Vangie asked. "When did she die? Is there a blood feud? Are you and Bryn a supernatural Romeo and Juliet?"

"Vangie!"

"All right!" She tucked a strand of hair behind her ear. "You can tell me later," she added. "Are you hungry? I brought lasagna."

"Yum."

We sat at the table. "Oh hey, did you remove those hexes?"

"Yes," she said, but looked away from me, and I wondered if she told the truth.

"Vangie!"

"I did. I swear. But in one case, I was a little late. One woman suffered dehydration and low blood pressure. As a precaution, they sent her by ambulance to Dallas. A bit of an overreaction, if you ask me. I hear she's fine now."

I sighed. "Don't ever do that again."

"Cast a spell?"

"Not that kind of spell. Duvall townspeople are off-limits."

She tapped her plate absently with her fork, thinking it over.

"Tell me about your stepmother and stepbrother. Why would they be plotting to kill you?" I asked.

She perked up. "I don't know, but they absolutely are."

"Mmm," I said, and took another bite. "What exactly did they say?"

"That they have to kill me."

"They used the word *kill*?"

"Yes. And Oatha can do it. She killed my father. I don't know how. But she did. I saw the triumphant look on her face when she heard he was dead."

"Even if she looked happy, it doesn't mean she did it," I pointed out.

"Oatha's family descended from a really nice line of Cajun witches. But Oatha's brother married a bad woman, a voodoo priestess. I believe Oatha is learning curses from her."

She traced a crisscross pattern with her fingers on the table.

"But there were no traces of the spell on your father's body. That doesn't seem possible if he was murdered by magic."

She waved a hand and then made symbols on the table. I realized she was playing tic-tac-toe on an imaginary board she'd drawn.

"Okay, let's say they do want to kill you. Why now? Has something happened?"

Vangie shrugged.

"You're engaged."

"They don't know that. I've never introduced him to them. And never will!"

"Let's assume they found out somehow."

"Oh, well then, sure." She made an imaginary *O* mark on her imaginary board.

"Then sure what?"

"Well, then they'd have a motive. It's in my father's will that if I get married, I get the house and all its contents."

"You get his spellbooks! And the house!"

"Yes. And most of the money."

"Oh my God," I said, my fork pausing in midair. "That's it. They probably found out."

"How could they? I'm very secretive." She paused, narrowing her doe eyes. "Unless they used one of my father's spells to spy. Maybe they planted something in my apartment!" She shook her head. "And no one believes me about them. They all think I'm crazy." She glanced back down at the table and finished her game with a flourish, giving herself a congratulatory thumbs-up.

I eyed her over the top of my water glass. "I can't imagine why."

"So now I understand why they're after me. And you figured it out," she said with a smile. "You're the best maid of honor ever! What kind of gun should I buy?"

"None. As a lawyer and a wizard, Bryn will sort this out. And I'll help him."

"The only real way to stop them would be to kill them. How will you do it?" she asked.

My jaw dropped. "That's not what I meant."

She played another game of tic-tac-toe with herself and then looked up. "My fiancé, Jackson, will be here tomorrow. He can't wait to meet you," she said with a bright smile. "He's probably going to try to convince you to relocate to Dallas to be our chef. My idea," she said. "I've told him how chaotic your personal life is."

"I'm not leaving Duvall," I said gently.

"It'll do you good."

"Even so, I'm staying put."

"You'll change your mind," she said softly. "Because we're such good friends. And because Jackson's very persuasive." She sighed dreamily, then looked sharply at me. "Don't fall in love with him."

"Oh, Vangie, I can promise you there is no way I'm going to fall in love with yet another man. My love life's been messed up enough. I'm trying to make it less complicated. Not more so. Besides, I'd never go after a friend's guy. So wrong!"

"Good." She smiled. "You couldn't anyway. I had health—well, mental health—troubles when I was young. Jackson had a blood disease when he was a boy. We both recovered, but he says the memory of being sick makes us birds of a feather. You weren't sick as a child, were you?"

"Nope. It turns out I was kind of indestructible."

"Well, there you are," Vangie said, satisfied.

"How about some dessert?" I asked, getting up.

"Yes, please." She played another game before taking the plate. After a bite, she moaned and then exclaimed, "Delicious! I'm going to love it so much when you move to Dallas."

I winced. Romantic relationships weren't the only ones that were exhausting.

10

VANGIE INSISTED THAT she keep me company for moral support. Since I didn't feel like talking, I put in a DVD of *Butch Cassidy and the Sundance Kid* and then promptly fell asleep on the couch. I was startled awake by a sharp prod in my side.

I opened one tired eye. "What?"

"They're here! What are they doing here?" Vangie demanded.

"Who?" I mumbled, sitting up. Hair hung in my eyes, like my vision didn't have enough trouble with blurriness from sleep.

"You didn't tell her I was here, did you?" Vangie asked, giving my arm a sharp pinch.

"Ow. Cut that out," I said, smacking her hand away. "I've been asleep. Who would I have told? The Sandlady?"

"You didn't call her earlier?"

"I don't even know who the heck you're talking about."

Vangie made a threatening pincer motion. "Tell me the truth. Did she call you?"

"For pete's sake," I said, shoving her away from me. "You

pinch me again, and I'll never make you another dessert for as long as you live."

Vangie sucked in a breath and widened her eyes, yanking her hand back.

Oh yeah, I can play rough.

"Now, who's out there? And what kind of weapon do I need?"

"It's Oatha Theroux, my stepmother. She's probably got Beau with her. I didn't see him through the peephole, but he's somewhere nearby. Let's go out the back and climb the fence. How tall is it? Can I climb it in these shoes?" She raised a lace-up platform boot.

I gave her leg a push to lower it. "We're not climbing any fence," I said. "You just keep your boots on." I stalked to the kitchen drawer and got my gun. I tucked it under my shirt. "This is where I live. I'm not fixin' to be run out of my own house. And nobody's going to run off any of my friends either. Especially when I'm busy watching—or sleeping through—a movie."

"Uh, Tammy Jo?"

"Yeah?" I asked, glancing around. "Where's Mercutio? Merc?" I called.

"I think he's out. He left a while—"

Mercutio bounded down the stairs. I bent down and stroked his head.

"Morning, Merc. We've got company."

"Oh, he's home. He's quite stealthy."

"That he is," I said fondly. Mercutio stretched.

"Tammy Jo, I'm just going to—um—I'll be here, but don't tell them that I am, okay?" With that, she opened a closet where I kept my mops and stepped inside. She pulled the door closed.

"For the love of Hershey," I grumbled, marching to the front door, where the knocking had gotten louder and more urgent. Mercutio hissed at the closed door.

"It's like that, is it?"

I had been reaching for the door handle with my right,

but switched to my left in case I needed my gun hand free. I opened the door and coughed at the putrid smell that wafted in.

Oatha had streaks of gray that had resisted black hair dye, wrinkles that had resisted Botox, and teeth that had resisted straightening. Her lipstick shade was the color of dried blood—more brown than red—and if she hadn't used at least six coats of mascara, she'd attached dead caterpillars to her eyelids. Her dark purple stretch top plunged farther than was decent unless you're working as a stripper, and somebody should've paid her bra's underwire overtime. Beyond all the Goth gone bad, though, the unsettling thing was the stench. When I was seven, we'd taken a class trip to Stucky Clark's family ranch. We'd discovered a dead cow covered in flies and baking in the sun. Oatha Rhodes smelled almost as bad as a bloated cow rotting in the Texas heat.

She sized me up and nodded. "Hello, Trask child. Is your mother or aunt here?"

I shook my head, taking a step back.

She sniffed. "Tell her to come out."

"Who?" I asked, peering past her. I didn't see the stepbrother yet.

"My stepdaughter."

"Who says she's here?"

She narrowed her eyes, caterpillar lashes shadowing her cheekbones. "I say so," she said with a hiss. "Beau," she called. "Ghosts. All around."

"Yeah, Momma," a voice to the left said.

I flicked on the porch light. I could just make him out. He wasn't very tall, but the glint in his eyes gave me pause, like a raccoon coming down with rabies, not quite crazed, but working on it.

"We'll come in," Oatha said, pulling the screen open.

I reached back for my gun but then dropped my arm. Keep your friends close and their enemies closer.

"Of course," I said. "Y'all come on in out of the cold. What can I make you to drink? Tea? Chicory coffee? I don't have beignets, but I've got three kinds of homemade scones and a torte that'll curl your toes or my name isn't Tammy Jo Trask," I said, my tone sweeter than vanilla icing.

"Coffee, yes," she said, walking inside.

Mercutio yowled and lowered his body as if preparing to pounce. "Mercutio," I said with a sharp shake of my head. He wrinkled his nose, and I understood his main objection might not be their magic but their terrible odor. Oatha really was refuse on two legs.

Beau followed her in, and his hair put porcupines to shame. At least he didn't smell like death. He smelled reptilian, making the alligator tattoo on his forearm really appropriate.

"Y'all come in the kitchen and have a seat," I said, afraid if they sat on the couches, I'd have to throw out the furniture after they left.

I quickly lit some scented candles with a glance at the closet where Vangie would be trapped until I got rid of her family. Of course, what I had planned was for her benefit, so I figured she wouldn't mind hanging out to hear it.

I put the kettle on and busied myself at the pantry. On the middle shelf, smack-dab in the center, was a small wooden cask that my friend Kenny who does woodworking had made me custom. I opened the tap and let four drops of amber liquid drip into the bottom of the French press.

I'd been drugged with truth serum by the president of the World Association of Magic. Ever since then, I'd been working on my own truth serum, knowing it would come in handy sooner or later. I'm good with recipes, so I was pretty sure I'd be a good hand at potions one day. I'd perfected a truth serum from my aunt Mel's spellbook and tested it out—with his permission, of course—on Bryn's friend Andre. I thought he'd tell me cute stories from when he and Bryn were kids or some good gossip from when they were in their early twenties, but mostly Andre chuckled nonstop and told me about spells he'd twisted around to use in physics experiments. On account of the fact that I couldn't even keep up with my high school science class, let alone a physics genius, I had to record the stuff he said and have him check it afterward to be sure he'd been telling the truth. It was kind of anticlimactic that way, but at least the potion had worked.

Now I could get to the bottom of whether Oatha had killed Vangie's daddy.

I scooped dark roast coffee and chicory into the French press and waited for the water to heat. I took down two mugs and one teacup. I put some loose mint tea into a teapot. When the kettle was hot enough, I poured the steaming water into both. I waited as the drinks steeped and nearly jumped out of my skin when I felt breath against the back of my hair. I turned and found Beau standing a couple of inches from me.

"Smells good, *chère*."

I wished I could say the same for the company. "Have a seat," I said, giving him a little push toward a chair and away from me. I noticed a clump of reddish brown clinging to Oatha's skirt. Was that what it looked like? Rotten flesh? Yuck! What kind of spells called for rotten meat? And couldn't Oatha have showered before she visited a person?

"I'll help you make the coffee. Add a little of this," he said, handing me a silver flask.

"If you say so," I said, taking it from him.

"You're not pure Texas witch, *chère*. You old world?" he asked.

"Wherever my people might be from," I said, "I'm one hundred percent Texan. Count on it."

"She knows where our Vangie girl is," Oatha said. Looking at me, she added, "You best not interfere."

"With what? What are you planning to do to Vangie?" I asked.

Oatha glared at me.

"Momma?" he asked, leaning forward to smell my hair.

"Beau," I said. "We don't know each other well enough for me to be able to count the whiskers in your mustache. Why don't you be a gentleman and step on back?"

"Who says I want to be a gentleman?"

"See how she tastes," Oatha said.

"What the hell?" I snapped as he grabbed my upper arms in a vise grip. Intent as he was on pinning my arms to my sides as he licked my neck, I guess he didn't expect me to react as fast as I did with a head-butt knee-slam-to-the-groin combination. He also might've forgotten about Mercutio. Merc's not full-grown yet, so people sometimes mistake him for a house cat. That's a mistake nobody makes twice if they get on the wrong side of his teeth or claws.

All I saw was a blur of fur as Merc landed on Beau's shoulder and bit down on his ear.

Beau dropped like a stone from my between-the-legs blow, but he hollered and reared forward at Merc's bite. He grabbed Mercutio and with three vicious jerks pulled Merc loose. It cost him an earlobe. He flung Mercutio, who sailed through the air, twisted in a half somersault, and landed on his feet. Those Cirque du Soleil guys had nothing on my cat. Merc slid backward a few inches before he got his grip on the floor, and then he was on his way back to us.

Oatha screeched a spell, arms outstretched. I slammed a palm into her back to send the spell wide. She knocked the table over to block Mercutio, and Beau clipped my leg, knocking me to the ground.

He backhanded me across the face and yelled a curse as he grabbed my hair. On the one hand, I was startled by the impact of the floor, the blow to my face, and the sharp stab of pain where his knee dug into my stomach. On the other hand, this wasn't my first rodeo. As he raised his hand to hit me again, I whipped out my gun. I shoved the barrel against his throat.

"You sure you wanna do that, *chèr*?" I drawled, pressing the gun against him hard enough to dent his flesh. He checked his swing and held out his arms in surrender.

"Momma," he said. "Enough."

She panted with rage.

Beau leaned forward and rubbed his thumb in the blood that trickled from my nose. Then he bent forward and kissed my lips. I hit him behind the ear with the butt of the gun. It was no love tap, and his head jerked from the force of the blow. He bit my lip maliciously before he tumbled off me and drew back.

The sound Mercutio made when he pounced from the counter would've been enough to send anyone running for cover, and Beau barely managed to dodge away. Beau grabbed a butcher knife from the block and held it out.

"Call him back or I'll gut him."

I grabbed Mercutio with my left hand. "No, Merc," I whispered frantically. "Not now."

Mercutio squirmed and hissed as they backed away. To Merc, no fight is over if his enemies are still walking. "Not now," I repeated, trying to soothe him.

"You'll regret this, you redheaded McKenna bitch," Oatha said. "I'll see you cursed. I swear it on all my dead."

"Y'all wanna threaten me, go ahead. But you might want to check the witch newspapers before you start a fight in Duvall where I've got the home field advantage. You won't be the first who've tried. Hasn't worked out for anybody so far."

Too late, I saw her going for the door. I released Mercutio and lunged forward but not before she got the closet open. Luckily, there were only mops and buckets inside. Vangie must've left when I'd gone to the front door to let them in.

"Gone," she announced, turning to Beau. "You have what I need?"

Beau wiped his thumb on an old piece of cloth that looked like burlap. "Yeah, Momma. She's all ours." He nodded menacingly at me. "You shouldn't have interfered."

I tightened my muscles, ready for another attack, and stared them down with a cold glare.

"See you soon, *chère*," he said as he backed out of the room, my butcher knife still in his free hand.

"Not if I see you first," I murmured. "By the way!" I called out as they crossed to the foyer. "We've got a grocery store and several boutiques in town that all carry soap. I'd appreciate it if you'd use some before you attack me next time!"

The only answer I got was the door slamming.

"You know what, Mercutio? I'm beginning to think Vangie might be right about her stepfolk being murderers."

Mercutio hissed and then drank from his water bowl, sticking his tongue in and out of the water more times than he needed to for a simple drink.

"He tasted bad, huh? I don't doubt it." I tucked my gun away and dabbed my nose with a wet washcloth. "Even though it must be convenient to have a deadly weapon like your teeth handy all the time, I bet there are some days when you wish you could just shoot people."

Mercutio didn't disagree.

11

I WISHED I could go back to sleep, but sometimes trouble was like a boulder rolling downhill. Once it got started, it was hell to stop.

The phone rang at ten thirty. I expected it to be Vangie calling me back, since I'd left her several voicemails, but instead it was from Bryn's house. I snatched it up.

"Hello?" I said.

"Tammy Jo?" It was Bryn's night security officer.

"Yes, Steve. What's up?" I tucked a strand of hair behind my ear.

"Are you planning on coming over here tonight?" he asked.

"I can be," I said, tossing the throw blanket aside. "What's wrong?"

"I think it would be a good idea for you to drop by. Mr. Jenson's worse, but he won't agree to see Dr. Suri."

My stomach lurched. Bryn had said Mr. Jenson had a cold. It shouldn't have been serious. Of course any illness could sneak up on an elderly person. "Bryn should tell Dr. Suri to come to the house so Mr. Jenson doesn't have to go out." I mounted the stairs.

"Yeah, it's not happening. Usually the boss is patient where the old guy's concerned, but he's a little 'the worse for whiskey' tonight. Did you guys have a fight or something?"

"Or something," I huffed, propping my phone on my shoulder so I could change clothes and talk at the same time. "But don't worry. I'll be over in a few minutes. Hold down the fort."

I tossed "just in case" sneakers into a tote bag. Bryn and Mr. Jenson will take me as I am, but for a sit-down talk with Mr. Jenson and a face-to-face with Bryn under the "he's probably really mad at me" circumstances, I wanted to wear something they'd really approve of. Some men bring out the worst. Some men bring out the Sunday best. Mr. Jenson brings out the "what would I wear for tea with the queen?"

I wore black slacks, a blue sweater with tiny pearls around the collar that I'd bought to wear to a baby shower, and a pair of black heels, not too tall, but not shabby either. They had eyelet lace at the edges, making my feet look extra pretty.

I brushed my teeth and hair and put on mascara and lipstick.

When I got downstairs, I tucked a gun and knife into the tote. Then I wrapped up some lemon pound cake with vanilla icing and several cranberry orange scones. I regretted that I didn't have time to make chicken noodle or vegetable barley soup. I really needed to freeze some for emergencies.

I called for Mercutio, but he was obviously out of earshot because he didn't bolt into the room. I locked the door and windows, thinking Merc would have to manage on his own till I got back or meet me at Bryn's. Merc's an expert at tracking me down.

I got in my car and decided not to take Main Street, knowing it would be the way people would expect me to take across town. I also figured I'd have an easier time seeing anyone who was trying to follow me if I was off the main drag.

I kept an eye on my rearview mirror but didn't see any

headlights. A block from Magnolia Park, I figured I was in the clear. A pinging sound on my roof made me reconsider. I zigged and zagged down the street. It sounded like hail, but it wasn't. I braked so I could get a better look at the nut that rolled down the windshield and off the hood.

"What the Sam Houston? Are squirrels on the offensive now, too?" I bent my head, straining to get a look into the trees. Not spying any warrior squirrels or other small fur-covered creatures, like hobgoblins, I started the car forward. Then I heard a thunk followed quickly by a second one that caused my car to lurch. As I rolled forward, I felt the car pull to the right and realized what the sound had been. I had a flat tire.

Damn it!

I threw the car into park and grabbed my tote. Not sure which weapon I needed, I tucked the gun into the back of my slacks, which I regretted wearing. First, because they wouldn't hold the gun as firmly in place as my Levi's, but also because the pants were a wool blend and therefore dry clean only. What the heck had I been thinking wearing angora and wool? Clearly, I hadn't totally gotten the hang of being under siege.

I wished I had a knife holder I could strap to my calf. Also, I really needed to think about getting a dagger or hunting knife. Since a butcher knife would've been too likely to cut through my tote bag, I'd settled on a steak knife, which against a rib eye on a plate would do just fine, but it lacked the length and razor-sharp edge I prefer to threaten a live opponent with.

A rock slammed into the passenger window and shattered it. I jumped, yanked on my door handle, and rolled from the seat into the street. I used the car for cover. Clearly whoever was attacking was shadowed by the trees on the far side of the car. Behind me on the driver's side there were houses where people were probably getting ready for bed or watching television.

"Let's take this fight outside the neighborhood," I called out in a whisper. "My neighbors have been through a lot, and I've sort of gotten a reputation of late that I don't want to—"

Another rock—a big one by the sound of it—hit the side of the car, crumpling metal. I winced, imagining the dent.

"Damn it!" I snapped. I had a huge deductible, and I wasn't set to cover any more bodywork on my car. I crept around to the back of the car, peering into the woods. That last rock had been too big to have been hoisted by a hobgoblin. Could it be Oatha and Beau? If so, where was their car? And how would they have known where to find me?

The night air was cool, crisp, and clean. I sniffed and then inhaled more deeply. Unless I was pretty far upwind, there was no way this assault against me and my Focus was coming from Vangie's nasty step-people. The air smelled earthy and fresh, like leaves after spring rain. I took off my fancy shoes and my footie nylons and slipped them into the tote. I'd be better off in bare feet in the woods.

"Trees," I whispered, inching toward them. "It's Tammy Jo Trask. 'Member me? I'm coming to visit. If you could see your way to giving me a hand against whoever's shooting at me, I'd appreciate it."

I sprinted from the street, over the lawn, and between two large trees. Most of the lower branches swayed out of my way, but one thick branch swung into my path. I couldn't stop in time and it caught me across the lower ribs, knocking me backward. I lost my breath when I landed.

"Mean," I complained, wheezing. I got up and moved forward gingerly, my ribs smarting with every step. The lone woody aggressor swung even lower, as if to trip me. I feigned turning but at the last second darted forward and hopped over the branch. I ran forward to be sure that it didn't catch me in the back. Unfortunately, I was no farther than a few feet when a vine caught my right ankle. I pitched forward, but instead of falling, I was scooped up by some kind of mesh and thrust into the air. A moment later, I bobbed like a rabbit in a snare.

"Oh," I said, swinging in the human-sized pouch I was caught in. "This is why you wanted me to go the other way,

Tree." I shook my head. "You were right. But you hit me so hard, I didn't realize it was a hint, not an assault. Next time, I'll know," I murmured.

I ran my hands over the mesh. It wasn't a fishing net. It was made of something soft, like finely woven silk lace. And it was coated with something that rubbed off on my hands and made my head buzz.

"Uh-oh," I murmured. "I need to hurry, don't I? There's something . . ." I twisted around for my tote. I opened it and found the steak knife. I poked its tip into the mesh, which actually seemed to push back. "No way," I growled, thrusting and sawing madly without making any significant progress. The satiny substance on the fabric clung to my skin, making it tingle and almost . . . shimmer.

"Tree," I said, trying to suppress giddy laughter that bubbled up like sparkling wine. "I'm having some problems here. Could you help? Could you drop this Tammy bag? Just swing it right off your branch?" I wiggled to get the pouch swinging. I felt the branch move and the pouch pop over a few feet. "That's it. Keep going! Whoa!" I exclaimed as I lost control of the swinging motion, and the pouch string twisted as it spun in a circle.

The whirling motion as the pouch's securing ropes unfurled made me lose all sense of place. I fell against the side of the pouch and had a vision, either a hallucination or a premonition, I couldn't be sure. All I knew was that I was on a blue and gray bridge that looked like someone had started to make a castle and decided to make a bridge instead. I ran because someone chased me. I saw the twinkling lights of a big city and knew that if I could just reach the street, I'd be safe.

I glanced down and saw my feet, which were tattooed with gold and green vines. I sprinted with a racing heart, hearing the pounding footfalls of my pursuers.

Run. Run faster!
Go, go, go!

In an instant, the bridge under my feet disappeared. I felt the pouch swing in a long arc and then I sailed through the air. I heard an angry voice, speaking a language I didn't understand. It sounded like Gaelic, which Bryn sometimes spoke. The trees made angry sounds in return.

My ears hummed. "Ours," the trees seemed to say. "Unlike you, she's ours."

"Aw," I said, wanting to give them a hug. Even the Duvall trees were loyal. I felt myself spinning end over end and then I hit the ground and rolled a few more feet. It took me a few minutes to fight my way out of the pouch. No wonder there's that expression, *madder than a bag of cats*. Being stuck in a bag is frustrating as all get-out. It could definitely drive somebody crazy.

When I had a Tammy Jo–sized hole in the top of the pouch, I shot through it and rolled away. The dirt and grass soothed my skin, which tingled to the point of pain. I landed in some fern fronds and would've lain there for a few minutes watching the stars dance in the sky, but I heard someone running toward me.

I might be out of the sack, but I wasn't out of the woods yet. Literally.

12

I ROLLED ONTO my hands and knees, scrambled up, and lurched forward, sprinting through the woods.

"Hello, dirt," I whispered breathlessly. "Show me the way to the muddy banks of the Amanos River."

I closed my eyes and concentrated on the feel of the earth beneath my feet and between my toes. It was almost like I was flying through the forest, like an Ewok on a *Star Wars* speeder. Everything whizzed past, chirping crickets and whirring wind all around me.

Can't catch me, I thought, and laughed.

I heard a male voice exclaim something in the distance and knew that branches and vines got in his way.

"Nope, can't have me. I belong to this town and it belongs to me."

I burst from the woods, my eyes popping open as I ran out of grass and landed hard in the street.

I panted for breath, the world spinning like the teacup ride at a carnival. I staggered across the street and for a few minutes I wasn't sure where I was, and I wanted to turn back to the woods. When I fell against a street sign, I held on and looked up. Sycamore Street. I was near the Amanos and near Bryn's house.

"Wasn't I going there?" I mumbled. My skin and clothes were covered in something that felt a lot like pixie dust but had a slightly tangy taste. The ground shimmered as if lit by a candle from underneath. "I'm not lost," I swore to myself, but my body was all kinds of crazy, jittering and weaving. It was like I'd drunk twenty tequila shots and then tried a hit of some scary wind-you-up drug like cocaine. I shook till my teeth rattled and my tongue did a dance against the back of my teeth.

"I gotta get this stuss—stuffs off me," I mumbled. "Before that guy catches up." I stripped down to my underwear and dove into the grass. I grabbed handfuls, apologizing for pulling it out, and rubbed it over my skin wherever it glowed golden.

After a few minutes, I was steady enough to walk. Barely.

I meandered down the street, glad when I got to Bryn's neighborhood. Whenever possible, I walked on the grass because the asphalt felt hard and cold and foreign against my soles. If I hadn't been raised by people, I would've made a good forest nymph. Or half-fae girl Tarzan. Being reared by apes didn't appeal to me, but chimps are cute. Or better still, I could've been raised by an ocelot. Merc could've been my stepbrother, the two of us a pair of cubs trying to make our way in a mad magical world. I giggled until my sides hurt and I fell over. I rolled around on the grass for a few minutes until I got my bearings. I grabbed my head to steady it on my shoulders and then stood. The world seemed to wobble, but I was pretty sure that I was the one wobbling.

What the heck had been in that mesh? I wondered as I watched my feet walk. I forced myself off Bryn's neighbor's lawn and crossed the drive triumphantly.

At the security buzzer, I busted out laughing. "Made it!" I clung to the post and hit the button.

"Took your time," Steve's voice said.

"Got a little side-sacked, sidetracked, Tammy-sacked, Tammy in a sack." I laughed so hard, I doubled over.

The gate slid open.

"Come on," I said to myself. "Pull yourself under control and get inside onto Bryn's properly—property." I took a deep breath. "Feet! Get going." But my feet weren't interested in the paved circular drive. My toes curled and inched toward the grass. "For pete's sake . . . and who is Pete anyway? Isn't he the daytime security guy?"

One of Bryn's neighbors' front doors opened. "Uh-oh. They'll see me! Get in there!" I hissed at my feet, which weren't working. I pitched to the side and let go of the post. I fell into a hibiscus bush and crawled through. Happy to be in the dirt, my feet started to work, but it was quite a long journey through the landscaping.

By the time I got to the house, I was bleeding from rose thorns and sticky with plant juice. I managed to force my feet onto the paving stones to get to the front door. I didn't want to ring the bell in case Mr. Jenson was resting. I tried the knob, which Steve had apparently unlocked.

The door swung open and I fell into the foyer.

"There," I said, blowing a lock of hair out of my eyes. "Made it." I dusted myself off. "Now if I were a Mr. Jenson, where would I hide myself?" I scratched my head. "If I were sick, I'd be in my bedroom in my bed." I forced myself to a standing position. "Now if I were a Mr. Jenson's room, where would I hide myself?" I looked around, disoriented. I could've sworn I knew the layout of Bryn's house.

"What the hell?" Bryn's voice boomed from in front of me.

"Holy shit," Steve's voice said from behind me.

"Hello, men of Bryn's house. Can you point me toward Mr. Jenson's room? I've come to check on him."

"Mr. Lyons," Steve sputtered.

"Tamara," Bryn said sharply. "Are you drunk?"

"No," I said, walking toward Bryn. "But I do smell whiskey. Who smells like the juice of the barley?" I asked. I sang a line from an Irish drinking song that I didn't even know I knew the words to and pointed at Bryn, adding, "It's you, isn't it, who smells like whiskey?"

"Don't stand there gaping, Steve. Get a blanket," Bryn said blackly.

"Don't yell at him. You," I said, poking my finger into his chest. "Don't be mean."

"What is this? What's all over your skin?" Bryn said, holding me away from him.

"A little dirt. And grass." I plucked a couple of rose petals out of the cup of my bra and dropped them. "Some flowers."

"Not that," Bryn snapped.

"Hey, what happened to my clothes?"

"Exactly what I'd like to know," Bryn said.

I looked down. My tiny undies barely covered my butt. I put my palms over my cheeks to cover them.

"Well, you know whose fault this is?"

"No, I don't."

"It's yours."

"Mine?" Bryn said, his brows shooting up.

"Oh boy," Steve said from behind me as he wrapped a blanket around me.

"Who do you think bought me all these lacy barely-there underwear? I used to wear plain cotton. When I wanted to get fancy I'd wear some with kiss prints or Longhorn symbols or even once pink-and-black leopard print. Sexy! But they always covered my butt as well as a bathing suit. But you didn't think that was good enough. And look at me now. I'm almost as bad as a stripper. Actually—" I glanced down inside the blanket, frowning. "I did get stripped. In fact," I said suspiciously, "I think I may have stripped myself." I exhaled a sigh. "Good grief. I'm a stripper. Can you even guess how that happened?"

"I'd rather not," Bryn said, turning and walking away. "Sober up in the library. Steve, you're responsible for her."

"He is not responsible for me!" I announced, trailing after Bryn, who mounted the stairs. My feet and legs tangled in the blanket and I had to grab the railing to keep from falling down.

"Steve, close your eyes," I said, dropping the blanket.

"Mr. Lyons?" Steve questioned as I darted up the stairs. "You want me to come up and get her?"

"Now, Steve," I said. "You and I get along fine because you know your limits. Don't make me get rough with you."

Steve laughed.

"Don't encourage her," Bryn said flatly, walking down the hall.

"Mr. Lyons?"

Bryn shook his head. "I've got it. Go back to your post, Steve."

I pursued Bryn until he paused and took me by the arm. He drew me into his bedroom and then into his bathroom. He pointed at the sunken tub. "Get in."

I glanced at myself in the mirror. My skin shimmered, my ear tips were slightly pointed, and my eyes glowed a tawny hazel. Ivy and fern fronds hung from tangled hair.

"Green's a good color for me," I said, touching a vine.

Bryn plucked the vine from my hair and dropped it in the wastebasket with a frown, then turned to the tub, flicked the drain closed, and spun the knobs, making the water gush. "I'm not going to tell you again."

"You're not the boss of me."

"That's certainly true. But right now, you look like someone crossed a cavewoman with a Bratz doll. In," he said.

"What's a Bratz doll?" I asked.

"A toy. My client's daughter collected them." Bryn dumped in bath salts. The water foamed.

"I'm not ready to take a bath yet. This dirt helped me out. It had my back. And my front," I said with a laugh. "And my backside."

Bryn reached over and unhooked my bra with a two-fingered pinch of the clasp.

"Hey," I complained as it fell on the floor. "I was wearing that."

I reached down, but arms came around me and a second later I sat in hot sudsy water. I glared at him.

"I thought I warned you—" I said, attempting to stand. The struggle was brief, but soggy, and when I surfaced,

I grabbed Bryn's shirt and yanked. He pitched forward and fell in.

"How do you like it?"

He ignored the question and instead grabbed a loofah thing and scrubbed my skin with it. Pretty soon, the tingling disappeared and the brown-and-gold bathwater ran down the drain. Bryn climbed from the tub and, without a word, stripped out of his soaked clothes.

I rested my chin on the edge of the tub and admired the view. "I should probably be annoyed that you're prettier than me, but I actually don't mind."

Bryn toweled his hair with a brief glance over his shoulder. "Don't."

"Don't what? Lust over you?"

"Don't flirt. Not after this morning. And not while you're under the influence of fae magic."

"Fae?"

"Yes," Bryn said. "What happened? Find another box of pixie dust and accidentally dump it on yourself?"

"Nope," I said, and then launched into a rambling account of my sacking.

Bryn shook his head with a grimace, then walked out of the bathroom, saying over his shoulder, "Wash your hair."

I refilled the tub and soaked awhile, then haphazardly washed and conditioned my hair. When I got out of the tub, I shucked my panties and walked into Bryn's room. I have a drawer and a small section of the closet, and that's where I was headed when the open suitcase on his bed stopped me in my tracks.

"Where are we going?" I asked. My mind darted to the vision I'd had of myself, galloping away from someone who was after me. That dream had been of someplace outside Duvall. What had I been doing on horseback, racing down a lane? I'd been riding a few times, but I was no Kentucky Derby jockey. That kind of pace would've scared me half to death, though I hadn't seemed scared in the vision. Was I going to learn to ride a horse while on vacation with Bryn? That sounded fun.

"*We* aren't going anywhere," Bryn said, tying his white terry-cloth robe closed. "I'm taking Jenson to Ireland, and then I'm meeting Andre in Gstaad."

My stomach lurched like I'd fallen from a cliff. Bryn leaving? *That's not right*, I thought.

Bryn and I were connected forever by the oath. I wasn't supposed to ever have to worry about losing him. He tossed a toiletry bag into the case as if he didn't know the new rules of our relationship, which of course he did since *he'd* been the one to tell me!

He clipped the suitcase strap over his clothes, and I was overcome with a possessiveness I hadn't felt since a girl tried to steal the Edie locket during third-grade recess.

Like the locket, Bryn wasn't allowed to disappear. He belonged to me.

Even as the logical part of my brain tried to argue that you can't own a person, another louder part yelled, *Yes, I can. Bryn is mine.*

I stared at him, practically speechless. The only thing I managed to say was, "No."

13

"NO, NO," I said again, walking to his suitcase. I scooped out clothes, fighting the tight strap I hadn't bothered to unclip. Some shirts fell from my arms to the floor. I grabbed them up into a rumpled heap, the buzzed fae part of my nature giving Bryn a defiant look.

"Get dressed," he said, grabbing the suitcase and pulling it away from me.

"You get dressed. I'm busy," I said, marching into the closet with the clothes I'd liberated. I hung them on hangers, shaking out the wrinkles.

"Tamara, goddamn it," Bryn said, stalking into the closet. He grabbed the first thing of mine that he reached. It was a silver and turquoise dress. He dragged it down over my head, covering my body, and then spun me away from him and zipped it up.

"What are you dressing me in this for?" I asked, giving a little twirl. The skirt flared. "Not like we're going dancing. You're not in a dancing kind of mood, are you?"

"Go down to the guest room and sleep off whatever drugged you. And while I'm gone, you should stay out of the woods. There may be more fae snares. Who knows if you'll be lucky enough to escape next time?"

"It wasn't luck," I said, blocking him from retrieving the clothes I'd taken.

"Cut it out and go downstairs."

"I'm not going anywhere. If I do, you'll keep packing. And that'll just make more work for me to unpack since you're not going anywhere."

"Listen," he said, lowering his voice. "I'm leaving. If I could take back what happened, I would, but I can't undo it."

"Take back what happened? You mean the fight this morning?"

"Further back."

I sucked in a breath. "You mean the vow?"

He nodded.

"That's not yours to take back. That was my vow. I made it."

"And you regret it."

"I do not. It saved your life."

"But you regret what it cost you."

"What it cost me?"

"Sutton."

"Oh," I said, remembering Zach for the first time. "It's true that I love Zach. Might always."

The look on Bryn's face just about stabbed me through the heart. He turned and stalked back into his room. In the closet, I still felt his power rolling over me. Magic that was angry and restless and passionate. Magic that made my ears ring and my feet want to chase him to the ends of the earth.

I don't love Zach the way I love you. Not anymore, I thought, knowing it was true. Bryn and I had been through too much together. We were the ladyfingers and coffee in a tiramisu dessert. Once the coffee soaked into the cake, there was no way to separate them.

I moved to the doorway and leaned against the jamb, watching him pack.

"You're wasting your time," I said, making my voice extra gentle.

"It's mine and mine alone to waste."

"You've got a right to be mad. If you still cared a lot about one of your exes, I'd be jealous, too."

"You warned me enough times that you weren't through with Sutton. I should've listened."

"I hurt you."

"Of course you hurt me," he said, pouring himself a whiskey. The crystal decanter was almost empty. I tried to remember how much had been in it the last time I'd visited.

"If you'd seen your face when you walked out of that house," Bryn said. "How much you didn't want it to be over between you and Sutton. It ripped the heart out of my fucking chest. I'd have done anything to have been spared that. I wish to the stars I'd never gone to that Halloween party."

I sucked in a small breath, feeling like he'd dumped ice water over my head. Bryn was always so smooth, able to handle anything. Sometimes I forgot that I had the power to hurt him. I took it for granted that I couldn't lose him. I'd been so worried about Zach ignoring me that I hadn't thought about what pursuing a relationship—even a friendship—with Zach might do to Bryn.

I sat on the bed, folding my hands on my lap. "I'm sure sorry you feel that way. That's not how I feel."

"How can you say that?" His magic snapped like a whip, sending a glass flying. He jerked the power back, and the glass dropped to the carpet without shattering, but reining the magic in had cost him. He vibrated with unspent emotion.

I spoke softly, trying to soothe him. "Zach was my first love and he's family. We had almost twenty years together and made lots of passionate promises. That sort of thing doesn't just go away."

"Tamara—"

"*But*—" I said, quick to cut him off. "If I had to choose

between him leaving town and you leaving town," I said, shaking my head. "It hurts to lose Zach and I'll sure miss him a lot, but he can go if that's what he needs to do," I said. "You can't."

"What are you saying?" he asked, becoming very still.

"You know. You're always two steps ahead."

"Tamara," he warned.

"I don't want you to go, and I won't let you."

"You can't stop me," he said.

"You sure?" I asked softly. I stood and walked to him. I took his face in my hands and kissed him. "I love you more than chocolate," I whispered, breathing in his magic and letting it mingle with mine. I blew against his lips, feeling the tingling warmth spread from my mouth to his.

He rubbed the kiss away. Had it tasted of the Never? Or was he just upset?

"If you knew that of the two of us he was the one you could live without, why the hell did you—?"

"I didn't know. I figured it out when I saw your suitcase." I shook my head with an exasperated sigh. "I've got recipes and spells and emotions all jumbled together in my head. I figure stuff out when it hits me, like the button popping up on a Thanksgiving turkey when it's all cooked."

"If it's so chaotic in your heart, maybe tomorrow you'll see Sutton and realize he's the one you can't live without."

"Maybe so. Faeries are mercurial, and I'm half. Maybe you'll never know from one day to the next what I'm going to do. God knows, sometimes I don't know myself. But I can tell you one thing," I said, taking a step back.

He raised his brows in question.

"If you try to leave, you won't get very far."

"Why not?"

"Because you want to stay, and now you know that I want you to stay, too."

"Why do you want me to stay?"

"Because I love you," I said.

"It's not enough to love me. Obviously."

"I love you more than anyone."

He scrutinized me. "Do you?"

"Yep," I said, putting a hand over my heart. "I swear to God and Hershey and all that's holy and delicious."

"To all that's holy and delicious?" he asked skeptically.

"Yeah, I swear on the important stuff."

I walked to the drawer, pulled out a pair of underwear, and slid them on. "Unpack, Bryn, we've got work to do. Later, if you want, we can make up in a way that's fun."

His hand shook a little as he ran it through his hair. "I've never felt this out of control in my life. Not even the times in college when I got dead drunk."

"Yeah, welcome to love. It's a mess."

He choked out a laugh. "That's your expert opinion, huh? Christ," he murmured. After a moment, he seemed steadier. "Come give me a kiss."

I looked over my shoulder at him. He watched and waited.

"I might still taste like fae magic."

"I'll risk it," he said.

I strode to him and planted a kiss on his mouth. His arms slid around me, and I felt restless magic, dangerous and delicious, slide against me.

I had to wrestle free. His eyes blazed blue with a look that promised the best kind of makeup sex, but I shook off the temptation.

"Later," I said firmly. "I need my brilliant-guy Bryn first."

"All right." He retrieved the fallen glass from the floor and set it next to the bottle. "And Tamara?"

"Uh-huh?"

"If you ever sleep with Sutton while you and I are together, I will kill him."

I huffed a sigh. "Don't you guys ever get tired of threatening to kill each other? There are more important things going on in Duvall than who I spend the night with."

"It doesn't feel that way."

"Yeah," I said. "Jealousy's the reason love's a mess. But

don't worry. You'll be okay," I promised, which made him smile.

DOWNSTAIRS, I PICKED up the security phone in the kitchen. "Hey, Steve."

He cleared his throat. "Hey, Tammy Jo. How are things?"

"Oh, yeah, everything's okay," I said. "Where's Mr. Jenson's room?" I asked.

Steve gave me directions. A minute later, I knocked softly on Mr. Jenson's bedroom door.

He invited me in, and I heard a deep, wet-sounding cough that worried me straight down to my toes.

"Hey there," I said.

"That's interesting attire for eleven p.m. Did you come from a party, Miss Tamara?" he asked, pausing between sentences to catch his breath.

"Dr. Suri's coming over."

"That's not necessary."

"I know it, but I can't talk him out of it now after I woke him."

He coughed. "You shouldn't have done so. This is just a bad cold. And if it isn't, well, an old man has to die of something," he said.

My jaw dropped.

"And," he continued after a pause, "a young man needs something to do."

"What young man? Bryn?"

He nodded. "Your preoccupation with your ex-husband's return has been hard on him. I realize you have to follow your heart, my dear, but I can't sit by and do nothing. Shuttling me to Ireland will take his mind off what's happening here."

I took Mr. Jenson's hand in mine and squeezed it. "He's so lucky to have you, but you don't have to worry. I'll keep Bryn busy. That's all settled."

"Is it?"

"Yep."

He sighed with relief. "If you aren't the death of him, you'll be the making of him."

"I don't know about all that, but we'll take care of us. You concentrate on getting better. Or we'll have to sit by your bedside and might miss saving the town next time around. You don't want Duvall's destruction on your conscience, do you?"

"Certainly not," he said with a slight smile. "It's good to have you home, Miss Tamara."

"It's good to have you home, too, Mr. Jenson," I said, giving him a kiss on the cheek. I pulled the covers up to his neck and left the room, closing the door gently. Back in the kitchen, I picked up the security phone and told Steve to get Dr. Suri to come to the house right away.

"Mr. Jenson will see him?"

"Sure thing."

"How'd you do it?"

"Made a promise he liked."

"A promise you intend to keep?"

"Of course. You don't lie to a sick-bed Mr. Jenson, Steve. It's against house rules."

"All right. Good to know," he said, and I felt him smiling.

"Hey, Tammy Jo?"

"Yes?"

"Welcome back."

14

IT'S NOT HARD to figure out how Bryn became a successful lawyer and top-tier wizard. Laser beams have less focus. As I rambled on, he managed to follow even my most wandering thoughts, which I appreciated.

I told him about the dustup with Vangie's stepmother and stepbrother.

"I wonder if the skeleton guy in the tree could have been some special zombie that Oatha raised to spy on my house. A creature who was stalking Vangie, maybe? I did meet Vangie and Skeleton Guy on the same night."

"Oatha's not powerful enough to raise and control a zombie that sentient."

"Not even if she used black magic she conjured with a smelly animal sacrifice?"

"Well," Bryn said with an uncertain shrug. "Depending on the size of the animal. It would almost have had to have been a human sacrifice."

I shuddered. "Hope not."

"While scanning for sources of magic in town to see if I could detect the spells that are affecting the Duvall ghosts, I did detect water magic. The Theroux family casts using water."

"Not water again! Not after the flood!"

Bryn smiled. "They're not using it to make rain. That's weather witches. Water witches harness the power of flowing water. They use it to power spells, the way you use herbs and I use the stars. The power drawn is the energy source, not the target result."

"Oh, right."

"It's possible it was used against the ghosts, but it didn't feel nearly powerful enough to have animated a collection of bones and to make it sentient enough to move around independently."

"Why would the Therouxs care about driving the ghosts out of Duvall?"

"Maybe they haven't driven them out. Maybe they've collected them."

My eyes widened. "To spy?"

"That's what the ghosts around here do best," Bryn said grimly.

"It seems like a lot of trouble. Couldn't they just use a strand of Vangie's hair to scry for her and track her down? She thinks they messed with her hairbrush."

"Sure, much easier."

"Although, she said she doesn't leave hair in the brush," I said, tapping a finger against my lip. "The other thing is that if they've heard that we use Edie and the Duvall ghost network to get information, maybe they don't want the ghosts loose."

Bryn ran a hand through his hair and nodded. "We'll investigate the Therouxs more deeply, but first I'd like to do a more elaborate spell to check the seals on the doors to the underhill."

The Unseelie fae whose territory we lived in were trapped behind magical doors. The "minor fae" who were small could slip through and around them, but human-sized fae couldn't. On Samhain and the winter solstice, the doors to the kingdom of the Unseelie would open, but Bryn's magic reinforced the seal to keep them closed.

* * *

WHEN BRYN WAS prepared to do the spell to assess the seal on the doors between the fae world and ours, I asked him to let me join him as he cast. Bryn's a good teacher. He writes the spell down, goes over it with me line by line, and tries to show me how to cast it. Unfortunately, I can't feel anyone's magic except his. Not even my own. So when it comes to controlling power and putting the right amount into a spell, it doesn't work out for me. I also can't separate the fae and the witch magicks on purpose. They tend to unravel when I'm really upset or scared. Luckily, Bryn can draw out the witch magic because it's perfectly matched to his own. He's celestial magic. I'm earth magic. Heaven and earth, aren't they just always paired up?

After my spell-casting attempts led to absolutely nothing, I sat on the grass and watched him do it, enjoying the feel of his magic sliding across my skin.

He shook his head. "I can't find a tear in the fabric of the spell that's reinforcing the doors. They seem to be tightly closed. None of the large fae should've been able to get through. If the skeletal creature you saw is Unseelie fae, he must have come through before."

"Or have a talent for crossing at points other than where the doors are." It was reportedly a rare talent. But I'd met one faery who could do it. Her name was Nixella, and she was child-sized, but deadly.

"Hey," I said, sucking in a breath as my body felt like someone was twisting my guts in knots. I grabbed my stomach and rolled onto the grass.

Bryn dropped next to me. "What is it?" he asked, putting a hand on me. He hissed in pain. "What's going on?"

The sensation shifted to my chest, and I couldn't breathe. It was like my lungs had been popped. I opened my mouth but couldn't make a sound. Bryn had one hand on his chest and one on my arm.

"Tamara!"

Then as instantly as it had started, the sensation disappeared. I drew in a startled breath. Gasping hard, I lay exhausted, clutching the grass. Bryn leaned over me, concerned.

"I'm okay now."

"Are you sick, sweetheart?" he asked, running his hands over my ribs and belly.

"No. Something happened. Something magical, I think," I said, looking around. The buzz from the fae mesh was almost gone, but maybe it had been poisonous. The strange thing was that now that the assault on my guts was done, I felt normal. If I'd been poisoned, shouldn't I have been getting worse?

"I don't feel any residual magic," Bryn said. "There's no spell on you. Unless I can't sense it because it was fae magic."

"Maybe, but it didn't feel like fae magic or taste like it. Usually I get a honey or fruity flavor in my mouth. And my skin shimmers or tingles." I took a deep breath, feeling my belly. It was fine. "Whatever it was, if it hit me this hard in the grass it must have been really powerful."

"What do you mean in the grass?"

I flushed. I hadn't told Bryn about my increasing connection to nature. "I've got earth and fae magic. I usually do well when I'm in the grass or dirt or among the trees, especially lately. What about a hex sent from far away? Vangie said Oatha's been studying curses." Oatha had sworn to get back at me, and she certainly didn't want me helping Vangie.

"Hexes and curses generally need to be cast in close proximity unless someone really powerful is casting them. And that would leave residual magic."

"Speaking of Vangie, I wonder where she is. Even if Oatha didn't hex me just now, Vangie was right about her and Beau being dangerous. They tried to kill me in my own kitchen, my favorite room in the house."

Bryn smiled in spite of everything.

I told him about her father's will and how they might have a motive to kill her now that she was engaged.

"I'll look into it."

"I lost my phone in the woods," I told Bryn. "Vangie might've tried to call me. I need to talk to her," I said, fingering the sore spot on my cheek where Beau had clocked me.

Bryn examined my face, scowling. "You're a little swollen where he hit you."

"It's much better actually. It throbbed like crazy and felt more puffy before I got caught in the sack."

"Christ, I'm sick of seeing you covered in blood and bruises. You know, we could just say to hell with this." He stared at me, and his voice softened. "We could leave, really leave here. I'd take you anywhere . . . show you the world. All you have to do is let me."

My brows rose. "Run away?"

"That's not how I'd put it."

I gave him a stern look.

"You're not even tempted? I wonder if that fae drug is still in your system," he said. "Because when I met you, you were more than ready to sidestep—"

"I've changed," I blurted. "And remember how we're the good guys? The good guys don't turn tail and run."

Bryn ran a hand through his hair. "I know all about fighting the good fight. I've done it for a long time. But I think many people would say we've already done our part. And nearly died doing it."

"I know," I said, touching his face.

Long before I'd taken up arms against evil, Bryn had fought the establishment for years as part of the Wizard's Underground. He seemed to prefer a clandestine approach to fighting bad guys. If we were law enforcement, Bryn would be a spy or an assassin. I'd be on the SWAT team.

I stood. "Let's go in and call Vangie's cell."

We went back inside Bryn's house, and I waited for him to find Vangie's cell phone number. I called her, and this time she picked up on the first ring.

"Oh, Tammy Jo, thank goodness! I have to—I'll be right there, Jackson," she called. "Tammy Jo?"

"I'm here."

"Jackson arrived early, and I can't talk about, you know,

magic in front of him," she hissed in a whisper. "He's only human, and I decided not to tell him about me being a you-know-what until after we're married, possibly for a few decades. I have, however, told him my relatives might try to stop our wedding. They might even try to say I was mentally incapacitated. We decided we should get married without delay. I'll pick you up at two p.m., maid of honor. So we can have our hair done at Johnny's salon."

"Vangie—"

"And wear a blue dress for good luck. Jackson likes blue."

"Listen, I believe you about your stepfamily. They are dangerous."

"Oh, I know."

"They attacked me—"

"And you survived! Well done, Tammy Jo! I knew I had the right witch as maid of honor."

"I'm saying you have to be careful. Maybe you and Jackson should come to Bryn's house."

Bryn's brows shot up.

"It's fortified," I said.

"And what a lovely location for the reception. I accept!" With that she hung up before I could say another thing. I shook my head and put the phone back in the cradle. "We should probably try to get some sleep. Big wedding tomorrow."

Bryn's expression was more than a little skeptical. The security phone rang. Bryn strode over and picked it up. He listened, his face growing concerned. He hung up.

"What?" I asked.

"We have a visitor at the gate, and he's here on a matter of life and death."

15

DOC BARNABY LOOKED dapper. After his wife's death, he'd been a mess. But since raising her as a zombie using stolen magic from me and accepting that she had to go back into the ground, he'd really pulled himself together. He'd started dating a younger woman, the Widow Potts, who's sixty-one. His silver hair had been trimmed short and he wore a blazer and bow tie with his jeans.

"Hi," I said, ushering him into the kitchen.

"It's nice to see you," he said, nodding at us with an approving smile. "I'm meeting my lady friend soon. We're going to have dinner and then play pinochle with some other Duvall seniors."

"So late?" I exclaimed.

"Sure. None of us sleeps much anymore," Doc Barnaby said.

"You said something about a matter of life and death?" Bryn asked.

"Well, death and afterlife apparently," Doc Barnaby said, accepting a slice of cake and cup of coffee. "I came to talk with you about Abner."

"Abner?" I asked.

"Abner Gillicutty. A town ghost. Don't you know him?" he asked, surprised.

"No. I only see the ghost of my aunt Edie."

"Well, since Halloween, the Widow Potts and I see a fair number of ghosts. Or we did. They're dwindling. And Abner ranted about some livestock that's been abducted, as he puts it. He's fearful that the dark witches who've come to town plan to slaughter the missing animals. Abner's quite attached to some of them. He was about to tell me where the animals had been taken when he disappeared. One moment he was shaking his phantom fists, the next, poof. Haven't seen or heard from him since."

Bryn and I exchanged glances.

"I would have talked to the police, but you see the difficulty . . ." he said, trailing off.

"No, you did the right thing. We're the ones to tell about bad witches," I said.

"This cake is delicious, Tammy Jo. Really tasty. I'm sorry my lady friend isn't with me. I'm sure she would've enjoyed it."

I strode to the fridge and took out a caramel apple torte. I put it into a cake carrier and handed it to Doc Barnaby. "For the card game. Tell the seniors I said hey."

Doc Barnaby beamed and gave Bryn a wink. "She's quite a find."

Bryn nodded.

"Well, I'm off," the doc said, and with that, he strolled out of the kitchen.

I glanced at Bryn. "Do you think we should wait until tomorrow to look for the missing animals?"

"No. If they are using animal sacrifices for black magic rituals so they can murder Vangie at a distance, we should stop them as soon as possible."

"I'VE HAD TOO much whiskey to drive," Bryn said, tossing me his keys. I caught them with raised eyebrows.

"I'm not drunk," he added. "But I'm certainly over the legal limit, and I'm sure if any of Sutton's deputy friends pulled us over, I'd find myself in jail."

That was certainly true. When word got out—which it probably already had—that I'd spent the night with Zach, who'd just gotten home for Christmas, and then the morning after I stayed at his place, I'd ditched him to go back to Bryn, well, Bryn and I wouldn't be winning any popularity contests with local law enforcement.

We approached Bryn's sports car. The shape of its headlights made it look predatory, like it was ready to attack the road. The doors opened vertically like an alien craft, and since it had enough power under the hood to practically launch us into space, that was fitting. I dropped into the leather seat and buckled myself in. Bryn joined me, leaning back in the passenger seat, relaxed. I liked that he was so comfortable with my driving. Unlike Zach, Bryn was always quick to acknowledge the things I was good at, like shooting and driving.

Bryn glanced over to find me staring at him. "Everything okay?"

I pulled the seat belt to give myself some slack and leaned toward the opposite seat. I turned Bryn's face and kissed him, my tongue playing with his. His magic slid down my throat, warming me to the toes.

"Yes," I said when I pulled back. "Everything's good."

Bryn watched me through lowered lids.

I brushed my thumb over his lip, wishing we had time for more kissing. "Sorry. I shouldn't wind up my toys if I don't have time to play with them."

"I'm not a toy," he said, pinning me with a dark look that sent a shiver of lust to all my sexy parts. "But you're welcome to play with me."

"Um—could you stop that?" I said, shoving the key into the ignition.

"Stop what?" His voice was low and smooth. Magic floated to me on warm breath.

"Stop seducing me with your eyes and voice and that

warm waterfall of magic spilling over me. I'm trying to drive," I said, putting the car in gear and rolling to the gate.

I buzzed Steve on the intercom. "We're heading out for a while. Be sure to let Dr. Suri in to see Mr. Jenson."

"I will, and be careful out there," he said.

"We'll give it a shot," I said. I pulled the car out onto the street.

"What's that?" Bryn said, putting a hand against the window.

I looked around. "I didn't see anything."

Bryn rolled down the window and a blast of cold air rushed in. "Stop," Bryn said.

I pulled up next to the curb three houses down from his place. "What's up?"

"Someone is using blood-and-bones magic. Part of this spell calls the spirits, I think."

"Can you tell where it's coming from?"

"Go to Riverbank Park," he said. "Let's see if it follows a path along the water."

He closed the window and I cranked up the heat, but a minute later we were at the entrance to the park.

"Wait for me," Bryn said.

"Nope. I'm coming with you," I said, grabbing a gun.

"Tamara, the magic's not being cast from the park. It's some distance away."

"If you say so, but I'm comin'."

He nodded, climbing out. I joined him on the dock that stretched out over the Amanos River and watched him call to the sky. Magic from the stars folded down on us like whipped cream. I edged closer to him.

"Yeah, sweetheart, come here," he whispered, catching my free hand. My breath frosted on the air and I shivered, pulling the borrowed coat tighter around me. My feet were freezing, but I let the magic flow and for a moment, I saw a kaleidoscope of color in the night sky, like rainbows shining through the dark.

"Wow," I said with a gasp.

He brought my hand up and kissed it. His breath warmed my skin, but nothing could overcome the chill.

"Got a signal?"

Bryn grinned. "I'm not a GPS device."

"You're not a space heater either. Hurry up if you can. I'm freezing."

"The blood-and-bones magic is gone, but there's water magic humming along the river." He stretched his hands out and whispered in Gaelic. His magic bent and feathered outward. He nodded.

"You have it?"

"Sure, I have it," he said with a cocky smile.

I rolled my eyes, but I smiled, too.

We returned to the car, and he directed me. "Turn left. The spell was cast from out of town," he said, his voice trailing off.

"Bryn?"

Bryn rested his head back against the seat.

"Bryn?" I said, reaching over to tap his thigh.

"Sorry. I'm struggling to stay awake."

"You can't fall asleep! You're the navigator!"

"I know," he said, giving himself a shake. "But I've been up since dawn. I had a fight with your ex and his bone-crushing amulet, I suffered the worst heartbreak of my life, and I worried Jenson might be dying. Half a bottle of Jameson's Irish Whiskey was supposed to cure me of being conscious, but you arrived and had other plans. My bed just keeps getting farther away." He rolled the window down a crack to blast himself with frigid air. His lids rose.

I stroked his hair. "I know you're tired. As soon as we spy on these death magic witches and possibly run them out of town, I'll take you straight home and put you to bed."

"Will you come to bed with me?" he murmured.

"Yes." *Eventually.*

"Turn right up ahead. Is that a new bracelet?"

"Um, yeah. Vangie gave me a charm bracelet," I said, giving my wrist a shake to show him. "Gracie Kramer had a charm bracelet when we were little. I always wanted one."

"Why didn't you tell someone? I'm sure they would've gotten you one."

"Edie said they were silly. She's a jewelry snob."

"She's also a bitch."

I sighed. I needed to remember to tell Bryn only good Edie stories. They clashed enough already. "She wanted me to have the good stuff."

"How old were you?"

"Seven."

"And you were supposed to hold out for diamonds, huh? I'm sure your mom and Melanie couldn't afford to deck a seven-year-old out in fine jewelry. And losing a fortune in precious stones in a sandbox or swimming hole would've been an incredible waste."

"They let me wear the locket sometimes. I never lost it," I said defensively.

"I'm just saying that a charm bracelet would've been more practical at that age, and the ghost shouldn't have criticized your taste, then or now."

"She can be great, too, you know. She always told me where they hid the sweets. She took me on pretend adventures around town and taught me the Charleston. We danced every day. From the time I was five until I was thirteen, Edie was my favorite person in the world."

"What happened when you were thirteen?"

"I grew up and things changed."

"What things?" When I didn't answer, Bryn said, "Sutton."

I nodded. "He was my boyfriend forever, long before either of us even knew what boyfriends and girlfriends did together besides kiss. Around thirteen, we started to figure that stuff out and then we wanted to be alone whenever we got the chance. Edie got in the way. On purpose, of course."

"Maybe she's not so bad after all," Bryn said.

I smiled.

"There," Bryn said, pointing to a light in the distance.

"What is that? There are no houses this far out of town. Isn't that the wetlands?"

Bryn nodded. "Someone's out there. That's a bonfire. Pull off the road and turn off the headlights. We'll walk."

"Walk?" I scoffed.

I sidled the car onto the shoulder and turned off the lights but kept the engine and its hot-air-blowing heater on. I had my spare tennis shoes and socks that I kept at Bryn's, but they wouldn't do me much good if I ended up walking through freezing swamp water.

"I don't think we want to walk far in this cold."

"If you want to find out what's going on, we can't drive. They'll see the headlights and will either leave or get rid of anything they don't want us to see."

"I really would like to find out what's going on, but it's so cold out there. What good will knowing anything do us if we turn into Popsicles?"

"You can wait here," he said.

"No."

"I grew up in Ireland and went to school on the East Coast. I'm dressed for the weather; I'll be fine."

"Against the cold maybe," I said. "But I need to stay with you to help with any trouble other than the weather."

"You know I can take care of myself, right?" he asked, amused.

"Yeah, against regular odds. Maybe there will just be a couple people roasting marshmallows, making s'mores. Yum, s'mores. I'm hungry again. But if they're making something else, like say black magic, and they don't want a witness, I'm going to be there to make them think twice about feeding you to the alligators."

"Alligators?" he asked.

"Yes, alligators. This is a Cajun witch and wizard. They could throw you in a trunk and take you back to Louisiana to feed to the alligators, of which they have many. Haven't you ever watched *Swamp People* or eaten French-fried alligator at a Cajun restaurant?" I asked, grabbing my socks and shoes.

"You don't have shoes on?" Bryn asked. "Why the hell not? You were barefoot in Riverbank Park?"

"I'll explain about that sometime," I said.

"Now's good," Bryn said.

"Not for me," I said. "If I'm walking across wetlands, I want to get it over with."

"Tamara," he said with a scowl. "I assume this is something I'm not going to like."

Exactly. "I'm ready," I said, getting out of the car. I heard him sigh as he climbed out.

"You know I'll find out eventually."

"Maybe," I agreed. "Or we might die first."

"That's what I love about you. You always look on the bright side."

16

WE WALKED ABOUT twenty-five feet before coming across a black F-250 whose license plate I recognized.

"You've got to be kidding," I whispered.

"What? Is that Sutton's truck?"

"Yep."

"What the hell would he be doing out here?"

"I guarantee he's not making s'mores," I said. "If I had to guess, I'd say he's out here the same as us, investigating."

"A bad idea. He has no experience, and no chance against magic this deadly."

"His bone-crushing amulet maybe feels different."

Bryn said nothing. We walked on until we came across another car, this one a BMW that I also recognized.

"A veritable parking lot," Bryn murmured.

"That's Johnny's car," I said. Johnny Nguyen owned the town's beauty salon that about ninety percent of the women and seventy percent of the men went to. Johnny was multi-talented. He also designed costumes and sets for the local theater group and for Halloween parties. And most recently, he'd started an event company called Johnny Time. The group got together to go jogging and do aerobics at the community center; they went on shopping trips to Dallas in a big bus and took tours of the hill country. I'd been saving up to join them, even though Johnny would've let me tag along for free because we're friends. He's sweet-natured that way.

Johnny also happened to be able to see Edie. Other than Zach, he was the only regular person who could. And Johnny dated a snarky, cross-dressing vampire named Rollie, who was six foot five if he was an inch and who made fun of anything that moved. Rollie and Johnny made as odd a couple as Bryn and I did, but it worked for them.

"I hope Rollie came out here alone. Johnny's not built for swamp fights."

"But you are? You weigh what? A hundred pounds?" Bryn said.

"A hundred and seven point five," I corrected, like that seven and a half pounds moved my fighting class up from lightweight to heavyweight. Bryn was not impressed. "Plus, Rollie shouldn't drag Johnny into a witch fight on a weeknight. Johnny opens the salon. For a long day of Duvall ladies bent on gossip and highlights, he should get a full night's sleep or he'll be tired."

Bryn's soft chuckle was drowned out by zydeco music and Rollie's nearby not-quite-whispered complaint of, "What the hell is this? Bramble? I think it snagged my shirt."

"It okay. I fix for you tomorrow."

"You don't have these iridescent sequins in your sewing box. I'm sure they were dyed in a special lot for Versace."

"Rollie, I fix for you. Now hush, I think we getting close."

"Johnny!" I called out in a whisper.

I heard rustling and the swish of fabric.

"Who's that?" Rollie demanded. "Oh look, it's our redhead. What are you up to, Miss If-he's-handsome-he-must-be-mine? We heard something about fisticuffs and a water hose—oh, hello, Bryn."

"Rollie," Bryn said.

"Come on over here, Tammy Jo, let's have a quick sidebar," Rollie said, grabbing my arm and pulling me aside.

"Hi, Rollie," I said, smiling up at him. As vampires go,

Rollie was medium dangerous. Johnny forbade him from biting people in Duvall, and Rollie complied. Mostly. With Rollie being a fork-tongued gossip and fashion critic, demons bowed down to him, and Johnny had no chance of keeping him under control there. As his friend, I'd been on the receiving end of plenty of critiques, but he'd also been sweet enough to fight monsters with me, so all things considered, I liked him a lot.

"Hi there, cupcake," he said, then paused to look me over. "Honey, what are you wearing? That coat doesn't fit. And is that one of the lawyer's college sweatshirts? It's hanging off your shoulder. Are we in a *Flashdance* revival, darling? What's next? Leg warmers?" He shuddered.

"I don't know what leg warmers are, but you can bet I'd wear 'em if I had 'em. It's freezing out here."

Rollie snapped a finger as he jerked his forearm to the side in a "not if I have something to say about it" gesture. "The reason I took you aside is I think you should know that Deputy Tightbuns is out here. Unless you brought a fire hose, maybe you'd better leave this little fact-finding mission to us."

"What facts are you trying to find? And how come?"

"Edie the ghost got Johnny all worked up. Something about animal cruelty and desperate witches."

So Edie had talked to Johnny about the trouble, and obviously to Zach, too, since he was out here. "Edie didn't tell me." Then I realized that of course she couldn't have. I'd been at Bryn's, where she couldn't appear.

"Oh no?" he said, making a sympathetic face. "Maybe she thought you had your hands full with, I don't know— your train wreck of a love life."

"Yep, probably," I said.

"I'm sorry I missed the bloody dogfight between your cop and your lawyer. A little violence is tasty," he said. "All those glorious muscles and torn clothes—were clothes torn?" he asked, clearly relishing the thought.

"Rollie! What about Johnny?"

"Right," he said, snapping his fingers. "I love Johnny. I do love Johnny. I've had my share of butch muscle boys and lords of the manor. I've had my share of intellectuals and artists, explorers and anarchists, princes and politicians . . . hmm, I've pretty much had my share of every kind of man. Immortality has its perks, and in Johnny's case, it's perkiness."

"Rollie, it's freezing out here!" I said with a dismissive wave before I marched back to Bryn and Johnny. "Let's go."

As we got closer, the conversation trailed off. I expected to smell something rotten, but instead the smell of roast meat and wood smoke filled the air.

They looked like a gypsy caravan with cars parked this way and that and multicolored tarps on four poles acting as makeshift tents. Lanterns burned, bottles of local whiskey and ale littered the tables, and a group of dark-haired men played guitars, an accordion, and a fiddle while women in low-cut sweaters danced near the fire. There was also an ash-covered pit, like the kind used to roast a pig. My stomach growled and my feet itched to do a little dancing. I couldn't help myself. Give me a pig roast, a crawfish boil, or any old backyard barbecue and I'm there with a tray of deviled eggs and a bounce in my two-step.

These were my kind of people. Just out to have some fun and some good food. It wasn't the usual weather for a cookout, but that's a can-do country attitude for you.

There were about a dozen people, and I didn't recognize any of them. What I did recognize were the contents of a narrow wicker basket that might have held umbrellas but instead had a bouquet of shotguns. I frowned.

Bryn tugged on my sleeve, and I realized that this wasn't the party we'd come to crash.

The four of us crept forward, giving the group a wide circle. My feet squelched in chilled mud. Rollie made small disgusted noises and huffed when I shushed him. Bryn's grip on my hand tightened as we entered a clearing. The back of my neck tingled and Bryn's magic sharpened as though he were focusing it for use. The aroma of charred meat and something sour filled the air.

"Blood," Rollie murmured. "Not my brand. Some kind of animal's been slaughtered."

"And gutted, from the smell of it," Bryn whispered.

I slid my hand free of his so I could be armed and ready. The smell turned rancid. This was the stench that had clung to Oatha at my house.

"Stay close, Tamara. A ritual sacrifice was done to generate power. And they dealt exclusively in the black on this site."

"Black magic?" I asked.

"The blackest, from the feel of it."

A light bobbed toward us and voices carried on the wind. A glassy-eyed severed horse head stared at me from the middle of a picnic table. I had to slap a hand over my mouth to cover my gasp.

Jars and bottles of I-don't-know-what surrounded the head. A tray of bloody entrails and another of bloody bones sat on either end. Bile clogged my throat, and I forced it back down.

I take it back. This is not my kind of party.

I recognized one of the approaching figures.

"Where's Bobby?" Beau asked.

"Taking a piss, no doubt," a man to Beau's left said. He looked like Beau, but a few years younger and a few inches taller.

"Bobby, *je suis prêt*," Beau called out.

"Ready for what?" Bryn murmured, translating handily for us.

"She got everything she needed?" the man with Beau asked.

"Yeah, stepsissy's in for it now."

"Nick of time. And the local witch?"

"The *belle rouge*? She won't be a problem anymore. We figured we'd have to deal with her if Vangie came to this town for her help. From what we've heard that little red-haired bitch never minds her own business, and she's got a way of bringing down people more powerful than she is."

I stiffened. The red girl witch who never minded her own

business. I didn't have to speak French to know who they were talking about.

"She sure gave you a good lick on that ear."

"Her wildcat did that. And that pussy suits her. She's a spitfire."

"Mmm, just the way we like 'em."

"You know that's right."

"Wouldn't mind a piece," the man said, adjusting the front of his pants. My stomach lurched, and I tightened my grip on the gun.

"I may break one off," Beau said with a lewd tongue gesture. "I've got a place all picked out."

They both laughed.

I grimaced and felt Bryn's magic sharpen with cold fury.

"Get the other side of the table," Beau said. When they were positioned at either end, Beau tucked the flashlight in his back pocket, and they tipped the table and moved it away from the pile of horse remains.

"You pour the gas. Let me see where the hell our dumbass cousin Bobby's gotten to," Beau said.

"Go on, cousin, I've got this," the other man said as Beau walked away.

A flicker of light, like a firefly, caught my eye. I recognized the shade of green, Edie's, and strained my eyes. I suddenly suspected that Bobby hadn't gotten lost while relieving himself against a tree.

I didn't see Zach until he was inches from Beau's cousin. The cousin never had a chance to say a word. Zach grabbed his throat and thunked him on the head in a simultaneous motion. The light dropped and so did the man. Zach's coat and shirt were open. Blond and muscled, with a face full of fury, he looked like an avenging angel. Or would have, if avenging angels had worn cowboy boots and brass Longhorns belt buckles.

The amulet against his chest glowed purple for a second, then went dark. He bent and rolled the man facedown. In seconds, he used a plastic tie to secure his wrists and clicked off the flashlight that had rolled free.

Yeah, he's got no business being out here, being totally inexperienced and all. He doesn't stand a chance, I thought with a smile, proud of his prowess.

Then a gunshot blasted the silence to hell.

17

BEAU FIRED THE first shot but hadn't hit Zach, who'd seen him raise the gun. Beau hollered for reinforcements. The partiers came running and they came armed.

As they fanned out, they extinguished their lights.

Bryn grabbed my arm and drew me to him. He whispered a spell, and magic closed around us.

"Concealment?"

"Yes, no need for them to find us before we want them to. They're looking for him."

"Zach?"

"The amulet should reflect the spells back on them."

"Maybe they'll shoot each other," I said hopefully.

Edie appeared, trailing a few inches behind an unsuspecting man. My jaw dropped when Zach appeared in the glow from Edie and swooped behind the guy. A crack on the head dropped him. Edie disappeared and reappeared behind another man.

"Beau! Edie, go for Beau," I whispered, but she was too far away to hear me.

"What?" Bryn asked.

"Edie's showing Zach where the bad guys are."

"This way," someone yelled. Suddenly flashlights turned in our direction, and they ran toward us.

I stepped away from Bryn and raised my gun.

"Dark," someone yelled, and the lights went out.

"Yeah, I don't think so," Bryn said. He flung up a hand and with a few words in Latin, the sky lit like it was the Fourth of July and full of fireworks.

Then the spells started to fly. I let loose a hail of warning bullets, and Rollie made a snack of a couple of sultry now gun-toting dancing girls.

Beau ran up, lit a match, and tossed it on the ground where the gasoline can had overturned. Flames burst into the sky, and Beau locked eyes with me.

"Oh, *chère*," he said with a crooked smile and a shake of his head. He made a lewd tongue gesture at me. A broken jar whizzed toward him, Bryn's magic. Beau deflected it awkwardly, and blood dripped from where it had sliced his forearm.

He let loose with what I'm sure was a nasty spell, but Zach stepped in front of me and countered it. Beau apparently felt the spell coming back toward him because he dove out of the way. A mountain with legs who was at least Rollie's height came forward. He cracked his knuckles with a nod at Zach.

Zach shrugged off his coat and raised his fists.

"He's not the prize," Bryn said, drawing me forward with him toward where Beau had disappeared into the darkness.

"Rollie," Bryn said, making a circular motion toward the caravan. "Get the license numbers of the cars, and if you spot a spellbook I want it."

"Edie," I called. Edie appeared near Zach. "Where did Beau go?"

Edie glided to us. "Who's Beau?"

"The weasel of a guy who set the fire. If his scary mother's not here, I'd bet he's in charge."

Edie looked around. "I don't see him. With all his magic, can't your candylegger find him?" Her gaze returned to Zach.

"Edie, you can't help Zach right now, but you can help me and possibly yourself if these people are responsible for the ghosts going missing."

"Tamara, talk less so you can pick up your pace," Bryn said.

I sucked in a breath and sprinted with Bryn toward the tents. The sound of cars starting made me wince.

Bryn slowed and came to a stop a few feet from the edge of the bonfire. "He's gone."

I doubled over, panting for breath with burning muscles. "Edie?" I said, but she hadn't come.

Spinning tires splattered mud as the partiers zipped away. *Damn it!*

Bryn met Rollie and Johnny in the main area under the tarps and started searching through the things that the fleeing caravan had been forced to leave behind. I didn't care to search.

I needed to know how Zach had fared against the big guy. I hurried across the cold marshy ground back to the clearing. With Bryn gone, his magical sky lights had faded. The gas fire had also burned out, but the smoky mess reeked. The single beam of light came from Zach's flashlight, and it made methodical sweeps over the ground where the fire had been. His lip was swollen and bloody, and his knuckles were scraped, but he had his coat back on and looked none the worse for having fought a giant.

"You okay?" I asked.

He looked at me. "Well enough. You?"

I nodded, not having been hit by any spells or shotgun pellets. Bryn's protection spells hold up against a lot, even when his attention's split so he can go on the magical offensive. I wondered how many other wizards could manage that.

"Find anything interesting?" I asked, walking over.

Zach shook his head and moved a few feet away. "I'll

concentrate better if you're somewhere else. You mind giving me some space?"

"You won't take away any evidence, will you? Bryn's been a trained wizard a long time. He might see something that'll help us."

Zach looked up and around. "Where's he at?"

"Checking the other area."

"He sure got over you spending the night at my place fast. Must come in handy as a lawyer being that cold-blooded. You sure you know what you're doing when it comes—" He bit off the angry words and shook his head, clenching his teeth. After a few moments, he exhaled. "I could use some room," he said softly. "Give me that, Jo."

His pain made my heart cramp. I swallowed and forced my voice to sound normal when I spoke. "Sure. If you find something important, send Edie with a message." I looked around, but she wasn't nearby. Where was she? How could she flit off when she was needed?

I walked past where Beau's cousin had lain. An impression marked the ground, and Zach's plastic tie lay severed in the center. The Cajuns had collected their fallen members and slithered away. I made a face and kept going.

When I reached the cooking pit, I found Mercutio pawing at the ash.

"Where have you been? It's not like you to miss a fight."

I bent down and rubbed his head. Blood spotted his whiskers. Apparently he'd been in his own fight. Or he'd been hunting. I ran my hands over his fur and didn't find any holes in him.

Bryn emerged from the tent with a shake of his head. "Nothing useful. Oatha took everything of magical importance with her. I'll walk to the other site to be sure, but I don't expect to find much." Bryn leaned over and stroked Mercutio's back. "Hello, Mercutio."

Merc meowed a greeting.

"Tamara's coming home with me. You're welcome to ride with us," Bryn said to my cat before walking away in a direct line toward Zach. My stomach tightened with concern.

I hurried over to Rollie and Johnny. "Johnny, I can't go with him. You go keep an eye on things. If he gets in a fight with Zach, give a holler."

Johnny set off in pursuit. "Mr. Bryn, I come with you."

Rollie grinned. "Is there any man who won't instantly do your bidding, Calamity Jane?"

"Lots. Beau punched me in the face and put his knee in my stomach. You can bet that wasn't my idea." I bent down near a garbage can, where I spotted something shimmery. "Rollie, come here with that light, would you?"

Rollie strolled over and lowered the camping lantern the Cajuns had left behind. I plucked a tiny plastic shoe from the ground.

"From a toy," Rollie observed.

"There weren't any kids out here," I said, looking around. I gave the garbage can a shove and it tipped onto its side. A mess of potato peels, spices, apple cores, and grease topped the pile, but beneath them lay a plastic tube for a Disney princess Barbie doll.

"Hey, Rollie, which princess was Ariel? The mermaid one, right?" I asked, pushing the garbage around with my foot.

"Yeah," he said, leaning over as I uncovered a headless dolly.

"Where's her head?"

"Her red-haired head," Rollie said.

We looked at each other. *Hellfire and biscuits.*

"Beau pulled my hair and made a point of smearing his thumb in my blood. I thought he was rubbing it in, literally, that he'd given me a bloody nose, but that's not it. He told his momma he got what she needed."

"You don't seriously think—?"

"Sure I do. And I bet the Disney people will be as furious as I am if Miss Oatha used a Barbie head to make a voodoo doll of me."

18

ZACH HAD APPARENTLY been walking away as Bryn got to the site, so a repeat of the morning was avoided.

When I rejoined Bryn, he'd found nothing useful in the smoking remains. He rubbed his eyes, and I felt his exhaustion. Using magic to fight, to shatter glass and fling objects and to shield against magic and flying objects, expended a lot of power and energy. He'd had two fights in one day and hadn't slept. I ran my hands up his arms and rubbed his shoulders.

"You need some rest," I said.

He nodded.

"Can you do one last thing for me?"

"That would depend on the nature of the one thing," he said.

My hands moved inward to massage his neck muscles. He leaned into me.

"Can you cast a spell to find out where Beau's gone? I'm pretty sure he'll rendezvous with his momma, and I need to know where she is."

"You need to know that right now?" he asked, and shook his head to answer the question. "We're going home."

"We are, but you're going home before me. I'll be there a little later."

"Why?"

"Well, it's possible—and I'm not saying it's for sure because what the heck do I know about making voodoo dolls—but it's just possible she made one of me."

"She wouldn't dare."

"She wouldn't?"

Bryn's face hardened. He looked dangerous. "She knows you're involved with me. Inviting my wrath would be really foolish."

"They didn't seem to have any reservations about fighting with you tonight."

"This was a small skirmish. They may claim they didn't know they were fighting me, and that I haven't laid claim to this land so they were within their rights to use it," he said. "But if they plan to attack you using a voodoo doll, they've seriously underestimated what my response will be."

I hugged him and gave him a kiss on the cheek. "Can you do a locater spell to find them? I'll just pop over to wherever they are and peek through a window to see what they're up to. If they're just making gumbo and drinking Armadillo Ale, no problem. I'll come on home and we'll sleep all night."

"And if they're doing something sinister?"

"If I happen to see a Tammy Jo voodoo doll, I'll steal her. If I don't, I'll spy and report back, so we can make a plan."

Bryn eyed me up and down. "You shouldn't go alone. I'll go with you, but once we return to my place, neither of us is getting out of bed before noon."

"Deal," I said, brushing my lips over his.

He inhaled, and I felt a tendril of magic edge toward him.

"You can take magic from me if you need it. You are doing a spell for me, so it's only fair."

He shook his head. "I don't need it. I just wanted a taste." He ran his thumb over my lower lip. "You always taste so good."

"So do you," I said, smiling as I stepped back. I swirled my finger toward the sky. "Find 'em."

He tipped his head up and whispered Latin words. I felt his magic pulse and sail outward. A sliver of moon sparkled overhead and made his skin glow.

After a few minutes, he opened his eyes and shook his head.

"They must be using all the magic they have to conceal themselves. It'll take a more complex spell to track them until they start casting again."

"If there is a voodoo doll and she uses it, will you be able to track her down?"

"Absolutely," Bryn said.

"Okay then. We'll sleep now and spell later, since I don't think they'll be doing more black magic tonight, do you?"

"I doubt it."

"I'm sorry we didn't save that horse. Shame on them!"

We walked back to the road and caught up with Rollie and Johnny at their car.

"I've texted you the list of license plate numbers I collected," Rollie said with a yawn. "It's pumpkin time for this Cinderfella. We'll call you later." Rollie folded his long body into the passenger seat of Johnny's little sports car.

We waved at them and found Mercutio waiting for us next to Bryn's. "You're comin' with us?"

Mercutio cocked his head and meowed.

"Oh, good," I said with a smile. I liked having all my guys safe and accounted for.

"I'VE GOT TO go back to the woods for my cell phone," I said with a shake of my head as we entered Bryn's home. "Should've already gone."

"Because you've had so much free time on your hands," Bryn said.

"Gotta make time. Without a cell, it's like living in the dark ages."

We went upstairs, stripped, and crawled into his bed. Within a couple minutes of closing my eyes, I was deep in dreamland.

I woke before Bryn did. I gave him a soft kiss and climbed over Mercutio. That's an advantage of having a king-sized bed. There's room for the king and a bunch of other people.

Bryn opened his eyes. "You're up," he murmured. "You need to call Vangie. She left a message around five a.m." He rolled to the phone and got me into the voicemail.

"Hello," Vangie said. "This is Evangeline Rhodes. This message is for Tammy Jo Trask. Hello, Tammy Jo. I've discovered something very important! I've tried calling you on both your phones to no avail. I really hope you haven't been killed! If you're alive, call me back right away!"

I tried calling Vangie's cell, but the call went straight to her voicemail.

"Hey, it's Tammy Jo. I'm alive. Call me back at Bryn's."

Bryn, still exhausted, went back to sleep. I ventured downstairs, wondering what Vangie had found that was so important. If I didn't hear from her soon, I'd have to drive to Dyson to the Bay Window Inn, where she'd said she was staying.

I made ham and eggs and tea and toast. I put everything on a tray and carried it to Mr. Jenson's room.

I knocked softly and found him awake and dressed in pajamas and a bathrobe. He coughed but had a little more pink to his cheeks.

"Morning, Mr. Jenson. I brought you some tea and breakfast. Can I come in?"

"Oh, Miss Tamara, that's very good of you, but we can certainly have breakfast in the kitchen."

"But I'm already here," I said. "You sit yourself down." I nodded toward the small table and two chairs in the corner of the room. He moved slowly, and I noticed the way he braced himself with a white-knuckled grip on the chair before he sank into it.

"What did Dr. Suri say? Did he give you some medicine?"

"He did."

I poured us each a cup of tea, adding honey and milk to mine. Mr. Jenson usually takes his straight up, but I had a small creamer that was a quarter full of Irish whiskey next to it.

"Would you like a teaspoon of whiskey in your tea? For your cough?"

"I would," he said. "And better make it a tablespoon."

I added some and stirred. He settled back as I buttered the toast and added honey to mine and blackberry jam to his.

Once we were all set, I munched toast and told him about our night. He listened, occasionally asking a question or murmuring his surprise about the goings-on. He ate slowly, but well enough to reassure me.

"It sounds like it was quite a harrowing night. It's a relief at least to know that you had each other."

Collecting the tray, I agreed. "Bryn and I make a good team. You go back to bed for a bit. The house is squeaky clean, and I took care of Bryn's breakfast. This afternoon, you should take a slow walk around the house for some exercise. It doesn't do to lie up in bed all day. 'Bad for the bones,' my granny Justine used to say."

Mr. Jenson smiled at me as I set the Dallas newspaper on his bedside table with another cup of hot tea. "Your grandmother sounds like a wise woman."

"Never knew her to be wrong," I said, giving his pillow a fluff. "You rest up. I'll see you later."

I took the tray to the kitchen. After everything was in a sink of soapy water, I picked up the security phone. "Pete, it's Tammy Jo."

"Good morning," he said. Pete and I had gotten off to a rocky start when he'd first been hired, but we'd settled that and got along fine now.

"If I'm not back by the afternoon, will you help Mr. Jenson take a walk through the house? He might be weak and I want someone with him."

"Sure. Where are you going?"

"Here and there."

"Don't forget to turn on your cell phone."

"Yeah, I'll see about that, too," I said, and he heard the pause.

"Have a heart. He won't be happy if he can't reach you."

"I'll do my best. Tell him there's a plate for him in the microwave. There's plenty for you, too, if you're hungry. Actually, I'll leave him a note on his dresser, so he won't be mad at you for letting me take off without saying where I'm going."

"He wouldn't get mad at me personally, but when he's pissed, the whole house is tense. Everyone prefers it when you're here."

"Except when he and I fight."

"Those flame out quick enough. You guys are good together. All the stuff you did when he worked that big case? The devil'd be wearing ice skates before my girl would set an alarm to make me dinner during an all-nighter."

"How many times a week do you laugh at her jokes like she's the funniest girl in the world? Or give her a present just because it's a Tuesday?"

"Hell, never," he said with a laugh. "Maybe I should, but she'd probably think I was up to something."

"No doubt. But she'd still like it."

"You're probably right. See why we all like it when you're around?"

"Later, Pete." I hung up with a smile and a roll of my eyes. Bryn's guys were well trained. It wasn't that I didn't believe that Pete had grown to like me, but roughneck Texas boys weren't known for laying it on so thick. I'd bet my double boiler his boss had put him up to that bit of sugar. The message, loud and clear, was that everyone at Casa Lyons wanted me there. And darn Bryn's clever lawyer tactics if that didn't just warm my heart.

I wrote a note, gave Bryn a kiss on the cheek and one for Mercutio. Then I went out and stole Bryn's car.

19

VANGIE HADN'T CALLED me at Bryn's, and I decided not to wait any longer. It would be safer for everyone if I found out right away what she'd discovered about her stepfamily. It would also be safer for her and her fiancé if they relocated immediately to Bryn's house.

Dyson was a cute little town, but it had nothing on Duvall. We had rivers and creeks, a magic tor, and several different prosperous businesses; Dyson had one main source of jobs, the branch of a big chemical company that I felt pretty sure was poisoning their lake given the weird reaction their cows had to drinking the water. Half were barren and half produced more babies and milk than anybody had ever seen. The citizens of Dyson didn't say a word. As long as their own kids were healthy and folks had work, they claimed it was fine by them.

Dyson had a honky-tonk, a ten-room motel, two diners, and a horse stable and cattle ranch. They also had the biggest collection of chemical hazmat suits in a hundred-mile radius. No, they weren't worried about that chemical plant at all.

As I rolled into town, I realized I wasn't the only one

whom Bryn's fancy car reminded of a spaceship; everyone on Dyson's main street stopped to stare as I passed. It wasn't the car to drive when I wanted to keep a low profile.

I pulled into a parking spot in the motel lot and watched the car door open. It moved vertically, like it was being held up and therefore reached for the sky.

I climbed out. The clear, sunny day made the grass look extra green. I smiled at the collection of chirping birds in the trees. It was like a movie scene. It could almost have been spring, except for the chill.

As I got closer I waved at the small white-flecked black birds decorating the trees in front of the motel office. Those sparrows were adorable. I hurried forward when I spotted a beautiful blue jay nearly twice their size about to dive-bomb them. Blue jays are pretty, but they're bullies. When the blue jay attacked, though, the little birds swarmed and pecked at it, going for the eyes. My jaw dropped as the startled blue jay fled, little dots of blood on its face.

The sparrows settled back onto the branches and tweeted away like they hadn't just been in a big bird fight. I loved that they'd stood their limbs against a bully, but that hardly seemed like normal behavior for little birds. Yeah, I had my worries over the chemicals that were in the Dyson drinking water.

The motel office had a bay window, as its name advertised, but the window faced the parking lot. I was no architect, but that seemed like a waste of a view to me. I strolled inside the office where coffee brewed and Danish was piled high. What the motel lacked in architectural sensibility, it more than made up for with pastry hospitality. I snagged a cherry Danish and bit into it. Not from-the-oven fresh, but tasty nonetheless.

Multicolored posters advertised bus tours to Dallas and one to, of all places, Duvall. I stared at the Duvall poster, which talked about sampling local pastries that were too good to be true, visiting haunted sites, traveling the flood route, picnicking on the "magical mountain," and driving by the mansions of the rich and dangerous whose secrets put all the reality shows to shame. Visits to the Armadillo Ale brewery and the Glenfiddle Whiskey Castle with tastings were included. *Learn all there is to know about our unusual neighbors to the west in one jam-packed afternoon and evening.*

"Good morning and welcome to Dyson," the young guy behind the counter said. He arranged a couple of welcome packets that he'd been bending down to get when I'd walked in. "Will you be needing a room? And if so, would you like a lakeside view? It's only twenty dollars extra, and now that the ducklings have hatched, there's a complimentary bag of day-old bread to feed them. They come right up to shore for it."

I was really tempted to go feed those ducklings, but I couldn't spare a half hour. I frowned. What was wrong with my life that I couldn't make time for baby ducks?

"I'm actually here to see about a friend of mine. Her name is Evangeline Rhodes."

"Miss Rhodes, you say?" he asked, flipping through a handwritten register book. "Oh, yes, she's our guest in number four, lakeside view."

I glanced out at the full parking lot. "Has your business picked up since the Duvall flood and fires?"

He nodded. "We're very sorry for Duvall's misfortunes, but it has meant a lot of business and tourism over here. Are you from Duvall? Wait, you've got red hair. Are you *the redhead*?"

"The redhead?" I echoed, taking a step back.

"Tammy Jo Trask, ghost whisperer, pastry princess, and femme fatale?"

"Femme fatale? Who called me—I mean her that? I'm sure that's an exaggeration. I'm sure she's just an average small-town girl."

His right hand popped up with his phone, and he aimed it at me. I had to dive through the door to avoid having my picture snapped.

"Femme fatale," I grumbled as I hurried to the metal stairs.

A pair of middle-aged ladies in khaki pants and hiking

boots walked briskly toward the motel. They lifted binoculars that hung around their necks. As they peeked through them, I thought for a minute they were spying on me, but then I realized they were looking at the birds.

C'mon now, I admonished myself in my head. *They're just bird-watchers! Don't go getting paranoid*.

"Look at the coloring, sister," one of the ladies said. "Definitely *Ammodramus maritimus nigrescens*, common name dusky seaside sparrow."

"I know they look like dusky seaside sparrows, but they can't be. Seaside sparrows are extinct. The last one died in captivity in 1987 at Walt Disney World."

"And yet here they are! An entire group! This will put Dyson on the bird-watching world map."

I smiled. *Well, what do you know*, I thought, proud of Dyson for having something no one else in the world had. And also proud of those little birds that weren't supposed to exist anymore. Good for them for deciding not to be extinct.

I climbed to the second story and hurried to number four. A row of cute sparrows sat on the rail and tweeted at me cheerfully. "People have tried to make me extinct, too," I told them. "Hasn't worked," I assured them as I rapped on the door. I glanced over my shoulder, relieved that the young man hadn't come out of the office.

Number four's door opened, and a man with blond highlights, a narrow nose, and a cleft in his chin answered. His flawless skin looked like it had been taken from a rubber mold. I studied him, wondering if he'd had plastic surgery. If so, I thought maybe he shouldn't have. His features were smooth and perfect, but the proportions were off. His nose bugged me. It was small, like it would've fit better on a ten-year-old girl than a man.

"Hello," he said. He had an appealing radio announcer kind of voice.

"Hi there. I'm Tammy Jo. Are you Jackson?"

"I am. Come in," he said, motioning me inside. He wore an oxford shirt with a Polo logo and matching cologne. "Where's Evangeline? Has anything happened?"

My stomach lurched. "Why are you asking me?"

"She went to meet you," he said.

"She did?"

"Yes, after she returned from Dallas."

"When did she leave to meet me?"

"Three—possibly four—hours ago. She doesn't sleep much when she's agitated or excited about something. I told her it was too early to disturb you, but she wanted to go to your town bakery and was convinced that you'd be awake early."

"I tried her cell this morning. She didn't pick up."

He frowned, drawing his thick and well-groomed brows together. "Well, she doesn't always answer right away if she's distracted. She's probably gotten sidetracked. It happens. She loses track of time and disappears for hours."

My heart thumped in my chest, and I ordered it to calm the heck down. Vangie had ignored my calls the day before, and she'd been perfectly fine. For all I knew she'd been waiting for me and had fallen asleep in her car. Or took up residence in the bouncy castle again for a nap.

I called Cookie's Bakery. The morning rush kept Cookie hopping, but she did bark into the phone that no strangers had been in. I sighed and hung up, glancing back at Jackson.

"Well, I'd really like to talk to Vangie, to be sure she's okay. My cell phone's growing grass in the woods—long story—so could you call Bryn Lyons's house or have Vangie call it when you talk to her?" I took the small pad from the table and wrote Bryn's number and address for him. "In fact, you can just go on over there whenever you're ready. Did Vangie talk to you about staying at Bryn's until after the wedding?"

"She mentioned it, but I'll wait to come until she's with me. Will you extend me the same courtesy of calling if you see her?" he asked, taking the pad and pen. He wrote his number.

"Sure thing," I said, taking it.

"I'm sure she's all right," he said, but I sensed that he was trying to convince himself more than me. "She believes her stepmother and brother followed her here. Anything having to do with the pair of them puts her on edge."

"With good reason."

He blinked. "Have you met them?"

"Yeah."

"Were they rude to you?" he asked, surprised.

"Were they polite to you?" I asked, equally surprised.

"I've never met them. But I thought Vangie might have exaggerated how unpleasant they can be," he said. "In pictures, Oatha Theroux is usually dressed in a 'ladies who lunch' suit, albeit with a skirt that's too tight. Vangie's stepbrother wears suits. He hardly seems like a thug."

My brows shot up like his. "Suits? I don't think so," I said. "They're more Louisiana swamp than Dallas swank. He's got an alligator tattoo! And I can tell you firsthand that Vangie didn't exaggerate about how bad they can be."

"Maybe I should call the police," he said.

"You could," I said. "But it's too early for a missing-person report."

He nodded, grimacing. "I'll check the local places around here. If I don't find her, I'll join you in Duvall."

"Okay," I said with a nod. I was already halfway out the door.

She's probably fine.

But given what I'd seen going on in the wetlands outside Duvall, I was pretty concerned. One time, I'd been kidnapped twice in one week and that hadn't even been after a night of black magic and burning horseflesh.

On the landing, I spotted half a dozen Dyson residents milling about the parking lot near Bryn's car. As soon as they saw me, they fumbled to get their cell phone cameras up.

"Hey, y'all," I said with a cheerful smile, but held out a hand to cover my face as their phones clicked.

"C'mon now, Tammy Jo," they protested. "You're the closest thing we've had to a celebrity sighting in Dyson."

I kept my chin tucked, so my hair hid my face. "I'm not a celebrity! I'm just like you," I lied.

"Then why not be sociable? Stop and pose for a few pictures."

"No time for pictures," I said. "And I'm not photogenic at all," I added, which was true.

"What in the world kind of car is that?" someone asked.

"The fast kind," I murmured. *All the better to get me out of here quick.*

I closed the door and almost ran over some toes as I peeled out.

20

THE DAY WARMED, so I tossed my jacket on the passenger seat. I checked the bakery, the bouncy castle, Bryn's house and mine. I didn't spot Vangie or her Bentley. I chatted with my neighbors. None of them had seen her. I frowned.

She could still be okay. Maybe she went back to Dyson.

I checked in with Jackson. He hadn't found her either. My heart sank a little. The more time that passed without her turning up, the more sure I became that something bad had happened to her. In Bryn's car, I shoved the sleeves of my jersey up, feeling flushed. Maybe we were going to have a heat wave. I hoped so. I was tired of the cold.

I drove to the edge of the woods where I'd had to leave my car. The car itself was gone. My brows rose and I looked around. Had my car been stolen? Who would steal a dented Ford Focus with a flat tire? More likely someone had seen it and called Floyd, the local mechanic, who'd towed it to his garage. I grimaced at the thought of what towing, tire change, and bodywork would cost me. I should really think about buying a different vehicle. Maybe something from army surplus, like a rusted old tank. I bet a tank's tread would stand up against bullets, arrows, and most things that my enemies could throw at it. Yeah, a tank would be a really smart way to go. I wondered what used ones cost.

The sun beat down on my head. I walked into the woods. The trees were quiet and still. Sleeping maybe? Did trees sleep during the day? I wasn't sure about that.

Despite the shade, my clothes were warmer than oven mitts holding hot cookie sheets. I tugged at the collar of my shirt.

"Something isn't right," I said, hurrying farther into the woods. "Trees, you there?" I asked. Not a whisper. Instinct made me turn toward the river. A sharp pain ran through my middle.

"Ouch," I yelled, falling to the ground. I rolled and writhed in pain. It was like I'd been skewered with a hot poker. The cuffs of my jeans burst into flames.

"Hey," I screamed, flapping my legs against the ground and heaping dirt on them. The flames died out, but my clothes were searing hot. I jerked off the shirt, toed off my shoes, and shoved my jeans down. The clothes caught fire again, and I kicked the jeans away and yanked off my socks.

My skin sizzled as I got up and ran toward the brook. I literally dove into it as my bra caught fire. I landed belly down and slid several feet. The cool mud soothed me. No wonder fancy spas can charge so much for mud baths.

Water steamed and rose in humid protest. I half swam, half dragged myself farther downstream to where the water could cover my whole body. When strands of hair burned against my back, I flipped over and dipped my head underwater.

The water around me bubbled and boiled, and I was afraid my skin itself might catch fire. Deep in my body, my organs warmed like they were being baked.

I lifted my head, gasping, and grabbed a tree root so I could dig my feet into the mud. My witch magic is from the earth and my fae magic is connected to it, too. At the moment, I needed to tap into any power that would keep me from being burned alive.

"Hi, Earth, it's me, Tammy Jo," I said. I wiggled as my panties sizzled. I dragged them off and tossed them on shore. Steam rose as they caught fire and burned in blue flames.

I don't know what's going on.
It might be a black magic spell.
If you could save me from it
That would really be swell.

I'm not exactly eloquent when I'm in a panic, or when I'm not, but I felt a difference right away. My tight skin still stung, but I didn't feel like I was being pan-fried like a fish. I panted my relief and let go of the branch.

"Thanks," I mumbled. The current picked up and I floated with it, dipping myself every few minutes to keep my burned skin cool. The water babbled over rocks and I knew by the sound that I was getting close to the place where the creek dumped into the Amanos River.

I'd have to get out soon. The Shoreside section of the Amanos River isn't fit for swimming. The current's too strong, and the river feeds into a big waterfall. Getting pulled over Cider Falls and dashed on the rocks below is a good way to get your bones broken to pieces.

I climbed out of the creek, muddy water dripping off all my naked bits. I needed to find the clothes I'd taken off the night before, so I'd have something to wear out of the woods. I looked around, trying to gauge where I was in relation to where I'd been caught in the sack.

I jumped when I spotted a figure leaning against a tree.

When I got over being shocked speechless, I yelled, "Hey, turn around!" and tried to cover myself with my arms.

He smirked, not bothering to so much as turn his head. He was handsome and blond with tan skin like he'd just arrived from a week on a Mexican beach.

He also glowed golden in the low light. *Not human, then*, I thought.

"Here," he said, flipping something toward me.

My palm shot out instinctively, but I pulled it back to

cover myself. An etched disc of green and gold landed at my feet, and he said, "A coin for a kiss."

"Not on your life!" I snapped. "You turn around," I demanded, shifting to conceal my private parts.

He raised his brows. "That accent's unbelievable."

"Not if you're from Duvall, Texas, which I am." I took a long step back. "Bye," I said, and dropped into the creek with a muddy splash.

The water swept me downstream, and I thrashed until I caught an overhanging branch. I had no intention of standing around naked, putting on a show for a strange man, but there was still the deadly river to be considered.

The golden guy jogged along the creek till he reached me. His color wasn't as unnaturally bright when he stood close, but his skin and hair still looked gilded.

He studied my face, stretching one leg behind him until he was down on one knee.

"Show me your left shoulder," he said.

Considering what he'd already seen, a shoulder hardly seemed like much, but I resisted just to be contrary.

"I'm not showing you a thing. You go on back to wherever you're from so I can get out of this creek and back to doing what I came out here to do."

"What are you here to do?" he asked.

"To get my cell phone and clothes."

He drew a quiver of arrows from behind his back and reached into a pocket on the side of it. He held up the phone I'd lost.

"Yeah, that's mine. Did you set the trap I got caught in?"

"What's your name?" he asked.

"Tammy Jo Trask. What's yours?"

"You can call me Crux."

"Are you a faery?"

The question seemed to amuse him because he smiled.

Splotches of faery dust dotted the bottom of his quiver. I recognized it from the Tammy sack. That *had* been his snare.

"Why were you trying to catch me?"

He didn't answer at first. He stared at me for a long time. "Are you the redheaded witch who fought Unseelie fae on Samhain?"

"No," I lied.

His grin widened. "I think you are. In which case, I was trying to catch the fae who's trying to find you."

I gulped. "Who says other fae besides you are hunting me?"

"Do you doubt it?" he asked, amused and smug.

"Who is it? A skeletal creature?" I asked, tensing so I could submerge myself if he tried to grab me. If it was between the faery I could see and the falls that I couldn't, I'd escape the guy first and worry about the other after.

He ignored the question. Instead, he said, "You interest me." He extended a hand. "Let me help you stay alive, Tammy Jo Trask."

"That's actually a full-time job. Someone just tried to burn me alive, and I don't think it was a faery."

"Were there flaming arrows involved? Or burning leaves?"

"Nope. My clothes burst into flames."

"Not of the Never," he agreed.

"No, I think a witch used a voodoo doll against me."

"Voodoo doesn't work on faeries."

"I'm not a faery. I'm a witch."

"One of those statements is true, but not both," he said, studying my face. "You're half of each."

I flushed. "Am not," I said, lying again.

"If there is a voodoo doll, it was certainly your fae half that kept you alive long enough to protect yourself. How well do you fare against iron arrows?"

"Not too well, I don't expect."

"Then my offer's a good one."

I shook my head at the outstretched hand whose long fingers beckoned me to clutch it. "That's sure sweet of you, but as you might've noticed, I'm naked in here. I'm not getting out of the water until I'm alone."

"You object to my seeing you naked?" he asked.

"Do you see a pole around here? I'm no stripper. I'm a pastry chef."

He let his hand drop as he stood. "I've tried pastries. I like them." He took a couple of steps back and set his bow and quiver on the ground. He slid off his brown tunic shirt, which looked like the sort of thing a medieval squire would wear. He hung it from a nearby branch, and I watched his lean muscles ripple, the tiny grooves between his abdominal muscles glinting golden.

He lifted his bow and quiver and walked several feet away, turning to the side.

I waited, but he didn't turn away completely. "I can stand here all day," he said.

Clearly, I'd gotten the best offer I was going to get. I hauled myself out of the water and scrambled into the shirt. It smelled of fields of warm grass, of sunshine and earth. Of honey and apples . . . For a moment, I stood in a field of heather far from Texas. A thistle bridge led to a door of woven vines and daisy chains. Sunlight streamed through the gaps. It smelled heavenly and I started toward the bridge, but before I reached it, it disappeared. I stood again in the cool Duvall forest under a canopy of brown and green leaves where sunlight could scarcely penetrate.

"You saw something just then. What?"

I opened my mouth, then closed it. I didn't have to tell this strange faery every little thing. In fact, I felt sure that I shouldn't. Faeries often try to trick humans. Especially when they're planning to kill them.

"Nothing. I was just thinking," I said, resting my hand on a nearby tree. The bark was solid and reassuring under my palm.

"Liar," he said. "And not a talented one."

"Thanks for letting me borrow your shirt. I'll leave it at the edge of these woods when I've changed clothes. I'll take my cell phone," I said, thrusting out my hand as I walked to him.

"What will you trade me for it?" he asked.

I rolled my eyes. "As you can see, I don't have a lot of

things to trade at the moment. I can make you a cake. I'll drop it off with the shirt at—um, you probably don't wear a watch to know the time, huh? How about at twilight? Right before the sun sets?"

"I'll accept a kiss in trade."

"Well, I'm not offering one."

"Then I suppose I'll keep this phone."

"I bet you don't even know how to work it. And if you did, who the heck would you call?"

"It plays music. I like music."

"The battery will be dead in a few hours, and then it won't play music or do anything else. It'll be completely useless to you."

"Even so."

"All right," I said, stepping forward with a smile. "I don't have time to argue with you. I need my phone."

He smiled and bent forward. I snatched an arrow from his quiver and pressed the tip between his ribs, hard enough to break the skin.

His breath came out in a hiss.

"How about this?" I asked, all saccharine. "I'll trade you your life for my phone."

He glared at me, but nodded.

"Drop the phone and your bow and back away."

He dropped the phone.

"Now your bow."

"No. Kill me if you will. I won't give up my bow."

"I don't want to kill you, but if I turn my back on you, you could shoot me with it."

"You have my word that I won't shoot you this day or night."

"But you're free to shoot me tomorrow, huh? What happened to your offer to save my life?"

"You answered my offer with a threat. It seems likely that you'll end up dead by my bow. But that won't happen this night. My word," he said earnestly. I believed him.

"Okay." I bent down and retrieved my phone. As I started

to stand, he shoved. He knocked my arm to the side so he didn't fall on the arrow as he landed on top of me.

I struggled, but he pinned my arms and his eyes flashed like smoky quartz. Then he kissed me, and he tasted like honey and sunshine even as he bruised my mouth.

I twisted my hand free to stab him with the arrow, but he caught my arm and slammed it to the ground, making my bones rattle.

A second later, he rolled off me and regained his feet. He grinned down at me. "You're exactly who you claim to be."

I cursed at him and rubbed the sweetness from my lips. "You do that again, and I'll poke more holes in you than a piecrust."

"I like huckleberry pie. I'd be pleased for you to make me one."

As if! Faeries are kind of psycho. One minute they assault you. The next they expect a pie?

"I don't think so," I grumbled, getting to my feet and brandishing the arrow as I fumbled through the leaves for my fallen cell phone.

"Until next we meet," he said, and then he disappeared between the trees and was gone.

Despite the fact that most of my skin felt sunburned, I shivered. The wind carried a chill that rustled the leaves.

Just great. A kiss-stealing killer faery. Why the hell couldn't supernatural creatures let me be?

I glanced down at my bare legs and grimaced. As furious as I was, there was someone who'd be even more furious about Crux than I was. Bryn. I dreaded telling him.

"If it's not one thing, it's a half dozen."

21

I LISTENED TO my messages on the cell phone. In the ones from Vangie, she said, "Tammy Jo, I just know there's a reason you're not around. I hope they didn't kidnap you. I sincerely hope that's not the reason you're missing." She paused. "I went to my father's house in Dallas and broke in. I've got a box—she hid it well! She killed him from a distance, and now I have the proof! Call me *as soon* as you get this message."

The message I left her said, "I'm so sorry I wasn't home when you came looking for me. I tangled with some people in your stepmother's family. I'm worried they might have gotten hold of you. Jackson—I met him—and I are worried sick. Call me as soon as you get this message. And about the proof, that's great! With that, we can get them locked up . . . or whatever happens to witch murderers."

I didn't want to waste time going home to change. So I showed up at Bryn's house half-dressed for the second time.

I peeked out into the sunroom and spotted Mr. Jenson. He wore his pajamas, bathrobe, and house slippers. Mercutio slept on the glider next to him. With an inhaler and a pot of tea on the side table, he sat reading a book. At least Mr. Jenson seemed okay, I thought, relieved.

I checked the library and found Bryn. He wore jeans and a gray sweater, and his skin was darker than normal.

"You've got a suntan," I said.

"So do you," he said, glancing at my legs. "Nice outfit. Are you auditioning for the role of Peter Pan or one of the Lost Boys?"

"I have a suntan?" I asked, partially closing the door so I could look in the round mirror behind it. Sure enough, I was suntanned—and a little shimmery. Momma and Aunt Mel were like most redheads; they couldn't get suntans. If they didn't use sunscreen, they turned red as raspberries. I'd always felt lucky that I didn't get sunburns, but now I realized it was probably because I was half faery.

"The winter sun doesn't cause a tan that dark. So why did I wake up an hour ago with a fever, looking like I'd just spent the day at a Playa del Sol resort?"

"Well . . ."

"Tamara?" He ran a hand through his black hair, and intense cobalt eyes studied me.

"Somebody, Oatha I think, tried to roast me," I said. "I went swimming and escaped."

He frowned. "I felt it. I cast a spell to protect us, which seems to have worked to some extent, but you were right. Oatha's amassed a lot of power from black magic."

"See! Yeah, so we have to figure out where she's casting her spells from. Not just for our sake, but because I think they might have kidnapped Vangie. She's got some proof against her stepmother. She got it from her dad's house in Dallas, and no one's seen her since early in the morning. She left Dyson to find me and vanished."

Bryn shook his head, frowning. "I spoke to Vangie's father's lawyer. She's right. If she dies before she marries, Oatha inherits everything. If Vangie gets married, the bulk of the estate, including the house, reverts to her."

"I don't understand, though. Even if they lost the house

and some of the money, couldn't they just steal his valuables and spellbooks when they left? They could've claimed Vangie was paranoid and deluded about things being missing, and people probably would've believed them over her."

"Ever since he died there's been a battle for control of his library, and there are several special provisions to protect it. Vangie's father seems to have stored his power not in the individual books, but in the room itself."

I shoved my hands through my hair. "So they have to keep the house to keep his power."

"The regional witches and wizards won't allow Oatha Theroux to keep the house if it's proven she killed Evangeline."

"A fat lot of good that will do Vangie if she's already dead! And if Oatha uses voodoo or some trickery, maybe you guys won't be able to prove she killed Vangie." I shook my head. "So they found out that she's engaged, and now they're desperate." I took a deep breath and blew it out. "Desperate people are the worst!" My hands fisted. "I have to find Oatha Theroux."

"I'm working on it, but they've moved since they cast the spell that burned you."

"Already? That was fast."

"It was, but they had to move."

"They did? How come?"

"Because my counterspell to their magic was pretty aggressive."

"What did you do?"

"I made their roof cave in."

"What?" I yelped. "Vangie might've been in the house with them."

He nodded with a grim expression. "I didn't know that at the time."

"All right, so first off we have to go to the house to see—"

"The firefighters and police have already been there. I spoke to Sutton. No bodies."

I stilled. "You talked to Zach?" My brows rose. "Zach talked to you?"

"Briefly."

"How was that?" I asked.

He shrugged. "He and I have one thing in common. We don't want anyone to kill you. I relayed our suspicions about the Therouxs. He was in a better position to check out the house after the roof caved in, so he went."

Bryn took a swig of coffee.

"Their concealment spell is a good one, and I've used a lot of magic over the past two days. I need to cast a power spell before I try to cast a spell to break their cover. Unfortunately, my power spells are better cast at night when I can see the stars."

"I don't think we should wait. Use my magic. Add it to yours so we can cast a good spell to find Oatha right now."

"Tamara—"

"I know," I said, strolling over to him. I slid my arms around his neck. "It's not the most romantic reason to fool around, but it's a pretty good reason to, don't you think?"

He stared into my eyes. "I'm not sure it's a good idea for me to drain a lot of power from you. I want you as strong as possible, in case Oatha Theroux tries to kill you using voodoo again."

"Believe me, I want to be strong enough to survive, too. But if we find Oatha, maybe we can stop her from ever using the voodoo doll again. And we can save Vangie if they have her, which I'm pretty convinced they do."

He nodded and his hand rested on my leg and stroked my skin, giving me goose bumps.

"Hang on till we have privacy," I said, grabbing his hand. "What are you wearing, by the way? Where are your pants?"

"Let's talk about that later," I said, leaning against him. When I kissed him, he drew back and licked his lips.

"What's on your mouth?"

"What?" I asked, running my tongue over my lips. I could still taste a hint of honey and salt. I wiped my mouth with the back of my hand. "It's a long story. We'll talk about it once we deal with the Therouxs."

He hesitated. "I don't want you to keep things from me."

"I won't. Just let's do the power spell first and talk later. I think I'll wash my face and brush my teeth." Glancing down at the smudges of mud on my legs, I added, "I'd better take another shower, too. I swear my skin's going to be drier than a lizard's before the week's out. Using that much shower gel scrubs away all the body's natural oils," I complained. "Come upstairs and you can put lotion on me in the places I can't reach."

He watched me cross to the door. "You think I'm that easy to manipulate, huh?"

"Well . . ." I said, cocking my head. "I think you're quick to help me when I need it. You don't want me to get lizard skin, do you?"

He arched a brow.

I looked over my shoulder at him and smiled. "Okay, stay here. I'll just come down with the lotion, but then we'll have to worry about security cameras catching us at whatever we end up doing."

Walking toward me, he said, "I'm not agreeing to do things all your way."

"Okay," I said innocently.

He paused, narrowing his eyes, and stood stubbornly in the library doorway. "You plan to make it hard for me to resist, don't you?"

I stopped on the steps with an impish grin. "Well, yeah. But if it's any consolation, I plan for us to have a really good time while I distract you."

He tried not to smile, and I added sincerely, "Also, I love you."

He sighed and joined me on the stairs. "Apparently sometimes, I am that easy."

AFTER MY SHOWER, I rubbed lotion on my arms. Bryn sat in a chair in the corner of the room reviewing a book with a ghoulish cover. He lowered it to watch me.

I wore a green and gold satin robe that I'd bought online. Sitting on the bed, I squeezed lotion on my calves and massaged it in. "Mr. Jenson looks better. That medicine from Dr. Suri must be helping. Do you know what part of India Dr. and Mrs. Suri are from?"

"No, why?"

"Because India's like Texas," I said.

Bryn barked out a laugh. "How so?"

"Well, Texas is big and has different weather and terrain and accents. So does India, right? And most importantly, different parts of India have different cuisine. If I'm going to make something tasty for Dr. and Mrs. Suri to thank him for making a house call, I have to find out what kind of spices they like best," I said. "I'll talk to Johnny. He can find out anything about anyone. It's the scalp massage. It's almost impossible not to let something slip when that guy's fingers are going to town. I've never been hypnotized, but it can't be more relaxing than fifteen minutes in Johnny's chair."

I started toward Bryn with the bottle of lotion in my outstretched hand, thinking he could put some on my back and we could get cozy, but I never made it to him.

The bottle of lotion fell to the floor as I was lurched off the ground, my stomach dropping like I was riding a roller coaster. A split second later, I was flung backward and slammed against the French doors. I guess they weren't locked because they banged open and my ankles hit the balcony railing as I flew over it.

An outstretched branch whacked my shoulders. It knocked the wind out of me, but I caught it. My fingers clamped down, and I dangled two stories above the flower beds, panting from the adrenaline rush.

"For the love of Hershey," I yelled as my body whipped back and forth like I was on a swing. I tightened my grip, making my hands grind against the bark, scraping them raw. My heart thumped in protest, and my palms grew sweaty.

No!

Falling twenty-five feet to the ground or being whipped

through the air and then slamming onto the lawn both seemed like scary options.

Bryn thrust out a hand, and his magic grabbed me. Then there was a tug-of-war. The towel came loose and fell into the flower bed, leaving me bare-assed . . . again. Not to mention that we'd just bleached those towels to get them pure white, and now look . . . Yikes, the ground was far away. *Don't look down!*

I jerked my gaze up and cursed a blue streak under my breath. I didn't want to make too much noise. If I did, Mr. Jenson might look up, and it was hardly dignified for me to hang from a tree in my birthday suit.

Bryn strained, whispering magic-laced words. My body swayed toward the balcony. If I got the tree to help, I could swing back to the house.

"Tree," I said. "Can you give me a swing toward the terrace? I'd appreciate it ever so much," I said sweetly.

The tree twitched its assent. The branch swayed back, dragging Bryn to the railing, and then thrust me toward him. I sailed forward and let go at the last possible moment, reaching out. Bryn plucked me out of the air and set me on my feet. He spun toward the south and drove magic out like a lance, his eyes glittering blue-black.

The magic slammed so hard into something my teeth rattled. For a split second, I saw inside a crumbling house. The Therouxs were there. Four of them fell to the floor and were deadly still. Oatha dropped to her knees, her face haggard and worn. She snarled, clutching her chest with her left hand. I saw a doll at her feet, the pretty plastic head attached to a cloth body. I opened my mouth to scream as she snatched it with her right hand.

In the next instant, I flew off the balcony. Bryn shouted and reached for me with his magic, but it didn't hold. It only caught the tips of my toes for a second. She'd thrown me in a blind fury. I rocketed over treetops with a deafening whoosh.

Flying is fun, but landing sure isn't. The ground raced up, but a pulse of Bryn's magic lobbed me skyward and out.

I landed in the Amanos River with a cannonball of a splash. The water felt a little less solid than concrete, but not much. At least three ribs cracked on impact and maybe my skull, too, because a few seconds after I plunged under the icy water, I went dead unconscious.

22

I WOKE IN a cocoon of blankets with an explosive head-ache that felt like a grenade had gone off in my skull.

Oxygen prongs blew air into my nose, making it itch, and Dr. Suri and Bryn stood over me.

"Tamara?" Bryn said, clasping my hand.

"That's my name. As far as I know," I mumbled, clutch-ing my head. I coughed, which sent knives slicing through my brain. "Ow, ow, ow," I whispered.

Dr. Suri flashed a bright light into my eyeballs, and I tried to squeeze them shut. "Don't do that."

"It's all right," Bryn said, pushing Dr. Suri's arm away. "I knew you would wake up," Bryn whispered, stroking my face.

"You were in a coma for three hours," Dr. Suri said. "A very deep coma."

"I think I should've stayed there for a couple more. My head's killing me."

I felt Bryn's lips against my forehead, and the verse he whispered delivered a sliver of soothing magic. I closed my eyes. "That feels better. Do that some more."

I felt the bed sag as Bryn sat next to me. "Give us a few minutes, Prashat."

"Of course," Dr. Suri said, and I heard him go.

Bryn's cool palms rested against my temples, his fingers gently stroking my scalp. He whispered a melancholy poem against my mouth, and magic eased into me. I gasped as my head tingled and went numb.

"Wow," I said, my lips abuzz. I noticed the pain in my ribs for the first time. "How are you? You okay?" I asked, knowing that our connection caused trouble for him, too, when I got injured.

He nodded. "My head hurts. My side feels like someone pummeled it with a bat." He raised his shirt, showing off a massive purple bruise that took up most of his right side.

"Matches mine?" I asked.

"It does."

"You fished me out of the water?"

"Just in time," he said. "Another minute, and you'd have gone over the falls alone. That I don't think . . ."

"You don't think I could've survived? Me either," I said, sitting up. "These swamp people witches are becoming a real problem." My voice was cool and hard.

"I agree. I'm fairly sure you were right about Oatha using a voodoo doll."

"I'm a hundred percent sure. I saw her. Had a vision clear as cable TV."

"I wrote a special protection spell. I'm not sure if it'll work, but—"

"Go ahead," I said. Bryn's considered one of the best spell writers of the age. He inherited the talent, along with his blue eyes, from his momma.

"It will hurt when I close it around you."

"Can't hurt worse than falling into the Amanos from halfway to heaven."

"The voodoo doll's been connected to you by the spell Oatha cast. If I cast a spell on your body that makes it pain-ful for anyone magical to touch you and link it to the doll, she won't be able to touch the doll again, even with an implement, without causing herself serious pain."

"Sneaky. I know I told you that you should only use your powers for good, but I've decided that sometimes there are going to be exceptions to that rule. Like when I've been thrown off a balcony, across the yard, and into the river. A self-defense spell with some bite is just what the doctor ordered. Or it would be, if Dr. Suri found out my injuries were voodoo-related."

Bryn left the bedside and returned with a yellow legal pad. He put a hand over me and read the spell in Gaelic. It was rather musical and flowed over me like oil. The magic warmed me until I was feverish and crackling with it.

I sucked in a breath, making my side sing with pain. I exhaled and concentrated on keeping myself still. The spell's energy changed. It became hot and sharp, like lots of pine needles dried on a hearth were poking me. I wiggled, feeling like a porcupine turned inside out. I hissed, but Bryn kept going. Once he started something, his concentration was a force to be reckoned with.

All at once, my body contracted, and I heard a loud pop. Then I felt better, or at least back to the level of uncomfortable I'd been before he started the spell.

Bryn set down his pad and stretched his finger out. The second he touched my arm, an electric shock zinged me. He jerked his finger back, rubbing his arm from hand to shoulder and shaking it. I guessed that he'd gotten a much worse shock than I had.

Bryn smiled, his eyes shining cobalt and rimmed with black. "Let her try to use that doll now."

"I saw several of her relatives laid out on the floor. I guess they were helping to protect her while she used the voodoo doll on me. They looked pretty dead to the world after you flung your magic at them. I wonder if they were just knocked out or if . . . ?" I trailed off.

It was Bryn's turn to be cool as a whiskey on the rocks. "They were accomplices to her attempted murder of you. Anyone who's seen a publication on the supernatural world in the past few months should've anticipated that we'd answer a mortal threat with deadly force."

"I suppose so," I said, still uncomfortable. Being in a shoot-out was one thing. To my mind, that was fighting in self-defense. But magic that killed from miles away? I shuddered. Technically, I guessed it was still self-defense. They'd attacked me from a distance; Bryn had attacked them back that same way. It just didn't sit well with me.

I glanced at him. These were the moments it was hard to trust him. I loved his mastery of words and the way he could draw me close without touching, but that kind of seductive charm was otherworldly. He'd lived in Duvall on and off since he'd been thirteen, but he wasn't like the rest of us. He was part Ireland, part Ivy League. His power didn't crave the sun like mine. His was night magic.

"We're so different," I said.

He leaned toward me, his expression softening. "That's why we're good for each other," he said. "Sometimes cold calculation is necessary. Treachery has to be answered with force. It's the only thing evil respects. But history has proven that power without empathy leads to massacre.

"Compassion's your heart's blood, Tamara," he said. "It gives you a valuable perspective, like when justice turns to vengeance. While I have you, I won't lose my way. You're my North Star."

I swallowed, tongue-tied for a moment. I thought Bryn gave me too much credit. I wasn't exceptionally good. I was like most people, basically decent and trying to do the right thing. Still, it was nice to hear that Bryn believed I was special. I wondered if that feeling would last. Would I be such a good moral compass if I pointed too far fae? That part of me didn't seem to have much conscience, and Bryn recoiled from me in that form. What if I couldn't stop myself from becoming . . . ? No, I could stop it. I was in control of my own self.

"That was really sweet. Thanks for saying it," I said, then puckered up and smacked my lips in a makeshift kiss. He smiled.

I rolled onto my uninjured side and levered myself into a sitting position with a huff of breath at the pain. "Has anyone heard from Vangie?" I asked.

Bryn shook his head.

"It's past the time she was supposed to pick me up for her wedding. She's not going to get married today," I said, then bit my lip, forlorn.

"Doesn't look like it," Bryn said, giving my hand a small squeeze.

I swallowed. "I hope Vangie's stepfamily's been distracted enough by you and me to leave Vangie unharmed if they've got her. But if Oatha can't use a Tammy Jo doll now to torture me with, I bet she'll be plenty mad when she gets back around to Vangie. The thing I don't understand is why they're attacking me if they've got her. They could just kill her and leave town."

"I don't know," Bryn said. "Maybe they worry that you'll make trouble once her body is found. That you'll testify that she told you they were trying to kill her and they attacked you in your house when you prevented them from finding her."

"Once her body is found . . ." I repeated, feeling the blood drain from my face. I pushed the covers down. "She could still be alive. We've got to find them."

"Tamara, I know you heal quickly, but even you need a few more hours in bed after suffering a concussion and a coma, and breaking half a dozen ribs."

"Half a dozen, huh? No wonder my chest hurts," I grumbled. I glanced down at my naked body and frowned. "For pete's sake, Bryn, how come you didn't put some clothes on me?"

"Clothes weren't a high priority when I carried you in here unconscious and half dead."

"Well, you knew I'd wake up eventually and then I'd want to be dressed," I said, wrapping the covers around my shoulders. "Can you do me a favor and go upstairs to get me some jeans and a shirt? And underwear and socks," I said, pulling the oxygen tubing off my head.

"About that."

"Yes?" I asked, going still.

"You don't have any jeans left."

"What?"

"Everything's ripped beyond repair. You're pretty hard on your clothes these days."

"I'm—" I sputtered. "I'm not hard on them. Other people are!" I clutched my wounded side and cursed. Over the past few months I'd been in so many fights. It was hell on a wardrobe. "So what do I have left here to wear?"

"Party dresses and La Perla underwear."

My hand was halfway to thunking my head when I jerked it back. That would be more hurtful than helpful. I licked my lips. "Okay then. I'll sure be sorry if any more of that expensive lingerie gets ripped to shreds, but that'll teach you not to buy me undies that cost more than the down payment on a used car."

"I had hoped that if any of that lingerie was torn off you, I'd be the one doing the tearing," Bryn said ruefully. "At least you look great in it before it's ruined."

"That's one way of looking at it. A guy's way," I said with a hint of a smile. "Can you go upstairs and grab me a dress to wear? Or are you too sore?" I asked, wincing at the way he grimaced when he stood. His sharing my injuries wasn't good.

"I'm all right." He walked to the door and paused. "Tamara?"

"Yes, Bryn?"

"I love you."

"I know," I said, smiling sympathetically. "It's your only dangerous vice, but you indulge like there's no tomorrow."

23

EVEN THOUGH I'D planned to head straight out after getting dressed, we only made it as far as the front door before I had to return to the guest room, gasping for breath. I did need more time to heal.

I eased onto the edge of the bed, my pewter dress with the beaded hem falling over my scraped knees.

"Bring me tea and cake," I told Bryn. "Or just cake. And the leftover chocolate buttercream frosting that's in the green Tupperware on the bottom shelf." When I'm recovering . . . or just having a regular day, I've found that a good dose of chocolate helps clear my head.

"How about some protein first, sweetheart? I'll scramble you some eggs."

"Oh my gosh, that's so sweet of you. You know what would be sweeter? If you brought me some frosting. If I'm going to get killed by swamp witches, my last meal isn't going to be scrambled eggs—no offense to chickens. In times of trouble, eggs are really better off as a team player. And the rest of the team is semisweet chocolate chips, butter, and heavy cream."

Bryn didn't looked thrilled about it, but he came back with a pot of tea, a slice of cake, and two teaspoons of extra frosting on the side.

"What's this? Are we on frosting rations? In case I'm too wounded to make more for a while?"

He leaned against the dresser and smiled. "I want you to have some appetite left for grilled ham and eggs."

"And I want you to stop confusing me with Mercutio. He's a cat, so he needs meat. I'm a half faery, so I need sugar."

He frowned, and I regretted mentioning my fae side. I needed to watch that. Or not. If Bryn couldn't accept me as I was, maybe it was better to know sooner rather than later.

I drank two cups of strong tea and ate my cake and extra frosting. Then I lay down and rested. While asleep, I dreamed of faraway places and heard a pretty female voice say in an Irish lilt, "There you are. Be well and step lively. Your wounds won't trouble us." I woke with the taste of honeyed apples on my tongue, and my skin glowed pure gold. The pain I'd had was much less. Fae healing of some kind?

Finding me awake, Bryn brought a laptop computer and a map into the room. When he opened an article with pictures of the Therouxs, I blinked and my jaw dropped.

"How old is that picture of Beau and Oatha?"

"A few months."

"No way," I said, leaning forward. "She looks at least fifteen years older now. Where are all her wrinkles and the streaks of gray in her hair? And his face looks so smooth. Where are the acne scars on his cheeks and the stubble and . . . That's not what they look like. Not at all. It's like they've been airbrushed twenty times."

Bryn narrowed his eyes.

"When you've seen them, haven't they looked all old and rough to you?" I asked.

"No, they looked like this picture."

I gasped. "How come I don't get the airbrushed 'I could run for political office' makeup and face-lift effect?"

"They must be using glamours to smooth out their appearance. To look more respectable to the police and witches who've investigated them. Maybe they can't maintain the glamour when they are casting these major spells."

"I need to talk to Edie. If we can't figure out where they are with a spell, maybe we can use the Duvall ghost network to track them down."

"I've got a pretty good idea where they are," he said, pointing to a map. The area he'd pointed to was about ten miles from Old Town. "Without as many members of their clan reinforcing the concealment spell, it'll be harder for them to hide."

I rubbed my ribs. The pain was much less intense. "Good, that frosting's kicking in. I'll be ready to go in no time."

A yowl from the kitchen announced sunset and that Mercutio was hungry. I glanced toward the kitchen. "Now there's someone who'll appreciate some grilled ham. Or some raw ham."

"I'll be back," Bryn said, leaning over. He almost kissed me, but the pop of a spark made us both jump. "Damn, I forgot the spell."

"It's like a chastity belt. Parents of teen girls would probably pay a lot of money for that sort of spell."

"I wouldn't do that to teenage girls. Or their boyfriends."

"Uh-huh. Let's see what you say when you have daughters," I teased.

Bryn paused in the doorway and looked back at me. "You think I'll be overprotective?"

"I don't know."

"When you're ready to find out, say the word."

I cocked my head. "Three hours ago I was in a deep coma and at the moment, if we touch, we get electrocuted. You really think it's a good time to talk babies?"

"You brought it up," he said in that "graduated with honors" lawyer tone. "I wasn't suggesting that we try to conceive them tonight." His tone was milk-and-honey, and as we'd already established, I went for honey above everything.

"It's too soon," I said, but hesitated as I pictured adorable babies with black hair and blue eyes. I blinked and shook my head. "Anyway, I wouldn't want to have kids if Edie couldn't visit."

Bryn frowned, but I saw the look on his face just before he did, and I knew that we had him.

Mercutio yowled.

"I better feed Merc before Mr. Jenson hears him and gets up to do it."

"You should stay in bed," Bryn said with a stern look.

"I'm feeling much better. And this is what happens when everybody in the house is sick or injured. Be glad you're not Dr. Suri. Imagine what he's got to deal with all day long. Doc Barnaby's hammertoes and Mrs. Schnitzer's lumbago and—"

"Okay," Bryn said, holding out a hand to stop me from listing the rest of Dr. Suri's patients.

I giggled, then strolled out of the guest room. I fed Mercutio and filled him in on my circus act from the voodoo curse. Then I went to check on Mr. Jenson. I found him settled on the living room couch under a blanket.

"Hi, Mr. Jenson. You feeling better?"

"Much better, my dear. How are you?"

"Right as rain and ready to rescue. My friend's gone missing," I added, checking my phone. No calls from Vangie. "Have you seen Bryn?"

"I believe he's gone outside to do a power spell."

"That's a great idea. They don't call Bryn a genius for nothing, do they?"

"They certainly don't," he agreed.

"You take care," I said.

"That should be my line to you, Miss Tamara."

"I'll do my best," I said, blowing him a kiss. I went outside and found Bryn standing on the lawn, wearing a thick knit turtleneck sweater over jeans. He'd laid his wool topcoat over a chair and I lifted it, inhaling its faint scent of Bryn and magic. I carried it to him and reached out. A warning crackle reminded me just in time that I wasn't allowed to touch him with the protection spell in place. I grimaced.

"You know, I'm not too keen on this spell. You're all magicked up and I want a kiss."

Bryn ran a hand through his black hair and smiled. "Rain check?"

I nodded.

He fell into step with me while Mercutio circled the area where Bryn had been casting spells. Merc's got a taste for magic that often comes in handy.

Bryn paused in the kitchen at the sound of Mr. Jenson coughing. I slowed, relieved when it got quiet again after a couple of inhaler puffs.

"He's okay," I said, but Bryn didn't move. "Are *you* okay?" I asked him.

"I want your opinion on something."

My chest warmed. Bryn wanted my advice? That was new, and better than Ghirardelli white chocolate baking chips. "All right," I said, leaning toward him for a smooch. My lips got a little jolt and I jumped. I stomped my foot and clenched my fists. "I hate this spell. Take it off."

"Tamara," he said, shaking his head. "I nearly broke my ankle dropping from the balcony so I could get to you." His wry smile faded. "By the time I got to the river, you were almost to the falls, your body limp and facedown . . ." Bryn became utterly still, his voice low and grim, like he could see it all unfolding again. "There was only a halo of red hair floating on the water. I thought you might already be dead and I felt . . ." After a few moments of silence, he shook his head and whispered, "Keep the spell a little longer, sweetheart."

I exhaled, blinking. I knew from experience that it's easier to be the one dying than the one watching the person you love die. "Well, if you're going to put it like that," I said with mock exasperation, "I guess I'll keep the dumb spell on. Now what did you want to talk about?" I scooped a handful of Hershey's kisses from a Saturn-shaped cookie jar I'd bought him.

"I'm not sure what to do about Jenson," Bryn said as we walked across the kitchen.

"What do you mean, what to do about him? He's on the mend."

"I know, but he's not young. This illness has taken its toll."

"He'll recover," I said firmly. That had to be true.

"He told me he wanted to go to Ireland."

"Uh-huh," I said, pausing in the hall. He stopped, too.

"His wife's buried there, which is what she wanted, but he's mentioned that it's hard not being able to visit her grave. I bought the land near the cemetery and had a cottage built for when he retires." Bryn glanced at the window, as if he could see clear across the ocean if he looked hard enough. "He should have retired long ago." Bryn folded his hands, rubbing the tip of one thumb over the base of the other. "Whenever he's said that I might be better off with someone younger, I've said the change would be a disruption to the running of the house and claimed I didn't have time for it. I thought he was trying to make it easy on me, to give me the option of replacing him. But now I wonder if he's tired and actually wants me to let him go. Maybe I've been selfish to keep him in Texas this long."

"Besides his wife, what people does he have in Ireland? Any kids or grandkids?"

"No, he has a niece and her family and some cousins in England. They send him Christmas cards. He mails them holiday gifts."

"Anybody you think he cares about more than you?"

Bryn shrugged. "They are his blood, and he's always said he wants to be buried in Ireland with his wife."

I leaned forward. "Being buried in a place and living there all alone waiting to die are two different things. I happen to know that the reason he was talking about going to Ireland right now was to give you a job, to take your mind off me and our problems."

"What problems?"

"The business with Zach."

"How did Jenson know about that? I didn't say anything to him."

"I'm sure he's got his ways of finding stuff out," I said.

Bryn nodded. "So what do you think? Would suggesting that it's time for him to retire be something he'd welcome? Or something that would hurt his feelings?"

"From what I can tell, you're like his grandson. I can't believe he'd be happier living in a cottage by himself. Maybe he'd get a lot of visitors over there and it would make up for missing you, but I doubt it. If it were me, I wouldn't be happy if I didn't get to see you, and we've only been together a few months. Mr. Jenson's had a whole lifetime with you. I think the best thing would be to take him to England and Ireland for a visit. You can size up his relatives and see what he thinks of the cottage. Then just tell him you'd prefer he came back to Texas to be with us, but you'll understand if he wants to stay there. See what he says."

"Jenson's of the old set. A butler doesn't talk to his employer about his feelings. It would make him uncomfortable."

I nodded. "Okay, I'll take care of it for you."

"You will? How?"

"I'll start taking over a few tasks around the house to lighten his load, but I'll ask for his advice a lot, so he knows I need him."

"You don't think he'll catch on to what you're doing?" Bryn asked.

"Sure he will. He'll know exactly what I'm doing," I said. "But he won't mind. Southern ladies and English butlers are actually a lot alike in the way they handle people."

Bryn smiled. "You think so?"

"Yep. I doubt he'll call me on it, but if he does I'll just tell him the truth. I never had a daddy or a granddaddy growing up, and I always wanted one. Mr. Jenson's the closest thing I've got. I won't give him up without a fight."

"From you, that would probably work," Bryn said, shaking his head in admiration.

"Yep. You're welcome," I said. "And here." I dangled a Hershey's chocolate by its tissue banner. "Here's a kiss from me."

He unwrapped it and dropped it on his tongue. After he chewed and swallowed, he said, "Thank you. That was exactly what I needed."

24

MY NEXT-DOOR NEIGHBOR Jolene was behind the counter at the local drugstore when Bryn and I went inside. I loaded my arms up with the leftover summer inventory of size six-seven flip-flops. She sure gave me a funny look as I bought fifty-three dollars' worth of rubber footwear.

"Honey, a pair of these should last you for a couple years. What in the world are you going to do with fifteen years' worth of flip-flops?"

"I like to have extra," I said, taking off my expensive high heels and putting my feet in a pair of sparkle-patterned flip-flops with *High Class* printed on the straps.

"That's a pretty dress you're wearing," she said, looking down at my flip-flop-clad feet. "Tammy Jo, honey, you know it's forty-eight degrees outside, right?" she whispered with a glance at Bryn, who was looking at the newspapers. "Your man is going to think you've lost your mind. For goodness' sake, put on some stockings and a pair of pumps."

"Oh, don't you worry about it," I said. "He already knows I'm crazy." I scooped up my bag of flip-flops and sauntered out of the store. I wondered how long it would take for the whole town to hear that I wasn't just off my rocker, I'd turned the thing over on itself.

Bryn, who normally cares about his reputation and town standing, just shrugged when I told him about my conversation with Jolene.

"These days, sweetheart, we've got to pick our battles. Gossip, no matter how malicious, won't kill us, so it's got to fall to the bottom of the priority list."

"Right, foes before schmoes."

Bryn laughed and was still laughing when he got in the car. Mercutio stood with his hind paws on my bag of flip-flops and his front paws on the dash, scanning for villains or small game. I leaned back, wishing I'd eaten more frosting, and rolled down the windows to see if the trees had anything interesting to whisper. I was disappointed by the silence. Not only weren't they whispering, but there were no cricket chirps, no rustling of wind, nada. It was definitely too quiet.

Mercutio made a noise of apprehension.

"Yeah, I think so, too, Merc. Something's not right." My muscles tensed as I saw a flash of green streaking toward us. "Stop the car."

"What's up?" Bryn asked, slowing.

"Stop the car!"

He hit the brakes hard, and we jerked to a stop. I opened the door and hopped out as Edie stopped twenty feet from me like she'd hit a wall. Her essence was thin as a veil. When she spoke her voice was faint enough to make me hold my breath so the sound of my breathing wouldn't get in the way of my hearing her.

"I recognize them, Tammy. It's just like that night."

"What night? What's wrong?" I asked, hurrying toward her.

"I finally remember what happened . . ." She looked up at the sky and so did I, but there was nothing overhead. "On the night I died."

I gasped and jerked my head to look at her.

She sagged. "Of all the nasty tricks—I can't . . . I'll come back," she said with a feathery voice. In an instant, she faded away.

"Wait!" I called, and then spun frantically toward the car. "You didn't do anything, did you? You didn't send her away?"

"No," Bryn said. "I didn't even feel her presence."

"Something's happened," I said, rattled. "She said she saw *them* the night she died. Who can she have meant? Maybe Vangie's family look like their kin? Or maybe something Oatha's doing reminded her of whoever killed her?" I slapped the car in frustration. "If they did anything to hurt her or drain her away, I'll make them sorry."

"Hasn't she gotten worn out from manifesting for too long before?"

"Yes."

"She may just need time."

"I know that," I said, and pursed my lips. "But I'm worried."

"She has the locket for protection. And ultimately, she is already dead, so there's not much that can be done to her."

I eyed him. "Given that some thought, have you?"

He held out his hands. "I'm just making an observation."

I dropped into the passenger seat. "Let's go," I said when Mercutio and Bryn were inside and the doors were closed. "Take me to the Therouxs." I glanced out the windows, scanning the road and the woods. "The spell that's hurting the town ghosts, what if it's powerful enough to get through the locket?" I bit my lip. "I have to find out what's going on."

Bryn didn't respond, which frustrated me.

"Don't you have anything to say? Something's wrong. Can't you hear how quiet it is?"

He gave me a sidelong glance. "It's always quiet at night. This is a small town."

"Yeah, but not like this. Usually I hear the trees and the wind, the brooks and rivers, insects and bats, even the ghosts. They all make small noises that I can hear and that Mercutio can hear. I bet if I asked Crux, he'd confirm it. Something is choking nature's voice into silence."

"Who's Crux?"

"He's a faery."

"What faery? Where did you see him?"

"In the woods. He's either hunting me or trying to help me. I'm not sure which. But he isn't doing this. No fae would ever do this," I said, extending a hand toward the windshield and the darkness beyond.

"Why didn't you tell me about him before now?"

"We were busy. That's the thing I was going to tell you later."

"It's later. And as a point of information, I'm never too busy to hear about a member of the fae who might be hunting you."

"There's not much to tell."

"Tell me anyway."

I chewed my thumbnail and looked in the rearview mirror. What had Edie seen that reminded her of the night she died?

I filled Bryn in on my meeting with Crux. Bryn bristled with anger, making the seat vibrate with magic. As I finished talking, Mercutio yowled and bonked his head against the windshield.

Bryn hit the brakes, and we came to a sharp stop. I opened the door and Mercutio darted out into the woods. I started to follow him, but Bryn said my name and made me pause.

"That's not the way to Oatha Theroux." There was no question in his voice.

"Are you sure?" I asked, even though I knew he was.

"Yes, I'm sure."

My hand hesitated over the door handle. "Mercutio's tracking something." I tipped my head, listening. "Could even be Crux."

"Do you want to follow him or to go after the Cajuns?"

I wanted to find Vangie. I pulled the door closed. "Foes before fae," I said in a tone that lacked any trace of cuteness.

Bryn didn't laugh this time. Neither did I.

THERE WERE AREAS where the creeks had overflowed during the town's massive flood that still hadn't dried out.

At the edge of this marshy area north of Old Town, the caravan of Vangie's stepfamily had assembled.

I checked my weapons, pulled a borrowed sweatshirt over my head so I could take off my coat for better mobility, and climbed from the car. Bryn joined me, and we rounded the house. The people were apparently packing up to leave since truck tailgates were lowered and trailers were open and half full.

Was Vangie packed among the stuff? Or was she tied up in the house?

I gave Bryn a questioning look, and he nodded at a truck that was parked away from the others. I marched over and we waited. Beau's cousin approached, carrying two suitcases. When he leaned to shove them inside, I came up behind. When he straightened, his head came into contact with the gun in my hand.

"Not a sound," I said. "Where's Vangie?"

"Who?"

"Evangeline Rhodes."

"Oatha's girl? How would I know? Haven't seen her in two years."

"Where's Oatha?"

"She's on her way back to her house in Dallas. Been havin' fierce chest pains." The look on his face said what he didn't. He wanted revenge. They'd like to kill me and Bryn for retaliating against Oatha and them.

"When did Oatha leave?" I asked.

"Around an hour ago. We're all clearing out of here. Two of our people had heart attacks today. We're taking 'em home to be buried."

I stiffened, knowing they hadn't had regular heart attacks. "Where's Beau?"

"He's packing one of the trailers. You wanna talk to him? Beau!" he hollered.

I thumped him on the head with the gun and he staggered. Bryn chopped him again and the man fell facedown. We heard footsteps running toward us, and we hurried around the house.

Shouts and heavy footfalls came from various directions. I realized it was likely going to be a repeat of the magic and gunfight of the night before. Bryn drew me into the house.

There were lit lanterns rather than electric lights burning. Bryn crossed the room and lifted an overturned box. On the floor was the Tammy Jo voodoo doll. So Oatha had left without it. If she'd actually left.

"Tamara, you should be able to touch it."

I stalked over and picked her up. The doll was cold but hummed with the spell Bryn had put on her. "I don't have pockets," I complained. "This is the problem with dresses." I tucked the doll inside the top of my dress, which was snug enough at the waist that she didn't just slide down and fall out the bottom. "Okay, got her."

Bryn walked around the room, whispering spells and touching surfaces. "There are traces of black magic, but I don't find any of Evangeline's here."

"Could they have had her locked up and gagged? Maybe in a trunk or something? They wouldn't have wanted her to be able to cast spells."

"If there was a binding spell done, it wasn't cast here."

Beau and several of his family members burst in, shotguns raised. I pointed my gun at his head and moved so that I was behind a tattered couch with exposed springs.

"*Chère*, we meet again," Beau said. His bruised and swollen face was in sharp contrast to the white wall behind him.

"Where's Vangie?"

"I'll take you to her. Just you and me. He stays here with the others."

"Absolutely not," Bryn said.

"You better do what I say, my friend," Beau said to Bryn. "You're outgunned."

"Am I?" Bryn asked coolly, and I felt his power rise and contract in preparation, like a snake coiling to strike.

Outside, a tailgate slammed closed and a motor started.

I stalked to the window. "She could be in that truck," I said. A busted-out window provided a big enough opening for me to climb through, but there were jagged shards of glass. I hit the biggest pieces with my gun, making them shatter and fall to the ground.

"Tamara," Bryn warned.

"I'll be right back," I said, climbing out. I ran, my flip-flops popping off in the mud. I reached the road just in time. The truck made a U-turn to flee the scene. I stalked forward, took aim, and blew a hole in the front driver's-side tire. The truck fishtailed and then jerked to a stop. I jumped in the back and checked through everything in the flatbed. If Vangie hadn't been cut into little pieces, there was no way she'd have fit in the luggage or boxes in the back, but I opened everything and checked. No body. No bones. Thank goodness.

The couple who'd gotten out of the truck's cab screamed obscenities at me and waved their guns menacingly. I figured if they'd planned to shoot me, they would've done it right off.

I climbed over the side of the truck and dropped to the ground. Where was she?

I looked through the broken window to check on Bryn. He and Beau were still talking, with a room separating them. Beau and his people seemed hesitant to attack, which made sense. I doubted they wanted Bryn to blast them with his heart-attack-inducing magic. If Bryn could keep them distracted for a few minutes, I could search for Vangie.

I rushed to a nearby car and leaned in its open window to turn on its headlights. They shined directly into the trailer across from it. My plan was simple. I'd check all the parked cars, trucks, and trailers. If I didn't find Vangie, Bryn and I could drive to Dallas and search Oatha's car and house.

I dug through luggage and overturned boxes in the next trailer and was just about finished when gunfire and magic exploded in the house. I jerked upright, raced to the end of the trailer, and jumped out.

The couple who'd been in the middle of changing their tire converged on the house at the same time I did. They opened fire on me. I dove behind a rusted car on cinder blocks. I returned fire, wondering how Bryn was faring in the house. He had a gun but was better armed with magic. It gusted like an icy wind.

"*Chère*, what are you doing out here?"

I jerked around to find Beau's gun pointed square in my face. I knocked the gun to the side as I dropped. Most of the blast went by me, but a few pellets caught the side of my upper arm, making it burn with pain. I popped to one knee and shot Beau in the shoulder and the leg.

He howled and fell backward, landing hard on the ground. I rose, heart hammering, and felt blood stream down my arm. Even with my pulse pounding, the wound didn't gush. Just a flesh wound. Thank goodness.

I stood over Beau. He screamed obscenities, clutching his leg.

"I got your thighbone, huh?" I asked, my voice low but agitated. "You shouldn't have snuck up on me and pointed a gun in my face." I lifted and lowered my throbbing shoulder. "And you shouldn't have shot me. This sweatshirt's not even mine."

I bent forward and pointed the gun at the middle of his forehead. "Do you want to be put out of your misery?"

"No!" he yelled, gnashing his teeth.

"How about some pain medications? Want some of that?" I poked his leg with my toe, not hard enough to jar it, but hard enough for him to feel the threat. He grabbed my ankle and looked ready to try to knock me off balance. I steadied myself on one foot. "Go ahead," I said in my best Clint Eastwood *The Outlaw Josey Wales* voice. "I bet I can put two bullets through your heart before I hit the ground." I paused. "Well, that might be overconfident. Maybe just one will hit its mark."

He snarled at me and let go of my leg. Sweat beaded on his forehead, and he wiped it away.

"Dr. Suri, our local doctor, has morphine in his clinic. He can probably be here with it in twenty minutes once I call him. But I'm not calling anyone until you tell me where my friend is."

He panted for breath. "She's in the back of the red trailer by the woods."

"And what about the Duvall ghosts? Where did your mother put them?"

He dropped his head back, cursing and gasping for breath. "Damn you. Goddamn you."

"Ghosts?" I repeated.

"I don't know what the hell you're talking about. She didn't call the dead. Why would she, you redheaded she-devil bitch?" Except he didn't say *bitch*. He used a four-letter word I've never used in my life and never will.

I leaned forward and slapped his face. "Call me that again, and I'll bust your other thighbone so you'll have a matched set."

He surprised me by laughing. "You should kill me, *chère*. Otherwise, one day you're going to find yourself naked and tied down and I'm going to—"

The rest of what he threatened to do made me want to shoot him in the groin. Then he grabbed for his gun. So I did.

He screamed, cursing me, God, and the devil, apparently undecided about who deserved the most blame.

"Yeah, I know. Look what you made me do," I snapped, shaking my head and kicking his gun farther out of reach.

He continued to wail in pain, and I knew there was no use trying to talk to him about anything. As I walked away, he yelled that I'd shot him in his left testicle.

"You're lucky. If I could've seen what I was aiming at, I would have shot the part you don't have a spare for," I called back.

Despite my tough talk, I felt a little shaky as I stalked away. Threatening to rape me wasn't the same as doing it, and his broken leg meant he hadn't stood much chance of getting the upper hand, so technically I hadn't been forced to shoot him. I could've kicked his gun out of reach. I saw that now.

But I reasoned, from the way he talked, that there were women who hadn't escaped him in the past. They'd needed an avenger. Also, he'd kind of been asking to get shot in the testicle, really. Why use rape threats to goad an armed woman who's already shot you twice unless you're looking for trouble? Yeah, I rationalized, it was partly his fault. Forty, maybe fifty-seven percent his fault.

I checked my shoulder. It throbbed, but didn't seem to be bleeding.

I held pressure and rubbed it as I hurried to the red trailer. I heard Vangie thrashing inside. "I'm coming, Vangie. Just gimme a minute." I shot the lock open.

It took some muscle to get the rusted lever up. I jerked the door open and there was just enough light to see the snapping jaws that lurched forward.

25

IN HINDSIGHT, I should've anticipated that Beau might try to trick me. And if I hadn't just shot him in the balls, I might've been clearheaded enough to realize that I should be a little careful when I opened the back of a trailer in whose direction he'd pointed me.

I'm pretty fast and I did get off two shots, but it turns out alligators are fast, too.

Really fast.

The gator was about thirteen feet long and a thousand pounds. He came out of the trailer like a claustrophobic who'd been trapped in a box for days. I jumped back, but when those jaws closed, he had me.

I was lucky that he hadn't had them fully open and snapped them shut or he'd surely have cracked the bone in my leg. Instead his momentum had been focused on escaping the trailer as he pursued me, and his head had jerked sideways when I shot his right eye out.

Still, once he clamped down and some of those teeth drove into my flesh, I screamed and lost my mind. I thrashed and clawed at the ground with my free hand, but that's just what a gator expects its dinner to do, and once a gator has a grip, it doesn't let go.

At first, pain and panic made me insensible, but then I realized he was dragging me. His massive tail thwacked the ground as he backed up and a spray of brackish water dotted my exposed body. He had most of my left leg between his jaws, and even trying to stop him from pulling me was excruciating since it tore my flesh.

I'd watched enough Nature Channel to know what he had planned. Alligators get their prey in a death grip, drag it underwater, and roll over and over until the prey drowns. Then they stuff their booty under a log or rock to let the swamp tenderize it. Even knowing I'd be dead when it happened, I couldn't stand the idea of a reptile eating the decaying flesh from my bones.

"No, no, no!" I screeched as water splashed over my kicking right leg and lapped up my side.

With a sharp yank, I was dragged in, my butt and belly submerged. My free leg kicked, hitting nothing but water. I could feel the current and knew we were heading into the creek. In another few seconds, he'd have me in deep enough water to roll and that would be the end of me.

I sucked in a breath and tightened my abdominal muscles. I levered myself to a sitting position and for a second locked eyes with his one good eye. I thrust the muzzle of the gun into his empty socket and unloaded.

The *bang, bang, bang* was followed by an empty *click, click, click*. The jaws tightened in one sharp bite and the gator slid backward, pulling me underwater. I felt the gator's body go limp, but he was by no means slack-jawed. I wondered if shooting him in the brain had caused him to go into rigor mortis around my leg.

I dropped the useless gun and grabbed the top of the alligator's jaw with both hands. I felt a splash next to me and wondered if it was a snake or something else coming to eat me. With my heart slamming in my chest and my lungs wailing for air, I pulled up with all my might.

I had to heave a few times before the top jaw loosened. Adrenaline drove my muscles and I contracted my hip and lifted my left leg, tugging it loose from the teeth that had been embedded within it.

I rolled free, got my feet under me, and kicked until my head splashed out of the water. I sucked air for several long seconds with every one of my muscles burning like I'd run a marathon. The rushing sound in my ears made it impossible for me to hear anything else, but I felt something slick against my arm and jerked.

It was Mercutio's head, and he meowed. I grabbed a clump of vegetation with one hand and the root of a fallen tree with another.

"Hang on," I said as Mercutio pushed against me. He wanted me out of that water. I was all for that plan, but my arms shook and it took me several tries to haul myself up onto the bank.

"Did you see him?" I said, panting. "A granddaddy alligator got me. He ate about a third of me in one bite." I sat on the bank, shaking. "Alligators don't play," I said through chattering teeth.

Something slithered toward me, and Mercutio rounded and chomped down. A water moccasin had come out of the creek, but Merc's as fast as a snake. He bit through its neck and shook it back and forth until the snake went limp and quit trying to bite us. Mercutio spit the snake out with a hiss.

"Yeah, I know, Merc," I said, falling back onto the muddy grass, staring up at the black sky and trying to catch my breath. "You don't play either."

A shotgun blast somewhere over my right shoulder made me wince. "Oh, for pete's sake," I mumbled. "I forgot we're in the middle of a gunfight." I sucked in a breath and rolled onto my side, making everything hurt. "The trouble is, Merc, I'm fresh out of guns."

As expected, Mercutio didn't see this as a significant obstacle. He waited for me to get to my feet and then padded along with me as I sneaked across the property toward the rusted car on blocks.

Beau's shotgun and whatever shells he had left seemed like a good place to start if re-arming myself was the plan, which it was. I found him only half conscious.

"Who's there?" he murmured.

I didn't answer. I picked up his gun and rifled through his clothes till I found a box of shells.

"No!" he said, realizing it was me. "I heard you screaming and that big old gator's thrashing tail hit the water. He got you."

"He did."

"He got you!" he repeated like I hadn't agreed with him. "You're at the bottom of the creek."

"Okay," I agreed amiably. The fight had gone out of Beau, and entering into a battle of wits with someone who's unarmed wasn't very sporting.

"You a ghost, *chère*?" he asked, his voice a soft rasp.

"Yeah. Where are the rest of the Duvall ghosts? I need to meet up with them."

"Gone."

"I know. Where?"

"I don't know."

"Your momma take them back to Dallas with her?"

His head lolled to one side and I thought he'd passed out, but he answered in a tired whisper. "No, nor that crazy bitch stepsister of mine either. We've been looking for her for days. Momma thinks she's got a charm to conceal herself from us. We thought you were helping her stay hidden."

Was that why they kept attacking me? And if Oatha didn't have the ghosts or Vangie then where in the world were they?

"All right, Beau, lie on down and rest so you don't give up your ghost, too."

His eyes shut, and Mercutio and I crept around the house, stealthy as spies. When we shoved our way into the house, however, there were only two men left standing. Mercutio bit the leg of one, which caused the guy to fall down. I stepped on his forearm to keep him from raising the gun, and I shoved my shotgun between the shoulder blades of his cousin.

The cousin who bled from several nasty lacerations lowered his gun.

Bryn had his back to the wall, which sported dozens of large holes, but his own injuries looked minor.

"Hey," I said.

His gaze traveled up and down me. The shredded hem of my dress's skirt hung in tatters, clotted blood clung to my shoulder, and fresh blood and muddy water dripped off my injured leg onto my filthy feet, making brown puddles on the floor. I imagine I'd looked better. I reached down and put pressure on the couple of punctures that were oozing the most blood. I hoped my fae super healing would kick in soon because now that the adrenaline was wearing off, I felt a little woozy.

"Are you all right?" he asked.

"All things considered, I can't complain," I said with a weak smile. "Better now that we've got things under control."

Bryn opened his mouth, but the sound of sirens drowned him out.

"Oh sure," I said wearily. "Now they show up." I shook my head. "That's just how I wanted to spend the rest of my night. Explaining myself to local law enforcement."

"Tamara?"

"Yep?" I asked, lowering the shotgun to point it at the ground. I leaned against the wall for support.

"You know what I want you to say when you're questioned?"

For a moment, I felt hopeful that Bryn would have the exact words to keep us out of trouble. He's a brilliant lawyer, after all. "No, what should I say?"

"Not a word."

I sighed and shook my head. "Oh good," I said. "'Cause the police take it so well when people refuse to answer questions about a shootout."

26

THE SHERIFF AND his deputies rounded up everybody who was left at the crumbling house and on the property. Apparently whoever had taken the bodies of the people who'd died earlier in the day had gotten away because there were no dead.

Everyone except Beau, his cousin with the cuts, and me was taken to the police station. Dr. Suri gave Beau a blood transfusion, a pain shot, a tetanus shot, and a shot of antibiotics. He shook his head, packed Beau's bleeding wounds, and packaged him onto a stretcher for transport to a hospital in Dallas.

When Smitty, one of the Duvall deputies, asked who'd shot him, Beau claimed he didn't know, saying it was too dark to see. He said it was probably an accident, just a misunderstanding. Even in shock and under the influence of morphine, he stuck to his statement. Then they put him in the ambulance and he closed his eyes. I don't know if he knew I was alive or not.

I was next on Dr. Suri's exam table. Smitty let out a strangled curse when he saw the teeth marks on my leg. He took pictures of my leg and of the shotgun wounds to my shoulder with a big police evidence camera.

Dr. Suri wasn't happy. "Where is Mr. Bryn Lyons?" he demanded.

"He's at the police station. Why?"

"What was this girl doing out of bed? She had a very bad head injury today. Very bad. And broken ribs." Dr. Suri shook his head. "Miss Tamara Trask," he said, pronouncing my first name with his accent so the first part almost disappeared and *mara* rhymed with *star-uh*. "What could you have been doing tonight? Staying in your bed, that's what I was telling you to do." He shined a bright light in my eyes and I blinked.

"Sorry, Dr. Suri."

"Now what has happened to this leg? It looks like something bit it very hard."

I smiled. I like Dr. Suri's accent. He talks really cute. Also, he'd given me a good idea.

"It was the alligator that ate the horse."

Both Smitty and Dr. Suri stared at me.

"Alligator?" Smitty scoffed.

Dr. Suri drew up a syringe of morphine, but I scooted away.

"No, no," I said. I knew I couldn't keep my wits about me if he gave me strong pain medicine.

"I have to clean these wounds. Without medicine, it will hurt very much," he said sternly.

I pushed the syringe away. "It doesn't hurt at all," I lied. "The ibuprofen and the blood and fluid you gave me through the IV made me feel all better." I clenched my fists to brace myself as he cleaned the wounds.

"What were you saying about an alligator?" Smitty asked, with his little spiral notebook and pen in hand.

"I don't see how it thought it could eat me after that horse. But it had me thirty percent eaten—thirty, maybe thirty-three percent—when it gave up. He was driving the horse trailer."

"Who was?"

"Or maybe he was the passenger."

"Who?"

"The alligator. The horse was maybe the driver. Till he got ate."

Dr. Suri had started cleaning the wounds, but that made him pause and shine the light in my eyes again.

"A bad head injury you say, Dr. Suri?"

"Very bad!" Dr. Suri confirmed. "She should be in bed." Dr. Suri made a motion for Smitty to turn around as he tugged the hem of my dress higher.

"I need to see her injuries," Smitty objected.

"Like hell," I said. "Out."

"Hang on."

"Please step out, officer," Dr. Suri said. "I will document the injuries in her chart. Go now. I have very much to do here."

Smitty grumbled but left the room.

Dr. Suri got me out of my ruined dress, which I kept silent about on account of him being a doctor and having already seen me naked once. When the half-Barbie voodoo doll fell out, his brows crinkled together. He picked it up and set it next to me.

"Oh, my friend gave me that. She's making homemade toys for the Houston Homeless. So far I think we're better off buying them from a toy store, but she just keeps going on. Some people are stubborn as all get-out."

I wasn't sure Dr. Suri believed a word of that, but I figured he'd just chalk up any crazy thing I said to my head injury. Sometimes concussions are handy.

He washed my wounds, put bandages on them, and gave me a shot of antibiotics in the behind, which hurt more than the scatter from the shotgun blast had hurt my shoulder. He put me in a clean patient gown and wrapped a white sheet around me.

Then he started asking me questions about who and where I was. I worried that if I seemed too out of it, he might ship me off to a Dallas hospital, so I answered all his questions right and added, "I'm feeling kind of better."

"I'm quite worried about you, Tamara. Quite worried."

"Thanks, Dr. Suri, but I'm doing okay. You patched me

right up," I said with a smile. "I sure appreciate it. And Bryn and I both appreciate you coming to see Mr. Jenson. He's doing really well. He follows instructions. I'll try to do better with that."

He nodded and gave me a bottle of pain pills. "I'll come to see you both. I expect you to be resting."

"Sure thing," I said, climbing off the exam table. "By the way, Dr. Suri, what part of India are you and Mrs. Suri from?"

"Punjab."

"What's it like there?"

"Hot."

"Like here," I said. "I told Bryn India's kind of like Texas."

Dr. Suri laughed. "Well, the heat, yes, but it's quite different otherwise."

"Sometime I'd like to see pictures and hear about what it was like growing up there. You think Mrs. Suri would mind if I came for a visit?"

"No, she won't mind. Unless you come before I say it's safe for you to be out of bed. That she'll object to very much."

"Got it. As soon as the police let me go, I'll do my best to get to bed." I tucked the Tammy Jo voodoo doll into the folds of my sheet and limped out of Dr. Suri's exam room. Smitty turned me over to another deputy since he was going to wait on the cousin with the cuts. Just as Beau had done, the cousin said he didn't know what had happened at the house. It was like everyone had a head injury.

When I got to the police station, Zach was there in plainclothes. And Bryn was in Sheriff Hobbs's office being questioned.

The young deputy named Garth helped me to a chair and I perched on it, trying not to sit on the spot where my antibiotics were making me sore.

Zach leaned against a post and listened.

"I don't remember what happened," I said. It was what I

answered every question with. When Sheriff Hobbs came out, I guessed Bryn had been just as unhelpful because the frown on the sheriff's face stretched practically to his collarbones.

"A man was shot three times, Tammy Jo. You know anything about that?" the sheriff asked.

"No, sir."

"Somebody shot him in the balls," the sheriff said.

I made a shocked sound. Zach raised an eyebrow.

"My deputies and I all agree that that particular injury seems likely to have come from a woman. Now maybe she had good reason to shoot the man in the groin."

"Maybe she did," I agreed.

"But whatever the reason, the whole truth's bound to come out."

I sincerely doubted that. Voodoo dolls, long-distance magic spells, sacrificing horses in black magic rituals? No, I didn't think the Cajun witches and wizards would have much interest in telling what had really happened while they were in town.

"Sure," I said, nodding.

"So why don't you just tell us why you shot Beau Theroux?"

"Me?" I asked with wide eyes. "Why in the world would I shoot him? It was probably one of those girls from Louisiana he had with him. Maybe he was two-timing somebody or something of that nature."

"Now, Tammy Jo, everybody out there had shotguns. And Theroux's wounds weren't from any shotgun."

"Maybe the people with other kinds of guns drove away. How many sets of tire tracks did you find?"

"What were you doing out there?" the sheriff asked impatiently.

"I don't remember. On account of my concussion."

"What concussion?"

"I got it today. Or I think I did. Dr. Suri said so."

"Who shot you?"

"Nobody."

"Deputy Smith said Dr. Suri plucked several pieces of buckshot out of your shoulder and arm."

"Was that what that was? And you say someone shot me?" I scratched my head, noted that my hair was stiff with mud and was standing up at odd angles, and stopped. "I wonder who it was. If you find out, I hope you let me know. I'll give him or her a real piece of my mind."

Zach glanced down at the ground, but I saw the corners of his mouth curve up. I continued to look bewildered for the sheriff.

The sheriff made an exasperated sound. "Sutton?" he said, whirling toward Zach.

Zach's smirk disappeared. "Yes, sir?"

"You take this girl on home. I don't trust these slippery— these tourists from Louisiana, and I doubt whatever happened out there was settled tonight. They could decide to pay her a visit to keep her from remembering what really happened, and the town council would never let me hear the end of it if I let someone from Duvall get killed in their own house. Come to that, neither would my wife. You take Tammy Jo home and you stay with her till I'm satisfied."

I protested, but the sheriff cut me off.

"None of that from you, missy. You're out of your head from a concussion. If you don't behave, I'll have Dr. Suri sedate you. From what I hear, he was madder than a hornet that you were out of bed at all." The sheriff adjusted his gun belt. "Go on, Sutton. I'm going to have another talk with our local lawyer. See if I can't get something useful out of him."

So it was a conspiracy, then. Sheriff Hobbs loved Zach like a son, and the whole town had heard that Zach was losing me to Bryn. This was the sheriff's way of giving Zach another crack at me with Bryn conveniently out of the way. Unfortunately, while I blamed my crime-scene confusion on a concussion, there was nothing I could do about it.

I had to hand it to Sheriff Hobbs. Sometimes he was as sneaky as Bryn.

Zach pushed off the pole and strolled over to me. He held out a hand to me. I frowned and shook my head. Bryn stood in Hobbs's office doorway, watching us.

"I'm okay." I ignored Zach's offered hand, standing with a grimace. "I can walk by myself," I said, limping. My leg and that shot in the butt really did smart when I moved. The pain was definitely worse now that the adrenaline had worn off.

"I'm okay," I repeated, squaring my shoulders and lifting my chin. I could at least make it out the door before I had to stop for a rest.

A second later, Zach swung me up in his arms.

"I can walk."

"Yeah, I saw. You think I've got all night to watch you hobble three feet?" Zach asked.

I folded my arms across my chest. "Put me down," I said under my breath.

"I will," Zach said, nodding at the deputy, who opened the door for us.

"Right now. Put me down right now," I said.

"You worried about what your boyfriend's going to say?"

"No, I'm worried about what he's going to do."

"To you?" Zach asked, his voice suddenly dangerous.

"No, to you."

Zach's stride turned smooth again. "No need to worry about that, darlin'. Everyone in town knows I can take care of myself, including Lyons." Zach opened the passenger door of his truck and set me inside.

When he got in the other side, closed the door, and started the engine, he asked, "Did you shoot Beau Theroux in the balls?"

"Yep."

"How come?"

"He made me mad."

"How'd he do that?"

"Shot me in the shoulder. *Tried* to shoot me in the face and threatened to do worse if he got the chance. I decided I'd arrange it so he couldn't make good on his threats of a certain kind."

Zach put the truck in gear and smiled. "That's my girl."

27

I WAS NOT Zach's girl, and we both knew it. I'd let him carry me out of the police station because there hadn't been a choice. I wasn't in any condition to kick and scream and force him to set me down.

Now that I was at home, though, I didn't a hundred percent trust us. Our final breakup was fresh, and I was determined not to let things get muddled. I sent an urgent text to Rollie, which said:

Need help. Come over quick. Wear sequins. Thanks!

If there was one way to unsettle a he-man football player cop from East Texas, it was to invite a cross-dressing vampire to the house.

As Zach and I made small talk, I worried about Bryn. What did he think about Zach carrying me off like that? Was he upset? Did he trust me to be alone with Zach? How could I expect him to, when I didn't?

I sent Bryn a text.

Hey, it's me, Tammy Jo. Got home safe. Nothing going on between me & Zach. I told Rollie to come over. We— Rollie and me—will come 2 your house. Call if u need

anything . . . bail money, another lawyer. A kiss. I love u.
Bye 4 now.

Zach didn't come over to snoop into what I'd written, but he watched me send it. Zach's not really much for spying. He's more into straightforward confrontations.

Mercutio, restless and angry, padded back and forth near the back door. I opened it, but he turned away, eyeing me and Zach.

"What's up with the wildcat?" he asked.

"I suppose he's on to something but isn't ready to chase it down yet. Or maybe he's waiting for me to recover a little. Merc's not overprotective, but he knows when I'm good to fight and when I'm not."

"He's your familiar?"

"Kind of. It's not like we read each other's minds or anything. Or leastways, I can't read his." I cocked my head, studying Mercutio. "I can't speak for him." I concentrated. *Can you read my mind, Merc?*

Mercutio glanced at me but didn't answer. Instead he hopped onto the counter and into the sink so he could rest his paws on the windowsill and look out into the yard.

"Thanks for the ride home," I said.

Zach crossed the kitchen and looked into the yard. Apparently not seeing anything of interest, he turned and came back to me.

"Whether we're ever together again as lovers or not, I meant what I said when I married you."

Together again as lovers? What the heck kind of dangerous talk was that? He'd said it had to be over between us, and he was right. No backpedaling or second thoughts.

My mouth opened but didn't have any words. I closed it for a moment and then asked, "You mean you'll always be there when I need you?"

"Yeah."

"That street runs both ways," I said, and cleared my throat. This was okay. I wanted us to be friends. Close friends. But not more.

He leaned a little closer. I took a step back and my butt

muscle full of antibiotics seized up. I pitched backward. He grabbed my arms and lowered me to the couch.

"Dang, that hurts," I said, lying half on my side and massaging my tush.

Zach's big palm came down over my hand. The heat of it seeped through the fabric of my patient gown. He gave a squeeze, and I would've jumped except for half my butt being in the middle of a seizure and his hand having a grip on it.

"That's a tough spot for a muscle spasm. Roll onto your belly."

"No way," I said.

He ignored my protests and pulled my hand free with his, then pressed his thumb down on a trigger spot.

I yowled, but the clenched muscle released and relaxed.

"Thanks," I said grudgingly, and pushed his hand away. He cocked a brow at my suspicious expression.

"How many times did you or a trainer help me work out a cramp after a game or a practice?" he asked. It was true. Zach had occasionally needed a rubdown from cramping muscles. "It ain't no big thing."

When I didn't immediately agree that his hand on my butt was no big deal, he added, "Girl, you really think I need cheap tricks to get my hands on your backside? What am I? Fourteen again?"

"No," I acknowledged, but I was anxious to change the subject. "So are you back to work at the station? Because I'd like to make a report."

"Oh, you would? You remembered some facts about tonight? I'm not sure it's a good idea to let that cat out of the bag."

"No, not about the shootout. About my friend Vangie. She's missing. She's been abducted, almost for sure she has."

Zach's amused expression disappeared, and he was all business. "Who's Vangie?"

I explained that Vangie was supposed to get married, but that no one had seen her since she'd gotten some evidence against her stepmother. I also told him about Edie disappearing and what she'd said. I figured if he and Edie were friends, he would want to know. And I didn't know whether Vangie's disappearance and the spell against the town ghosts were related.

Zach raised his brows. "Edie said she saw 'them' the night she died?"

"Yes."

"Can't be. The friends who were with her the night she died were all investigated and had alibis for the time of her death. Not to mention that they'd all be around a hundred and ten years old. It stands to reason that anyone she saw that night is dead by now."

"How do you know that the people Edie visited with on the night she died were investigated and had alibis?"

"I got the case file."

My jaw dropped. "You—you got an almost-ninety-year-old case file from New York City?"

He nodded.

"How?"

"You of all people should know I can turn on the Southern charm when I need to," he said with a flash of a smile.

Yes, I did know that. All too well.

"Well, I'd like to read that file. She's my aunt," I said, annoyed that Zach seemed to know more about a piece of my family history than I did.

"I'll show it to you sometime."

"I want a copy." I pulled the gown down to cover my legs to the knee. "I'd like it right away."

"I can't see how her murder could have anything to do with what's happening to the ghosts in town. That voodoo priestess witch Oatha probably has some provenance over the dead. I'd expect she's the problem for the local ghosts."

"According to her family, Vangie's stepmother went back to Dallas, suffering from chest pains and running scared, no doubt. Bryn made the Tammy Jo voodoo doll untouchable and attacked them with strong magic."

"Maybe she took the ghosts with her. Your aunt tells me there are ways for witches to trap ghosts. If Beads hasn't shown up by tomorrow afternoon, I'll drive to Dallas and have a word with the witch."

"You'd do that?" I asked. "For Edie?"

Zach nodded. "I denied she existed for a long time and was a bad husband to you because of it. I'm not going to say Beads and I always get along. She's a real pain in the ass sometimes, but she's your kin—even if she is only a ghost— and I've got plenty to make up for where you're both concerned. Going to Dallas ain't no big thing and would be a good start on me making amends."

I smiled at him. "I feel like I've grown up a lot over the past few months. Seems like you have, too," I said. "I'm a little bit proud of us."

He grinned. "Darlin', you shot a man in the testicle tonight and I was happy about it. I think we've got further to go before anyone nominates us for the maturity hall of fame."

I sniffed. He had a point. "I shouldn't have shot him when he was unarmed, but he made threats and reached for a fire-arm. Probably I shouldn't be carrying a gun, but lord knows sometimes I need one. A sassy personality and a snappy come-back don't go far against shotguns and voodoo magic. Still, I do have a bad temper sometimes. If I weren't me and it were up to me, I don't know that I'd give myself a gun permit."

This made his smile widen.

I drew my brows together. "I'm gonna have to think on that."

"Well, don't give yourself a headache. Some assholes need shooting. Beau Theroux obviously did."

"You're only saying that because I'm a girl. If a man had shot an unarmed man in the nuts, you would've locked him up."

"That would be true most of the time," Zach agreed. "But not necessarily always. If someone small like your friend Johnny was getting the hell beaten out of him and he shot someone to get away," Zach said with a shrug, "I wouldn't expect the prosecutor to throw the book at him under those circumstances."

"That's a good point," I said. The doorbell rang. "Speaking of Johnny."

"You expecting Johnny Nguyen?" Zach asked, walking to the front before I could shove myself off the couch.

"Maybe Johnny will be with him. I'm expecting his boyfriend, Rollie."

Zach opened the door as I hobbled across the room. I tilted my head and sure enough Rollie stood in the doorway, all lean and lanky six and a half feet of him. He wore tight black pants with a fuchsia sequined shirt. He'd used dark eyeliner, thick mascara, and bright pink lip gloss. He wasn't pretty—his face was way too angular and masculine for that—but he was sure striking.

"Well, if it isn't Bo Duke. How's the butch life treating you?" Rollie asked.

"Well enough. And you, Stretch? What are you working on? A *Rocky Horror Picture Show* revival?"

"Only if you'll play Brad Majors in my big seduction scene," Rollie said, reaching out to give Zach's face a stroke. Zach caught Rollie's wrist before the fingers reached him, but he didn't look like his grip was meant to crush Rollie's bones. That, I thought, was progress.

"Easy there, Romeo," Zach said, returning Rollie's arm to his side. "I'll never be that good an actor."

"I'm sure if you—" Rollie began, but Zach had turned toward me.

Zach leaned over and gave me a kiss right on the lips. My brows shot up.

"See you later, baby girl."

My tongue darted out reflexively to catch the taste of him, and then I shook my head at him and myself. "Zach! No kissing on the lips anymore," I exclaimed.

"You're right," Zach said with mock regret. "But you know I've got that habit of collecting a little sugar from you when I'm going off to work. It'll probably take me a while to break myself of it. I'm sure Lyons will understand, him being so understanding about the other night."

I gave Zach's shoulder a shove. He didn't budge. He just

smiled. "Still, no sense pushing our luck. You probably shouldn't mention to him about me massaging your butt earlier."

Now I knew he was talking to bait a trap for Bryn, figuring that Rollie would let it slip if I didn't.

"Is that flavored lip gloss you're wearing, Rollie? It sure smells delicious. Is it raspberry? If Zach needs a little more sugar before he goes, maybe you should give him some, too."

Zach immediately put his hands out in surrender, but he didn't look worried. "I'm going." He nodded at both of us and walked out.

"Oh my," Rollie said. "What's gotten into the butch boy beautiful? Look at him connive like the cast of *Dynasty*! We have to keep him away from that ghost of yours," Rollie said.

"What? Why?"

"Because we used to be able to see him coming like a freight train, straight ahead and packing a punch. Poking Bryn with a crooked stick is hardly his style. That's got Edie written all over it."

"They have been spending time together," I said worriedly. "And being friendly with Edie certainly got me in plenty of trouble over the years." I hobbled to the kitchen.

"Why are you limping? And why do you smell like sewer water and dried blood?"

"Come inside, I'll fill you in," I said. "I've got to do a spell to try to find my friend."

"A spell? Does it call for a fabulously dressed vampire?"

"No."

"Then why the order to wear sequins?"

"Edie's not the only witch in this family who can scheme. I needed to run Zach off before I got into trouble with him. Sorry about making you rush over, but thank you for coming right away. I owe you a favor, okay?"

"Oh, I don't care about that. But why run him off?"

"Because I'm with Bryn now."

"So that's been settled?"

"Yep," I said, trying to sound completely confident.

"Good to know," Rollie said thoughtfully as he joined me in the kitchen. "So the handsome deputy's available then?" Rollie asked, leaning languidly against the counter like I ought to grab a camera and take his picture.

"Well, he's available to women, I suppose," I said, not really wanting to contemplate Zach's future love life.

"Hmm. Yes, to women," Rollie said, leaning over to check out the shelves of witches' herbs that I took bottles from. "Anything in there for a love spell?"

My brows shot up. "Rollie, you better behave."

"I'm just kidding. I don't need love potions to get a guy. Besides, something really tiresome has happened."

"What?"

"I fell in love," Rollie said in an exasperated tone. "With a tiny hairdresser," he added, shaking his head. "And now I'm thinking of doing something drastic and permanent."

I grinned. "Like getting married? It's legal in some states. Wanna look on the Internet to see which one's closest?"

"Marriage, God no! This from the girl who got divorced before she was old enough to rent a car." He yawned and half-reclined on the counter. "I said permanent, Tammy Jo. I'm thinking of making him a vampire."

My jaw dropped. "Does Johnny want to be a vampire? Who would open the salon? It's got all those windows."

"Details," Rollie said with a dismissive wave of his hand. He yawned. "So do you need help with a spell or what?"

"Nope, but I like your company. Stay and visit."

"No, Zach's gone. My work here is done. And the truth is I'm feeling a few pints low."

"Do you need blood? Are you out of your supply?" I asked, alarmed. There was no blood bank in Duvall. He usually brought some with him.

"No, I've had plenty. It's some kind of supernatural chronic fatigue syndrome. It hit several of us in Dallas. I thought I was better, but I've come down with it again here."

"I didn't know vampires could get sick."

"We usually don't. The coven's investigating. It would

normally have caused high hysteria, but people were too exhausted to fuss. Everyone lounges for hours like models posing for a Hippolyte Berteaux painting. Very sensual. Anyway, the sickness doesn't last, so there's nothing to worry about. Johnny got me a gorgeous silk peacock kimono. I'm going to his condo for a lie-down before I drive to Dallas. Bye, darling," he said, giving me an air kiss.

"Rollie, you said it's a supernatural illness. Are you sure?"

"Not really," he said, walking down the hall.

I trailed after him.

"The coven thinks it's caused by a spell. I'll hear more details when I get home," he said.

"Someone's attacking vampires with a spell? Who do they think is doing it? A Dallas witch?"

"Dunno. I'm so tired," he said, putting the back of his wrist to his forehead like he'd wilt. "Leaving now," he announced, sashaying out of my house with sequins sparkling.

I clucked my tongue and turned to Mercutio, who sat on the bureau. "Merc, what do you think about that?" I demanded. "Edie got exhausted and faded away. Other ghosts lost energy and disappeared. Now vampires are feeling run-down, too? Ghosts are dead. Vampires are undead. Both are afflicted by some energy-zapping affliction. Coincidence?"

Merc cocked his head.

"You know," I said, pausing with a grimace. "The trouble arrived when Vangie did. From Dallas." I frowned. "I hate to suspect her, but she did hex townspeople with the flu . . . What if she wasn't abducted? What if she's hiding out? Sucking up death juice for some death magic spells? Maybe to use on her stepmother and stepbrother?" I couldn't decide which worried me more: Kidnapped Vangie or Necromancer Vangie?

Either way I had to find her. I filled a large glass bowl with water and grabbed a pair of pillar candles and the other ingredients I'd decided to use for my location spell. In the past, I'd tried spells from borrowed spellbooks, but one of the instructional books for young witches that I'd been studying at Bryn's had said that witches should choose spells with ingredients that they were drawn to. None of the herbs I'd used in the past had been especially meaningful to me, so I decided to modify the spell to make it more suited to what I like.

I put a jacket on and filled a bag with my supplies. Mercutio joined me outside. I sat down and burrowed my feet in the dirt. I lit the candles and placed them to the right and left of the bowl. I took off my charm bracelet, which was the only physical link I had to Vangie. I arranged it in a circle on the bottom of the bowl.

I added three drops of almond oil and then three drops of vanilla, which looked like swirling smoke in the water. Then I put in a dozen mini-marshmallows. Mercutio sniffed the bag and skewered a marshmallow with one of his sharp canine teeth. He tried to chew the marshmallow, but it didn't work. He resorted to rubbing his tooth with his tongue and making faces that said he didn't care that much for mini-marshmallows after all.

"Yeah, that's gonna be hard to get off. Sticky, huh? But good."

Merc gave an annoyed yowl.

"Sorry! They are really good in s'mores and hot chocolate, though. And I needed something that floats," I said, defending my decision to use marshmallows.

Mercutio was still annoyed, but I knew he'd get over it if I got us on the right track for an adventure.

"Hi, Earth. It's me, Tammy Jo," I said. "As usual, I could use your help. My friend Vangie's missing, and I need to be shown the way to her. So I'm going to say a spell, and I'd appreciate it if you'd help my magic arrange the marshmallows in the right direction."

I took a deep breath and swirled the water, then stared into the bowl, letting my eyes cross and uncross till they were unfocused. It was a little like looking at one of those Magic Eye posters where it starts out looking like a computer-generated kaleidoscope and the next thing you know there are flying eagles or jumping dolphins.

I breathed in a slow, steady rhythm.

Vangie, my brand-new close friend
If I had a letter I wanted to send
I'd need directions to where you are
So show me a map and tell me how far.

I let my muscles go limp and waited. After a few minutes I saw Vangie. She wore an ivory-colored gown and lay on some sort of bench. Her long hair spilled over the edges and swayed in the wind. I didn't like the look of her skin, which was pale and slightly gray. My stomach clenched worriedly. That's not a good color for anybody. There's a reason you never see a foundation shade called Bride of Frankenstein.

"Oh," I said, clutching the sides of the bowl. I couldn't take my next breath as I waited to see if Vangie would take hers. When her chest finally rose, I exhaled, my hands clammy with sweat.

"Alive," I said. "Thank goodness, Vangie. Thank goodness. You just hang in there. Just keep on breathing. And if you're not too tired, maybe you could breathe a little faster."

Merc made an impatient sound. I looked up and narrowed my eyes at him. "She looks half dead and not in a Sleeping Beauty suspended animation kind of way. She looks like her makeup artist is Tim Burton," I hissed in a whisper.

Mercutio dipped his head.

"Now where are you, Vangie?" I asked, looking back at the marshmallows floating on a vanilla almond oil slick. I blew softly on the marshmallows, and they swirled slowly in the bowl. "Show me the way to my friend."

I sat staring for several minutes, but when the water stilled, the marshmallows clumped together. An image of the town appeared on the bottom of the bowl, like I was looking down into a magical snow globe, and the cluster of marshmallows rested above the town like clouds. They didn't move even though the water swayed in the bowl. I pushed them to the side, but they floated back to the spot where they'd been and stopped.

Mallows mark the spot?

"Northeast. North even of the golf course. What's up there besides the river?" I murmured. "There aren't even any roads," I murmured, and looked at Mercutio. "I don't know, Merc. You think these marshmallows are really trying to tell me something? Or is this just a sweet and soggy mess?"

I pinched a mini-marshmallow between my thumb and index finger and dropped it inside my mouth. It was slightly slimy. I let it melt a little on my tongue before I swallowed. It slid down my throat, and despite the chill, I felt a little warmth deep in my gut. An urge pulled me northeast. Yes, that was the way to go . . . the spell was clearly working.

Suddenly Mercutio sprang toward the door, ready to proceed.

"Okay, thanks," I said, patting the earth. "Follow the mallow it is."

Before I could reach the house, however, the smell of honey and apples hit me, and I heard humming. I looked around sharply, but I was alone. Then I pictured myself lying in the arms of a tree. Words seemed to slip from my lips, but I couldn't make them out as I placed my arms around my ash tree. My skin tingled and warmed, like there was sunshine on my back. I glowed faintly and the bluebells began to ring in alarm.

"A faery is near. And it's me," I whispered to no one.

I shuddered, and the glow faded, but the ache from my wounds had lessened. *Healing magic*, I realized. I felt energized and a little . . . invincible.

I sucked in a breath and looked at Merc. His head was cocked. The bluebells quieted.

"I'm all right." I ran a hand through my hair and picked up the bowl I'd dropped when I'd been in the semitrance. "I have always healed fast, Merc, but there is something going on. Some power is fortifying me and making me more fae on and off. The true fae are immortal except for wounds made by iron. So I guess I wouldn't heal an iron arrow through my heart. But I swear the other injuries just don't stick around as long as they used to. I just wish I knew why this is happening. And I wonder if there will be a price to pay? There usually is one."

28

I WAS DETERMINED not to ruin any more good clothes. I stripped out of my patient gown and threw it in the hamper. After a fast shower, I put on underwear, a sports bra, and an old pair of cotton pajama pants and its matching striped shirt. Then I hooked the charm bracelet around my wrist.

Merc gave me a funny look, and I sighed.

"What? It's nighttime. People wear pajamas at night-time." I pulled on a raggedy sweater and was ready to tackle the next part of the evening. I hoped I wouldn't run into anyone besides Vangie, who I figured would be too busy being grateful at having been rescued to question my decision to leave the house in PJs.

I didn't have a gun, so I armed myself with a crossbow I'd bought two weeks earlier and took the custom-made quiver that I'd had Georgia Sue's momma quilt for me out of some cupcake-print fabric. The quiver was lined with vinyl and held a dozen arrows. Merc eyed the bow.

"I know it's bulkier than a gun, but it's what we've got on hand."

Speaking of not having the normal equipment, when I was at the police station, I'd learned that my car with its flat tire had been discovered and taken to Floyd's garage as I'd suspected, which was a relief since it hadn't been stolen, but also a problem because it was locked up. Since Bryn's car was way back at the site of the battle with the Cajun witches, I'd need some other transportation. Even though some of my pain had eased and my muscles didn't seem to be cramping anymore, I knew I couldn't walk all the way to the northeast side of town. There was nothing to do but steal a car.

Doc Barnaby, who once drugged me to use my blood to raise his wife as a zombie, was my neighbor. You'd think we wouldn't be friends anymore, but he did it because he missed her so much. It was the most romantic zombie-raising I ever heard of, and I forgave him for poisoning me.

Returning Zombie Mrs. Barnaby to the grave had gotten me in tons of trouble, so I figured that he couldn't in good conscience begrudge me a little grand theft auto. I used a spare key to get into his house, careful to be quiet so I didn't wake him. I found his car keys and took his 1987 Buick LeSabre station wagon out of the garage. The custom paint job was brown on top and blue on the bottom, which I didn't think looked all that good together.

I let Mercutio in with a warning. "No scratching the dashboard. This car's real old. Some people like the doc call it a classic."

Merc made a skeptical sound.

"Yeah, classics are in the eye of the beholder, apparently." I swiveled the wheel and rolled out of the driveway as quietly as possible.

I drove across town while Merc licked his paws. I studied him for a moment. Mercutio spent more time grooming himself than any guy I knew, even Bryn on a court day. Why would a wildcat who spent half the night stalking rodents and lizards need to be so fastidious? Heaven forbid Merc should get into a fight with dirty feet.

He paused with his tongue above his ankle, glanced over at me, and then gave his shin a lick.

"You know, Merc, Doc Barnaby's not the only guy I know who's quirky."

Mercutio meowed.

"I know it's a cat thing, but it really would be faster and less gross to just take a shower. Think about it, okay?" I cleared my throat. "So according to the vision from the magic marshmallows, Vangie is barely breathing and probably in a coma. I don't think she did that to herself. Not when she was looking forward to getting married. No, I'm pretty sure she *has* been kidnapped. I assumed that if anyone snatched her, it would be her stepmother and stepbrother, but Beau claimed they couldn't find her. If not them, who? What about her plastic-faced fiancé?" I glanced over at Mercutio. "Vangie said he didn't know magic. She would've known if he did, right? The thing is, Merc, when a woman meets up with foul play, it's always a good idea to suspect the husband or lover. Zach and a bunch of detective stories taught me that. But if Jackson was after her money, wouldn't he wait till after they were married to kill her? So he could inherit it?"

Mercutio thought about it in silence.

"The answer is: Yeah, he would. It's still possible her stepmother grabbed her, bespelled her, and left her for dead. Oatha might be setting up an alibi for herself. If the coroner says that Vangie died while Oatha was safely back in Dallas, Oatha could get away with murder, right?"

Merc meowed.

"Right. Of course, if Oatha and her people did leave Vangie alone, that'll make rescuing her easier for us."

Merc agreed.

I pulled Doc Barnaby's station wagon up to the curb outside the golf course, got out, and tucked the keys up under the bumper. If I carried them, they'd be too likely to get lost.

With some major effort, I climbed the fence. Mercutio watched me with interest and, to his credit, no mocking. Then he darted through the iron rails as easy as can be.

"I'd like to see you do that if you were human-sized," I grumbled. We hurried across the course. As a sport, golf never seemed like much exercise to me, but after five holes' worth of walking I changed my mind.

"I could steal a golf cart," I said, swinging my flashlight

from side to side. "But I guess they're locked in the club-house garage, which is out of our way." If I'd thought the club would have an all-terrain vehicle, I'd have taken the detour. But since we'd have to go on foot outside the course, it didn't seem worth the effort.

When we finally got off the golf course and into the woods, I found several trails. Mercutio had caught the scent of something, and he led the way.

"So let's say it wasn't Vangie's steps who took her. And let's assume it wasn't her betrothed. Who does that even leave?"

Mercutio yowled, and I blinked.

"Who?"

Whiz, whiz, whiz came the arrows, one, two, three, pinning my pajama top and sweater to a tree I'd been passing.

"Hey!" I yelled, trying to jerk free. Cotton tore, and cold air nipped at my side.

Mercutio rushed forward, and Crux emerged from the woods pointing his bow and arrow at Merc. I yelled and Mercutio darted away. Crux lowered his bow, apparently not intending to shoot Mercutio, but not intending to be chewed on by him either. Crux grabbed my bow, which I'd barely had a grip on with my sleeve stuck to the tree trunk.

He tossed my bow aside.

"You!" I said. "What are you doing?"

He smiled. "Sneaking up on you, which you make quite easy."

I glared at him. He removed the arrows that pinned me and in the process made rips in my clothes. He dropped the arrows into his quiver.

"Turn back," he said. "You're not to continue this way."

"Why not?" I said, poking a finger through a quarter-sized hole. "You ruined my pajamas!" I said, shaking a fist at him.

He leaned against the curve of a tree. "If you want to stalk things in the night, you should stop talking and listen."

I closed my mouth and did just that. All I heard was the normal rustling and whispering of trees and grass and vines.

"Who covered you in a magic spell?"

"No one," I said, taken aback. "Oh, wait." I realized
Bryn's spell might still be on me. The one that protected me
from malicious voodoo doll magic. "None of your business.
What are you doing out here? Did you kidnap my friend
Evangeline?"

It made some sense. Witches and faeries didn't get along.
Vangie was a witch. This guy was a faery.

"Not I," he said.

"Do you know who did?" I demanded.

"By name? No," he said. "I've seen him, though, and
you're no match for him, Halfling, untrained and noisy as
you are. Return to your home."

"I'm not returning anywhere. I had to steal—I mean
borrow—a car and walk about a thousand miles with a sore
butt to get here. I'm fixin' to find my friend."

"No."

I tried to stroll past him to where my crossbow lay, but
his arm snaked out and caught me around the waist and
yanked me against his body.

"If you want to be a match for a warrior, you'd better get
one to train you."

"Like who? You?"

"Yes."

"I don't think so," I said, kicking and thrashing. I elbowed
him in his ribs, but he barely acknowledged the blow. When
my foot thumped him between the legs, his breath came out
in a whoosh and he dropped me as he landed on his knees.
Nice to know faery men weren't so different from regular
ones.

I dove forward, yanking an arrow from my quiver with
one hand as my other grabbed the bow. I had it loaded by
the time I rolled onto my back. I aimed at him but found he
was already aiming at me.

"Dang. You recover fast."

"Lower your bow," he said menacingly. "I'm a fae knight.
You're a Halfling. Obey me now or the punishment will be
flogging with a thorny switch."

"You can kiss my antibiotic shot."

He quirked a brow.

"My butt," I clarified.

He moved in a blur and an arrow shot through the edge of my shirt. I tried to roll, but it pinned me. A moment later, he flung me over. My bow hit the dirt and bounced out of my grasp. A second later, the back of my shirt was pulled up and something swished across my back. The stings were razor sharp and stole my breath. I screamed and heard Mercutio's matching rebel yowl. Crux jerked and yelled something—probably a curse—in a foreign language. Mercutio had jumped on his back and been flung off.

Mercutio landed and sprang back at him. Crux threw an arm up and deflected Mercutio. Crux cut the drawstring of my PJ bottoms. I struggled and they slid down. Then warm lips landed on my penicillin-filled butt cheek and kissed it.

I howled in fury, arched, and twisted. My fingers grabbed his hair and yanked, and Merc landed on his back. Crux grabbed my wrist with one hand and jerked. I came away with a clump of his hair for my trouble and he yelled some more.

He rolled free and jabbed Mercutio with an arrow. Merc twisted, but his teeth sank into Crux's neck.

"Cat!" Crux roared, whipping him with an arrow shaft. "I'll kill you if you don't let go."

I jumped to my feet, which ripped my shirt open. My pajama bottoms fell off and tripped me as I launched myself forward. *Naked again, darn it all.*

I grabbed a loose arrow and went for Crux's throat. He disappeared and reappeared a few feet away. My momentum carried me into a tree trunk with a slamming force and I fell back, the arrow stuck in the bark.

"Sorry, Tree," I murmured, dazed. A moment later, I whirled. Crux raised an arrow to skewer Mercutio, and I launched myself off the ground, grabbing Crux's arm with both my hands and hanging with all my weight. Jerking his arm down pointed the arrow at the dirt and away from Merc.

"Stop, Merc," I yelled, but Mercutio's teeth tore flesh as he jerked his head and then hopped off Crux.

Crux's neck bled reddish gold, and he gasped for breath. He dropped to his knees, clutching his neck with both hands.

Then he laughed, reinforcing my belief that faeries are crazy. Mercutio and I exchanged a quick look.

Crux wheezed in a breath, nodded at us, and disappeared.

"Lunatic faery! There's no disappearing in fighting!" I yelled. Mercutio and I stood back-to-back and circled, watching the woods, waiting for the next attack. "Show yourself and fight like a man! Or a manlike creature!" When at least ten minutes had passed and my heart had stopped hammering, I said, "Mercutio, I don't know that he's coming back. I think maybe we won. What do you think?"

Mercutio licked blood from his whiskers.

"All right, then. Victory it is." I glanced down at my undies and torn shirt and sweater. "Yeah," I said. "Except for my clothes, we're totally triumphant." I twisted and my back stung. I walked over to where my pajama bottoms were and found a discarded rose stem. The thorns were tipped with my blood.

"That faery is a real asshole," I snapped, but the stinging cuts on my back didn't hurt that much. I climbed into my pajama bottoms and had to knot the drawstring to hold my pants on my hips.

I collected my bow, quiver, and flashlight. "Let's get on with finding us a Vangie."

Merc finished grooming, got up, and led me farther north. We'd probably walked for about forty minutes when he stopped and pawed the ground.

"What did you find?" I asked, pointing the flashlight down. There was dried brown stuff, the color of steak sauce, staining the tall grass. I crouched and there, tangled among the grass blades, was Vangie's charm bracelet. For a moment, my heart stopped, but then I reasoned that at least now I knew we were on the right track.

"Good job, Merc. You found clues," I said, grabbing the bracelet and tucking it into the pocket of my pajama top. "What do you think of that brown stuff? Not A-1, I don't guess. Is that blood?"

Merc yowled.

"Yeah, I figured." I took a breath. "Is it Vangie's blood?"

Merc's tongue tip touched the grass and his head bobbed.

"Not good. At least there's no fresh blood. This could've happened anytime yesterday. Probably during the abduction. I saw her tonight in the marshmallow bowl, so she's still alive. I know it," I said, trying to stay positive. "Let's keep going. Let's rescue her."

Mercutio turned and plowed through the grass. I followed him until we hit a trail that led to a small clearing. As soon as I got free of the tall grass, two trees' worth of dusky sparrows fluttered from the treetops and flew away chirping.

"What the Sam Houston?"

Mercutio crouched. Merc taking that posture meant trouble, so I turned off my flashlight, tiptoed to his side, and dropped down to one knee. As my eyes adjusted to the darkness, I waited.

Wings fluttered and a whistling sound rang out. Mercutio's body tensed and so did mine. I loaded the crossbow and rested it on my elbow to steady myself to take aim.

The creature's skeletal face grimaced in the sliver of moonlight. It was Skeleton Guy from my tree.

Something slammed into us with a gust of hurricane-strength wind. I fired the bow, and the arrow arced up even as I tumbled backward. Mercutio landed on top of me and we scrambled into the tall grass for cover.

"Magic," I realized. "He hit us with magic."

Mercutio crouched, baring his teeth.

"Hang on, Merc," I said. "Let's think this over. This might not be the best kind of fight to jump into. What do you say we sneak around him and just keep on going?"

Mercutio stalked through the grass. So far, he was going with my plan, which surprised me. But once the creature landed in the clearing and we got behind him, Mercutio went flying out of the grass toward it. Mercutio hadn't been going along with me. He'd just been getting into position. Cats like to attack from behind.

"I thought we were leaving!" I hissed when he landed on

the skeleton creature with a clatter. A pulse of magic flung Mercutio backward. I barely managed to catch him before the thing turned.

"I told you we should've kept on going," I said, dropping Mercutio to the ground. I loaded an arrow in an instant and let it fly, but a wave of the creature's bony hand sent it wide.

"That's really not good," I said as the arrow poked into the ground several feet behind Skeleton Guy. The creature raised its chin and its teeth clattered. A roar of wind issued forth, its intensity hot and blistering.

"Shoot," I said, dropping down to brace myself and shield Mercutio as it rolled over us, searing my skin. I dragged us behind a tree, panting. "I think we're gonna need a bigger bow."

29

I RAN OUT of arrows, and it quickly became apparent that fury and a can-do attitude weren't going to cut it. Skeleton Guy just kept coming. He was strong and magical and didn't have any muscles or flesh to get pierced or pummeled. I was pretty sure that the only thing keeping me from being reduced to pulp was Bryn's protection spell because zaps of electricity popped off me when Skeleton Guy tried to pound on me. The spell's energy drove him back. Sort of. I needed to crack his bones to really slow him down.

I swung my empty crossbow and knocked him aside and then scooped Mercutio up and dove into the tall grass, panting and sweating despite the cold. I had to do something. I had to try a spell.

We can't win on strength alone against this bony ape.
Got nothing else to try right now so know we must
*   escape.*

The skull came barreling into the grass right above us. I gasped and flung us back, the rest of my impromptu spell whistling past my lips.

Good guys win, let me make this clear
Shrink that spellcaster, now disappear

The creature froze, gnashing its teeth and looking from side to side. I'd hoped to shrink him or at least to shrink his magic. Even better would've been if I'd made him disappear, as I'd once done to my town nemesis. At first I'd thought I'd disintegrated her, but she'd actually been shrunken down to a bite-sized candy bar. Unfortunately, Skeleton Guy didn't look the slightest bit smaller. He just seemed confused because he didn't come barreling into the grass after us.

I took this as a sign from God and the universe to haul butt out of there. Mercutio writhed to get free, but I clutched him to my chest and held tight. He might not know when to quit, but I did. Before we went head to skull with Skeleton Guy again, we had to figure out what he was and, more importantly, what his weaknesses were.

I raced through the grass due east to the Amanos. A few times grass crunched behind us, and I pictured him hot on our trail. When the river came into view, I didn't slow. My legs pumped, my chest heaved, and I ran straight off the bank.

With a freezing splash, we landed in the water. The shock of it made my whole body clench. Up to my chin in cold water, I howled and sputtered curses. I let go of Mercutio, who made furious sounds, too. He's not crazy about being submerged at the best of times.

Why do I keep ending up in the water? Winter's no time for swimming.

The sweater grew heavy and dragged me down. I pulled it off, and my cramping fingers released it. The current was fast, especially with water levels still high from the flood. We were swept past the golf course in a matter of minutes.

As soon as we got to the residential area of Shoreside Oaks, Mercutio swam to the bank and got out. It was a good idea, since my limbs were almost completely numb with cold, but I knew I couldn't jog through Bryn's neighborhood in my torn and soaked pajamas. I was surprised Mercutio didn't run alongside me. When I was in the river, he usually stuck with me, making sure he was there if I needed help. This time, though, he sauntered along, falling behind, like he didn't even care if I made it out of the water alive. He was obviously mad as hell that I'd abandoned the fight.

"C'mon, Merc, don't be mad! We couldn't beat him. Even you know we have to retreat sometimes to live to fight another day—or night, as the case may be."

Mercutio ignored this and took off.

My teeth chattered, and I huffed a sigh. "I don't care what you think. Bryn's going to agree that mine was the better strategy. You just wait and see."

When I got near Bryn's property, I swam upstream to slow myself down so I didn't slam into the dock. It's always tricky to get out of the water near Bryn's because the current's really strong with Cider Falls half a mile downstream, trying to suck everything over it.

The current swept me toward the dock, and I managed to get my arms around a strut. With a fair amount of effort, I hauled myself out of the water and onto the dock. It was tough work given how tired and injured I was. I couldn't wait to get inside and get warm.

I shuffled through the grass to the house and knocked on the back door, hoping the police had released Bryn. If they hadn't, I would have to put on a party dress and go get him. The police would never get anything useful out of him anyway, and they'd probably be ready to give him up by now.

I knocked again and the back door opened. Bryn stood in the doorway with a blank expression. He didn't say a thing.

"What?" I demanded. "I wasn't with Zach. I fought a pissed-off fae and a pissed-off I-don't-know-what—the skeleton creature."

Bryn looked around behind me, like he thought I might've brought them along. Then he stepped back and closed the door.

My jaw dropped open in surprise. "What the hell?" I snapped. "Has everybody lost their minds?" I lifted my fist and beat on the door.

He jerked it open.

"Are you kidding me? I'm hurt and I'm freezing. Are you really—"

Bryn whispered a spell, and I felt the magic reach out and pass me. A little pulse of light lit the grass, and he looked past me, like he was looking right through me.

"Bryn?"

He didn't answer. Slowly, he began to close the door again.

"Holy moly!" I squeaked, and Bryn had no reaction to that at all.

The spell didn't work on Skeleton Guy; it worked on me. For the love of Hershey, I made myself disappear.

I shoved my hands against the door and kept it from closing. Bryn stilled after lifting a hand, ready to blast me with a spell.

I touched his arm and a zap of magical electricity arced between us. His brows shot up.

"Tamara?" he whispered.

I tapped the door with two quick raps.

"You're invisible."

"Apparently so," I said, exasperated, but of course he didn't hear that. My knuckles made two taps on the door.

He shook his head. "How in the world did you manage that?" he wondered, taking a step back.

"A spell gone wrong. As usual," I explained with a shrug he couldn't see. He stopped and I bumped into him, causing a big zap that made us both jerk away from each other.

He stood staring past me, thinking. "I don't know how to undo what you've done. Maybe if I remove my protection spell it will disrupt the invisibility one." Then he whispered a spell in Gaelic.

His magic melted off me like warm chocolate. I took a deep breath and waited.

"I still don't see you," he said. "Try touching me. Let's see if my spell came off."

The tip of my finger stretched toward him and with a tentative touch that didn't zap us, I confirmed that his spell was gone. I stepped forward and kissed him, tasting him and his magic. He shivered, his hands finding my sides and exploring my body as if to confirm that I had the right shape to be Invisible Tammy Jo and not some other random invisible girl who wanted to smooch him.

After the kiss, he rested his forehead against mine. "You're cold and wet and taste like the river. I guess there's going to be an explanation for that."

I gently pinched him twice.

"Rendering yourself invisible should've taken an incredibly complex spell. Did it?"

With a thumb and forefinger, I plucked at his skin once. I wondered how I knew one pinch or knock meant no and two meant yes. Maybe I'd seen it in a movie?

"Of course not," he said with a rueful smile. "Every time I start to forget that you're not an average witch, that you are in fact closer to a force of nature, you do your best to remind me."

"This wasn't my fault," I protested, and gave him a slightly harder single pinch.

"I didn't say you do it on purpose," Bryn said.

I frowned, thinking it wasn't too fair that he could argue with me when he couldn't even hear my side.

His hand slid down and clutched mine. "C'mon. Let's get you a pen and paper, so you can write down what happened."

"Good idea," I said, following him down the hall and into his study. He sat me in his desk chair, saying it was really strange not being able to see me, and it would be nice if I could sit in one place so he'd know where to face when he talked to me.

I gave him a quick double pinch. "Boy, too bad I didn't make myself accidentally invisible when the Conclave was in town and I needed to spy on them. Like this, I could be the best spy ever. Or the best cat burglar."

He set a pen and blank piece of paper in front of me. And then grabbed a throw blanket from the couch and wrapped it around my shoulders.

"Not that I would rob people. 'Cause, hey, one of the good

guys here. But I could be as good as a ghost or a fly on the wall at collecting gossip in this nobody-can-see-me state. Vangie would envy me. She loves eavesdropping."

I wrote a short version of what had happened and the spell I'd said to try to get rid of Skeleton Guy. I drew an arrow next to Crux's name and a scary-faced little skull next to the words *Skeleton Guy* like I was one of those guys who works for the Internet and makes the icons for e-mail. The pictures did dress it up a little, and I started to draw Merc, too. I only got the ears and part of his face down before Bryn cleared his throat impatiently.

"Um, yeah, okay. You're right. This is no time to get Google-logo artistic on things." I lifted the page to Bryn, and he took it.

Bryn read it over. He pointed at the partial drawing. "What's this?"

I took the paper and finished Merc's cat body and put whiskers, spots, and stripes on him.

"Mercutio," Bryn said. "So you drew as part of the spell? In the grass? Did you use a stick?"

I pinched him once.

"You didn't draw as part of the spell?"

I pinched him once again.

"So why are you drawing now?" he asked.

I bent over the paper and wrote, *For decoration*, adding another whisker to Mercutio's cute little drawing face.

"Tamara," Bryn said in a disapproving tone. When Bryn's working, he's very serious. I don't hold as strictly to seriousness myself.

I glanced up at him, sympathizing with the poor guy. "Invisible Me is just as exasperating as Regular Me, huh?" I patted his hand. "Sorry about that."

Bryn's expression softened, and he caught my hand and lifted it to his mouth. He pressed a kiss onto my skin and let it go.

"I love you, too," I whispered, and then because sometimes he's got to put up with a lot, I bent over the paper and wrote the words.

He read them and smiled. "All right, let's see what we can find," he said, walking to the floor-to-ceiling book-shelves that take up one wall of the room.

I wrote another note on the paper.

Making me visible again isn't actually my highest prior-ity. I need to find Vangie and to do that I need to get past Skeleton Guy. Actually, now that I know he can't see me, I can go back for her while you stay here doing research. By the way, can I borrow a gun?

I hopped up and carried the paper to Bryn, tapping his shoulder to get his attention. He took the sheet and read it.

"The gun's not a problem, but I should go with you to find Vangie."

"No, this is a job for the one of us who's invisible." I pinched him once.

He frowned. "I don't like the idea of you going alone. If you got hurt or were captured, I wouldn't be able to find you or even see you if you were lying ten feet from me. It's—"

I took the sheet back to the desk and wrote: *No one can get me since no one can see me. I'll be okay. I'm going!*

Bryn came over to see what I'd written. "You'll be okay, huh? Because you never almost get yourself killed when you're out of my sight."

I huffed and picked up the pen. Having an argument with Bryn was even more aggravating than usual when I had to stop and write everything out.

Then it occurred to me that I didn't actually need to negotiate. I could walk out any time without him even know-ing it. Of course that would've been bad manners.

I was about to ask again for the gun, but then I realized that like the pen and paper, it wouldn't be invisible. Skeleton Guy and anyone else who wanted to get in my way, like Crux, would be able to spot a gun and track my movements by it.

Never mind about gun. Can't risk it being seen. I'll dry the clothes I have on and then head out. I promise to be careful.

Then I drew a heart and a chocolate kiss next to it.

He sighed, but nodded.

I left him and took a shower while my pajamas and underwear were in the washing machine. Afterward, I tossed them in the dryer. I got a blanket from the guest room and wrapped it around me and used a hair dryer on my hair. It felt wonderful to be warm and dry.

An idea occurred to me. Ever since Bryn and I had mixed magic, he'd been able to use magic to do violence from a distance. But he also knew spells to heal. What if he could do some distance healing on Vangie? Or a protection spell? Also, taking a little of my witch magic away would make me more fae and hence give me better reflexes and even better healing abilities if I came up against Skeleton Guy.

When I went back to the library, the corner of the blanket dragged behind me.

Bryn looked at me. "That's a strange effect. Almost ghostly. With the fabric trailing behind you as a train, you're like a phantom princess, or a phantom bride."

I smiled because that reminded me of the story *The Princess Bride*, and I loved that movie.

I crossed the room to him with a pen and paper in hand. I wrote a line and held up the paper.

Want to fool around for a good cause?

The corners of his mouth quirked up. "The cause doesn't have to be good. Or even exist."

I smiled and wrote to him that I wanted him to take some power and use it to do a protection or healing spell on Vangie. I gave him Vangie's charm bracelet for a physical link to her.

"From a distance," Bryn said, his expression clouding. "I can try, sweetheart, but I'm not sure it'll work."

Take magic from me so you'll have a lot of juice. I won't need it. I'll be better if I'm more fae anyway. Fae Tammy is tougher than regular Tammy.

He frowned. "I wouldn't take that much. To leave you pure fae? No."

I took a step back. "You really hate that part of me, don't you?" I demanded, knowing he couldn't hear me. "It's not a small part that you can pretend doesn't exist. I'm *half* faery.

And there's nothing anyone can do to change that. No matter how much you all want to!"

Tears stung my eyes.

"Tamara?"

I grabbed the paper and scrawled a message in big letters.

I expect you to do whatever it takes to help Vangie. By the time I get back here, I'll be back to normal and you won't have to deal with the fact that I'm a half-breed.

He scowled. "Don't refer to yourself that way."

Why? It's the truth, I wrote.

He closed his eyes, like he had to focus to not lose his temper. "You know why. That term has a negative connotation."

According to you, Edie, Momma, and Aunt Mel, being fae has a negative connotation.

I shoved the paper against his chest. He opened his eyes and read it.

His covered his mouth with his hand for a moment and then nodded. When he dropped his hand, he said, "I apologize. I never meant to make you feel that way. I was raised to be wary of the fae. All Association witches and wizards are trained to be, and there's no denying it makes us prejudiced against true fae. That doesn't mean that those of us who are mixed race, and I include myself in that group, should be forced into a position of shame and denial. I really don't care that you're half faery. I swear on the stars and everything I hold sacred. The reason I don't want to drain away your witchcraft and leave you pure fae is that your humanity is an essential part of who you are. The fae side makes you powerful. I know it's saved your life, and I'm grateful for that. But when the faery emerges without anything to counter her, the things that make you *you* recede. I lose the witch whose magic matches mine. I lose the woman who loves me. And because I don't know where she goes during that time, I'm afraid I won't get her back."

I pulled the paper away from him gently and wrote to him.

It doesn't work that way. I'll always come back to you.

"How do you know?" he whispered.

I just do.

I pushed him toward the couch. He didn't resist. He sank onto the cushions, looking up. I straddled his thighs, sitting on his lap, and brought the blanket over our heads. Cocooned in the thick cotton with him, I leaned forward, unbuttoning his shirt as I kissed his neck. He exhaled loud enough for me to hear and his lids drifted closed.

When we'd fooled around in the past, his magic had enveloped us and pushed the rest of the world into the distance. This time was different. His magic stayed with him, delicious and just out of my reach. I tried to inhale it but could only taste the spicy tendrils that rode his breath. It made me restless and determined. I'd always been able to share in his power when it combined with mine, but I guessed that now it couldn't find mine. His magic clung to him like he'd been dipped in caramel. I could taste it but couldn't drink it in.

I eased his shirt off and bit his collarbone, causing a sharp intake of breath from Bryn. He tightened his grip on my hips and swung us sideways. Tangled in the blanket and a little breathless, we twisted until we were lying lengthwise on the cool leather, mouth to mouth, heartbeat to hammering heartbeat.

The blanket, partially pinned beneath us, was like a snake coiled around us.

"Christ," he swore, impatiently yanking the blanket's edge to give himself room to maneuver. I laughed softly. He couldn't hear me of course, but he felt it. "You'd better not be laughing," he said, giving my butt a pinch.

"Ow," I said, and treated him to a warning smack.

With the flick of a button and the *snick* of a zipper, he freed himself from his pants. The top of the blanket slid down and a bit of light exposed his mussed hair and the hollows above his collarbones as he poised himself above me. His eyes glittered sapphire and I lost myself in them. He really was better-looking than any guy had a right to be. I slid my hand down and curled my fingers around him. He sucked in a breath and then bent his head, finding my mouth and claiming it in a soul-searing kiss.

When our bodies locked together, I felt his magic and our heartbeats throb deep inside me. Neither of us moved, savoring the moment. We hadn't been this close for so long, and I'd missed him, missed the feeling of his body against mine. My fingers traced his spine as his teeth caught my earlobe and bit down. I gasped and arched.

He laced his fingers through mine and pressed my hands against the armrest above my head. When his hips moved, he whispered Gaelic words in my ear and magic speared me from the inside out, making my body clench tight as a fist. My breath caught, and he nodded with a dark smirk.

"We belong to each other, Tamara." With his breath silky and hot against my cheek, he said, "You hold my heart hostage, but I can enslave you, too."

I struggled against him, testing his grip. He didn't let me escape. The strength of his body and his magic bore down on me, like a summer storm battering a ship.

My body met his, reaching and recoiling, until the intensity was white-hot and almost unbearable, until every part of me belonged to him just as he'd promised. I shattered into climax with a scream he couldn't hear. He certainly felt it. My body pulled his with me, love and lust and magic flooding me.

Afterward I felt as if I'd melted onto the couch cushions like the wax of spent birthday candles left too long to burn. He released my cramped hands, which dropped behind my head. Limp and panting, I couldn't decide whether I wanted to get revenge on him or give him a present. Maybe both.

He moved his lips along my jaw to find my mouth. "I love you, sweetheart," he said, kissing my bruised lips lightly before giving my hip a squeeze and adding with a crackle of magic, "I'll always fight to keep you."

"Yeah, I love you, too," I said. "But I'm going to make you pay for being so great in bed. As soon as I can move my legs again."

He sat up and, with the blanket strewn across his lap, he

dressed. I watched him, for once able to stare without being caught. He had good looks that were kind of mesmerizing, but I also liked the way he moved, with a masculine grace that emanated sexiness and hinted at the magic that could extend from his lovely tapered fingers.

I sat up, thinking I'd steal a few more kisses, but then the dryer buzzed. He glanced up with a frown, buttoning his shirt.

I climbed off the couch, draping the blanket around me and dragging it along.

"Tamara, be careful out there tonight."

I turned and strode back to him. I gave him two quick pinches to promise I would take care and then added a kiss for good measure before I left him with his books.

It was nice to put on clothes that were hot from the dryer, but that cozy feel was short-lived. I dropped the blanket in the guest room and went to the kitchen. I braced myself as I opened the back door. I huffed angrily at the gust of cool air. It was frostily inconvenient to have to run around without a sweatshirt or coat.

I shivered and exited the house, deciding that I wasn't going to have to worry about being killed by arrows or magic. I would probably die from exposure.

30

I JOGGED THROUGH the woods. Partly because I was in a hurry, partly because when I ran I felt less cold. I half-froze crossing the golf course. There was no protection from the wind.

I trembled and tried to keep my teeth from chattering. I didn't want Skeleton Guy to find me by sound waves, like a bat or something.

North of the golf course, I entered the woods again, but when I crossed the small clearing it felt like my senses were muffled, almost like my ears were filled with water. I doubled back to the clearing and at a certain spot that I stepped across, my senses went back to normal.

"Witch magic," a familiar annoying voice said.

I jumped and spun toward a nearby tree. Crux leaned against it. His neck was red and raw where Mercutio had torn it, but the flesh was nearly healed.

"You can't see me. I'm invisible."

He grinned. "You're invisible to humans," he said.

"And to witches and wizards," I said, raising my fists in case he planned for us to tussle again. The soreness in my butt and back had gone away. I didn't want Crux starting it up again with a bite or a thrashing. I widened and planted my feet.

"Witches and wizards are human," he said, shaking his head at my ready-to-rumble stance.

With him still half-reclining against the tree, I felt ridiculous keeping my fists up, so I dropped them and straightened. "How come I'm not invisible to you?"

"Because you concealed yourself with fae magic, and being fae and stronger than you, I'm not affected by it."

"I concealed myself with fae magic?" I asked, impressed. That actually made a lot of sense. I'd done a number of spells that were really simple but did powerful things. That wasn't the way witches' magic worked. To do a really powerful spell using witch magic, a person had to use a complex, tricky, and perfectly planned spell.

"Do you happen to know how I undo the fae magic that makes me invisible?"

"Sure."

"Wait," I said, putting out my hands. "I don't want to be visible yet."

"I'll bet you don't. You want to wait until you're sure you're past the lych."

"The what?"

"The lych. The skeletal wizard you and your cat ran into earlier tonight."

"How did you—?"

"I told you to turn back. You should've listened."

"You *ordered* me to turn back. I don't take orders from foreign faeries. America's a free country."

He rolled his eyes. "Freedom's an illusion."

"Since I got away from you and went on my merry way, freedom feels real enough to me," I said, waving my arms to show how unchained they were.

His smile disappeared. "You escaped, but that doesn't make you free. It just makes you a particularly slippery fugitive."

"Hmm. I don't agree with that, but you're entitled to your

opinion since America's a, you know, *free* country," I said with a defiant quirk of my lips.

He smiled, too.

"So undoing the invisibility spell," I began. "Just how would I go about that later on?"

He folded his arms across his chest. "Here we reach an interesting point in our negotiations. I have something you want. There are some things I want as well."

I narrowed my eyes suspiciously. "Such as?"

"An end to hostilities. I want you to offer me friendship and hospitality."

"Hospitality?"

"I want you to invite me to stay at your home."

My eyebrows shot up. "I live in a house full of witches. It's got a bluebell plant spell that goes off like a fire alarm when a faery gets near it."

He shrugged. "I can cut through that magic. The witch who laid the spell isn't even here to reinforce it."

"How do you know I'm not the one who put the spell on?"

He laughed.

I folded my arms across my chest, mirroring him. "You know," I said in a faux sweet tone, "you're kind of a jerk."

"That I am," he said, not taking the least offense at the insult, which was even more proof; only a really big jerk would agree to being one.

I waved a dismissive hand. "I don't negotiate with jerks. And I definitely wouldn't invite one to be my houseguest."

"You'll be stuck. Indefinitely invisible."

"Nah," I said, walking away. "The spell will rub off eventually. My magic's kind of wobbly," I said, which was true, but of course, the last time I'd made someone disappear and turn bite-sized, it had stuck really well. It had taken us weeks and a dangerous adventure to lift that spell. What if I stayed invisible for months? That would be a complete pain in the behind.

I stepped tentatively into the territory where my senses muted and then back. I squatted down, looking at the ground, trying to find a line or symbol marking the transition.

"It's the lych's magic."

"It is? Is it poisonous?"

"Not to fae."

"Well, that's okay, then, right? Since I'm half," I said. He shrugged.

"What is a lych anyway?" I asked.

"If you offered me friendship and hospitality, I'd be very generous with information."

"Yeah, you're just the guy to help me out," I said. "Rose-thorn-wielding, arrow-shooting, cat-threatening faery that you are." I stood. "The truth is, Crux, I recently met an alligator who tried to swallow me in a single bite. He was more trustworthy than you." I took a deep breath of fresh forest air before I stepped across the invisible line into the muted world of lych magic.

He chuckled. "The alligator's in good company. Like him, I enjoyed the taste of you. Swallowing you in one bite, or several, would be a pleasure."

Lecherous jerk. I blushed, frowned, and kept walking.

"You can't ignore me forever," he called.

"You're likely right about that," I said. "Eventually, I'll probably shoot you. Or run you out of town. Or both."

He laughed, and that annoying sound was the last thing I heard as I ventured deeper into the heart of a sensory wasteland.

THE NIGHT FELT full of cobwebs, like my skin was covered in cotton candy. I rubbed but couldn't get the film off. The air thickened and clogged my mouth and throat. I had a really strong urge to turn back before I suffocated, but buried somewhere deep in my belly was another instinct. It said to soldier on. It told me I was getting close.

I put my palms out in front of me as though pushing through muck, but then my feet stopped. I looked down at the edge of murky mud that my toes curled back from.

Knowing how fond of mud my toes are, this struck me as weird. I inched back and crouched down, eyeing it suspiciously. I reached out and sank my finger into the grime. It was cold and heavy as death. I jerked my hand away. The tarry mess clung to my finger. I wiped it on the ground, getting as much off as I could in the damp grass.

I was not going through that mud, but the instincts that had carried me through the crossing didn't want me to turn back. The marshmallow still warm in my belly drew me north. I squinted, trying to see through the dark fog. There didn't seem to be anything in front of me. Just more of the same terrain that I'd come through, but I heard something through my clogged ears. I held my breath and cocked my head, listening.

Tweets.

In the distance, birds chirped.

Those little guys again. They'd been near Vangie's hotel room, too. Were they watching over her? Like a fallen Snow White?

I had to go on, but I misplaced my hand as I tried to stand and it sank to the wrist in that lifeless bog. I didn't have any doubt that if the mud pit was deep enough, my body would sink like a stone in quicksand.

I walked the edge, and it seemed to go on forever, like an unending line in the forest, like a moat as long as the wall of China.

Can't go around. Can't go across.

I glanced at a large tree.

Have to go over.

I climbed, my bare legs scraping bark. I paid them no mind. When I was around ten feet up, I crawled out onto a thick limb. Too bad Mercutio wasn't with me. This maneuver was just his style. Plus, I think he would've appreciated my nimbleness. The limb grew narrow, but I balanced like a gymnast on a beam. Well, kind of. I didn't walk out there on my toes; I inched out on my belly like a worm. A worm with hands and feet clutching the branch. Okay, maybe Mercutio wouldn't have been that impressed.

At the end of the branch, it dipped toward the ground. I dropped off the side, dangling by my arms. I swept my toes over the dirt. Definitely not a Tammy-Jo-swallowing mud moat. I let go and landed solid.

I turned and stepped forward, feeling a pop. My ears cleared, the air thinned to normal, and the smell of gardenias and death hit me like a fist.

I let out a slow breath and tiptoed forward. A tent shimmered into view, like a desert mirage. One second there'd been nothing, the next a large white tent that could've slept at least ten people appeared right in front of me. Black sparrows were in all the branches of the surrounding trees. I narrowed my eyes. Not only weren't the seaside sparrows extinct, Duvall and Dyson seemed to be infested with them. Why was that? I wondered.

I crept forward and turned sideways to move the tarp as little as possible as I entered the tent. There were half a dozen burning oil lanterns and in the center of the room, Vangie lay as I'd seen her in my vision, pale and unmoving.

Small feathers lay scattered around her, and clusters of wilting gardenias stretched from her waist to her throat. A crown of them had been placed on her head since I'd last seen her. Moving closer, I pushed the gardenias aside and found several small splotches of dried blood on her chest. I clenched my teeth. Somebody was in big trouble when I caught up to him.

I bent and touched her cool skin. Under her jaw, her pulse throbbed, though faintly. She wasn't gray as she'd been in my vision. I tilted my head and studied her. Her skin was as white as a pearl and silky smooth.

I lifted her gown's neckline and looked inside, finding a circle of thin cuts. How deep were they? *Not very*, I thought. They were arranged in a perfect little oval, like an Art Deco jewelry design. I imagined someone performing a blood ritual. What kind of spell had she been used for? I wondered with a shudder.

All right, then. We're getting the heck out of here.

I grabbed the flower crown and dragged it off her head.

Tossing it aside, I whispered her name. She didn't respond. I shook her shoulders.

"Vangie, wake up," I said louder.

She lay still as a corpse.

"Evangeline! Open your eyes!" I hollered.

Then I remembered that she wouldn't be able to hear me anyway since I was invisible. I slapped her cheeks lightly, but that didn't work. I pressed down on her chin. I didn't spot any pieces of poison apple in her mouth. *Just checking*, I thought with a shake of my head.

I swiped the gardenia petals off her and saw blue bruises on her neck. She'd been sliced *and* choked. I stiffened with fury.

"C'mon, you have to get up," I said, pushing hard on her collarbones. She bobbed. My brows shot up, and I lifted the willowy fabric of her dress so I could see what she lay on. It was an air mattress, like she was on a deadly supernatural camping trip.

"All right. I'm not a faery prince, but for all I know I could be a faery princess. I never knew my daddy or his people. I suppose I could be royalty. Nobody's said I'm not." I bent and kissed her. My lips tingled, but hers didn't even twitch. She tasted like menthol cough drops and Bryn's magic. His spell must have worked, at least a little. That's why she didn't look as dead and gray. If I could get her back to his house, we could do more magic spells to heal her and maybe she'd be okay.

"Well," I told her. "I didn't expect a kiss from me to work, but a kiss from the rescuer always does the trick in movies, so I had to give it a shot."

I heaved a sigh and decided to try a spell.

Digging my toes in the dirt, I said, "Hi, Earth. It's me, witch-fae Tammy Jo Trask again. I don't think me being invisible means you can't hear me. Pretty sure you're stronger than any magic, witch or faery. I've got to get my friend out of here, and she's a little too big for me to carry. Anyway, if you're not busy, I could use your help." I cleared my throat. "Here goes."

I bent close to Vangie's ear.

It's not morning, but it's time to get up.
This creepy camping is no fun.
Defy the lych and wake on up.
We're leaving on the run.

Nothing at all happened, except that I slapped my hip in frustration and cursed a little.

"Well, Vangie, you can be stubborn about staying unconscious if you want, but I'm not leaving you here." I ripped the hem of her dress and tied the fabric around the handhold at one end of the air mattress. I dragged the mattress into a position that was on a direct line to the tarp door and then hooked the torn fabric over my shoulder. I leaned forward and pulled. It was slow work hauling that mattress over the ground, but I got it outside.

I was fairly sure that the air mattress would float over the mud, but I ripped some more strips of fabric and tied them together. I hooked the tree branch with an end and gave a tug to slip the knot into a tight noose.

"Okay, Vangie, here we go," I said, kneeling on the mattress next to her calves and pushing us out onto the moat. The stinking mud glopped up the sides of the air mattress. I gagged and wrinkled my nose, trying not to breathe too deeply.

I pulled and paddled us until the mattress bumped against the other edge.

"Good," I murmured. "I'll just climb off." I crawled over Vangie, but all of a sudden the mattress jerked. I fell forward, my elbows on the regular ground, but the mattress popped out from under me and my legs fell into the mud. I yelled as the mud sucked me down. I had to battle my way out of the muck, and by the time I did, Vangie and the mattress were almost out of reach.

Skeleton Guy was on the far side of the moat, hauling Vangie and the mattress away.

I dove forward and grabbed the fabric hooked to the handle on my end.

"You let go! She's my friend! You're not keeping her!" He couldn't hear me, which was lucky, but also unsatisfying.

Skeleton Guy yanked and I had to let go or fall into the bog. If I fell all the way in, I knew I'd drown. That mud was too thick and foul.

I needed to knock Skeleton Guy into it. I ran and jumped, grabbing the fabric hanging from the tree. I swung like Tarzan and kicked Skeleton Guy. My feet sank into the nearly translucent flesh that apparently sometimes covered his bones. It was like he was made of Jell-O.

"Gross!" I yelled, yanking my legs back.

Fleshy Skeleton Guy dropped the mattress and fell back, clutching his middle.

"What are you?" I demanded, trying to rub the gelatinous goop off my legs.

He whispered a spell and magic blasted the area. I'd swung back over to the ground under the tree, then dropped and rolled out of the line of fire. The smell of decay from the mud was mixed with a weird cloying perfume smell. Crushed gardenias, I realized.

The mud and goop dried, feeling like sugar glaze on my limbs, making me itch. I scraped at it and stood. My nails dug into a very itchy spot and I hissed at the burn. I felt wetness and knew I'd scratched hard enough to draw blood. Blurred images flashed before my eyes. I squinted but couldn't make out the details, except that I'd left Texas.

Wind whipped all around my head, and screeching birds flew with beating wings toward me. The sparrows circled, then dove and pecked at my legs. I beat them away.

I inhaled a breath of gardenias and rotten eggs, and I saw a girl on a bed of leaves. She lay next to a pond in a park. On every side, tall buildings loomed, and on a bridge crossing the pond, a row of sparrows watched. A blond man with his back to me scattered gardenia petals on her body and whispered.

I strained my eyes, studying the fallen girl. The vision was hazy, as if behind a veil. Stars dotted the misty sky. The constellations sparkled, pulsing with power. I followed their light down and saw her face.

Edie.

It was my very own aunt Edie. She lay perfectly still with alabaster skin and dark waves clinging to her shoulders.

"No!" I screamed as the figure flourished a knife and bent over her. He cut with care like a master painter at his canvas. Slivers of pain sliced me. *Stop it!*

The image disappeared with a pop, and I was back in Duvall, clutching my chest. I jerked my hands up. No blood. I was okay, except that I was sure I'd seen Edie's murderer preparing to kill her. I felt cold all the way to the marrow of my bones.

Skeleton Guy and his rotten magic were connected to Edie's death. Had he been there? Was he the legacy of her murderer? All that was left of a monster?

And Vangie, his latest victim. How much longer did she have before he killed her?

I rushed around the tree and back to the moat.

"Don't you dare! I'll kill you!" I screamed. Unfortunately, threats are a lot more effective if the threatened party can hear them being made.

Skeleton Guy didn't look up. He pulled Vangie off the mattress and carried her away. I ran and jumped. I sailed over the moat, almost making it all the way across. One leg sank into the mud, but my other foot made it to the bank. I sprang forward, dragging my leg free.

I sprinted after Skeleton Guy, but he disappeared. Light from the stars beamed down, and I zipped through the trees.

I couldn't find Skeleton Guy and Vangie in the woods. "Where is he, Trees? Where did he go?" I panted, listening for a hint. The trees remained silent under an oppressive spell. "C'mon!" I yelled, my hands in fists, my muscles tight.

Minutes ticked by, and I raced left and right, straining my eyes for a sign of them. In the distance I heard a car motor.

A car motor?

I was pretty sure that Skeleton Guy couldn't drive. Did he have a master who had been waiting for him?

"No!" I yelled, stomping my foot. I ran toward the sound, but it faded away before I reached the clearing. I'd lost her. I shoved my hands through my hair, raking my nails over my scalp. I'd lost her to a murderer, and I had no idea how much time she had left.

31

ON THE WAY back to Bryn's, tears spilled down my freezing cheeks, and I tried to organize my thoughts. I couldn't ignore the fact that Crux had shown up right around the time that Vangie had been abducted, and he claimed to know what the creature was that had taken her. Did he have something to do with it? Or was he really in Duvall for some other reason? And, if so, what?

As brilliant as Bryn was, there was no way he could help me with fae magic or politics. I realized I did have a way to get information on the Unseelie court. There was a small fae operative named Nixella Pipken Rose that I'd defeated. I could summon her.

"Nixella Pipken Rose, come to me."

Nixella appeared, instantly furious, as usual. She was the size of the average six- or seven-year-old, but her skin was as green as a ripe avocado, and she had fingers and toes that were twice as long as a human's. She sneered, baring her teeth, which were pointed to needlelike tips.

"How dare you!" she yelled. "You have no right to call me to you. No right to use my name. You promised not to! When I took your cat out of that burning house."

"Oops. I forgot about that."

"Stupid, stupid witch," she said, giving me a vicious shove.

"Hang on, Nixella, I have a question for you."

"Why would I answer your questions? I wish you were dead," she snapped.

"Yeah, well, you may get your wish, but before that we could make a trade. There must be something you want?"

She paused, some of her anger cooling. "You only have one talent."

"I do?" I asked, trying to figure out which magical thing she thought I did well. I couldn't imagine.

"Yes, stupid witch. You make sweeties."

"Oh, right. I am talented at that."

"I want vanilla cake with vanilla icing," she said. "No, honey cakes with extra honey. No, spice cake with sweet creamy cheese frosting."

"I can do that. I'll make you a cake."

"Not one! A bunch of pastries. No, a stacked cake."

"Sure."

"Taller than me."

"Taller than—"

"Taller than me! I get to pick the layer cake's flavors. As many as I want."

"Okay," I said. "But first, you have to answer my questions. What is the faery knight Crux's mission in Duvall?"

She froze. "One of the golden knights is in Duvall?"

"You didn't know? Your queen sent him."

"My queen? She did not! If my lady highness could command a golden knight, she would order him to kill the Seelie Queen and when he came to report his triumphant success, she'd have him skinned and mounted on a torture cross."

My brows shot up. "Isn't Crux an assassin of the Unseelie court?"

Nixella shook her head.

"Then who is Crux?"

"Crux is a knight of the Seelie court. Part of the golden trio, which we hate more than all others."

"The golden trio?"

"Caedrin, the tracker. Crux, the trainer. Colis, the tree-keeper. The reported favorites of their queen. They're deadly and kill all Seelie enemies, including our own great assassin, Bitter Nole. If given a chance, I would cut the heart from Crux's body, burn it black, and serve it at a party to mark the anniversary of Nole's death."

"You said Crux is a trainer. Who does he train?"

"Seelie spies and assassins. Where did you see Crux, worthless witch? In the woods? How far from here? What was he doing? What did he say? Tell me everything, and I'll see that you're rewarded."

I pointed and explained about running into him in the woods. The Unseelie fae weren't my allies, but neither were the Seelie. If the Unseelie wanted to run Crux off, that would suit me fine.

"Nixella, I'm invisible to humans."

"Yes, I see the spell." She tilted her head. "It looks rather . . . golden. Did Crux help you with it? You must never align yourself with the Seelie. Not if you expect to live here in our territory. The queen doesn't like witches, but she tolerates your kind as long as you don't damage what's ours, the trails, the woods . . . She suspects that nature will kill you all eventually, so my lady highness doesn't trouble herself about you. But any ally to the light fae—that would be—" She pursed her lips. "No, she would never suffer a Seelie friend to live."

I nodded. "I'm not planning to align myself with any faery court," I said, deciding that it was in my best interest to change subjects. "Can you tell me how to remove this spell?"

"To undo what's done, you must return to the spot where it was laid."

My mind reeled. "Go back to the location where I did the spell? What if I don't know exactly where that was?"

She smiled. "Then we'll call you the Invisible Witch."

"Can you find the spot, Nix?"

"I don't want to find it!" she said petulantly.

"That wasn't my question."

"You smell like witches' death magic. You stink!" she said, pinching her nose.

"C'mon, Nixella, please lead me to the spot where I put the concealment spell on myself," I said.

"For two mountains of pastries, bigger than me?"

"Done."

Nixella huffed and then took off. I raced to keep up. She may be small, but she's sprightly.

By the time I reached the spot, I was out of breath and muscles I didn't even know I had burned like crazy.

"Nixella, a friend of mine was kidnapped by a skeleton creature. Is that someone from the Unseelie or Seelie court?"

"No."

I rested my hands on my knees, sucking air. "Do you know what a lych is?"

"No. Don't know and don't care. I'm leaving now, you wretched witch. I'll leave you a list of what I want for layers and then a week later, I'll collect my bounty. If you don't have it for me, I'll stab you in your fat human heart with another poison arrow and push you in the bog until you're more than dead."

"More than dead?" I murmured skeptically.

She scrunched her face in a furious expression.

"Right, sure. Well, thank you for your help, Nixella. I'm going to make you frosting so sweet, your teeth will think it's Samhain all over."

"You better or it's the bog for you," she said, and disappeared.

As always, she was the picture of Southern charm.

I straightened and rolled my shoulders to loosen them. I dug my toes into the dirt and stretched out my arms.

I made myself invisible,
Though I did not mean to.
I want myself revealed;
Bodies should not be seen through.

I couldn't tell if the spell had worked or not but figured that I'd given it my best shot for the moment.

I stretched and took off for Bryn's place. Unfortunately, when I arrived, I would have to tell him it was necessary for me to return to a place he wasn't fond of. Zach's house.

32

I REACHED BRYN'S property at sunrise and ran into Mercutio. I knew right away that the spell to make me visible had worked because he darted over to me.

I gave him a quick hug and then filled him in on the night. He yowled and yawned and followed me into Bryn's kitchen. I ducked my head and avoided eye contact with the cameras. It was nearly time for the security guy switchover. Steve from nights would go home, being replaced by Pete on days. I hoped they were debriefing and not looking at the monitors since I was disheveled and filthy in torn pajamas.

I went upstairs to Bryn's room, where there were no cameras. The bed hadn't been slept in. *He must be exhausted.*

After a hot shower, I dried my hair, then put on a plum satin dress, underwear, and a borrowed maroon sweater and sweatpants. I added a pair of thick gym socks. Passing a mirror, I shook my head.

"You look silly," I said to myself. But the part of me that had been freezing all night didn't care. I was layering up for warmth. And also if some of my outfit got destroyed, I'd still have something left to wear, I decided hopefully.

Downstairs, I found Mercutio asleep on the kitchen floor

and stepped over him. I made myself toast with butter and honey and then went to the library. Bryn slept in a big leather chair with his feet resting on the matching ottoman. A two-foot-tall stack of hardcover books sat next to him.

He looked as sweet as the honey I licked from my lips. I hated to disturb him, but I needed to. I bent and kissed his neck just below his ear before I said, "Hey, can you wake up?"

I squeezed his arm and jostled him gently.

"Hey, Bryn?"

His black lashes stayed stubbornly against each other. I gave him a harder shake.

"I'm up. What time are closing arguments?" he mumbled.

I smiled and kissed him again. His lids rose, and he licked his lips as I leaned back.

"I'm sorry I had to wake you up."

"Come closer," he said, catching my arms and pulling me into the chair. He kissed me and curled me against his chest.

I snuggled with him for several moments, then leaned my head back. "It sure would be nice if we had time to fool around and then get some sleep."

"Don't we?"

"I'm real sorry," I said earnestly. "I'll make it up to you."

"When?" he asked, staring at my mouth.

"Soon," I said, rubbing my thumb over his lower lip. "I promise."

He sighed and closed his eyes.

"I know you're tired, but I need to talk things over with you. Then I'll leave you alone to rest."

"Ask."

"What's a lych and how do I kill one?"

His eyes opened. "A lych?" He sat forward. "That term sounds familiar. Where—?"

I opened my mouth, but he held out a hand to stop me.

"Wait, let me think. Lych," he murmured, rolling the word over on his tongue. "I read something. Where?"

I could practically see the wheels turning in his head. After several more moments of struggling, he blinked.

"I remember," he said, nodding his head. "There hasn't been one in hundreds of years, if ever. The only thing I've ever read that referenced a lych was written in the 1600s. I was doing research and came across it in an archive. I'd never heard the term before. More digging revealed a few legends that source materials thought were likely fictitious."

"The faery guy said the skeleton guy's a lych."

"How could that be possible?" Bryn murmured. "From what I read, a lych is a powerful wizard who's made himself immortal by taking an undead form."

"Like a vampire?"

"Not exactly."

"Do lyches have to feed?"

"According to legend, yes. I think in that account the lych used death magic to transform himself and then had to periodically reanoint himself with power at a terrible price."

"What price? Do they feed on the magic of pretty young witches?"

"Maybe," Bryn said, nodding. "I think in the story, the price of power was the death of innocent people. But how could a lych exist now and live undetected? If he stalks witches in urban areas, someone would see him. If he kills them, someone would investigate and track him down."

"I think this undead wizard guy's been killing girls for decades. Maybe centuries. I think he's the one who killed Edie."

Bryn's brows rose. "What makes you think so?"

I explained about the vision I'd had when my blood mixed with the mud and his body goop. "His magic is celestial, so he does his spells outside. Edie's body was near a pond."

"A pond? I thought she was killed in Manhattan."

"There's that big park in the city, right?"

"Central Park," Bryn said with a nod.

"Are there any ponds in it?"

Bryn nodded. "But doing a ritual in Central Park without being discovered is hard to imagine."

"Not if he did a spell to repel people. There was a big

moat around the place where he was keeping Vangie. It smelled bad and made me want to turn back. I bet if I'd been a regular person, I would have."

Bryn rubbed his eyes. "That may have worked. Complicated rituals might take an hour or two to complete, but if he did them in the dead of a winter night when very few people would've been walking through the park, a repulsion spell could've given him the cover he needed."

"Can you research how to kill it?"

"I can try," he said. "There's nothing about them in modern books. I'd imagine that's by design. They must have been so dangerous that the leaders of the World Association of Magic decided to wipe away any reference to them."

I climbed off him. He ran his eyes over my outfit and cocked a brow.

"I'm tired of being cold."

"Sure, but one of your layers doesn't have to be a cocktail dress. I can lend you a wool coat, and a hat and gloves to go over the sweats."

"The coat and gloves will be too big on me and might mess up my fighting or escaping moves." I twirled and kicked to show him how quick and mobile I could be in my current outfit.

Bryn smirked. "All right." He rose from the chair and walked to the bookshelf, then shook his head. "I don't have a single volume that includes information about lyches. I need a library with archives." He turned and walked to his computer. "Some old documents have been scanned to preserve them. I don't have clearance, but Andre could get me into the computers at WAM Headquarters through an electronic back door."

"Be careful, though. I don't want you guys to get in trouble," I said, walking to the door.

"Where are you going?" he asked.

"I'm—" I only hesitated a second. "I'm going to Zach's."

Bryn's hand reached for the phone, but fell as he turned. "Why?"

"He has the case file on Edie's murder. I want to read it. There might be some clues."

"Is that likely? The police won't have had information about the magical aspects of the case."

"Probably not, but I should look it over. The police might not have known the magical significance of things, but they recorded their observations. Edie saw something she recognized. Maybe I'll notice something in the reports."

Bryn nodded.

"You can come with me to Zach's if you want."

"No. He'll be more cooperative if I'm not there." He studied me for a moment. "You said you've made your choice. I trust you."

I smiled, proud of him. In his place, I don't know that I could've been as calm. I pressed my fingers to my lips and blew him a kiss. "I'll be back soon," I promised.

On the drive to Zach's house, the adrenaline had worn off and the honey toast had kicked in, so my eyes tried to drift shut. My exhausted body wanted to do a Sleeping Beauty impression.

No! I pinched my thigh and sucked in a breath at the pain. *Yep, that worked. I'm awake.*

Since the lych creature relied on celestial magic, I hoped sunrise had foiled his plans. My arrival had forced him to move Vangie from the site where he'd started his ritual. The staging had been pretty involved with its repulsion spell, tent, and flowers. It would take some time and effort to get another place ready. If I could figure out where he'd gone with Vangie, I'd have all day to find her and defeat him. If I didn't find him by sunset, though, I bet he'd finish his power-stealing spell, and that would be the end of Vangie.

I didn't even have a locket to preserve Vangie's soul in. My understanding was that my great-great-grandmother Lenore had tethered Edie to the locket so she wouldn't be lost or destroyed by the deadly magic on her. It had saved her since the nature of her death had somehow made it impossible for her soul to cross over naturally to the other side.

I shivered. There was nothing more terrible than imprisoning or destroying someone's soul. Lenore's protection spell allowed Edie to roam the world and to interact with some of the living and most of the dead on earth. Other spells, malicious spells, that held a dead soul didn't allow any freedom or peace. A soul could literally be held prisoner while it relived the trauma of the death of its body. Bryn's mom's soul had been kept that way. I'd felt her pain and would never forget it. If that was what Skeleton Guy had in mind for Vangie, there was nothing I wouldn't do to stop him.

I shuffled up the walk to Zach's, then knocked twice and rang the bell.

He answered the door in sweats and a T-shirt with sleep-tousled hair. "Who dressed you?" he asked. "Rollie the vampire and our gym coach from middle school?"

"Bite your tongue. Rollie would be furious if I let him take the blame for this outfit."

"So what gives?"

I waved a hand. "It'd take too long. I came to see the police file on Edie's murder. I have reason to believe I met her killer last night."

Zach stepped back and waved me inside. "Tell me what happened," he said.

I rubbed my eyes as I entered. I took a deep breath and rambled for several minutes. It wasn't the most coherent story ever, but I covered the highlights.

"Birds, huh?" Zach said, running a hand through his unruly curls. "There was a bird guy . . ."

"A bird guy?" I echoed.

"They found a couple of feathers beneath her body. The guy claimed he'd given her feathers for the fringe on her dress and that they must have come loose and been in the bedding."

"She died in Central Park."

"No, her body was found in her own apartment."

"He must have moved it."

Zach studied me. "There's physical evidence to support that. The back of her dress had loose dirt on it. Since she'd been dropped off at her apartment and had been found there, the New York detectives didn't give it much thought. But the timeline of her movements didn't explain it. I wondered when she was outside lying on her back on the ground. And why? Did she lie down on a whim to look up at the stars? Or was she pushed down or dragged through the dirt?"

"Why would her killer move her, though? Pretty risky to carry her from the park to a building. Why not just kill her in the park and leave her body there?"

Zach shrugged. "Maybe he didn't want the body to be found right away? Edie was known for disappearing. Under normal circumstances, her body could've stayed undiscovered for days."

"Was she found right away?"

He nodded.

"How come?"

"Her sister sensed something was wrong and went to the apartment. She let herself in using a spare key that Edie had given her. Edie's body was still warm. The police believe that the murderer left by the fire escape when he heard someone at the door."

"Still warm?" I paused. "So he didn't kill her in the park. He took her to the apartment to finish whatever he was doing," I said. "Maybe that's why Vangie's not dead. Perhaps the ritual is done over time. For part of it, he needs the night sky. For part of it, he needs something that's found indoors."

My stomach clenched. So the lych might already have a second location ready. Was he killing Vangie even now?

"We have to hurry," I said breathlessly. I felt dizzy and sick all at once, and my leg ached.

I must have gone very pale because Zach put out a hand to steady me. "Easy, girl. Sit yourself down," he said, steering me to the couch. "I'll get you some juice."

"And the file. Hurry, Zach." I pulled up my pant leg and my eyebrows shot up. The gator wounds on my calf that had been almost healed were fiery red and swollen, and there were small black rings around each one. I laid a hand on my thigh and pressed. The thigh wounds had been deeper than the calf ones, but they didn't hurt. It was that fetid mud that my lower leg had been dipped in. I'd known it was full of poisonous magic. My calf had been submerged and now its wounds were infected. I put a hand to my head and wondered if I had a fever. My hands felt icy cold against my brow.

I yanked the pant leg down when I heard Zach coming back. I didn't want him to get distracted. I took the glass of orange juice, but before he could sit I said, "I've got a little headache. You think you could spare me an aspirin?"

Zach gave me a speculative look and didn't set down the file before he left the room. Did he think I'd take off with it? I guess maybe he had his reasons for not trusting me, but it bugged me.

I leaned over to the phone and picked it up. I called Bryn's house, and he answered on the second ring. "Hey there, it's me. That mud moat I told you about, I think it had poison magic in it. No wonder it smelled like sewage. The part of my leg that went into the mud is infected. The wounds are red with black rings around them. Can you look into the cure for that after you check on how to kill the lych?"

"How do you feel?" Bryn asked.

"All right, except a little dizzy. And my leg smarts like nobody's business. Gotta go," I said, hanging up as Zach returned. He glanced at the phone, but said nothing.

I gulped down the aspirin and orange juice. He sat next to me and opened the thick file. It contained copies of really old papers. Some of the print was smudged and faded. I lifted the top pages close to my eyes.

I read through the police timeline of Edie's last night. She'd been at a party, gotten drunk on bootleg liquor, and gone home around one thirty in the morning. A man named Tim Pate dropped her off. He walked her to her door to make sure she got inside but said he didn't go in. He'd been a main suspect, but the clothes he'd worn to the party hadn't been bloody. They hadn't found the weapon on him or at his apartment. And friends who'd seen him later that night said he'd acted normally. Also, Pate didn't have a motive. No one had ever seen Edie argue with him.

According to the report, Pate had been one of the few guys Edie knew that she hadn't had a volatile affair with. It was pretty clear from the documents that the police thought Edie was a shrewish tart with no respect for her father or any of the men in her life. There was a definite tone to the report that suggested she'd gotten what she deserved. It shocked me to read it. In the pictures from the crime scene she looked so young. Also, I knew she'd had her reasons for rebelling. Her daddy had been mean and abusive. Besides, no matter what Edie was like, no one deserved to get stabbed to death. I wondered how hard the police had worked to solve the case. Maybe not very hard at all.

Zach shuffled through the pages and held one out. "Here."

The faded handwriting was hard to read. I made out: *Frederick J. Greer. Calls himself "Freddie." He has aviary— fancy bird coop upstate. Claims he gave the victim a collection of feathers for use as fringe on designer dress. Feathers on bed under her from dress or from him?* At the bottom of the page there was a note that the detective had left a message for Greer's alibi, another flapper. It never said whether the alibi had checked out.

I flipped to a picture of Freddie Greer, and my breath caught. I'd seen someone who looked a lot like him. "Oh my God. How much do you want to bet that the *J* in *Freddie J. Greer* stands for *Jackson*?"

"Why?"

"Because I believe I've met Freddie Greer's grandson. Or maybe his great- or double-great-grandson." I looked up. "Vangie's fiancé, Jackson. Supposedly he doesn't come from a magical family. But of all the women in New York, Freddie befriends Edie? And of all the women in Dallas, Jackson romances Vangie? Do you think it's a coincidence that both the Greer men found witches?"

"Hell no."

"Me neither. Jackson must've gone to a lot of trouble to

conceal his magic. It's hard to do. But if your grandfather is a serial killer of witches and you're his apprentice, you don't want covens examining your family tree."

Sweat popped up on my forehead, and I had to lean back to keep from falling over.

"What's wrong? You've looked pale since you got here," Zach said, putting a hand on my arm.

"I'm all right. I think the aspirin's breaking my fever."

"What fever?" Zach asked. "If you're sick, you should be in bed."

A knock at the front door made us both look. Zach rose and crossed the room. When he opened the door, Bryn stood on the porch.

33

"SUTTON," BRYN SAID with a nod.

"You're kidding, right?" Zach asked, his voice grim.

"You're supposed to be doing research," I said with a frown.

"I'm here because she's ill. For her sake, invite me in," Bryn said.

Zach glared at Bryn, but Bryn's expression was so neutral he could've been his Swiss friend Andre. Zach took a step back and opened the screen door.

Bryn strode to me and dropped to a knee. He pulled the legs of the sweats up and examined my leg. I peeked at it. The black splotches had grown larger.

"I know who has Vangie," I said. "She's got a fiancé whose name—"

"I don't care about Evangeline Rhodes right now," Bryn said.

"Well, I do. Plus, she's the key," I said, pulling my leg back as Bryn traced one of the black rings. "Ow. Don't press those. Listen, the undead guy, the lych, he must be a blood-and-bones wizard."

"You said he used celestial magic," Bryn said.

"I think he started that way, but he deals in death magic, too." I shivered, and my stiffening muscles ached. "Cold in here." I rubbed my arms. "The lych is stealing energy from the ghosts and the vampires. Dominion over the dead and undead, it's blood-and-bones magic, right?"

"Sometimes." Bryn closed his hands around mine and grimaced. "You're chilled."

"The bastard's made me sick and tired, too. I have to stop him!"

"Tamara, for God's sake, stay calm. You need to conserve your strength." Bryn yanked out his keychain and opened his Swiss Army knife. He made a slice in the sweatpants and tore the fabric in two all the way to my hip.

"Hey," I complained with a shudder. "I told you I'm cold."

"Don't you think I know? Don't you think I can feel it?" Bryn said, and I heard the concern in his voice. Sure, he could feel it. We were connected.

"Do you feel bad, too?" I asked, worried.

Zach put a blanket around my shoulders and then squatted next to Bryn to examine the snakelike black marks slithering up my thigh.

"Do you need to know the spell that was used to poison her to undo this?" Zach asked.

"I don't think we have time to track down the killer to find out what spell was used. This is spreading too fast. We have to do something right now."

"Like what?" Zach said.

"I'm okay," I said stubbornly. "Being half faery makes me half invincible, right? This had to be witch magic. It can only kill half of me, right?"

Zach looked hopeful, but Bryn looked worried and gripped my arms tight enough to bruise.

"Did you hear him recite a spell? Think back. Anything you tell me could be helpful. Concentrate."

"Hmm. I can't remember—"

Spots formed in front of my eyes, and my eyes rolled back.

When I opened my lids again, I lay on the couch. My

arms and legs ached and my tongue throbbed and tasted metallic. I swallowed bloody saliva and wrinkled my nose.

"What happened?" I asked, my voice slurred.

"Get the amulet," Bryn said. "It counters magic. Let's see if it'll slow this down."

Zach sprinted out of the room.

"What happened?"

"You had a seizure."

"That's some fast-acting poison," I mumbled. "You've got to hand it to that Skeleton Guy."

Zach reappeared seconds later. "You better stand clear," Zach told Bryn.

Bryn ran a hand over the side of my face. "If it hurts, I'm sorry." He backed away. To Zach, he said, "Go ahead."

Zach put the amulet over my head and slid it inside my clothes. The second it touched my skin, I howled. That thing burned like an oven set at six hundred degrees.

I clutched my chest and closed my eyes at the blinding light. Zach grabbed my hands and gripped them to keep me from hauling the amulet off.

"Lyons?" Zach called. "Is it helping or making things worse?"

I heard a thumping sound and pain shot down my legs. Bryn staggered backward into the wall, his breathing harsh. He recited a spell and a pulse of cool magic blew over me. I reached up, trying to put my fingers into the cold rush of power . . . anything to escape the pain.

"Hang on, sweetheart," Bryn said, and then he groaned.

My skull felt like it would split in two.

"Sutton," Bryn gasped. "How do the black marks look?"

"Better," Zach said, "but her skin smells like it's burning."

"I feel it," Bryn said. "Take the amulet off. Let me try something."

Zach removed the necklace and stepped back.

"There are times—" I mumbled, lifting my clothes away from the blistered skin on the top of my left breast and collarbone. "There are some times when the cure is worse than the disease."

"Back away for a minute," Bryn said to Zach. "Stand in the kitchen doorway."

A moment later, I breathed easier. My eyeballs felt scratchy and sore, and opening my lids was like having someone poke them with daggers. I cursed and tears welled, but at least they washed away some of the grit. Bryn's face swam into view.

"Here's what we'll do," Bryn said. "I'll draw off your witch magic. Then you'll be more fae. It should help."

"Go ahead," I said, puckering my lips.

Bryn whispered a spell in Gaelic and then kissed me. I felt his magic curl down my throat, and then he sucked it back into himself. I didn't resist. I pushed my tongue into his cool mouth. Moments later, the pain eased. I held tight.

Bryn pulled away and rocked back on his heels.

"How do you feel?" Bryn asked.

"Like I could eat you like a chocolate pastry," I said with an unsteady chuckle. All the pain from moments before had faded; like sound underwater, it was muted to nearly unnoticeable. Being fae had its advantages.

Bryn exhaled, and I sat up. The skin of my arms glowed like a golden sunrise. By contrast, Bryn's skin was pale, almost ashen, but he didn't fall over. That man had a will of iron. *Iron*, I thought, wrinkling my nose. *A will of steel*, I corrected.

My heart thumped, and I gave a little cough as I stretched. The dark marks receded to tight little whorls around the bites, like cinnamon pinwheels.

"I'm better," I said. "I'd like a weapon. A longbow and a quiver of arrows." I locked eyes with Bryn. He really was beautiful. Glittering sapphire eyes and hair jet as stones at the bottom of a riverbed. "You'll get a bow for me, won't you? From the arsenal in your house?"

Bryn swallowed. "I will. You'll come with me and pick out what you want."

"I don't think so," I said, wrinkling my nose. "Your house isn't friendly when I'm like this."

"Tamara—"

"No," I said. "You'll be tempted to trap me, to keep me safe. I won't be a prisoner."

"So you'll wait here for me?" Bryn asked.

"Sure," I said, waving a hand. "I'll be here." But I already felt the pull of the woods. I needed to be outside, to feel the rush of raw earth, pure and powerful, between my toes. It would do me a lot more good than a blistering amulet. "And bring Merc. We might need his help tracking the wizard."

"Sutton," Bryn said. "Fae are mercurial and their consciences aren't fully formed. When she's like this, she can be unpredictable."

"I can handle it."

"Don't handle it too well, or our ceasefire will be short-lived," Bryn said, and without waiting for a response, he left.

I turned my attention to Zach. He was definitely as handsome as any human had a right to be, but the amulet lay dull as lead against his skin, casting a smoky shadow over him, dampening the gold of his skin and curls.

"You should take that off," I said, nodding toward his chest.

"You started to tell us where you thought we could find Jackson Greer and his grandfather."

"The younger Greer and the girl were staying at a hotel in Dyson," I said. "But since the sun's risen, I can't see the lych carrying an unconscious and almost-dead girl across a parking lot in broad daylight. If the younger Greer is still at the hotel, we could get him. If the old lych cares about him, he'd be a good bargaining chip to draw the lych out. Then I'll kill them, and the ghosts will be freed. If there's still enough life left in her, the shy witch will wake up." I clapped my hands against each other in a "that's that" gesture.

Zach stared at me. "You don't sound like you."

I ignored his observation. "Once I deal with the lych, I can get on with more important things." I stood.

"What important things?" Zach asked.

"Catching a fae warrior in a snare and finding out what he wants with me," I said with narrowed eyes. "And paying him back for thrashing me." My voice had a fiery note that crackled on the air.

"For thrashing you?" Zach asked.

"Not your worry," I said, putting out a hand to prevent him from moving toward me and bringing the amulet closer. I went to the back door and opened it. I inhaled deeply. "That's better. Even from here, I can smell the pine needles. Almost the winter solstice. It belongs to the Unseelie, but all transitions are cause for celebration." I stared out into the yard, deep between the trees. There was a sliver of yellow, like sunshine. The gilded grass would lead to faraway lands, I decided. Prettier than Duvall. Much prettier. I leaned against the door.

"Tammy Jo, do you remember being in love with me?"

I turned my head and studied Zach. "I remember," I said, but it felt like that had been lifetimes ago. "If you took off that amulet, I'd probably remember better."

Zach's palm covered the amulet. "I've become attached to this thing."

I shrugged. "You're too human for her anyway. She doesn't always see it, but it's true."

"For her?"

My brows crinkled. "For me. I'm her. I'm Tammy." I laughed softly and shook my head. "It's the strangest thing . . . like emotional amnesia. My head remembers, but the rest of me . . ." I shook my head.

"You said Lyons is part fae."

I smiled. "He's a little bit fae. One quarter. It's buried really deep."

"So he's more wizard than fae. A lot more. And fae hate wizards . . ." he pointed out.

"Yes, that's supposed to be true," I said.

"But you don't hate him? Not even when most of who you are has been drained away?"

"Oh no," I said. "It's like when I was little. One time we went shopping at the mall in Dallas. I saw the prettiest pair of pink patent leather shoes with gold roses studding the heels. I stood staring at those shoes until Momma dragged me away.

'I just bought you a pair of shoes and two pretty dresses,' she said. 'I'm sorry, honey, but we can't afford those.' 'Could we take the other ones back?' I asked. She frowned and said, 'We can't return the dresses. You need one for your birthday party. You've outgrown your old ones.' 'I'd rather have the pink rosebud shoes,' I told her. She shook her head and said it didn't make sense. She thought the stuff she'd bought was just as pretty and that three things were better than one. I didn't think so. It was so sad to leave the mall without the pink shoes.

"None of the gifts I got made up for it. From the moment I'd clapped eyes on those shoes, they were the one thing I wanted more than anything else." I shrugged. "Bryn is the grown-up version of those patent leather shoes."

Zach shoved his hands in the pockets of his jeans, looking like he'd swallowed a bug.

"Sorry," I said.

He shook his head. "Don't apologize. The truth goes down hard, but it makes things easier in the end."

"I'm going to take a walk. I won't go far."

His quick nod told me what he didn't say: At the moment, he'd be happy to be rid of me.

34

"WHAT'S HAPPENING?" BRYN asked me when he found me twirling circles in the woods.

"There's a faery path here," I said with a wide smile. I bent down and brushed a hand over a row of dandelions. Glowing golden, they tickled my skin when I touched them. It was the most amazing find ever. My gaze darted along. The dandelions stood in a line, like soldiers, marking the path. I wondered how I'd missed them before. My witch magic, no doubt, had been obscuring my faery senses. It was a real problem.

"See these?" I said, pointing.

"What? The broken weeds?"

"Broken?" I murmured, cocking my head. Did they look trampled to him? They had been a little limp as I'd approached but became perfect when I stepped onto the path. *Camouflaged*, I realized, since faery paths were kept hidden.

"Come stand here," I said, beckoning him. "Right next to me. It's a thin path that'll lead out of Duvall. A Seelie path that I don't think the Unseelie know about. I bet they couldn't find it with a magnifying glass and the greatest tracker they've got. Jerks." My brows drew together. Why did I dislike the Unseelie so much? Other than trying to kill me that one time when I blocked them from coming into Duvall, I'd never even met any of them besides Nixella. Still, they *were* the enemy. I knew that as surely as I knew that up was up, down was down, and chocolate was heaven.

"Come away from there," Bryn said, holding out his hand.

"Not yet. Have a look, Bryn. Can you see the trail? I see heather in the distance. I think the path leads all the way to the British Isles. You're from Ireland. You're one quarter fae. Squint your eyes."

"Tamara, come here. We have things to do, remember?"

"Yeah, but this is incredible. It feels like home!" I enthused, but even as I said the words, I knew they didn't really make sense. Duvall was home. Always had been. Hadn't it?

The path has a secret. It's the key to filling the emptiness inside me. You know something's missing.

For a blink, I saw myself. I had green eyes and gold hair. In the Never, I'd be transformed.

"I can catch up with the lych after," I said. "You should smell it. The air's so fresh here, like cars and factories were never invented. It's fantastic. C'mon, I want you to feel—"

"Tamara," he said sharply, making me turn my head. Bryn shoved the sleeve of his sweater up and showed me a dark circular mark on his forearm. The poisoned magic he'd taken from me had infected him. "We need to catch up to that lych sooner rather than later."

There was still a slight ache in my calf, but it didn't trouble me. "I feel fine."

"I don't."

I glanced longingly at the wisps of green and gold curling through the woods. But the pull of Bryn was stronger even than the path's. The bluest eyes, the blackest hair, the cleverest wit. Magic dusted him like powdered sugar. I sighed and stepped off the path. The lantern glow of the dandelions faded. The air's purity drained away so that it wasn't so achingly fresh. As it became regular old air again, I felt Bryn more clearly. A fair trade.

My toes dug into the dirt as I approached him. I put my

hands on his cool cheeks and pressed a kiss to his lips. He tasted of peppermint cocoa. My arms slid around his shoulders, and I licked magic from his lips.

It took him a moment to untangle my arms and draw back.

"For the love of St. Patrick—" he murmured, rubbing a thumb over his lips dazedly. "You taste like the ocean at night with a side of melted caramel."

I smiled at him and laced my fingers with his, holding his hand tight. "Did you bring me a bow and arrow?"

"Do I deny you anything you ask for?" he said ruefully.

I brought his hand up to my mouth and kissed it. "Let's go find us a lych and put him where he belongs. In the ground with the other skeletons."

"I've found spells that may help, but apparently lyches are almost impossible to kill."

"Well, then we'll be well matched because so am I almost impossible to kill."

"Overconfidence is dangerous in battle, Tamara."

"So is an iron arrow between the eyes." As we walked toward the house, I said, "I don't want Zach to come with us. That amulet of his gives me a headache."

"Is that what you told him?"

"No, why?"

"I don't know. He seems subdued."

"Oh, that. I think I hurt his feelings when I told him you were the shoes."

"I'm the shoes?" he asked, glancing at my bare feet.

I opened my mouth to explain, but I didn't have time because Zach walked out the back door with the file.

"Lyons, take a look at this photograph."

"Bryn, did you bring Mercutio?" I asked.

"He's asleep in the car."

"Good, let's go."

"Hang on," Bryn said, taking the picture from Zach.

"Does there seem to be a pattern to the way the gardenias are laid out around Edie's body?"

Bryn stared at the picture for a moment and then said,

"Yes, it's Taurus. The Pleiades, the seven sisters. They're sapphire blue stars, which are fairly near the earth."

"The constellation Taurus?" Zach asked.

Bryn nodded. "Yeah, I'm surprised you saw that."

Zach shrugged. "If he performed a killing ritual, it stands to reason that nothing would be random about the arrangement of the body."

"These flowers can be used in sex magic," Bryn said.

"Gardenias," I put in with a nod.

"He may be using carnal energy to boost his power enough to perform the transformative killing spell. A ritual to suck the life force from a dying body and to absorb it into one's self requires a massive amount of energy and concentration. It's probably why he's doing things in stages. The winter solstice is a good night to draw power from Taurus."

"The solstice, that's tonight?" Zach asked.

"That's tonight," Bryn confirmed.

I patted the air next to Zach's arm. "Thanks for the help. We'll take it from here," I said, snatching the file from him.

"I don't think so," Zach said. He grabbed the edge of the file and held on so I couldn't pull it away.

"Vangie's my friend. Edie's my aunt. Black splotchy poison's my disease. That makes Skeleton Guy mine, too. He wants to come to Duvall on safari? I'm just the one to show him the big game around here are armed."

Zach and Bryn both looked at me like they didn't recognize me. I gave them a sweet smile. "If you want to look at this file, Bryn, go ahead. I'll wait for you in the car. Remember what I said about that necklace not driving with us." I let go of the file and snagged the keys from Bryn's pocket.

"How long until Tammy Jo's back to normal?" Zach asked.

"Hard to say," Bryn said.

"How can you stand her like that?"

I glanced over my shoulder and raised my brows in question. Bryn exhaled, half-sighing, half-smiling.

"When she's at her best, so am I. When she's Bonnie, I'm Clyde."

Penetrating the emotional numbness, warmth spread through my chest, and I smiled at Bryn and winked.

Zach shook his head. "There's only one version of me. And there's only one version of her that I like."

"Maybe that's why he's the shoes and you're not," I called over my shoulder as I walked out the front door.

Mercutio woke when I climbed into Bryn's car. He yowled a complaint and hopped into the empty driver's seat.

"Sorry I woke you," I said.

Mercutio licked my arm and made a face. Like all the guys in my life, Merc didn't like me to turn fae. I couldn't see why. I gave his head a pat and updated him on the Freddie-Jackson connection.

Mercutio listened and meowed his understanding. It didn't take Bryn long to join us in the car. I rolled down the window and leaned back against the headrest. With the sun streaming through the windshield and the smell of the woods wafting in, I relaxed. It seemed like a good time to get a few minutes' sleep on our way to Dyson.

I spotted Zach's truck in the rearview mirror. "He's following us."

"I know."

Zach was far enough away that the amulet didn't bother me. And he might be a help later. "Okay," I said.

I closed my eyes and floated between consciousness and sleep. I felt Merc's soft fur against my arm, but I smelled rain, moist ground, and horses. I heard the *clomp, clomp* of horseshoes against a winding road. I sat in an open carriage, bouncing softly with craggy rocks and a smattering of grass on either side of me. Drizzle matted the heavy braid of my hair against my neck. I glanced at my hands on my lap. I didn't recognize them. My fingers were longer, the fingernails more rectangular than normal.

I jerked awake, startled.

Bryn glanced over with a questioning look.

Words popped into my mind and a sense of déjà vu. The winding road had been familiar, but wide awake now, I knew I'd never been there in my life.

"Where's the Gap of Dunloe?" I asked.

"The Gap of Dunloe is in County Kerry in Ireland. Killarney. Why?" Bryn asked.

I cocked my head and couldn't keep from yawning. Fatigue, heavy as molasses, weighed on me. "I dreamed about it. Could be that I'm going to visit there. My double-great-grandma was a seer. I've maybe got her gift. It seems like it's kicking in."

"Am I with you in the premonition?"

"Not that I've seen, but you must be somewhere nearby."

"Why do you say that?"

"Because if I were leaving the country, you're the first thing I'd pack."

He smiled. "I'd be happy to show you Ireland, sweetheart. But I'm not sure we'd agree on the places to visit."

"You mean you wouldn't want to walk any faery trails?"

"Exactly."

"Don't worry. I wasn't thinking it through earlier when I suggested we follow that Seelie path. It just felt so . . . familiar, like coming home. But that's crazy. Some sort of faery enchantment probably, to trick me into going there, which would be dangerous. And if I went, I wouldn't want you with me. I definitely don't want them to see you."

"Why not?"

"Edie and Aunt Mel are right. Faeries are possessive. If they figured out you're a little bit fae, they might use it as an excuse to try to keep you. That would be a problem."

"It would be," he agreed.

"Yes, because you're mine."

He laughed. "Tamara, they wouldn't want me for romantic reasons. They'd likely torture me for information on the World Association of Magic and then kill me."

I glanced over at him. "She wouldn't want to kill you."

"She who?"

"The woman who runs the place."

"The Seelie queen?"

I nodded. "Yeah, Ghislaine. I think you're just her type."

His brows shot up. "How do you know her name?"

That was a very good question. I tried to remember if I'd heard it sometime. Not that I recalled. "I guess I'm not sure that is her name, but I think it is."

Bryn frowned. "Has she entered your dreams? Has she spoken to you?"

"I don't think so, but I know what faeries are like. I think one day soon she's going to send guys to chase me halfway around the world. Crux might already be here for that exact reason. I don't trust him."

Bryn blew out a slow breath as he turned off the car. "We can't let the fae distract us. We have to concentrate on the problem at hand. We'll deal with the faery threat afterward."

"Okay," I said.

"Just like that, huh? You can put them out of your mind?"

"Sure," I said with a wave of my hand. "I've been mostly ignoring them for days."

I got my bow and arrows from the trunk and followed Bryn to the hotel room.

Bryn used a spell to open the door. A blast of something spewed out. It didn't hurt, but Bryn grabbed me and yanked me out of the doorway, and Mercutio hissed and darted away. I smelled sulfur, rotting flowers, and musty feathers. I coughed.

"More poison?"

I peeked into the empty room before Bryn dragged me back. Zach jogged up the stairs, covering his mouth and nose with his T-shirt. He went inside and came back out a few seconds later.

"Nothing useful left behind," Zach said, then made a gagging sound and spit on the ground.

"I'll have to try a scrying spell," Bryn said.

"No need. I think Mercutio knows the way," I said, nodding. Mercutio had returned to the car and was standing with his paws on the dash. Mercutio can track magic better than a bloodhound can track fallen game. And he's cuter.

"I'm starving. I'd give anything for some biscuits and honey right now. Or a chocolate cupcake." I put my bow in the trunk and added, "Or a box of chocolate truffles." I closed the trunk. "Or a stack of pecan pancakes drowning in maple syrup."

"I get the idea. If we pass the market, I'll buy you something sweet."

"I have a lot of good stuff at my house."

"Tamara, we don't have time. Remember that we're still going to try to save Vangie's life?"

"Sure, but when Vangie wakes up, I bet she'll be really hungry," I said, finding it hard to concentrate when I was desperate for a treat. I was still a bit off. No more tripping through the dandelions after getting a poison kiss from Zach's amulet. "Every time I wake from a coma, as soon as I'm over the nausea, the first thing I want is some cake."

Bryn shook his head, climbing into the driver's seat. I whispered to Mercutio that if he could see his way to navigating us past a bakery, I'd be forever grateful.

Mercutio meowed, but then the first thing he did was lead us to the highway out of town. When the exit for Duvall popped up, I licked my lips, but Mercutio didn't want us to get off. Instead he directed us onto the expressway.

"Where in the world are we going?" I demanded.

Mercutio didn't answer.

"Well, wherever it is," I said crossly, "I hope they have pastries."

BRYN'S MAGIC AND I guess my own witch magic seeped back into me on the drive because I felt more emotional and a little feverish by the time we stopped for gas. I bought a packaged brownie. It was full of disgusting preservatives that made me frown, but the rush of sugar did perk me up.

I leaned against the car, and Zach and I exchanged glances.

"Hey," I said.

"Hey, yourself," he said, swiping his credit card.

"Bryn thinks we might be headed to Evangeline's

apartment in Dallas. Since Edie's body was left in her apartment, maybe he finishes them off at home where there's a concentration of their magic."

Zach tipped his cowboy hat back an inch and nodded. "Makes sense." I caught him looking at my legs. I'd gotten rid of the torn sweatpants, so my dress covered my thighs but my calves were bare. The red wounds had scabbed over, but the dark circles had grown again to the size of silver dollars.

"These teeth marks might scar," I said, glancing down. Normally I healed so well my skin wasn't left with evidence of my misadventures.

"Something to remember the gator by. He's luckier than most," Zach said, filling his tank.

"Meaning?"

"Meaning there's a part of you that's obviously Tefloncoated. Maybe you were just killing time with me until you could afford a shinier pair of shoes."

I sighed. "You can't listen to her."

"To who?"

"To the faery girl. I think there's something kind of wrong with her. Hate to say it, but she's maybe a little bit of a sociopath." I chewed on my lip.

"She's a part of you," he pointed out.

"Yeah," I said with a huff of breath. "It's worrisome." I walked around the pumps to his truck and leaned against it. "The regular part of me loved you and always will. The faery girl part of me doesn't seem to know what love is."

"She likes Lyons well enough."

"Well, she likes pretty shiny things. He fits the bill. Plus, he doesn't wear an amulet that repels her."

"That amulet may have saved your life."

"It did. Thank you for that," I said softly.

"You're welcome."

"Bryn's okay, you know. I think he'd be your friend if you'd let him."

"Oh, darlin', that friendship's about as likely as the devil getting invited to a prayer revival."

"If you guys both tried—"

"Not going to happen. Lyons is too smart to forget we're rivals. He's okay with me coming along today for two reasons. First, because I'm wearing an amulet that worked against the undead wizard's magic. And second, because you chose him, and he wants to rub my nose in it so I don't forget."

I sighed, knowing Zach might be right. I rested my hand on Zach's forearm and kissed him on the cheek. "One day you're going to fall in love with someone else, and I'm going to hate her guts."

"Promise?" Zach asked with a smile.

"Yep." I walked around the pump to Bryn's sports car and climbed in.

Mercutio licked my hands and made a noise of satisfaction. "Yeah, Merc, it's me," I said, bending my head and touching my nose to his fur. "And I think we'd better get a move on. My leg's starting to ache again something fierce."

Bryn returned to the car with a cup of coffee for each of us. Mine was a mocha, and I licked the whipped cream off the top.

"Thanks," I said.

"Everything all right between you and Sutton?" he asked.

"Nope," I said, taking a swig. "That was a consolation kiss."

"So where's my real one?" he asked.

"The car has tinted windows. If I kiss you, he won't even know."

"I don't care if he knows or not."

I rolled my eyes but leaned toward him and brushed my lips over his.

"You call that a kiss?" he demanded.

"We're on a timetable, Bryn. I promise if we survive, I'll kiss you a whole bunch."

Bryn's hand slid behind my head and held me in place while he gave me a deep kiss that made our magic twist all through me. Afterward, I had to gasp to catch my breath.

"If we don't survive, I want the last real kiss you ever gave me to have been memorable."

"And longer than the one I gave Zach?"

"And longer than the one you gave Zach," he agreed.

I smiled. Bryn started the car, revved the engine, and zoomed us out of the parking lot. I rolled my eyes, swigged my mocha, and watched Zach and the gas station disappear from the rearview mirror.

Bryn's phone buzzed in his pocket. "That's probably Zach, wanting to know what's up," I said, reaching into Bryn's pocket.

But the text wasn't from Zach. It was from Rollie.

SOB undead wizard in Dallas commands the dead. Call so strong am leaving home without tweezing brows. Help! RIGHT THIS MINUTE!

"Holy smokes," I said.

"What?"

"Rollie's in trouble."

"Rollie?"

"How many vampires are there in Dallas, Bryn?"

"I don't know. I'd guess forty or fifty."

"Oh, boy," I said.

"What?"

"We've got a new problem. I think the lych wants protection. He's drafted a vampire army."

35

AS WE APPROACHED the exit for Vangie's building, my jangled nerves had me squirming in my seat. Bryn pulled off the road so I could take over driving and he could check in with witches and wizards in Dallas. Most of them weren't friends with Vangie, but they did respect Bryn and pledged their help.

Bryn texted Vangie's address to Zach and included a warning about the text from Rollie, but when we reached the turnoff to Vangie's place, Mercutio put a paw on the wheel to keep me from turning. He batted the dash.

"Wait, where are we going?" I asked him, not leaving the expressway.

"Farther west," Bryn said, watching the signs. "Maybe to her father's house." And sure enough we exited on a road that drove out into the country where there was only an occasional huge house.

Bryn sent texts updating everyone just as a winter storm rolled in. I shuddered. I'd hate being out in a downpour. Probably suffering from post-traumatic-magical-storm-floods-Duvall syndrome.

Streaks of lightning filled the sky. I jerked at the thunder. "Not again," I grumbled. Bryn looked tense, too.

I drove partway up the dirt road leading to the ranch and pulled over. In the distance, we watched figures milling about outside Vangie's family mansion.

"Those vampires aren't nearly as graceful as Rollie."

"That's because those aren't vampires," Bryn said.

"What? What are they?" I asked.

"Zombies."

"No!" I yelled. "Not zombies! Zombies are almost unstoppable, and I didn't bring any passion flower potion with me."

"Passion flower potion?"

"It's what I used to put Mrs. Barnaby back in the ground."

"Mrs. Barnaby was raised using your blood. These zombies weren't."

"Meaning what?"

"Meaning no potion you made would put them back in the ground. To put the zombies down, the master must be defeated."

"I—well, how could Skeleton Guy raise them using his own blood? He's all bones and squishy Jell-O flesh. He doesn't bleed. I doubt there's been any fresh blood in him for a long time."

"I don't know."

"We've got arrows and bullets, but they won't work that well against zombies. What we really need is a flame-thrower." I licked my lips. "You didn't happen to bring one, did you?"

Bryn gave me a look and ran a hand through his hair.

"So, um, what's the plan?" I asked, peering out the windshield at the loping zombies. I didn't let their shuffling fool me. Behind the blank expressions was a gonna-tear-you-to-pieces attitude that was really irritating.

"I suppose, as usual, we'll have to improvise."

I took a deep breath and blew it out. "All right."

"We can mow them down," he said, but I started the car

and drove it off the road, scraping the expensive undercarriage on the tall grass.

"What are you doing?"

"I'm driving us to the barn."

"Why?"

"Because any Texas barn worth its salt will have things we need. Like axes for chopping up wood . . . or zombies. And cans of gas."

Bryn grimaced. "Let's try really hard not to light anyone we care about on fire, including ourselves."

"I like the plan so far."

IN THE BARN, we worked quickly. I collected rope, small jars used for canning, gasoline, and two axes. I put gas in the jars and used bits of unraveled rope as wicks.

A group of sea sparrows swooped in. Freddie Greer's legacy?

"What are you doing? Get out of here!" I said, shooing them even as the zombies watched their flight path. "Go on!" But it was too late. The zombies headed straight for us.

"Damn birds. How'd you like to be extinct for real?" I yelled, looking up. In an instant, I realized that when Edie had tried to warn me about the lych, she'd looked up, too. When she'd said she remembered them from the night she died, she meant the birds. She'd seen the sparrows.

The zombies cut us off on our way to the car, and we had to hack at them with axes. Just as we got overwhelmed, Zach's truck barreled in and ran over several of them.

Cracked bones slowed them down but didn't destroy them. They crawled toward us, dragging their rotting bodies.

"Gross!"

I lit the wick on a jar and flung it at a pair of half-broken zombies. They exploded into flames that blazed ten feet tall.

"Ashes to ashes, dust to dust. You'll thank me later!"

The birds circled, like an avian beacon. The lead bird's glowing green eyes gave me pause. Clearly supernatural.

I raced over to the car, got my bow, nocked an arrow, and shot it. It skewered the bird, which fell from the sky.

"Whoa," Bryn said, putting out a hand. "I felt the lych's power lessen when you shot the bird. What made you do that?"

"They're troublemakers. I thought they might be his eyes out here."

More zombies lumbered toward us as the sparrows scattered and dive-bombed the ground, the zombies, and us. The attacking birds seemed excited about the potential feast. I swung my bow, knocking them away from me.

I hurried to the downed bird. I didn't have a lot of arrows and needed to reuse them. When I reached it, a couple of wisps of breathlike mist rose from the bird. A green orb formed and my jaw dropped. The glow took on an Edie shape and then she appeared.

"There you are! I was so worried about you," I said. "But what were you doing leading zombies to us?"

"I couldn't control myself. That bastard has so much power! Stolen power, I might add."

The sound of flesh thumping flesh made me spin to the right. Zach and Bryn fought the zombies, throttling and hacking them up while trying to avoid coming within reach of their bone-crushing grips. Zach spotted some downed branches. He cut them into three-foot clubs, doused them with gas, and lit them. He rushed back to Bryn and handed him one. Flaming torches were a better weapon than axes. I rushed over to grab a branch, so I could help before rain put them out. There'd been only a few drops so far, but I expected a shower any minute.

"Tammy Jo, wait. Don't waste time with the zombies. Come this way. Bring that rope. You have to get to the second floor."

"Why?" I asked, running after Edie as she floated toward the house.

"I know him! I recognized the birds, but he's become so powerful. He was obsessed with birds, especially the sparrows that were going extinct. He was determined to preserve them. That fixation with a dying breed came from the fear of his own mortality. Freddie had hemophilia, like the Romanovs. He'd even consulted Rasputin, looking for a cure. In the end, he took a skeletal form as his salvation. He killed me to do it."

I jerked toward her, nearly tripping on uneven ground.

"I was so drunk after the party. He knocked on the door. It was strange for him to drive into the city so late at night, but I let him in. Then I passed out. And never woke again. He stole my life."

A zombie lurched out from the corner of the house. I dropped to the ground and rolled to avoid getting grabbed. They're strong, but not as fast as faeries or vampires. I jabbed it in the neck and knocked it down. The rotting smell stunk to high heaven, and I had to resist the urge to pinch my nose.

Zach sprinted over and swung the axe. The zombie's severed head fell off its shoulders, and he set the pieces ablaze with his torch. Bryn sent a flash of magical fire to burn others that stalked toward us.

"Edie, you all right?" Zach asked. It began to drizzle.

"For the moment," she said. Another zombie surge made Zach turn away. "Tammy, come on. Freddie's got vampires on the main floor guarding the stairs. You'll have to climb."

"Climb?" I murmured, following her to the house.

"He's up there," she said. "In the library. It's full of power. There's very little time left. If he gets Evangeline's soul and her magical legacy, you won't be able to stop him."

"I might need Bryn's help to defeat that lych. Normal weapons can't defeat them. Not having flesh and blood makes them invulnerable and immortal. Bryn's got a spell to draw the celestial magic away to weaken him."

"It won't work. Freddie's real power is from death magic now."

I knew it!

"The candylegger won't be able to pull it away. It's woven into his bones. This way," Edie said. "Hurry. I need you to distract him."

A group of vampires spilled from the house. "Wait!" Rollie yelled, tackling a thin young vampire whose fangs were bared. A blond vampire with high cheekbones and sleepy eyes barreled toward me. Others rushed at Zach and Bryn.

I raised my bow.

"Don't hurt them!" Rollie yelled at us. Bryn leveled spells that knocked over some of the vamps like bowling pins, but I felt a waning of Bryn's energy. Fighting with magic expels so much of it.

The blond vampire's long legs ate up the ground.

"You have to shoot him," Edie said.

The boy's glazed eyes were as blank as a zombie's. I hesitated, lowering the bow a fraction of an inch. "I don't think he knows what he's doing."

"A lot of good that'll do you when he rips out your throat," Edie said.

"Stop!" I yelled at the blond vamp. "I don't want to have to shoot you."

He didn't slow. I took a deep breath and shot him in the leg. He screeched with fury, and Rollie, who was trying to subdue some of the other vampires, clucked his tongue at me.

"Sorry, Rollie!" I hollered. "He was going to kill me." I tied the rope onto the end of an arrow and shot it into the second-story windowsill.

I pulled on the rope to be sure that the arrow and rope were secure. "I hope this holds," I mumbled, going hand over hand up the rope while walking up the wall. The sill creaked. I clenched my teeth. "If I fall, I'm going to break my neck," I said.

"Then hurry up," Edie encouraged.

My foot slipped and I swung into the brick, scraping my arm. "Ow!"

I struggled to get my feet back against the wall. My palms sweated, and I slipped down a few inches, burning my hands. I gripped the rope hard, glancing down. The ground was about twenty feet below me. I inhaled and held my breath, looping the rope around my wrists to keep from slipping farther.

The looped rope strangled my hands and slowed my progress but steadied me. Rain blurred my eyes.

"Come on!" Edie said.

"I'm not Batman. Or Spider-Man . . . or Mercutio." I blew hair out of my eyes, frowning. "I was never the best climber. Just ask my high school gym teacher."

"You're doing great," Edie said. "You're almost there. Pull yourself up. You can do it!" She vibrated with excitement and encouragement.

My arms shook, but I gave Edie a lopsided smile. I never thought I'd see the day when she'd do the perky cheerleader routine. It was sweet of her.

I finally reached the top and dragged myself up. My arms wobbled, and I thought I might lose my grip on the slippery sill. I tightened my muscles and clenched my teeth, determined not to fall. If I wanted to climb ropes in the future, I'd need to add some chin-ups to my fitness routine. I'd also need to add a fitness routine.

I put one knee on the arrow and one on the sill, balancing precariously. I hooked the bow over my shoulder with the quiver of arrows. My damp fingers tried to burrow under the window frame to lift it, but it turns out the outsides of windows don't have any handles.

"I can't get a grip."

"Tammy, the window's locked."

"Locked?" I snapped, grabbing the frame to steady myself. "Then how am I—?"

"Break the glass. Hurry! He could see you any minute and one blast of magic will knock you off the ledge."

"Swinging my bow will also knock me off the ledge!"

"Tammy Jo, please! There's no time."

"I think there's a reason successful people make plans," I mumbled, getting my bow free. "Improvising is dangerous." To break the glass would take a hard swing and if the window didn't break so that I could fall into the room, I wasn't sure I could keep my balance. My heart thumped and my lips tingled. I wished I'd had my feet in the dirt to give myself a power boost.

C'mon, Earth, help break this glass.
I need some power to save my ass.

I swung the bow and as it connected, I felt a blast of Bryn's magic. The glass exploded into the room and I plunged forward.

I landed on the floor and tiny shards of glass cut into my skin in at least a dozen places.

I rolled and sprang to my feet, raising the bow. Jackson Greer leaned over Evangeline's body. As soon as he saw me, he brought his arms into an *X* across his chest and literally faded before my eyes into the lych.

What?

I froze for a moment and then let an arrow go. It whizzed through him, splattering some goo on the wall. The lych lurched forward and slammed into me. I flew backward and hit the wall. The bow dropped and so did I. He landed in front of me and I rolled away between his legs and darted forward. I grabbed the bow and swung it. It knocked against his bony legs. The translucent part of him melted away to leave only bones. He clattered against the floor like a giant white cockroach and then rose. I swung at him, but he knocked the bow from my hands.

"Breathe, Evangeline!" Edie yelled.

The lych spun around and waved a hand and then closed his fleshless fingers in a fist. Edie grabbed her throat as if he were choking her.

I clambered to my feet and barreled into him. We both fell forward into the wall. I turned. Free of his death grip, Edie rose to the ceiling.

"Go, Edie. Go back to the locket where you'll be safe."

"I won't leave you alone with him."

The skeleton hands closed around my throat in a crushing grip. I grabbed the bones and pried at them.

"No!" Edie screamed. She moved into the empty cage of the lych's skeleton and stretched along his bones.

The hands released me and reached inside the lych's rib cage for her soul. I wheezed out a breath and rolled to

Evangeline. I flung myself on her body and scattered the gardenia petals and feathers away from her.

The lych spun toward us and breath roared from him. Magic blistered my skin and he squashed Edie's essence.

A coppery mist rose from Vangie's body, and her spirit materialized next to her body.

"Oh, no! No, Vangie! Get back in your body."

The lych flung me against the wall. I slammed into it so hard the plaster crumpled. Pain roared through me and my vision blurred.

A moment later, the young human form of Jackson Greer reappeared. Edie glared at him.

"Please," I whispered. "Please, Edie, go back to the locket." She faded slightly but didn't disappear.

Jackson Greer stared at her. "Hello, Edith. I always knew I'd find you again. A killer never forgets his first."

"You bastard."

He raised his hands as if he could take her by the arms. She recoiled, floating away from him. "It's been so long. At first, I wasn't sure the magic I sensed was yours. I followed it and waited. You weren't at the house, but I spotted you eventually. How did you get out of your sparrow?"

"You couldn't hold me. You're pathetic," Edie said, then turned to Vangie.

"Pathetic?" he yelled. "I'm immortal."

"Thanks to me. Thanks to power you've stolen rather than earned."

"I wrote a spell capable of things that have never been done before or since. It could have gone wrong and killed me along with my victim. I'm a master wizard, one of the greatest who's ever lived. I committed the perfect crime. Over and over! The police never came close to catching me, nor the witch covens anywhere I've been. I created a form that didn't exist before my spell. A shape-shifting lych! It's a spell-casting triumph."

"Congratulations. You're a freak and a parasite," Edie said dismissively. I swear she could rub the shine off an Olympic gold medal. For once, it was satisfying to see her do it.

Jackson, who'd probably been waiting years to brag to someone, reddened like a boiled lobster.

"Evangeline, let's go." Edie stretched out a hand, but Vangie's ghost turned dazedly toward Jackson, who walked stiffly away from them and bent to rearrange the flower petals into a star chart on Vangie's body. "I have to finish this, Edith, but don't think I'll forget about you after this is done. 'A locket,' your niece said. It won't be hard to find. I always suspected Lenore had used an object to tether your soul to her. Back then, I didn't dare get close; she had the sight. I had to conceal myself around her. I'm more powerful now. None of the witches in your family stands a chance."

"Vangie, he's trying to get your soul," I murmured, staggering to my feet. "You have to get back in your body. And, Edie, you have to warn Aunt Mel about him. Go now!"

"You never loved me," Vangie screeched. "You tricked me. Liar!" she yelled. "You killed me!"

"Go back to your body, Vangie," I cried. "You can still survive," I said, stumbling toward her body. I shoved Jackson away and pumped on her chest and blew breath into her mouth. "Don't die."

Greer's eyes were as hard as glass beads. "Beautiful and strong. You taste of McKenna magic, too." He leaned forward and a cold fishy tongue licked my cheek. I jerked back and punched him right in the face. Blood squirted from his nose.

He backhanded me, but I launched forward and knocked him to the ground. We rolled over and over, and he took the lych form again. He was unbelievably powerful as Skeleton Guy. He slammed a bony fist into me and pain exploded in my chest. I couldn't breathe, couldn't move.

He changed again and returned to Vangie's body.

Get out, I mouthed. "Go to the locket with Edie," I whispered.

Vangie's spirit was pale with shock, but she kept circling Greer, accusing him of betraying her.

"You have to go. He'll trap your soul and destroy it," I said, holding my ribs, trying to catch my breath. A black haze settled on the room as he rearranged the petals, and sparrows flew in on an icy wind. They tweeted, cheerfully sinister.

I realized that he had to be in human visage to complete the ritual, otherwise why would he keep changing back to his human form? The lych form was much more powerful. Once Vangie's soul had been taken, he could stay a lych and kill me, too.

Greer began to cast a spell over Vangie's body.

"Tammy, stop him," Edie said, her essence incredibly faint.

I rolled onto my side, the pain like a lance through my chest. Jackson turned and grabbed my quiver of arrows and yanked it from my grasp. Blood still gushed from his nose, and he tried to stem the flow with one hand while he kicked me in the ribs.

"Stay still!" he screamed. "You unworthy quiff. You're all whores. Sucking the magic from the earth."

I felt another rib crack and my insides bruise. I reared up and hit him in the gut with my fists. He doubled over and roared.

"I'll haunt you the rest of your life!" Vangie screamed at Jackson. "I'll never let you rest."

"If you stay here, he'll trap you," Edie said, trying to catch Vangie's phantom hand to entice her to leave.

I rose to my feet, coughing. Blood splattered from my lips and I realized I was bleeding inside. I swayed from the pain and the fear.

"He needs her body for the final draining," Edie said, her voice barely a whisper in my head. "We must not let him have it."

Jackson turned into the lych. I staggered back, watching Edie's green orb drift toward Vangie's body.

The lych had lost some of its quickness, but his hands were still strong. They choked me, squeezing my neck until the world spun, blackening.

Vangie's body rose behind him, ashen as a corpse. The eyes held a glint of life, and a hint of green glowed from

Vangie's sockets. Edie! Edie, who barely had any energy left, had animated Vangie's body to help me!

The body fell forward, its entire weight landing on the skeleton. Startled, he released me as he fell to the side.

He righted himself and grabbed Vangie's body, dragging it over his shoulder and slamming her head against the floor.

I tried to roll away, but he caught me and struck me in the face. I lost consciousness.

When I woke, the pain in my chest and belly was unbearable. He'd stabbed me and left the knife buried to the hilt. My mouth worked, but no sound emerged.

Jackson Greer's battered face hovered above mine. He whispered over my mouth, and I felt my soul being ripped out.

My vision wobbled, and I saw the green hills of Ireland. I raced along a path on the back of a horse. My hair was encased in vines and cascading behind me. I smelled rain and moss.

My fae hands came down on the dagger's handle. The blade was lodged right under the tip of my breastbone. He'd killed me.

At his command, the witch part of my magic ripped away. In the distance, Bryn fell to the ground, his magic being drawn into Jackson with mine.

No!

Despair swallowed me.

Greer howled in delight.

I felt Bryn's stolen breath rush in through the window on a wave of cool celestial energy. I sucked in a wisp, but Greer dragged away the rest. Tears sprung to my eyes. I'd let Greer kill me and kill Bryn, too, by default, robbing the world of Bryn's brilliance and all that he was and could be.

Bryn reached out for me. For a moment I saw his face as clear as the room around me. A cold fury at the thought of him dying balled in the pit of my stomach.

No, I thought. *I won't give him over to a murdering parasite.*

Help me, I called in my mind. I saw myself on horseback. Hazel green eyes stared directly at me.

Stab him, the me on horseback said. *Kill him*. My voice held a note of Ireland, a bit of Bryn.

I closed fists around the dagger hilt, locking eyes with Jackson Greer. I think he saw that a piece of me remained, a fae piece that couldn't be ripped out by wizard's magic. His eyes widened.

He should've fled. I wasn't strong enough to chase him. But he stayed and spit out a spell, his nose dripping blood in an endless faucet. He'd tasted my fae magic and wanted to consume that, too.

Frail, diseased human, I thought in disgust. *Like so many of your kind, you're a greedy fool.*

In his lust to stay young and alive forever, he grasped for more, for faery blood. He should've been satisfied with what he'd already taken.

You should've run, I mouthed.

He didn't see my hands.

I dragged the blade from my body, and my arm struck, lightning quick.

Words died on his lips, his mouth falling open in shock. He struggled to speak, to finish the spell, but I'd scored him too deep. I'd cut right through his windpipe. Air rushed out through his neck, spraying blood everywhere.

He grabbed his throat, his lips moving wordlessly. He wanted to call the lych, but he couldn't change without the spell being spoken. The form that helped him heal and kept him invulnerable was out of his reach now.

Bryn's magic brushed over me and gusted out the window and back to his body. I felt the pulse of our connection in the ring on my right hand. Bryn drew in a deep breath, awake and alive, though perhaps not for long.

I slumped back, breathless. When I'd pulled the dagger from my body, I left a large hole in a big vein in the back of my body. The severed vessel poured blood. I shivered, dying, but I felt magic emerging from dozens of places at once, from Greer's bones, from his birds.

I smiled and licked my own blood from my lips, tasting specks of iron. "I kill you, Frederick Jackson Greer. And with your death, I release the souls of your victims, including my aunt's. Edie is avenged."

I stared at the ceiling, watching the color drain from the circling birds. I heard Jackson's body fall, and the birds fell to the floor dead, too. The spirits that had been trapped in the sparrows misted the room, the faces of beautiful young girls emerging in a swirl.

My heart slowed, and I heard Edie crying. "No," she sobbed. "Don't you dare die. Tammy, don't you leave me."

The room spun, and bright lights danced before my eyes. Pain faded, and my body shuddered. Lighter than air and shimmering, I could go anywhere. In an instant, I could travel the world at the speed of sound. I heard distant drums.

In the next moment, I was sucked down into blackness, a hard thump rattling my soul. And then another and another. My heart, I realized. It beat stubbornly in my broken chest.

I fell to my side and curled into a ball, pinching that bleeding vein deep in my body. I felt dizzy, so very dizzy, like most of my blood had already drained away. Time ticked by as I faded in and out of consciousness.

The next thing I saw was Bryn's face near mine, whispering frantically. He forced magic into my body. Pain screamed through me, but I breathed and twitched.

"Not iron," I rasped. "The blade . . . not iron."

I closed my eyes, Bryn's plea for me to stay with him ringing in my ears.

I'll try.

36

I WOKE IN Bryn's bed. I thought maybe I was dreaming, but I moved and felt a stiff pain in my chest. I ran a finger over it, feeling scabs. A silk and velvet coverlet lay over me with a dozen smooth stones arranged in a constellation on my torso.

"I'm alive?" I turned my head. Mercutio lay on one side of me, Bryn on the other.

"Yes," Bryn said, tracing a finger lightly over my cheek. "How do you feel?"

"I hurt," I said. "But I'm okay." I struggled to sit up, the pain making my breath catch but not bad enough to knock me back down. "How long was I asleep?"

"Days," he said, sitting up, too.

I rubbed my breastbone. "Getting stabbed to death hurts," I complained, feeling dizzy as I stumbled to my feet.

Bryn shot from the bed to my side and steadied me with a hand.

"I'm hungry," I murmured.

"I'll bring you up some food."

"Something good. Something sweet," I said, shuffling

into the bathroom. I had to pause to catch my breath. "I'm not all the way healed."

"I don't imagine you are," Bryn said, watching me.

"I'll just take a shower for a minute," I said, the stale smell of blood and death in my nose. Bryn had washed off a lot of the ordeal, but not all of it.

"I'll help you," he said.

"I'm okay," I said. "You can help me by getting me toast and jam," I said. "And a cookie. I'd do anything for a cookie." It took me a few minutes to get undressed.

"Watch her, Mercutio," Bryn said. "Don't let her fall."

Mercutio marched into the shower with me. "You don't like water," I reminded him as I turned on the hot water. Merc yowled but stood guard at my feet.

I lathered my hair and skin until I smelled spicy and good, like Bryn's shampoo and soap. I wrapped myself in a robe and sat in the slipper chair in the corner of the room, admiring the bouquets of flowers lined up on the dresser. I couldn't have had more if I'd actually died.

Bryn returned with a tray. Biscuits with butter and half an inch of raspberry jam on each. A stack of warm chocolate chip cookies. A glass of milk and a cup of cream tea. I ate and drank every bit.

Pretty much as soon as I finished, I felt a ton better. "We won," I said with a smile. "Again."

He nodded, watching me.

"How about Edie and Vangie? Are they ghosts?" I'd seen that bright light. I'd felt the souls of the slain girls going into it.

"Evangeline's alive, but she's in a coma. No one's seen Edie."

I tucked a strand of hair behind my ear. "Edie seemed too weak to make it back to the locket to regain her strength. I think she crossed over to the afterlife." My voice broke, but I cleared it. "Which means she's okay. She's finally been set free." Tears stung my eyes. "I set all his victims free so they can rest in peace." I bit my lip hard. "I'll miss Edie. I know she was already dead, but she was alive to me. And with me my whole life," I whispered, a tear spilling over my lashes.

Bryn nodded. "I know you'll miss her. But you saved Evangeline's life and rescued the souls of the other girls. At least a half dozen of them."

"That's good, then," I said, swallowing hard.

"It's Christmas," Bryn said.

I wiped a tear from my cheek. "Oh no," I gasped. "I didn't have a chance to get people's presents."

Bryn laughed.

I rubbed the moisture from my face. "I've got to stop leaving my shopping till the last minute. I never know when I'll end up in a coma and miss all the last shopping days! Georgia Sue's going to be so mad. You can bet she's got my present all wrapped and ready. What in the world will I tell her?"

"I took care of it."

"You took care—what did you do?"

"I gave her and Kenny a present from both of us."

I smiled. "From both of us," I said. "Now the whole town's gonna be gossiping about how we're officially a couple." I licked my lips. "But it was sure sweet of you. What did we give them?"

"Plane tickets."

"Plane tickets!" I said with a gasp.

"A vacation to the Caribbean. She mentioned once that they never had a real honeymoon."

"Bryn! You can't do that. I have to be able to pay you back. I can't afford to give people honeymoon vacations for presents."

He shrugged. "When she realized you were so sick, she came every day, bringing casseroles and flowers. She told me stories about all the hard knocks you'd taken as a kid and how you'd recovered without a mark. She told me to try not to worry and talked so much that it was a distraction."

"Georgia Sue's tuna casserole," I said with a laugh. "I'm so sorry."

"She's not much of a cook," Bryn agreed. "But she and I have got a lot in common."

"You and Georgia Sue?" I asked surprised.

"We're both crazy about you. We both think I'm the right man for you."

"So that's how she won you over," I said with a smile and a shake of my head.

Bryn went down on one knee in front of me. "I'm glad you're awake. I need you to do something for me."

"Bake you a thousand cakes? Because that's probably how many it'll take to cover the cost of a beach vacation for two people."

"Tamara," he said, cutting me off.

I blinked.

"I love you," he said.

"Well, I love you, too, but that doesn't give either of us the right to go on a spending spree like there's no tomorrow just because one of us destroys a wizard serial killer and ends up in a coma. If you give people vacations every time I go into a coma, Duvall will be half empty."

Bryn smiled. "I want something."

"Uh-huh. What's that?" I asked, studying his face. His cobalt blue eyes stared into mine.

"I want something more than I've ever wanted anything."

My brows rose. "Be careful what you wish for. You wanted to bind us together, and that's very likely gonna get you killed before you turn thirty. Almost did a couple of days ago."

"I don't care how long I live," he said.

"What kind of thing is that to say!" I snapped, glancing at the ceiling. "He didn't mean that, God—universe . . . God and the universe."

"I need you to marry me. Whether I live for fifty more years or only fifty more hours, I want to do it married to you."

A thrill shot through me, my excitement a runaway train for several seconds. *Hold on!* I chided myself, forcing the pleasure of knowing he wanted to marry me aside.

I cleared my throat, remembering how I'd felt when he fell. The pain of knowing my death could kill him had been one of the worst moments of my life. If I loved him, which

I did, shouldn't I try my best to keep him safe? Even if that meant keeping some distance between us?

"I love you so much," I said.

"Good. Say yes."

"But listen, of the two of us, I'm supposed to be the impulsive one. You're supposed to be the one who thinks things over carefully and logically, who doesn't rush into stuff. I'm liable to get you killed. Is that really a quality a man should look for in a wife?" I asked. "I think there's probably a way for you to unbind us if you wanted to, Bryn. Some brilliant, complicated spell that only you could write? C'mon. Tell me the truth."

"No."

"No, you won't tell me the truth?"

"Will you marry me?"

"I'm dangerous for you. I know it. When the witch part of me died, it killed you, too. If Greer had been out of my reach, if he'd lived, you'd have stayed dead. It was this close," I said, making a tiny space between my thumb and forefinger. "You being bound to me, it's not safe."

"I don't want safe."

"Can you undo the oath that binds us?"

He hesitated and then said, "Maybe."

"Will you try?"

He shook his head. "Tamara," he whispered.

"Yes?"

He entwined the fingers of his left hand with the fingers of my right. Our bands clinked, sparking magic. "The bond saved my life once. I accept the consequences if it one day ends it. Especially since it allows you to draw power from me when you need it."

I squeezed his hand. "It slowed down my death, so I had time to heal?"

He nodded. "Let's stop talking about the magical bond." He ran a hand absently through his hair. "I'm not just a wizard bound to a witch. I'm a man in love with a woman."

I became very still, holding my breath. Tears burned my eyes.

"I'm not happy unless you're with me."

I shook my head. "You could have had any girl in the world, and you go and pick the one who's probably going to get you killed. I'm just like one of those black widow spiders. You must be out of your mind."

He waited, gorgeous and determined. And I already loved him too much. The thought of losing him, of not seeing him as much as I wanted to, created a hollow in my throat that stretched clear down to my belly. What good would it do to wait? A part of me knew that I would never willingly give him up.

Are you sure, Bryn? I thought, searching his face. I saw the truth there. He was sure. Deep in my heart, so was I.

"Oh, Bryn," I said. "I'm afraid I have to say yes."

He blinked. "Yes? You'll marry me?"

I nodded with a shrug. "I already told you, you're mine. We might as well make it official."

He grinned. "I am yours. I freely admit that. I'd appreciate it if you'd acknowledge that you're mine, too."

"I said I'd marry you. The rest is implied."

He arched a brow that said he wasn't satisfied by that answer, but he didn't argue about it right then. Bryn's a lawyer, so he can save up arguments and spring them on a person any old time. It's a problem.

He kissed the fourth finger on my left hand and slid a ring on it. The stone was sunshine yellow.

"It's a diamond?" I asked.

"Canary yellow," he said with a nod.

It stretched from one knuckle almost to the other, sparkling like a shooting star. "Expensive, huh?"

"Try not to lose it," he said, giving me a kiss. Then he turned my hand over and a gold chain poured into my palm. "The necklace is for when you're cooking. You can hang the ring around your neck."

I closed my fingers around the chain and turned my hand over to look at the big diamond.

"How much did it cost? Ten thousand dollars?" I asked, looking up at him.

He smiled, and I knew it cost a lot more. "Twenty?" I asked nervously.

"Hello, darling," a familiar voice said from the doorway. Bryn and I both turned. I expected to see Edie's ghost, but Evangeline leaned against the door frame.

She held her head high as her gaze traveled lazily around the room.

My jaw dropped. *Oh my God.*

"You're awake," Bryn said, standing.

"So it seems," she said, her voice dry as a gin martini. The woman in the doorway was definitely not the shy, slightly unbalanced Vangie. The woman in the doorway had confidence in spades and grace to match. She could've balanced in stilettos on the head of a pin.

"It's great to see you on your feet," Bryn said. "I brought you here to recover because I know you don't trust your stepmother and stepbrother. I hope that's all right with you."

"Sure," she said. "Have I interrupted something?"

"Actually," Bryn said with a smile. "We just got engaged."

She strolled in, bold as brass, and lifted my hand. "Very nice. Ninety thousand?"

Bryn nodded.

"Oh my God!" I said, snatching my hand back to look at the ring, feeling dizzy.

"Congratulations," Edie said to Bryn. "You don't deserve her."

I shot her a look, and Bryn raised his brows. "And here I thought you had a crush on me."

Vangie's head tilted slightly. The wide-eyed look was a bit like Vangie's, but the smile was pure Edie. I swallowed.

"I need a little fresh air. Is it okay if I borrow your car?" she asked.

"Sure," Bryn said. "The keys are downstairs."

To me, she said, "See you later, darling girl."

I stared after her for a long moment. How sure was I that it was Edie in Vangie's body? *Very* sure.

To Bryn, I said, "I believe she just stole your sports car."

He chuckled. "I don't think so. She buys Bentleys. They're enormous. I don't think she's in the market for a two-seater."

I wondered if Edie had ever even had a driver's license. Cars were new in her lifetime. She'd been from a wealthy family, so they might've had a car, but her father had been old-fashioned. I suspected that she'd been picked up and driven wherever she went.

"That car's pretty zippy. I hope she doesn't crash," I mumbled.

Bryn gave me a questioning look.

"I'm not sure that was actually Vangie anymore." I took a deep breath and then explained that Edie had been in Vangie's body when I killed Greer and apparently she still was.

What had happened to Vangie? Was she a ghost? Or had she crossed over? Bryn and I had no idea.

The giant diamond caught the light and sparkled bright as a camera flash. *For the love of Hershey!*

I slid it off and held it out to him. "That's the prettiest ring I ever saw, but you got carried away. I'll never be able to wash a dish without having an anxiety attack about dropping it down the drain. Can you trade it in for something smaller?" I asked.

"You like the yellow color? Rather than white?"

"I do," I said, looking at it. "It's all golden and sunny." I touched my fingernail to the faceted edge. "I like this rectangle solitaire style. It's real elegant."

Bryn slid the ring back on my finger.

"But it's too expensive. People are going to think I'm a gold digger. Plus, think about all the rolling around in the dirt I have to do. And the baking. I work with my hands. This kind of ring belongs on a princess or someone like that. Somebody who isn't so rough-and-tumble."

"As soon as I saw that ring, I knew it was the one I wanted to give you. Just like the first time you kissed me, I knew you were the woman I wanted to marry."

"Aw!" I said, and gave him a quick kiss. "But you being

romantic and sweet isn't going to distract me. I can't walk around wearing a ring that costs as much as a house! Besides, if I kept it, you'd get the wrong idea. I wear Levi's and cowboy boots. Half the time, I go barefoot. I'm not fixing to let you dress me up like a Barbie doll in designer clothes once we're married."

"You don't have to wear designer clothes if you don't want to," Bryn said, pulling me close to him for another kiss. "But you would look beautiful in couture dresses."

I thought of the drawer full of fancy lingerie and knew we were going to have a lot of fights about money. I frowned. "And another thing," I blurted out. "I want a prenuptial agreement."

Bryn just laughed.

I HAD ONLY two dresses left in the closet at Bryn's. I stared at the rows of his designer suits, his silk ties and Italian shoes. There was a small desk inside the walk-in closet, and I leaned on it, my palms pressing down on the wood.

"We'll move that desk to the room down the hall," Bryn said. "That way we can fit another dresser in here."

I touched a finger to the brushed silver frame of the mirror above the desk. The magic mirror is where I'd first met his friend Andre, another wizard. I supposed we couldn't have that kind of mirror in the closet if I was going there to get my clothes when I wasn't dressed.

Bryn leaned against the doorway, wearing a black bathrobe. He was as handsome as ever, and his smile was sweet and sated. We'd had slow, delicious sex, and the magic that had passed between us helped my healing. There would definitely be advantages to living with Bryn, but I did feel a little worried about how fast it was all moving.

"I never thought I'd live in a mansion," I said, taking a black cocktail dress from the hanger.

"Do you want me to sell this house? We could pick one out together," he offered.

I blinked. "You'd give up this house? And leave all the

custom work you've had done to it? And all the magic spells you invested into it?" I shook my head. I reached behind me for the dress's zipper, but Bryn stepped forward for it. I lifted my hair, and he raised the zipper and kissed the back of my neck.

"Wherever we live has to feel like your home, not like a place you're visiting."

"I'll talk it over with Mercutio," I said, putting my feet into the pair of black satin pumps that went with the dress.

"Are you sure you don't want me to come with you?" Bryn asked.

"Pretty sure," I said.

I was going home. Well, I was going to Momma and Aunt Mel's Victorian. Aunt Mel was supposed to be at the house by six in the evening, and I wanted to bake a cake and make a blender full of Brandy Alexanders so she'd be in a really good holiday mood when I told her about me getting engaged to Bryn.

"I think I should talk to her alone at first," I said.

Besides telling Aunt Mel about the engagement, I wanted to examine the locket that used to be the anchor for Edie's soul and to tell Aunt Mel about Vangie's body possibly being the new Edie locket.

Wow. Edie back alive! And where had she gone? It was Christmas. We were her family. And now Bryn would be, too. Oh boy. Holidays were going to be very interesting. If people didn't get along, I'd be caught in the middle, like a flaming marshmallow in the center of a s'more.

S'mores. Yum.

I'd have to make things work.

I turned and gave Bryn a kiss. "I hope that Aunt Mel will get used to the idea really quick and that she'll be willing to come over here for Christmas dinner. If not, I'll stay there until around eight or so and then come back with a suitcase."

Bryn nodded. "I love you."

I smiled because I believed him. I slid my arms around his neck and hugged him. "I love you, too." With a last quick kiss, I slipped out of his arms and left the room.

At the bottom of the big stairwell, Mercutio gave me a look and meowed.

"I don't have any jeans here," I explained. "Besides, it's Christmas. For once, it actually makes sense for me to be in a fancy dress."

The diamond ring sparkled, and Mercutio batted it with a paw. "Yep. A whopper, right?" I said, going outside. Mercutio joined me in the Focus. "I could buy about eight copies of this car for the price of the engagement ring." I shook my head. "So whatever we do, we can't lose it in the woods or at the bottom of the river." I took a deep breath. "It's going to be kind of nerve-racking."

Mercutio licked his paw. He doesn't concern himself with jewelry. That's one lucky thing about being a jungle cat. He's already all decorated with spots and stripes. He doesn't need bling.

We drove across town in a companionable silence until I said, "Yikes!" and slammed on the brakes.

Years ago, Miss Jolene's fiancé left her at the altar and a month later married her sister. Since then, every Christmas when her family got together, there was a knock-down, drag-out fight that spilled out onto the lawn.

I rooted for Jolene, her being my neighbor and the wronged party, but I didn't get actively involved in their shenanigans unless there was blood or broken glass. So normally I wouldn't have stopped to watch, but this fight had an unexpected fixture. A ghostly spectator sat in a lawn chair, her head turning back and forth to watch the players like she was at a tennis match.

Vangie wore a long black skirt and an Indian-style headband with hanging feathers. From dusky sparrows? Her shirt might have been purple. Hard to tell since it was buried under about seventeen multicolored scarves. She was a kind of hippie Pocahontas. When she saw me, she waved cheerfully and sprang from the chair with her arms outstretched. She flew toward me Superman-style.

"Hi, Tammy Jo."

I recovered from my drop-jawed expression and glanced

around to be sure none of the lawn combatants were watching us.

"Oh, Vangie! You're a ghost."

"Yes," she said, beaming.

"I'm so sorry. Edie stole your body. I don't think she meant to."

"Not to worry. You killed Jackson. That's what matters. And look at me," she said, giving a twirl. "No one will ever be able to lock me up again. Straightjackets? Electroshock therapy? Sensible shoes? All a thing of the past. I'm free! I can go anywhere I want. I can eavesdrop on the president of the United States. Or the president of WAM! I'm free!"

"I—well, I guess that's one way of looking—do you want me to see if Bryn and I can get you back in your body?"

"Good God, no! Haven't you been listening? No more worries about steprelatives trying to kill me. No more lonely nights in my apartment trying to drown out the voices in my head. There's no problem with brain chemistry when there's no brain. Oops, hang on," she said, whipping her gaze to the family on the lawn. "Here comes Jolene's granny with a frying pan. See you later!" Vangie sailed right into the cluster of yelling, pan-waving people.

"Wow," I mumbled, returning to the car. "Vangie's a ghost and she likes it, so everything worked out . . . I guess?" I said to Merc.

He meowed speculatively as I pulled the car up to the curb in front of our house. *Our* old *house*, I corrected in my mind.

"We'll have to wait and see if Vangie changes her mind about wanting to be a ghost. Not that I'd know how to swap her into a body. I bet that sort of spell would take more juice than a New York City power grid's got."

I unlocked the front door, and Mercutio and I went inside. We had about an hour before Aunt Mel was due to arrive.

"I don't think I should be wearing the ring when Aunt Mel gets here. She'll spot it right away before I get a chance to fill her up with ice cream liquor drinks. I'll just put it on the gold chain Bryn gave me and hide it inside the dress at first."

A noise made me freeze in the foyer. My eyes narrowed, and Mercutio made a low growl and crouched.

I heard the hum of the television and relaxed. "Hang on. It's probably Edie," I said. "She knows where to find the spare key. Or Aunt Mel's home early." I set my keys down and walked to the living room.

Sitting on the couch with his legs stretched out in front of him was Crux. He was drinking orange juice and watching an episode of *Dancing with the Stars*.

Mercutio hissed, and I grabbed Merc.

"Hey, what do you think you're doing here?" I demanded.

Crux turned his head. "Watching the box."

"You didn't help me turn visible, and I definitely didn't invite you to be a houseguest."

"What's that yellow gemstone about?" he asked, nodding toward my hand.

"It's my canary bird engagement ring. If you don't leave, I may punch you with it. It's a diamond. It'll probably put your eye out."

Mercutio squirmed and yowled. He wanted to take a bite or two out of Crux. "Hang on, Merc. You'll snag my dress! I have to take care of the clothes I have left."

Crux rose, tall and handsome, radiating gold and magic. "Who gave you the ring? The wizard?"

I nodded.

"You have to give it back."

"I tried to," I mumbled. "He's stubborn as a box of rocks." I walked to the bathroom and dropped Merc on the floor. "Stay in there for one minute," I said, using my leg to block him from darting out before I closed the door.

"Look, I'm pretty busy. I'd appreciate it if you'd go now before Mercutio tears up the wallpaper trying to get out here to kick your butt."

"I'm not leaving yet," he said, walking closer and leaning against the counter. "You'll have to take off both rings. The band on the right hand, and the diamond on the left."

"Why would I do that?"

"Because you're Seelie fae."

"Am not."

"You are. And the queen will never allow you to marry a wizard."

"The queen? I don't even know her. I'm American! We don't have kings or queens. It's against our Constitution."

Crux grinned. "You may live here, but this is not your homeland. We're older than the human race. First and foremost you belong to us."

"I don't belong to anyone," I snapped.

"So come and tell her. See what happens."

"Did she send you here to get me?"

"No," he said. "I stumbled upon you."

A loud bang on the door made me jump. Crux's gaze slid to the foyer. Another loud thump rattled the walls. Mercutio yowled and rammed against the bathroom door.

"For the love of Hershey, now what?" I said, marching down the hall.

I opened the door, and *I* fell inside.

Actually it would turn out not to be me, but it was an honest mistake. She looked a lot like me. And she *felt* like me.

In one instant, my whole life changed. She was what had been missing for so long. The two magicks inside me uncoiled. The sunny fae part surged forward; the shady one fell back and to the right side. It mirrored the girl's own divided magic.

So many green vines tangled through her strawberry blond hair it took me a moment to realize her hair was much lighter than mine. Still there was a flame tint to it, enough red to make it Trask hair. Her eyes were a little different, too. Hazel green, like crushed grass mixed with crumbled fall leaves. My own eyes were more gold-flecked brown. There was maybe a little green to my gold, but not much, not like hers.

In a realization that hit me harder than a lych's fist, I realized that the girl I'd seen riding the horses and being chased across bridges hadn't been me. It had been this girl. She'd been the one helping me tap into my fae power, helping me to heal my injuries. And she'd been the face I'd seen when I'd called for help as Jackson Greer killed me. She'd told me to stab him. Had maybe even given me some strength to help pull the dagger from my body. I owed her my life.

I smiled at her, and her eyes twinkled.

Staring at her face delayed me from looking the rest of her over, but after a moment, I looked down. She wore a ragged brown calfskin skirt and a black T-shirt with a picture of a rock group named "the cranberries" sitting on a couch. The lower right edge of her T-shirt dripped beads of crimson, speckling her skirt.

"You're wounded," I said with a gasp.

"Aye, a bit," she said, waving the bow in her left hand as if the wound she held with her right was nothing. "But I made it, didn't I?" she said with an Irish lilt. "Do you know me then?" she asked a bit shyly.

"Not your name," I said. "But I recognize you."

"My first name's Kismarley, but I go by Kismet. You and I, we're sisters. Twins, it seems."

"I never knew," I said. "But something's always been missing. And twins run in our family. All the way back! I should've guessed—"

She leaned against the wall like she needed it to hold her up. "You weren't to know. Neither was I at first."

A gold coin clattered to the floor at our feet and I turned.

Crux's eyes were fixed on Kismet, who sucked in a startled breath.

With a cool smile, he said, "Coin for a Kis?"

It was exactly what he'd said that first time he'd seen me. He'd told the truth when he'd said he hadn't come to Duvall for me. He'd been tracking my sister and had mistaken me for her.

Kismet pushed me aside, loaded an iron arrow in her bow, and aimed it at Crux's heart.

"You will go back and say you couldn't find me," Kismet said in a low, very dangerous voice. Her green eyes shone hard as emeralds.

"It's no use, Kis. Ghislaine knows I'd never stop tracking my quarry until I'd found it. She knows I'm in this town and that you were on your way here."

"She can't. No one knows that."

He cocked a brow and made a sweeping gesture with his hand. "I caught you. You can't pretend I haven't."

"I'm not caught," Kis said, giving the tip of the arrow a little bob. "If I kill you, she'll never know where I am."

"It's too late. I told her about Tammy."

She let the arrow fly. It whizzed through the air, barely missing him when he flung himself to the side.

He scowled, standing with the liquid grace of a dancer. "You'll return to the Never," he said. "Both of you."

"We will not!" I snapped. The Unseelie fae lived under Duvall, but the Seelie fae—my kinfolk—lived across the Atlantic, under Ireland and Scotland. "I'm not leaving Texas and my—my sister's staying here in Duvall with me if that's what she wants. Nobody's taking her anywhere she doesn't want to go."

Crux folded his arms across his chest. "Caedrin will be sorry to hear that, since if you don't come back they'll kill his love."

"That's not our problem," I blurted, too distracted to recognize the name at first.

"His love is named Marlee."

I froze because that was the one thing he could've said to change everything. There was no way in the world I could stay in Texas if somewhere across the ocean, a faery queen planned to kill my momma.

"Oh," I said. "Well, that changes things."

"No, it doesn't," Kismet said. "She chose to enter. We'll not risk our lives to save her, mother or not."

My brows shot up. "Um, that's not actually how our family works."

Her cool green gaze didn't soften.

Oh boy.

"Let me make you something sweet. It'll make you feel better," I said. *It'll make me feel better, too.*

"I'd like pie," Crux said.

"You can starve," Kismet and I said at the same time. She smiled at me, and I smiled back.

Crux appraised me coolly. I shrugged at him, but in the end, I did serve them each pie and cookies. Even though I didn't like Crux, if I had to go into the Never, I wanted every faery I knew on my side.

I dumped ice cream and brandy into the blender and turned it on. As it churned, I called Bryn.

"Hey, it's me. Tammy Jo."

"I know," he said with a chuckle. "How's it going?"

I chewed the corner of my lip. "This day's been full of surprises. Remember how we talked about going to Ireland?"

There was a pause before he said, "Yes."

I turned off the blender. "Well, it turns out we might be going sooner rather than later."

"We are not," Kismet said.

"Why?" Bryn asked, apparently not having heard Kismet in the background. "When?"

"Well, I might be. You might decide not to."

"Why is that?" His light tone didn't cover the wariness in his voice.

I poured Brandy Alexanders into glasses. "My momma's in trouble. I have to help her."

"Your mother. Where is she?"

"That's the tricky part. Underhill, I guess. I've got to get some more details about it. Listen, though, you don't have to go," I said, licking brandy shake off my finger. "Really. I'll understand. I know how you feel about the fae, and I don't know how this trip will affect me. I might not be myself." I frowned. Maybe it really would be better if he stayed home.

"When you're at your best, so am I. When you're Bonnie, I'm Clyde, remember?"

"I thought maybe you just said that to needle Zach. I didn't know whether you really meant it."

"I meant it." He sighed. "I just didn't expect to have to prove it so soon."

"I know. First a coma and now this! Luckily we got engaged, or Christmas would've been ruined."

Bryn laughed. "Yes, so lucky. I'm sure we'll be the envy of all our friends."

I knew he was being sarcastic, but as I took a swallow of my ice cream drink, excitement bubbled inside me. I had a new fiancé and a new sister, and it was likely that soon I'd be on my way to see Momma, who I'd missed every day for more than a year. I was lucky to be alive. *Really lucky*, I thought, running a finger over my healing wounds.

"Yeah," I said. "No doubt we will."

From national bestselling author
KIMBERLY FROST

Halfway Hexed

· *A Southern Witch Novel* ·

Pastry-chef-turned-unexpected-witch Tammy Jo Trask is finally ready to embrace her mixed-up and often malfunctioning magic. Too bad not everyone wants her to become all the witch she can be. One thing's certain: this would-be witch is ready to rumble, Texas style . . .

Praise for the Southern Witch series

"An utter delight."

—Annette Blair, national bestselling author

"Full of action, suspense, romance, and humor."

—*Huntress Reviews*

penguin.com

facebook.com/ProjectParanormalBooks

M938T0811

*Welcome to Duvall, Texas, where new witch Tammy Jo Trask
has just unleashed an accidental Armageddon…*

FROM
KIMBERLY FROST

BARELY
BEWITCHED

A Southern Witch Novel

When Tammy Jo's misfiring magic attracts the attention of
the World Association of Magic, or WAM, a wand-wielding
wizard and a menacing fire warlock show up to train her for a
dangerous—and mandatory—challenge. But is there more to
their arrival than they claim?

The town comes unglued when a curse leads to a toxic
spill of pixie dust and the doors between the human and faery
worlds begin to open. To rescue the town and to face the challenge, Tammy needs help from the incredibly handsome Bryn
Lyons, but WAM has declared him totally off-limits…

PRAISE FOR KIMBERLY FROST

"Frost can tell a tale like no other."
—*Fang-tastic Books*

"Filled with humor, sass, and sizzle!"
—*The Romance Readers Connection*

frostfiction.com
penguin.com

M1379T0913

In the small town of Duvall, Texas, the only thing that causes more trouble than gossip is magic.

FROM

KIMBERLY FROST

WOULD-BE WITCH

A Southern Witch Novel

The family magic gene seems to have skipped over Tammy Jo Trask. All she gets are a few untimely visits from the long-dead, smart-mouthed family ghost, Edie. But when her locket—an heirloom that happens to hold Edie's soul—is stolen in the midst of a town-wide crime spree, it's time for Tammy to find her inner witch.

Tammy turns to the only person who can help: the very rich and highly magical Bryn Lyons. He might have all the answers—and a double-oh-seven savoir faire to boot—but the locket isn't the only heirloom passed down in Tammy's family. She also inherited a warning: *Stay away from anyone named Lyons…*

"Delivers a delicious buffet of supernatural creatures, served up Texas style—hot, spicy, and with a bite!"

—Kerrelyn Sparks, *New York Times* bestselling author

frostfiction.com
penguin.com

M1378T0913